Acclaim for Catherine Friend's
Hit by
How I Learned
and Lov

D0819396

"What happens when you take a c [...] ng
with many high hopes and her partner of twelve years, on a Minnesota
farm?...enjoyable, enlightening and even laugh-out-loud hilarious *Hit
By a Farm*." – *Curve*

"If you've ever hungered for books about day-to-day realities of long
-term lesbian relationships, what makes them work, what happens in
the years after you start keeping your underwear in the same drawer,
this book is for you. And somehow, it's such a wholesome, Midwestern
tale that it would also be a perfect book to give to anyone who can't
quite imagine what two women do with each other." – *Books to Watch
Out For*

"I'm reading a book now that I ration out 10 pages a day because I'll feel
bereft when it's gone: it's a memoir of two lesbians who go into sheep
farming in Minnesota and I just really like both of them." – Garrison
Keillor, *New York Times Book Review*

"*Hit By a Farm* goes beyond funny, through poignant, sad and angry,
to redemptive: all the things that make a farm—and a relationship—
successful." – *Lavender*

"[A] charming memoir…[with]magical moments." – *New York Times
Book Review*

"...A thoroughly engaging romp for all, but a must-read for any city
girl who's ever whiled away an hour or two dreaming about the bucolic
existence of her rural sisters." – *Bust*

"Catherine Friend is a luscious writer. She packs this memoir of two
women starting a farm together in Southern Minnesota with hilarity,
tenderness, grim reality and suspense…This memoir is, hands down,
the best story I've read in ages." – Ellen Hart, author of *Night Vision*
and *Iron Girl*

"Offbeat and candid memoir of a relationship tested by the rigors of
sheep farming in Minnesota." – *Star Tribune* Best of 2006 Minnesota
Authors

Visit us at www.boldstrokesbooks.com

THE
SPANISH
PEARL

by

Catherine Friend

2007

THE SPANISH PEARL

© 2007 By Catherine Friend. All Rights Reserved.

ISBN 10: 1-933110-76-7
ISBN 13: 978-1-933110-76-9

This Trade Paperback Is Published By
Bold Strokes Books, Inc.
New York, USA

First Edition, May 2007

This is a work of fiction. Names, characters, places, and incidents are the product of the author's imagination or are used fictitiously. Any resemblance to actual persons, living or dead, business establishments, events, or locales is entirely coincidental.

This book, or parts thereof, may not be reproduced in any form without permission.

Credits
Editors: Cindy Cresap and J. Barre Greystone
Production Design: J. Barre Greystone
Cover Graphic: Sheri (graphicartist2020@hotmail.com)

Acknowledgments

I deeply appreciate the steady voice of editor Cindy Cresap, the thoroughness of copyeditor J.B. Greystone, and the chance to be part of Radclyffe's amazing vision. Bold Strokes has been a dream to work with.

I also owe a huge thanks to Ann Monson, Janet Lawson, Cindy Rogers, Pat Schmatz, Tif Boyd, Emily Kuntz, Kathy Connelly, and Carolyn Sampson for reading early drafts of this novel, and pushing me to keep going. I'm grateful to Richard Fletcher's *In Search of El Cid,* the book that reminded me how much I loved the Spanish history I'd learned in college.

And finally, many thanks to "my" librarian, Jeannie Johnson, who successfully found me all the obscure reference books I requested when I wrote the novel, like *A Dictionary of Andalusi Arabic*, then found them for me again when I needed to verify my work. Librarians rock.

DEDICATION

"Love at first sight is easy to understand. It's when two people have been looking at each other for years that it becomes a miracle." – Sam Levenson

For Melissa…for our miracle

CHAPTER ONE

Time. All I needed was a little more time to get used to the idea of me, Kate Vincent, being a parent. It wasn't that I didn't like the idea of giving a little boy a much-needed home—I did. And adopting was going to make my partner Anna so happy. She was wacko for kids, volunteering for the after-school reading program and helping out with story hour at the public library. She actually knew how to talk to kids. But me, driving around with a Parent bumper sticker on my car? More time, that was all I needed.

Unfortunately I was out of time, because today was *the* day. Too terrified to get out of the hotel bed, I reached under my pillow to re-read the letter from Arturo, opening it quietly so I wouldn't wake Anna. An adult at the orphanage had obviously penned the letter, but the paper was brightly decorated with Arturo's five-year-old kid art: *Dear Señorita Anna and Señorita Kate—*

Anna was officially going to be the adoptive parent, so Arturo would probably start calling her "Mom." When we returned to Chicago, I'd file for joint custody, but what would Arturo call me? "Mom Number Two?" "Kate?" "My other mom?"

Please come visit me, the letter said. *Thank you for the photo of Max. He is a big dog. I like big dogs.* Right now back in Chicago, my black lab Max was sleeping at my best friend Laura's house, dreaming of having his own little boy to play with.

I know I will like America. Are there caves in America? My favorite place to visit is the big cave. The adult scribe had written in parentheses that Arturo meant the Mirabueno Cave on the western edge of Zaragoza. *The Palacio is nice, but not as much fun as the cave.* I loved how the letter was half little kid, half travel guide. *When you come to Zaragoza, you should go to the big cave.* Yes, I should, Arturo, if I could only get out of bed.

I finished the letter, folded it up, and let the mega-panic flow through me. Anna and I were two hours away from becoming adoptive parents, and I was sick with excitement and high with terror. No, that's not right. I was sick with terror and high with excitement.

I pulled the pillow over my head to shut out the traffic noises outside our third floor hotel room. Zaragoza, Spain sounded just like Chicago. It had been Anna's idea to adopt, and since she supported me, the starving artist, I'd felt it was important to support her desire to have a family. My best friend Laura said that was a dumb reason to adopt, but who listens to their best friend's advice?

Once Anna convinced me, she started checking at Illinois adoption agencies. Since the entire country had its boxer shorts in a bundle over gay marriage, two women adopting would surely destroy the world as we knew it. I got tired of the raised eyebrows and stern looks.

Because Anna taught Spanish History at Northwestern, she began looking to adopt a child from Spain. I was still dragging my heels a bit because, when it came to kids, my usual confidence withered into a hard, tiny raisin rattling around inside my body. But then Señora Cavelos from El Orfanato Benévolo de San Estéfan in Zaragoza, Spain, sent us a photo of five-year-old Arturo standing against a peeling plaster wall, hands stiff at his sides, brown hair combed back, dark eyes wide open, and wearing the most serious smile I'd ever seen. His blue jacket hung loosely on his small frame, a red bow tie tipped crookedly under his chin, and one navy knee sock slid down his calf. I moved my art studio from the spare room into the basement and turned the spare room into what I hoped would be a five-year-old boy's nirvana, complete with race car wallpaper, dragon-shaped headboard, and a baseball bat and glove. I hoped mixing all those themes wouldn't give the little guy nightmares.

A car honked outside, and I groped the bed behind me for Anna's comforting curves. Nada. I rolled over and faced a note, which read: *Dear Kate, Have gone downstairs for breakfast. Join me when you're up. Love, Paloma de Palma.*

I smiled. Paloma de Palma. It was all the rage for college professors to publish scholarly works, then pen a bloody mystery or trashy romance under a pseudonym. Anna had ached to join their ranks, so one night we had polished off a bottle of Chardonnay and come up with her romance novel pen name, Paloma de Palma. She liked teasing me about having an affair with the mysterious de Palma. Me—have an affair? Nope. I was a one-woman woman.

Moaning, I rolled out of bed, then stood in front of the mirror, inhaling deeply. Did I look like a parent? Unruly brown hair curling around my neck, a pleasant enough smile, decent curves, average smarts, but no athletic ability whatsoever. I hated skiing, hated softball, and as for Laura's passion, horseback riding, forget it. What sane person gets on top of one thousand pounds of beast and says, "Giddiyup, horsie?"

What did parents look like anyway? They drove sensible cars and ate vegetables with every meal, balanced their checkbooks every month and never doubted their parenting abilities. That described *my* parents, but Holy Frijoles, it didn't describe me. I drove a black Thunderbird, ate vegetables only at gunpoint, used my unopened bank statements as door stops, and my Parental Doubt-O-Meter was off the scale.

Somehow I managed to drag myself into the minuscule shower and get cleaned up. Expecting another Zaragoza scorcher like yesterday, which we'd spent in an unairconditioned office drowning in adoption paperwork, I pulled on khaki shorts with huge cargo pockets, then cinched the narrow leather belt. I tugged on a dark purple T-shirt, blazoned with a perfectly reasonable message about our nation's current president and his demented policy advisors, and matching purple socks. I added wallet, passport, tissue, chewing gum, and a Snickers bar for Arturo to my fanny pack. At the last minute I threw in some Benadryl because Señora Cavelos's office reeked of mold, and then added the note from Paloma de Palma as teasing material for Anna. I still felt naked without my cell and Blackberry, but hey, I was on vacation, so I'd left them at home.

Anna had already finished her breakfast and was reading a newspaper. She glanced up, her blond hair swinging like a curtain away from her face, then checked her watch. "Cutting it a little close, aren't we?" As a starving artist-type, I felt compelled to live a less-structured life than Ms. Punctuality, which was yet another difference between the two of us. Sometimes I got frustrated with Anna, but I loved her. She was steady, sweet, and loyal.

I'd barely started on my eggs and toast when Anna put down her paper. "How about another history lesson?"

"No thanks," I said. History just wasn't my thing. I spoke fluent Spanish thanks to years of high school and college Spanish, but my interest stopped there.

"Kate, it's important for Arturo to know Spain's history."

"Babe, I can see only one use for history. Say you're walking down a dark alley and some guy jumps out, sticks a knife in your face, and growls 'Tell me the year the Moors invaded Spain or you're dead.' You wipe the sweat from your eyes, then squeak out—" I waited.

"711 A.D." Anna loved showing off.

"Right. 711. Satisfied, the guy lets you go."

Anna's smile made me feel good whenever it appeared. "Here's another use for history," she said. "You're on *Jeopardy* and it's Final Jeopardy and you've got $10,000 riding on this answer: The Christian soldier credited with beginning the drive to kick the Moors out of Spain."

I gulped the last of my orange juice and flashed her my most charming grin. "Who is Rodrigo Díaz, otherwise known as El Cid."

"Wow. Not bad."

"Are you kidding? You've made me watch that El Cid movie a hundred times, which is only bearable because Sophia Loren is so hot."

A wistful look passed over Anna's face. "I do love that movie, but I still think it was a horrible mistake to kick the Moors out of Spain. They were more advanced and more civilized, and I think the whole country would have been better off if the Moors had remained in power."

I checked my watch. "Righto. And when you're done fantasizing about the totally impossible idea of changing history, maybe we could get ourselves to the orphanage and pick up our son."

"Our son." Anna hugged herself. "I love the way that sounds." We grinned like fools, and I stuffed my fear deep into the tips of my Doc Martens.

❖

I glared at Señora Cavelos but she just shook her alarmingly hairsprayed head. "I'm sorry," she said. "We cannot release a child if he's running a temperature."

"It could just be the excitement," I said. Maybe if we found her a new hairdresser, she'd relent.

She fussed with her papers, her hands like two nervous moths fluttering over her desk.

"With any temperature above normal, we must keep and observe the child."

"But—" I stopped at Anna's light touch on my arm.

"No, Kate, fevers in children are serious. He should be kept quiet until his fever drops."

Señora Cavelos beamed at Anna. "He's the only child in the infirmary, so he'll have plenty of quiet. He'll be fine in a day or two. Then we can complete the adoption, and you can take him back to America."

We left her office and I closed the door behind us. "Well," Anna said. "I guess we're tourists today."

"Babe, look." I nodded toward a small white sign at the base of the staircase, which read Enfermería.

"You aren't suggesting we kidnap him," she said, incredulous.

"No, but we can visit."

"Kate, no, we can't—" but I was already heading for the staircase. I couldn't get this far and not meet him. I'd burned up all my terror cells this morning and had nothing left for tomorrow. Besides, the poor kid had to be as anxious as we were. A smile and a hug just might help. Anger and frustration and excitement drove me, the rule-breaker, up the stairs and into the infirmary, but then I froze at the sight of a lone boy sitting on a narrow bed with tight-as-drums hospital corners and sunshine streaming in through the bank of windows.

My mouth fell open. I moved my jaw but nothing came out. As Anna reached me, struggling to catch her breath, the boy turned toward us, brown eyes curious and unafraid. He looked at the photo in his hand, then back at us, eyes now big as Sacajawea dollars, mouth rounded to a perfect 'o.' He held the photo we'd sent him. I think I forgot to breathe.

"Arturo?" Anna stepped forward. The boy jumped off the bed and flew toward us. As Anna swept him up in a huge hug, something stuck in my throat. "Oh, Arturo," Anna crooned. "We are so happy to finally meet you." She squeezed him, his thin arms tight around her neck.

When two sparkling brown eyes peeked at me over Anna's shoulder, I still couldn't speak, so I winked. Arturo giggled into Anna's neck. She introduced herself, kissing his cheek, then reached for me. "And this is Kate. We are so excited you are going to join our family."

Arturo slipped into my open arms as if he'd been doing so all his life. "Kate," he said joyfully.

"Arturo," I whispered hoarsely as I held his slender frame, inhaling strong soap, warm child, and crayon wax. He squeezed me just as tightly as I squeezed him. The lump in my throat got bigger so I stepped back, blinking furiously.

Anna held Arturo's hand and stroked his hair. "How are you feeling?"

"Better, but the big, scary nurse makes me stay in bed." He pulled us toward a small table at the end of the long room, where he'd scattered a box of crayons.

"I drew this all by myself. It's not done, but you can have it." He thrust the thin paper toward me.

Three stick figures held hands under a lopsided yellow sun, and a stick dog sat nearby. Anna's yellow hair stuck out like spikes, Max's eyes glowed orange, and the little boy had brown hair like Arturo. The remaining figure, who must have been me, lacked a head, which bothered me a little, but I was pleased Arturo shared my interest in art.

"It's lovely," Anna said. "You're a very good artist."

"I can draw race cars, too," he said, face round and flushed. Shyly, I touched his silky hair. Score one for me and my race car wallpaper.

"Young man!" boomed a voice from behind us. "What are you doing out of bed?" Windows rattled as a uniformed nurse stomped down the aisle. With a guilty grin and adorable yelp, Arturo flung himself onto his bed, laughing as the gruff nurse, fooling no one, lovingly tucked him in. We only had time to kiss his forehead before she hustled us out, complaining of unauthorized visitors.

We fled the building, collapsing on the steps outside. My hands and head tingled. "Anna, you were great. You really know kids."

She smiled, panting from our run. "I earned my spending money by babysitting. You delivered papers." I *had* babysat once, but I'd never told her, or anyone, what had happened. It had been a close call, and I still had nightmares now and then about overflowing bathtubs and unsupervised toddlers. Anna tapped Arturo's drawing, still in my hand. "Most of you is missing."

"He can finish it later." I carefully folded the drawing and stuck it in my fanny pack. "I can't believe this amazing, adorable kid is going to be our son."

Anna hugged herself. "It's going to happen. It's really going to happen."

For Anna's sake, I hid my terror. I could do this. I could love this little boy and be a fine parent.

Twenty kids screamed from the orphanage's soccer field, so Anna had to raise her voice. "Since we can't take Arturo home today, let's tour the Palacio de la Aljafería. It's one of the few Moorish palaces left in Spain."

"But Arturo's favorite is the cave," I said. "Let's go there first." We spoke in English, which I hoped gave us a little privacy among the social workers in practical shoes hustling past us to the orphanage, or from the small, dark man sweeping the sidewalk.

Anna waved a slender hand. "Kate, I didn't come to Spain to visit a wet, dripping cave." Her mouth settled into that iron thin line I'd seen her use on difficult students. I moved aside as a delivery man pushed a cart past me, wheels clattering on the broken flagstone.

"Cave," I said.

"Palace," she snapped.

"Anna, yesterday we toured three cathedrals, one Roman forum, and four historical sites. It's my turn now."

Anna growled, dropping onto the granite steps. "You are *so* impossible."

"Me?" I sat down next to her, stretching out my right leg. My sore heel throbbed, and I wished I'd seen a doctor before we left Chicago, but when the orphanage said 'come,' we came. I untied my Doc Martens and rubbed my heel as we watched the traffic in silence. At 10:30 a.m. Zaragoza was a snarl of honking cars and lumbering buses. Two crows fought over a soggy cracker on the orphanage's lawn.

"Poor Arturo," I muttered. "We'd all counted on taking him today."

Zaragoza glowed brown, probably because all the buildings seemed constructed of the same light chocolate brick. Even the air radiated brown, as if the hot bricks had melted into the exhaust-filled air. Behind us the janitor's broom bristles rasped like a rhythmic cymbal; soon we'd have to get out of his way. I took a deep breath. "Anna, let's do both. Cave first, then the Palacio."

Anna rubbed her long, slender nose, which curved slightly near the end, a feature that didn't mar her good looks, but only made her more intriguing. "Okay, but the Palacio de la Aljafería is more important. El Cid lived there during his exile from Castile in the 1080s, over nine hundred years ago." Hands on wide hips, Anna thrust her pointed chin out slightly, a warning sign I knew well. Short and cool, Anna kicked her uncanny ability to sway people into high gear.

I put on my shoe. "Enough of El Cid. The guy's really starting to get on my nerves. I want to go to the cave." I didn't put my foot down that often, but I was determined to see Arturo's cave before we left the country.

"No go cave," came a low male voice from behind us. The man had stopped sweeping and stood frozen, broom hovering above the sidewalk. A deep frown furrowed his tanned, lined face. His silver-streaked black hair was combed straight back.

"What?" I asked.

His fierce black eyes, shiny as wet marbles, bore into me. "Do not go Mirabueno. Cave dangerous." He smelled of onion and garlic.

My gaze met Anna's. Did she put this guy up to this? No, her brows knit together with irritation. "Don't worry," I said. "I've been in lots of caves."

"Not Mirabueno. No go," he said.

The small man, in his early sixties, wore a blue service uniform with Roberto stitched in orange on the pocket. Another man, also dressed in the same blue uniform, called to Roberto from the side of the building. Roberto gave us one last fierce glare. "No go," he warned, then left us with our mouths hanging open as he trotted out of sight.

How much more melodramatic could you get? I turned to Anna. "Did you have anything to do with this?"

"Don't be ridiculous. Now forget the cave. Let's catch the bus to the Palacio."

I had this handy stubborn gene that rarely made an appearance, but when it did, Holy Toledo, it really kicked in. Anna didn't want me to go to the cave. Some weird stranger didn't want me to go to the cave.

Ha. That meant I was headed for the Mirabueno Cave, and right now. Nothing was going to stop me.

CHAPTER TWO

Nothing except Anna, that is.

"If we can't agree on this," Anna said, "how will we agree on issues concerning Arturo?"

"What issues?"

"Private vs. public schools. When to discipline and how. Soccer practice or piano practice. Choir or band."

"Anna, this isn't—"

"Yes, it's a perfect example of how we need to work together."

I sighed heavily and could feel a Moorish palace in my immediate future. I wasn't giving up so easily, however, so I dug into a pocket, pulled out a euro, and balanced it on my thumb. "Call it."

"Tails." The coin twisted in the air.

I peeked under my palm. "Damn." Anna laughed, satisfied. As we walked away from the orphanage, I looked over my shoulder. Roberto worked on the far side of the soccer field now, but he stopped to watch us leave. A strange shiver crawled up my spine.

While standing in the bus's packed aisle, I breathed through my mouth to avoid passengers' failed deodorants and dense, flowery perfumes. I stretched my heel again, wincing. We crisscrossed the Rio Ebro twice, once on a concrete bridge with a huge steel superstructure, the other time on a low stone bridge arching gracefully over the brown water.

As I stepped off the bus, the breeze cooled my neck. Intricate iron balconies dripping with fragrant red begonias and pink bougainvilleas jutted out over the crumbling sidewalk as we wove our way through the sidewalk crowded with Zaragozans. In another block we reached the Aljafería. Its brown ochre stone walls rose twenty feet, and diamond bastions jutted out from each corner. A drab grassy plaza ran around the back of the building.

At the entrance a young woman behind a glass enclosure tore herself away from her *Estrella* magazine long enough to take our euros and toss us each a floor map; we entered through a long, cool hallway. The rich scent of orange trees, roses, and lavender hit me as we stepped into a huge sunlit room. My head dropped back as I gazed at the ceiling. Intricately carved cedarwood columns dripped down from carved ceiling panels, the carvings a lush intertwining of ropes, flowers and geometric shapes.

"Incredible, isn't it?" Anna said. Arches drew us out into the courtyard, where orange trees fluttered in a gentle breeze, and the sounds of the city outside faded to a dull hum. Blue and yellow tiles wove their way around the courtyard. A massive fountain sprayed in the courtyard's center, the mist raising rainbows.

"Not bad," I said, unwilling to admit the palace's stunning beauty, knowing she'd find some way to rub it in my face. "Maybe we should explore this on our own." Anna nodded, so I opened my map and tapped one spot. "I think I'll check out the harem quarters first."

Anna snorted, but rewarded me with a thin smile as I walked away. I wandered through the labyrinth of small rooms, narrow hallways, frustrated with my sore heel. Up narrow staircases, then back down. Empty fountains graced the larger rooms. A lingering scent of lemon floor cleaner bit the air. I stopped and imagined people living here— smells of burning oil lamps, cinnamon and cloves, spicy lamb stew, sandalwood, eucalyptus.

I passed a small room with a charming round window and stepped inside. The stones around the window were cool and rough under my fingers as I leaned out over an inner courtyard. An odd feeling washed over me as I turned to survey the room, one that left me warm and content. Maybe it was leftover happiness from meeting Arturo.

After a short climb, I finally reached the harem quarters, where sunlight streamed into a large courtyard with a raised platform in the center. Small ornate fountains anchored each corner of the courtyard. Arching columns formed a covered walkway around the outside edge. Pungent boxwood, recently trimmed, rimmed the exposed courtyard.

I stepped through an opening in the boxwood, then ran my hands over the warm, irregular blue and yellow tiles on the raised platform.

"*Muy bonito, no?*"

My hand flew to my throat as I whirled around. An older man sat on a bench under the covered walkway. His black pants disappeared in the shadows, but his plain white shirt glowed. When I stepped into the shade to see him more clearly, he patted the stone bench next to him.

"*Sí*," I said, "*es muy bonito*." I sat down, slipping easily into Spanish, then inhaled sharply as my bare legs touched the cold marble.

"This is where the Moorish emirs kept their women." The man waved a pale hand toward the other side of the courtyard. "The women lived in small apartments lining the courtyard. They bathed down that hall, and they ate together in a room through that hallway."

I leaned back, soaking up the lacy wood carvings arching from column to column. "Why didn't the emir live closer to his...women?"

"Even a Saracen emir requires his peace and quiet. Court eunuchs would escort the woman of choice to his quarters." He chuckled, revealing fine white teeth. His aftershave reminded me of polished leather.

"Eunuchs, huh?" I slipped off my shoe and rubbed my heel. "My kind of man," I muttered under my breath.

"Eunuchs were the only men who could be trusted to guard the harem. Many of the women met lovers using secret passageways the poor emirs knew nothing of."

The man opened a paper bag, offering me a small, brownish pear. I accepted gratefully. Sweet juice dripped down my chin and hands as I chewed. "How do you know so much about this place?"

"I am a volunteer guide here. My name is Carlos Sanchez."

I wiped my sticky hand on my shorts before shaking his gnarled hand and sharing my own name.

"Come, I will show you." He stood and led me down a narrow hallway to a large room. "This was the bathing area. The women simply had to touch a carved panel on that far wall, and a small opening appeared so they could sneak out of the harem." On our way back to the courtyard, he waved toward a small room. "And in this room, a tile in the floor released the door to a secret passageway below the floor."

I stepped into the small room and gazed up, marveling at the carved peacocks strutting across the ceiling. "You seem to know the palace well."

"I have lived in Zaragoza my entire life. As a child, I played with my brothers and sisters in the ruins of this palace. To see it restored makes my heart grow in happiness."

Back at our bench, I tried to imagine the courtyard filled with a harem. "What about the cave at Mirabueno? Did you ever play there?"

Carlos shuddered. "Caves are dark and damp and full of bats. And what if one got lost?"

"With a light and a map, you won't get lost," I said. Carlos shrugged and handed me a chunk of white cheese. At least he wasn't warning me away melodramatically like Roberto. "I am eating your lunch," I said.

"I always bring enough to share."

"You come every day?" I chewed slowly, savoring the sharp flavor.

"The past still exists here, in these walls, these tiled floors, the very air we breathe." He sighed. "The Palacio is a symbol of the beauty and violence that built Spain. Its history stretches back to the fascinating time of Rodrigo Díaz, also called El Cid."

I tried not to roll my eyes. Yet another member of the El Cid fan club. Help. Someone get me out of here. Despite the pear and cheese, my stomach rumbled. "Very interesting, Carlos, but could you recommend a restaurant nearby?"

"There you are!" Anna appeared in the courtyard, so I introduced them, then made the fatal mistake of mentioning that Carlos was a history buff. Anna grabbed his hand, drawing him back down onto the bench, and within seconds they were boringly deep into a discussion about El Cid and some Moorish guy named al-Mu'tamin, and his wacko brother. I shook my head. Who would voluntarily fill their heads with this stuff? I boldly interrupted. "Excuse me, but too much information, people. Let's just keep it simple, shall we? Christians were the good guys. Moors were the bad guys."

Carlos shook his head. "Not necessarily. There were some very fine Moorish emirs and some brutal Christian kings."

"Okay, well then, at least we know the Christians always fought the Moors, and vice versa."

Anne frowned. "Not always. Sometimes a king and an emir would join forces against another king or emir. Remember that Spain wasn't yet a country, but just lots of kingdoms fighting each other for land and power."

I threw up my hands. "And this, ladies and gentlemen, is why history makes me crazy. If you can't tell the good guys from the bad guys, how can you possibly make sense of what's going on?"

When Carlos and Anna exchanged one of those 'she's-cute-but not-so-bright' looks, I decided it was time to visit a cave.

"We should get going," I said firmly.

Carlos stood up, stretching out the kinks in his aged back. "Before you go, I'll give you a quick tour." As we walked, Carlos pointed out the original walls. He led us past reproductions of museum paintings, stopping at a painting of courtyard arches. "This one confuses scholars. The paint analysis puts it in the late eleventh century, but it uses perspective, something that didn't start appearing until several centuries later." Something about the painting drew me to it, and I stood studying it. The artist's loose style was similar to my own, sort of, and I liked the romance of the blue and black arches. I peered more closely at the faint scrawling in the corner. Most of the name had been chipped away by time, but the initials were clear: *To E—, KV.*

I took a step back. "Wow."

"What's up?" Anna asked.

"Look. KV. Those are my initials too."

Anna didn't respond because she and Carlos had slipped back into history mode again. Finally, I lightly touched Anna's arm. "Look, since you're not interested in the cave, and I've had just about enough of El Cid, why don't you spend the afternoon here, and I'll visit the cave on my own."

Anna brightened. "Are you sure? You can find your way okay?"

"No problem. I checked the bus schedule earlier."

I shook Carlos's hand, thanking him for the tour, then turned to Anna. "Okay, I'm off to catch Bus 22. We'll meet at the hotel at three o'clock."

"Don't be late," we both said automatically.

❖

Bus 22 stopped at the foot of a steep, narrow street with a faded *Cueva* sign pointing up the hill. "Mirabueno," called the driver, and I followed ten tourists off the bus. My heel stung a bit, and I should have taken some ibuprofen, but I had nothing to wash it down with.

"The guidebook didn't say anything about this climb," complained an American woman with back-combed blond hair in front of me.

"This can't be good for my legs," her stocky husband replied, his bald spot already shiny with perspiration.

I trotted up next to them. "Actually, a climb like this is good for the tendons and muscles in your calves."

"An American!" The woman practically hugged me. "Honey, we haven't seen an American since we got to Zaragoza; just French tourists who look at us as if we're carrying some horrible disease or something." We talked as we scaled the hill. Joe and Lois Whipple, retired dentist and dental hygienist, lived in St. Petersburg, Florida, and adored traveling to offbeat places in their quest to collect a bumper sticker from as many tourist caves as possible.

"We have twenty-seven now," Lois said, touching my arm confidentially so I could share in this incredible accomplishment.

By the time we reached the top, sweat pooled around my waistband.

"Damn, Lois, this cave better have a bumper sticker after this torture." Joe wiped his face with a handkerchief.

The hill rose maybe twenty feet above us. A pathetic smattering of tourist carts selling tourist crap lined the wide concrete sidewalk. After I bought a small purple plastic flashlight with batteries, a Lion King key chain for Arturo, and a postcard of the Aljafería for Anna, my fanny pack bulged at the seams. The Whipples cackled with delight when they found two different bumper stickers.

I turned to survey the city. Through the yew trees below I could see where the bus had stopped. A short stretch of the Ebro was visible but then disappeared in the jungle of buildings. On the distant horizon, one hill stood higher than the rest of the city—I imagined this hill held the Aljafería, but of course the wall of apartment buildings hid it from view.

"Come on, Kate," Lois said as she gently took my elbow. "Let's go inside. You're practically melting."

The cool air inside raised delicious goose bumps; I took a deep breath. No musty, moldy smell, so the cave had fairly good air circulation, probably thanks to holes or vents in its roof. We stood in a large rock cavern with bare electric bulbs turning our faces into ghoulish, gray masks. I lifted my sore heel off the hard-packed dirt floor.

Our tall, skinny guide introduced himself as Jaime, then switched on a massive flashlight. We followed him through a narrow passageway to a series of natural steps worn into the rock. Two overhead strings of bare bulbs lit the path. After descending at least twenty feet, Jaime led us into a cavern stretching five or six stories above our heads. Massive waxy stalactites glimmered in the light. Below them, minerals pooled, building up stalagmites of fragile pink, sea green, and coffee brown; no wonder Arturo loved this cave. Roberto's odd warning made no sense. This cave was perfectly safe. A hollow dripping echoed against the cavern's smooth, moist walls. Overall, a very normal cave.

As we ambled from cavern to cavern, my heart rate slowed and my mind cleared. I must have been a cave dweller in a previous life. When Lois worried about getting lost, Jaime shook his head. "There is only one path through the caves, and you are on it. When we reach the end, we just turn around and retrace our steps."

After an hour, pain shot through my heel. Why had I let it get this bad? I drifted to the back of the group, trying to stretch my Achilles tendon as I walked, but it didn't help. The whole heel was already too inflamed. The path, enclosed with a faded yellow rope, held no benches or rocks on which I could rest. When the group turned a corner ahead, I stopped. How dare my body interfere with this day.

Hands on my hips, I surveyed the mid-sized cavern; its smooth, concave walls sloped gently up to meet the ceiling twenty feet overhead. When I turned, a ray of light caught my eye. Six feet up the left wall, sunlight filtered through a natural vent and lit up a narrow ledge where dust danced in the light. The ledge wasn't really a climb, but just up a few natural steps in the wall. Voices faded as the tour moved farther ahead. When they returned, they'd see me and I'd hear them. All I needed was a short rest. Of course leaving the path violated cave etiquette, but my throbbing pain overruled my ethics.

I slipped under the frayed yellow rope, using my nifty purple flashlight to light up the rock floor. Up two steps, and I sat down on the ledge, loosened my shoe, swung my legs up, and lay down. The rock radiated surprising warmth from the little bit of sunlight reaching it. I settled back, surprised my foot felt better already. Black graffiti spoiled the rock directly overhead. "If you are lost, only at Altamira can you find your way home." I snickered. The graffiti sounded like a self-help book.

I closed my eyes, inhaling wet rock and sweet earth. Not a bad place for a little meditation. My body relaxed into the ledge's crevasses;

a sigh escaped along with the week's tension. Nothing disturbed me for about sixty seconds, then a high-pitched whine pierced the cavern. My eyes flew open. The sunlight above me flared into a blinding white. I covered my eyes against the burning, then felt myself starting to spin. The shrill whine nearly pierced my eardrums as I spun faster and faster. God, I must be sick. Centrifugal force tugged at my ankles, and my heavy head threatened to fly right off my body. I flung my hands onto the rocks overhead to stop the spinning, but touched nothing. I grabbed for the rock ledge beneath me, but my hands scrabbled against air. My stomach roiled as I spun faster, crying out. The blinding whiteness bore down on me. I screamed, then everything went black.

❖

When I came to, I rolled on my side and threw up. I gagged on the acrid taste, coughed, then wiped my mouth on my arm and lay back. Jesus, my forehead burned. How had I gotten the flu? The thought of that horrendous spinning forced me onto my side again, where I pressed my cheek against the cool rock while my stomach turned flip-flops. Finally the nausea passed and I rolled onto my back again, opening my eyes to total darkness except for the weak shaft of sunlight above me. Great, I get sick and the cave has a power failure. Maybe I should have stayed at the Palacio with Anna.

Gripping the rock, I sat up, then doubled over, clutching my throbbing head. When I could breathe again, I fumbled in my fanny pack for the flashlight. The same path snaked through the cavern, but without the yellow rope. Had my group already come past? Did they coil up the rope at the end of the tour? A hollow 'drip, drip' echoed somewhere off to my left as I shone the flashlight on my watch. Three o'clock? But I left the path for the ledge at one o'clock. Oh my god, the cave employees must have closed the cave for siesta and gone home.

I fought an unfamiliar panic. I had a flashlight. I had a candy bar. But did I have enough strength to walk back to the entrance? Would the cave reopen after siesta? Probably not—it wasn't a hot tourist attraction. It could be morning before someone opened up the cave again. I slid gingerly off the ledge, trying not to think about what beasts might be sharing the cave with me. I knew bats wouldn't really harm me, but the last thing I needed was to be dive-bombed by an army of them. I stumbled down the two steps to the path, turned my back on the weak shaft of light over the ledge, and headed back toward the entrance.

I focused on the path, trying to ignore the dripping blackness around me. How had the others come back without me hearing? Perhaps at this very moment Joe and Lois Whipple were pressing the Zaragoza police to open the cave and search for me.

The flashlight trembled as I felt my way along the passageway. What was Anna doing right now? How long would she wait before getting help? Would she get help at all, or assume I was off exploring somewhere?

Something soft fluttered past my cheek. "Shit!" I stopped, trying to calm my racing heart. While it wasn't likely I'd have a heart attack at thirty, this would be absolutely the wrong place to have one. I'd die, the rats would have me for lunch, and all the rescuers would find would be a purple plastic flashlight and a Lion King key chain.

"Stop it," I commanded, my voice a terrifying echo. The path began to climb and lighten enough that I could see the walls, and the floor softened as I struggled through more loose sand than I remembered. I turned the corner and shouted with relief—the entrance room. Flecks of dust sparkled in the light from the open door. I ran for the light, stumbling out into the warm, blinding sunlight, then covered my eyes, dropping to the ground in relief, pushing back sudden tears. The vendors didn't need an overly-dramatic American staggering from the cave, crying in relief.

While I waited for my eyes to adjust, the wind murmured through the trees. No one approached me, asking "*Está bien?*" in a concerned voice, so I finally opened my eyes a crack. The vendors had all left, taking their carts with them. When I shifted onto my knees and realized the sidewalk was gone, I opened my eyes all the way. No tacky signs announced the cave. I stood shakily. No road snaked up the steep hill toward the cave; below me was only a brilliant jade river lined with thick yews and cottonwoods. A town capped a hill miles away, a white structure standing higher than the other buildings.

"Jesus," I muttered. I'd taken a wrong turn and come out the wrong entrance. Cussing, I started to circle the hill. Zaragoza would be on the other side. But after trudging through thigh-high grass to the other side, I stopped. Nothing but rolling hills, with a few wheat fields scattered here and there. For Pete's sake. Had I found a tunnel into an entirely different cave? I continued plodding around the hill until I reached the first entrance, just an opening in the rock wall. Where the hell was Zaragoza? I sat down. My head hurt. My heel hurt.

Time ground to a total halt until I realized my watch no longer worked. A rabbit hopped past, freezing when she smelled me. While two crows fought in a tree overhead, I strained to hear traffic noise. I sat high on a hill overlooking a wide river, which ran east and west. The distant town, blinding white in the afternoon sun, lay to the east. North of me, the river valley stretched itself thin, then folded into large, rough hills. The clear sky was almost unbearably cerulean blue.

No rescue came. Was Anna worried? Neither of us believed that "Knight in shining armor" crap, but I could have used some help. I should start walking, but to where? The white town to the east?

The sun dipped low enough so that the air began to cool and unfamiliar indecision paralyzed me. I stretched, walked around awhile, then returned to the cave entrance, where I sat against the gritty rock outcropping, pulled my bare legs up tight against my chest, and wrapped my arms around them. Soon, violent shivers racked my body, a reaction to more than the cold. The deafening silence rattled me. Where was Zaragoza? Why couldn't I figure out where I was? Finally, crickets and frogs began a symphony. I rested my head on my knees.

I felt it before I heard it. Faint pounding vibrations from the ground beneath me. A train? No, too irregular. Just like in the movies, I pressed an ear to the ground. Horses—lots of them. I leapt to my feet. Hooves thundering, men shouting, metal clanking. The trees below blocked my view, but the group had to be coming around the base of this blasted hill. I grabbed my fanny pack, fumbling with the strap. I would have preferred a bus, car, or taxi, but if it was to be the Spanish cavalry, fine. Half sliding, half running, terrified that they'd pass without stopping, I scrambled down the hill.

CHAPTER THREE

When I reached the bottom of the hill, I was still alone. I turned left around a thicket and stopped. Three men were taking a communal leak, backs to me, thank goddess, so I waited politely, taking in their odd costumes, until they put themselves back together.

"Man, am I glad to see you guys," I said.

All three whirled, eyes wide, drawing swords from scabbards at their sides. In four flying steps they surrounded me and pressed their swords against my chest and back. Two of the men wore black, filthy leggings and knee-high leather boots. Long-sleeved coats of chain mail clinked softly as they stared. Ragged surcoats brushed their knees.

When I knocked aside their heavy props, their eyes widened further. "Look, cut the historical re-enactment for a second. I need to hitch a ride back to Zaragoza."

Blank stares. The third man was young, his deep coffee skin smoother than mine had ever been. The boy wore a saffron robe, mud-stained, with matching turban. The fake sword in his hand curved nastily, but this concerned me less than the hungry way he stared at my knees.

"They're called 'knees,'" I said. The boy's eyes bugged out.

Then it hit me. I spoke English. No wonder the two chain mail guys looked at me so stupidly. "Excuse me," I said in Spanish, "but I seem to be lost. Could I hitch a ride back to Zaragoza with you?"

The two men looked at each other, then behind me to see if any more women might come barreling down the hill. The shorter, older man rubbed a full brown beard sprinkled with some disgusting remains from his dinner. The taller man, with unkempt ratty blond hair and a five-o'clock shadow, stepped closer, speaking in an odd but understandable Spanish dialect. "You need help?"

"Yes." What a nimrod. I was out in the middle of nowhere by myself. What did he think I needed—a French vanilla latte?

He stepped even closer, which my nostrils instantly regretted, then he actually leered at me. "Oh, señorita, I can give you exactly what you need." He grabbed both my arms, squeezing hard, then bent toward me with fetid breath. I twisted and kicked, but he crushed me to his reeking chest, his mail and scabbard digging into my side.

"You son of a bitch, let me go." If this was some historical reenactment, they were going too far.

The other man laughed, revealing yellow teeth. "Fadri, you ugly camel, you'll never match Luis's skill with women." The boy kept staring at my knees as I struggled, until his eyes rolled back in his head and he dropped over in a dead faint.

"Fadri! Enzo! Let's go!" The shout came from around the base of the hill. The blond goon began dragging me toward the voice; the other tossed the passed-out Arab over his shoulder.

I lashed out with my feet, but the laughing man held me tight against his chest. When we rounded a massive outcropping, I stopped struggling. On the slope below milled fifty or so horses, two-thirds ridden by grimy white guys in chain mail, the rest ridden by bearded black and Middle Eastern guys dressed as Arabs. Fatigue etched every face. Leather shields hung from most saddles. Dust clung to untrimmed beards and sweat-stained leather tunics. Filthy rags were wrapped around a few arms and legs, dramatically colored with ketchup. Fifty male faces turned toward me, each pair of eyes staring directly at my breasts, which strained against my T-shirt. A small cold bubble of fear formed in my chest.

Leather saddles creaked, a few horses snuffled noises, a few stamped the ground impatiently. "Hey, Fadri," one man called out. "Are you going to share her?"

Raucous laughter rippled through the group and my mouth dropped open. This just could *not* be happening. A slender man exactly my height stepped forward, leading a towering black horse. "Fadri, must you hold the woman so tightly? I do not think she likes you."

The men laughed again, but the moron loosened his hold enough so that I could pull my arms free. I turned to the slender man, taking in his short black hair, fierce black eyebrows, and surprisingly full mouth. Calm, self-assured, he stared back with startling light blue eyes.

"My name is Kate Vincent," I said in Spanish. "I've become separated from my group and need a ride back to Zaragoza."

The man's clear gaze held mine for a moment, then he looked toward the unconscious boy. "Enzo, dunk Hamara in the river. That should revive him." Half the riders whooped and urged their horses toward the river, choosing a dunking sideshow over me.

"Kate Vicente, you are in luck, for it so happens we are returning to Zaragoza. Our raids on La Rioja were successful, but Gonzalez may be behind us, so we ride hard. You are welcome to be our...guest as we travel." He finished tugging on long, thick leather gloves, stained dark.

"Thank you," I replied, vaguely uneasy but out of options.

My nostrils told me the pungent Fadri had stepped up behind me. "Can I keep her?" he asked. "She can ride with me." At the touch of his meaty hand on my ass, I clenched my fist and spun around, landing a solid punch on his filthy jaw. Fadri staggered, then tripped backwards.

I rubbed my stinging knuckles, then leaned over the stunned man. I briefly reviewed my limited vocabulary of Spanish cuss words, realizing I only knew enough for a clichéd threat. "You touch me again, you filthy bastard, and I'll kick you so hard you'll choke on your own balls."

As Fadri flew to his feet, face red, the slender man stepped between us and said, "Fadri, she will ride with me."

Fadri's face fell, but he did not challenge the smaller man. With a resigned shrug, he returned to his horse and I could breathe again.

"My name is Luis Navarro." He gave a slight bow. "For your own safety, I ask two things of you. First, do not leave my side." He didn't take his amazing eyes, lightly flecked with smoky gray, from mine, but I could feel his mind sweep toward fifty obviously undisciplined, uncouth men. Actors? If not actors, then what? I nodded. "Second," he said as he moved to his saddle bag and pulled out a small bundle, "put these on." He handed me a long, blue skirt and a white tunic, which brought more ribald laughter from his men.

"Luis has so many women he carries spare clothes for them," one shouted.

"El Picador is ready for anything, even naked women!" called another.

I examined the coarse, hand-made clothes. "What's wrong with my own clothes?" Luis moved closer. "Woman, you are nearly naked." His long black lashes blinked once. I expected a smile, but none followed, only one raised eyebrow.

I tugged the skirt and blouse on over my head, instantly grateful for the extra layer of warmth. But my brown Doc Martens and purple socks looked ridiculous under the calf-length skirt. "You and your friends are very strange."

"We must ride." When he led me back to his horse, I stared up at the black monster. Please, God, not a horse. Maybe if I waited another hour a bus would come by. But when Luis moved to help me, I grabbed the saddle, pulled myself up, and flung my leg over the beast's massive back, ignoring the men's gasps. I settled the skirt around me as best I could, but my knees showed again.

"You do not want to ride sidesaddle?"

"God, no."

Shaking his head, Luis mounted behind me. A dripping wet Hamara, his turban slipping off to reveal tight, black hair, rode beside us and fixated on my knees once again. When he looked up, I winked, which nearly de-horsed him.

We rode for over an hour, not speaking. Rather, Luis rode and I bounced. My inner thighs burned raw, my ass hurt from smacking the iron-hard saddle, and my back ached from holding myself erect so I wouldn't lean back against Luis and make something *else* erect. At least he didn't smell as badly as the others. Dusk began, deepening the lavender sky to a rich indigo. Would I get back to Anna before dark?

The black horse beneath us showed no signs of tiring, even though his broad neck glistened. "So, what's your horse's name?" I finally broke the silence, my voice jiggling.

"Matamoros," Luis said, only inches from my ear. Moor-killer. How lovely. The sun sank lower, throwing blackish purple shadows up the tight river valley. Still no sign of civilization. A tiny suspicion tugged at a corner of my mind, but it was too fantastic to consider. Maybe I had been drugged, kidnapped, then transported to a remote area.

By the time Luis raised his hand and the men reined in their horses, my butt burned. "We camp here," Luis barked. "Enzo, set up guards on those two hills and along the river. Send two men back one league to warn us if Gonzalez is foolish enough to attack. Fadri, put the prisoners near that ledge, with double guards."

Five of the men had their hands tied and lashed to their saddles, a procedure that seemed unusually cruel for a historical reenactment, with a chain mail goon leading each horse. The prisoners played their role well, appearing, even in this poor light, as fatigued and filthy as the rest of the men. The first four who passed sent convincing looks of hatred toward Luis, and one muttered a curse, to which Luis did not respond. The fifth prisoner flashed me such a charming grin I nearly smiled back. "Luis, you dog. Why do you always get such beautiful women?"

"Because, Nuño, I surpass you in charm, good looks, and wit."

Nuño leaned closer, his brown eyes warm above a beard gone wild. "I think your charms for women lay much lower than that."

"Ach!" Luis slapped Nuño's horse playfully. "Be gone, you barbarian."

A laughing Nuño joined the others. "Where are you taking them?" I asked.

"To al-Mu'tamin."

The name sounded familiar. "What will he do with them?" Might as well play this guy's game.

"Execute them, torture them, or ransom them. Perhaps all three."

"So why is that prisoner Nuño so friendly?"

Luis's chest rose and fell with a deep sigh. "He is my best friend, woman."

Before I could respond, he slid off Matamoros and helped me down. My knees buckled underneath me; helpless, I crumpled to the ground. "Holy Mother of God," I said. "I feel as if I've given birth to the damn horse, not ridden it."

A flash of amusement crossed his face, but he turned away. I rubbed my arms to warm them. "When do we reach Zaragoza?" I asked as the men jerked filthy blankets off horses so sweaty steam rose in clouds off their backs. Luis barked a few more orders, then squatted beside me, steel blue eyes boring into mine. An owl hooted from the hill beside us.

"Tomorrow, woman. Zaragoza remains in danger, so we cannot be away long."

"My name is Kate. Stop calling me 'woman.'"

Despite the two thin white scars running across one tan cheek and over the bridge of his slender nose, Luis's face was androgynous, skin smooth as a woman's, eyes defensively fierce. He sort of reminded me of a pissed-off Johnny Depp, and I wondered if he'd ever been harassed by other men for being too pretty. He rested on his heels, almost cat-like in his quiet confidence, then he lifted one corner of his mouth. "Kate."

I accepted the tin cup of cool river water and drained it, too thirsty to worry about bacteria. "So, what's your game? Historical re-enactment? Actors in a festival or something?"

He stared at me, then drained his own cup. "We are soldiers, nothing more."

"You mean you are pretending to be soldiers."

His fierce black brows pulled together briefly, then he shrugged. "I brought these lances on a raid to help them relax. Life in Zaragoza has been tense lately."

"I'll bet." This guy refused to step out of character even for a second. With the darkness, most of the men had stretched out, and a few had begun snoring. "I have to pee."

Luis surveyed the grassy hill behind me. "Follow me." We picked our way around bodies and saddles then walked twenty yards up the hill, where Luis stopped. "Fine. Do what you must."

I snorted. Not a tree or bush within hundreds of yards. "I think not, Señor Picador. Over there, up on that hill."

He stopped me with a rock hard hand. "No, your silhouette may be visible to Gonzalez if he follows. Here is fine. Darkness gives you privacy."

Creep. "Turn your damn back then." The men below paid no attention. I struggled to pull my shorts down, yet stay covered by the cumbersome skirt. Christ. My kingdom for a smelly Port-a-John. I ended up peeing on one sock and shoe and the hem of the skirt. Wet fabric slapped my calf as I stood and zipped up my shorts. "Great, just great," I muttered.

"I am so glad you feel better," Luis said. I could hear the twinkle in his eye, even if I couldn't see it.

"Jerk," I said in English. Back at Luis's saddle, he spread out a woolen blanket for me. "*Gracias*," I said as I sat down. But then he knelt, seized both my hands, and with two flicks of a rough, scratchy rope, tied my wrists together. "Hey!" I tried pulling back. "This hurts." He looped the other end of the rope around his waist.

"I would hate for you to wander away in the night and get lost," he said, dropping down beside me.

"I'm your guest, remember?"

He rolled away. "Good night, Kate."

I glared at him, then stretched out on my half of the blanket, a prisoner after all. I shifted, trying to get comfortable on the hard soil and dry, prickly grass, but no luck. A million stars shone overhead, more than one should be able to see with light pollution from Zaragoza, wherever it was. Was Anna out combing the countryside for me? Had she alerted the authorities? The US Embassy? While I fumed, the men around me snored, and the guards talked quietly. I unzipped my fanny pack, ate my candy bar, and entertained myself with thoughts of revenge. At the first town we reached, I'd scream for the nearest cop and have Luis & Company arrested. These pricks didn't know who they were messing with.

❖

I awoke to shouts in the early dawn as Luis rolled to his feet and yanked me up, nearly tearing my arms from their sockets. "Hey!" I cried.

He grabbed his saddle and raced for his horse, and since I was still tethered to his waist, I stumbled along behind him. "What of our guards?" Luis shouted.

"Must be dead," Enzo replied as he raced for his own horse. Terrified shouts and alarmed whinnies filled the cool air as Luis dragged me over to the prisoners.

"Enzo, you and two men take the prisoners ahead to the Narrows. Wait for us there. Take the woman as well." He untied the rope between us and grasped my waist, but before he could throw me onto the saddle, a commanding shout rang out above the chaos.

"Navarro!" Sound died as all eyes turned to the edge of our encampment, where a large man in full armor stood in his stirrups, his white horse prancing. Forty men on horseback fanned out behind him. "You are trapped. Return my men and I will let you live."

Luis, ramrod straight, glared back, a muscle twitching in his fine-boned jaw. "These prisoners are the property of the Most Respected al-Mu'tamin, emir of Zaragoza and all of western Andaluz. I will not release them without his authority."

"Then you will die," growled the man.

Luis shook his head, a wry smile flashing briefly. "Not today, Gonzalez."

"Who is that?" The scowling man pointed a gloved finger at me. "Another woman you've ruined?"

Luis's grip on my waist tightened. "Your Marisella came to me willingly, Gonzalez. Do not blame me if your fiancée figured out you are an uncouth bastard." Rude laughter trickled through Luis's men and the furious Gonzalez plunged his gray-speckled horse into the crowd, heading straight for us. Luis threw me onto the horse behind Nuño, the friendly prisoner with the black beard. I yelped as my tailbone hit the saddle but grabbed Nuño's black leather belt to stay seated.

Luis pulled a massive sword from his scabbard and raised it high. "For Rodrigo and Mu'tamin!" Luis's men raised their swords and a terrible, wrenching roar filled the valley as both sides collided and the air rang with steel. Gonzalez slashed his way toward us in a realistic imitation of a demon possessed. My pulse raced as I searched for a TV camera recording the dramatic scene. What the hell was this? An elaborate war games setup? Reality TV? A Middle Ages Survival show gone overboard?

While Enzo and his men struggled to get the prisoners mounted, I watched the fighting, marveling at the realistic choreography. These guys were good. Luis yanked a man off his horse, and the two clanged heavy swords together. Soon both men stood chest to chest, swords overhead locked together at the hilts. Sword in one hand, Luis pulled a dagger from a thigh scabbard with the other and thrust it through a rip in the man's mail. Blood spurted from the chest wound. Luis pulled out the dagger, then slashed open the man's throat.

"Jesus Christ!" I cried.

"El Picador strikes again," Nuño said. "Hold on. We go." With our horses' reins held by Enzo and his men, we galloped down a slope. I looked back to see the broad-shouldered Gonzalez leap from his horse and slash at Luis's head with a massive sword, but then we raced into a grove of trees, and lost sight of the fighting. I gripped the horse with my knees and clung to Nuño, who smelled no better than Fadri the Blond Moron.

"God damn it. Shit. Shit. Shit," I cursed in English. This was *no* historical re-enactment. Maybe reality TV, but where were the cameras? We rode hard, with Nuño's black boots firmly in the stirrups, my feet flopping around like noodles. By the time we stopped at what must have been the Narrows, I blinked back tears of pain and shock.

Enzo pulled me roughly from the saddle; I collapsed on the ground.

"Enzo, be gentle with Luis's woman," Nuño scolded as he too dismounted. Left on the ground, I curled up, too tired to care how pathetic I might look. Enzo and his men began tying the prisoners to a nearby stand of trees as I eavesdropped, confused by all the names. Enzo and Luis and the Blond Moron, Fadri, were good guys, while Nuño was a bad guy, a prisoner, but also Luis's friend. The Christians were taking Christian prisoners to a Moor. If they were trying to recreate history, they were doing a good job, because none of it made any sense to me.

"Enzo, do not do this," one of them pleaded. "We are Christians. You are Christian."

Enzo tied the last knot with a vicious yank, his face solid but rough, as if the stone carver had quit before Enzo had fully emerged. "You are a coward. Shut up." I began working at the knot holding my own wrists together.

"You follow an infidel. Luis has abandoned us. He has abandoned his faith."

Despite Enzo's even tone, his broad face, lined with age, flushed red. "Luis is no infidel, you pig."

The prisoner laughed, a short, staccato sound. "Look where he has led you. You live in exile from Castile, banished from your homes. Instead, you live with Moors in a Moorish castle. You probably *bathe*. You share a table with those infidels. It sickens me to think you probably share their women as well."

Enzo's palm cracked across the prisoner's face. "We wait here for Luis," Enzo said, then he stomped away to water the horses in the nearby river. I finally pulled my hands free, wincing as I rubbed my wrists.

"Luis Navarro will not survive today's battle," one of the other prisoners called. "Gonzalez will kill him."

Nuño's harsh laugh matched the iron in his voice. "Even if Gudesto Gonzalez had the skill to kill Luis, he lacks the courage. No, hear this.

Luis will ride through that ravine shortly."

I lay on the ground, breathing in the fishy river, the cool earth, the moist grass beneath me. A red-tailed hawk shrieked overhead. I closed my eyes. Maybe when I opened them, Anna would be kneeling beside me, concerned eyes moist with relief. She'd sit me up, wrap her arms around me, and tell me how frightened she'd been. But then my muscles began to cramp, so I opened my eyes. No Anna. Nothing had changed. Enzo and his men still tended the horses at the river fifty yards away. Nuño and the other prisoners had expanded their bickering to include some king named Alfonso.

I sat up. We had stopped in a deep, narrow section of the valley. Twenty feet away the trees thickened into a forest that rose up the side of the valley. A woman posed little threat, so no one watched me. I stood casually, stretched out my stiff legs and back, then with a last look at both groups of men, I dashed for the trees.

My stupid skirt caught on the underbrush a few times but I yanked it free, quickly scrambling high enough they wouldn't have seen me if they'd looked. Hot, sweaty, panting, I reached the top and started running through the long grass, keeping the river to my left so I wouldn't get lost. Below me, out of my sight, hooves thundered toward the river. The grass caught at my legs and feet as I ran faster.

"I told you!" Nuño's triumphant voice drifted up the hill, faint but still clear. "I was right, you idiot. Luis has survived."

I sprinted toward a grove of trees far off to my right, the only place to hide in this sea of grass. An angry shout down by the river pushed me to run faster, since Luis would know by now I'd escaped. Heart pounding, lungs burning, I stumbled but caught myself. The trees seemed miles away.

Minutes later hoofbeats pounded behind me. I reached the trees with the lone horseman nearly upon me, so I headed for the low hanging branches. Someone dismounted with a grunt. Too terrified to look back, I crashed through the brush.

"Stop!" he commanded, but I kept going. "Please."

Stunned at the polite request, I did stop, turning to face a panting Luis. His face, tunic, and leggings were blood-spattered, as was his brown cape, which fluttered behind him in the breeze as he approached, eyes sunk deep with exhaustion. "I do not have time for this. I have wounded men."

"Let me go," I said between gasps.

He wiped his face. "No, we must ride to Zaragoza. My men need tending."

I put my hands on my hips. "I am not coming with you. I am not your woman." My heart pounded. I couldn't outrun him.

Luis's eyes widened. "I did not say you were my woman."

"Nuño did."

He shook his head, smiling. "Nuño likes to tease. You are not my woman."

"Good. Glad we cleared that up." When I whirled to run, I suddenly couldn't move. A massive dagger, still vibrating, pinned my skirt to the tree trunk behind me.

Luis shrugged modestly. "So sorry. I am good with a knife." Damn it. Luis gripped my wrist, released my skirt, then slid the dagger into his thigh scabbard. He dragged me back to his horse at the edge of the grove.

The thought of mounting a horse again filled me with such despair I gripped Luis's mail tunic. "You don't understand," I cried, shaking him. "For nearly twenty-four hours all I've experienced is dark caves and sweaty men who fart in their sleep and spit and are covered in fake blood and carry phallic swords and throw daggers. I can't take this much longer." The last came out as a sob.

Luis patted my arm. "I do understand, Kate. We will return to Zaragoza, where there are many women in Mu'tamin's harem. You will like the harem. Come."

"No, please let me go."

Luis removed my hands from his neck. "No. We might have a use for you. Come."

A use for me? Once again I straddled the goddamned horse, Luis's arms around me holding the reins. I pounded the wide saddle front. Where was Anna? Why did I feel so utterly alone? Numb, I fell silent. While I floundered in some totally confusing charade, Arturo waited. Waited to show me the next drawing he'd made of his new family. Waited to introduce Anna and me to his friends. Waited to put his small hands in ours and walk out the door of El Orfanato Benévolo de San Estéfan. Waited for a plane ride across the ocean and his own room complete with race car wallpaper and a friendly black lab named Max.

I heard the hoots and catcalls as Luis and I returned, but did not respond. I saw the men's wounds, still bleeding through filthy wrappings, but felt nothing. Given the earlier scene I'd witnessed, the blood must be real. My ass surely hurt as we rode until late afternoon, but I felt nothing. I saw the massive wooden waterwheel floating on a river raft. I saw acres of orange groves, of wheat fields, and hill after hill of grape vines. I saw white city walls as we approached what Luis claimed was Zaragoza. I saw the distinctive towers rising up from a sparkling white palace high on the hill. I saw donkeys and ox carts. I saw women, veiled and smooth and light on their feet. I saw street vendors selling lemons and pomegranates. I saw children and dogs and goats running alongside us. I heard Arabic music down one street, a lute of some sort and a drum. I smelled rich spices. I smelled rotting human waste.

Luis must have helped me off his horse, for I found myself walking through a palace gate. Luis led me into a brilliant courtyard crowded with ferns, low benches, a massive central fountain with water rising fifteen feet, and men, more men. He led me into a huge room off this courtyard, where a bear of a man, dressed in a copper-studded leather tunic, sat at a carved desk muttering over his books. Luis brought me up to the desk, then bowed slightly. "My lord, the five prisoners have been put in the dungeon for al-Mu'tamin. This woman we found wandering alone by the cave."

The tall man stood, grunting as he readjusted the scabbard belt around his thickening waist. A ragged salt and pepper beard, braided at the tips, reached mid-chest, but his graying hair was clipped as short as Luis's. He squinted and stepped closer, hard eyes raking over every inch of my body, not as a man would look at a woman, but as a man would look at a horse.

"Her name is Kate Vicente," Luis offered.

The man grunted again. The fountain just outside his door pattered gently as the water spouting from a fish's mouth fell back into the basin.

Somehow, finally, I found my voice, which cracked from my long silence. "And who are you?" My foggy brain struggled to make sense of all this. The instant Luis had sliced that man's throat open, I knew this was not an historical re-enactment.

Luis touched my arm. "This is my lord, Rodrigo Díaz of Vivar. The Moors call him al-Cid."

Al-Cid...El Cid. An invisible vise clamped onto my chest, squeezing off my breath. I tried to speak, but my voice squeaked once, twice, then nothing. I'd gone too long without food or a cell phone, too long without a Diet Coke or email, too long on a horse, too long without a jet roaring overhead, a billboard trying to sell me car insurance, someone's boom box blasting at me. So I took a long look at the man before me, then did what no self-respecting lesbian should do. I fainted.

❖

When I opened my eyes, the ornate ceiling overhead seemed vaguely familiar, one of peacocks strutting and displaying. I jumped when the cool cloth touched my forehead, but a toothless camel-colored woman, wrinkled as a Shar Pei, pushed me back down on the lumpy divan. She scolded me in Arabic, dabbing my temples and wrists with the rag.

"She says you rode too long and too hard." Luis rested on a stool against the opposite wall of the small room, long legs crossed at the ankles, clothes and face clean, a bandage wrapped around one arm.

"That was your fault." Now that the guy had cleaned up, his androgynous beauty reminded me of the early Elvis, too pretty to be a man, too handsome to be a woman.

I rubbed my aching temples but the woman slapped my hands away, muttering "*Mah, mah*," and wiped once again with the cloth. The room glowed like warm honey as the sun from the adjoining courtyard streamed into the windowless room. Along with the sun, there drifted in the murmur of relaxed female voices. Two children ran by my open doorway, followed by a tiny gazelle. Three brilliant blue parrots flew past, then two screaming kids, then something that looked like a monkey. I felt like Dorothy looking out the window of her spinning house. Nothing made sense. I moaned. "Where am I?"

"The harem of al-Mu'tamin." Luis dismissed the woman with a terse Arabic command, and she bowed before leaving. "He indulges his women, so it is a bit wild in here."

I held my hands over my eyes, easing the headache some. "What do you want?"

"To know more about you. Why were you by yourself?"

"I was lost."

"Where did you come from? Where were you going?"

I raised up on one elbow. "Do you interrogate all your guests?"

Luis shrugged, eyes icy in this light, face cold as a marble statue of a Greek god or goddess. "I think we both know you are not a guest."

God, my head hurt. I lay back down again. Name, rank, and serial number only. "I was exploring the cave. When I came out—"

"Are you married?"

"Yes."

"Where is your husband?" Luis tapped his long fingers together, fingers that had held a dagger hilt and sliced open a man's throat.

I hesitated. "My husband is...working. I'm here with a friend."

"And where is that friend?" He leaned forward, leather tunic creaking softly.

"Good question." Hopefully tearing up all of Spain to find me.

"Who sent you? Alfonso? Gonzalez?"

I tried massaging the tension from my neck. "You're giving me a headache. Please leave."

In two strides Luis leaned over me, frowning fiercely, hands pressed against the divan on either side of my head. "What are you hiding?"

Anger darkened his features as he hovered above me. Enough of this asshole's game. I knocked one arm away and sat up, so he backed off. When I swung my legs down and touched the cool tile floor, I stared stupidly at the pair of thin gold slippers on my feet. Not my shoes. Not my clothes. Instead I wore filmy daffodil trousers and a jade drawstring blouse that barely covered my breasts. I glared at Luis, who actually blushed.

"Zaydun changed your clothes. I looked away. Really, I did." He folded his arms, scowling eyebrows black slashes across a tan forehead. How ironic for a kidnapper to defend his integrity.

My clothes and Doc Martens lay in a stack in the corner, but my fanny pack still circled my waist, so Zaydun must not have figured out the modern clasp or the zipper. "Look, Johnny, I've had enough of this. Let me go."

"Your husband will pay a ransom."

"I don't have a husband, you imbecile."

"But you just said—"

"I lied because I wanted you to leave me alone."

Luis dropped beside me on the divan, leaning close enough that I could smell mint on his breath. "You claim neither father nor husband. You cannot be a nun because of your clothing. What then? A whore? A spy?"

I pushed him away again, pleased when his eyebrows arched at my strength. "I am none of those."

"The options of a woman are few. Wife, daughter, mistress, whore, or slave."

"You are disgusting." I stood, hands on my hips.

Luis rose, grabbing my shoulders with steely hands. "Rodrigo thinks you a spy. For this you can be executed." He lifted a lock of my hair. "You are an attractive woman. For this you could be sold as a slave or a harem whore. Tell me the truth, or one of these will happen to you." Something earnest replaced the anger in his eyes.

"I have told you all you need to know. Let me go home. You can't hold me here."

"Where is home?"

"The moon."

"Bah!" Luis stomped toward the courtyard, whirling around in the doorway, cropped black hair nearly bristling with frustration. "If you do not help *me*, I cannot help *you*." He clapped his hands and the toothless woman returned. He pointed at me, barked something in Arabic, then stormed away, boots drumming on the tile floor.

Zaydun clutched my wrist in her chapped hand and pulled me out into the courtyard, where at least fifteen women, ranging from pink-skinned to deep copper, lounged on massive pillows, some smoking Turkish pipes, others playing with children, some speaking Arabic, others sharing secrets in a Slavic language. When I appeared, all fell silent. Zaydun led me around a corner fountain misting droplets of warm air that settled on my bare arms, then into a room with a small tiled box resting over a covered channel in the floor. Water gurgled through the channel. Spicy sandalwood candles nearly obscured the musty smell of old urine.

"*Mirhadun*," the woman said, nodding. I shrugged. "*Mirhadun*," she repeated.

"Fine, whatever you say. *Mirhadun*." Gums working furiously, black raisin eyes scolding, she steered me toward the box, turned me around, yanked down my flimsy pants and pushed me back onto the box. I yelped at the frosty tile, but understood; the pile of withering grape leaves on the floor must be the Charmin. Not needing an audience, I stood, pulled myself together, then let Zaydun lead me back to my small, doorless room, where she presented me with a tray of oranges, plump brown dates, slices of round, thick bread, honey, and a carafe of rose liquid. At least I wouldn't starve.

After she left, I consumed everything on the tray, down to the last drop of the smooth pomegranate juice. A more noble woman would have refused to eat until her captors released her, but starving myself would bring me no closer to Anna and Arturo. The rough, moist cloth felt good as I cleaned my sticky fingers.

When my bladder screamed for release, I had no choice but to head for the *mirhadun*. The unfamiliar Arabic and Slavic languages again ceased when I appeared in the courtyard. No one met my eyes; one woman even scurried her children out of my way. As I skirted the courtyard, vague familiarity plagued me. This was like a movie set, maybe a replica of the Palacio de la Aljafería?

After my business, I explored my windowless prison. Two smooth-skinned black men guarded the harem's only exit. One tall and pudgy, the other short and pudgier, the men wore flowing magenta pants, gold embroidered magenta vests; their ebony chests were bare.

Taking a deep breath, I approached them, smiling. "Good day," I said, then aimed myself right between them. Smooth as oil, the two men shifted, filling the entire doorway with their bulk.

"*Laa*," the taller said, shaking his head. Neither met my eyes, but instead looked past a point above my ears, ebony statues. Defeated, I returned to my room and curled up on the hard divan. The dusk cast enchanting blue shadows on the white walls and yellow-tiled floor and my full stomach purred. The soft wool robe over me chased off the evening chill, yet I ached to be back in the cold, damp darkness of the Mirabueno cave listening to Joe and Lois Whipple wax euphoric about cave bumper stickers, the last time anything in my life had made sense.

CHAPTER FOUR

It took me two days to figure out the tall black man's name was Suley, the shorter was Abu. Both women and children bossed the men around shamelessly. One woman called Abu to fan her, another for Suley to rub her feet, another for Abu to hold her child while she talked. Suley and Abu moved around the harem on silent gold slippers, their voices low and respectful. Some women even walked around topless in front of the two men, but Suley and Abu didn't seem to notice. Could these poor men be eunuchs? Did they still *do* that? Was I in some pocket of Spain that wanted to recover its Moorish roots? I'd once read about a town in Mexico founded by Italians that stayed Italian over the centuries. Even today people born there considered themselves to be Italian, not Mexican. Another, less plausible, totally fantastical explanation kept creeping in, but I repeatedly pushed it away. Time travel was for rabid fans of *Star Trek* and *Stargate*, not for me.

I began the next two mornings by standing so close to Abu he had to look me in the eye.

"Good morning, Abu." Then I'd drag over a stool, climb up into Suley's face. "Good morning, Suley." I would touch my chest. "Kate." Every time I went to the bathroom or walked the harem to stretch my legs, I made sure I greeted them. I tried asking to use the phone, but they didn't seem to understand either *telefono* or my mimicking the use of a telephone. They both just shrugged.

The third day I lectured the men on their civil rights, explaining Mandela's success in South Africa, translating Martin Luther King into Spanish as best I could. Both pairs of brown eyes flickered toward me once or twice, which made my spirits soar. Progress.

The women, however, were another matter. Other than Zaydun, who scolded me every time she brought me food and water, no one spoke to me. One woman with rosy cheeks and black curly hair looked at me a few times and almost smiled once. Her two children owned the only friend I had, the shy gazelle who would peek in at me now and then. With a piece of bread, I was able to coax her near enough to examine her wide black eyes and tiny black nose. But after a few minutes, she'd whirl and bound out the door, dainty black hooves clicking on the ceramic tiles.

Time slowed as I paced the length of the harem courtyard. Was Anna looking for me? How had she explained my absence to Arturo and Señora Cavelos? Were the Zaragozan police and US Embassy investigating my kidnapping? As I worried, I did feel a sliver of relief that I wasn't locked in a dank abandoned warehouse overrun with rats, but in a lovely prison. Sunlight filtered down into the harem through upper windows covered with white marble latticework, draping the rooms in lacy shadows. Soothing water splashed playfully in the huge center fountain. I lay on my back and marveled at the carved mahogany ceilings, burnished honey tugged down into fantastic sculptures by gravity. Whenever I inhaled deeply, something one just did not do in Chicago, my head filled with lavender and mint and eucalyptus and sweet almond. When it rained, I sat in my room and watched the rain splatter and bounce on the courtyard's bright yellow and blue tiles.

Careful not to stare, I enjoyed watching the black-haired woman with her boy, about Arturo's age, and the girl, perhaps a year younger. She hugged them, stroked their heads, but snapped "*Barakah*" when they'd chased each other screaming around the fountains too long. Once she caught me watching and deep dimples lit up her face, a trickle of water for my parched soul.

I ate baked meat pies, spiced rice, and a type of pancake stuffed with almonds and drizzled with honey. I couldn't see outside, but I could hear. Five times a day a man's mournful song rang out across the rooftops, and the women retired to a room to pray. The city fell almost silent toward the heat of the afternoon, then came alive, people shouting, hammers bashing, animals bawling, when evening came. But I heard no mowers, saws, drills. No backfiring cars, no honking horns. Now and then a lone trumpet called in the distance, followed by Arabic-sounding drums and pipes.

After four days of the silent treatment, I thought I would go crazy. Using awkward hand signals, I asked Abu for something to draw with. He returned with a stump of thick charred wood from the kitchen's fire pits, and I began drawing on my walls, sketching Anna's face, my dog Max.

"*Bazi*," Zaydun said when she peered inside, nodding with approval. Soon she returned with an armful of ivory muslin riddled with holes, likely nibbled out by tiny mouse teeth. Zaydun was obviously free to leave the harem.

I considered the cloth. "No stretched canvas?" I asked. "No sketchbook? Perhaps a Yellow No. 2?" It didn't seem too outrageous a request, especially since there was probably a Wal-Mart within a few blocks, an oddly comforting thought even though I never shopped there. Just because I was stuck in some weird place didn't mean the rest of the world wasn't continuing on as normal.

When the eldery woman frowned at my request, I said, "*Gracias*," and touched her arm briefly.

Her black eyes dropped shyly. "*Alalah*." She helped me rip the damaged fabric into an assortment of square, rectangular, and odd-shaped scraps. "*Titammu*," Zaydun said as she stuck the charcoal into my hand, which I assumed meant "draw," so I did.

Drawing helped pass the time, but my mind still spun. Would Señora Cavelos explain to Arturo that I had disappeared, that I didn't abandon him? Would Anna be allowed to take Arturo on her own? San Estéfan's permitted single adoptions, so there was no reason she couldn't. Would she think I'd gotten cold feet and run off? True, I'd been a little nervous as we'd neared the adoption, but I was dealing. I would never just freak out and run away, which was sort of what my own parents had done. Both worked sixty hour weeks, Mom in advertising design, Dad in nursing. Both worked out at the club three times a week, Mom was on three non-profit boards, Dad took classes, and I drifted, just one more of life's details struggling for a time slot in my parents' DayTimer planners.

Sometimes I'd even thought of myself as an orphan. No wonder Arturo had captured my heart. My resolve to return to him deepened.

But it had been six days since I'd seen Arturo, six days since I'd said good-bye to Anna in front of the Palacio, and I hadn't seen anything but this courtyard for days. The morning of the fifth day in the harem, I folded.

I stood before the ever-present Suley and Abu. I pointed to myself, then pointed out the doorway. Both shook their heads, but now at least they looked at me, and I swore regret shone in Suley's warm eyes. I pointed through the doorway again. "Luis Navarro?" The men looked at each other, then back at me. I repeated my request.

"Luis Navarro," Suley said. With just the slightest of winks, he bowed, then disappeared down the hallway. While I waited, I told Abu about Harriet Tubman and the Underground Railroad. His brows knit together as he struggled to understand my tortured explanation. Finally I heard boots on the hallway tile.

But instead of Luis, the form that filled the doorway was another man. I stared at him, and quickly recognized the man who'd five days ago screamed at Luis as he and the others had attacked us. The tall man carried himself like a soldier, his massive gray-brown cloak swirling around his calves, dull copper mail clinking as he flashed me a charming smile, then bowed deeply.

"Oh," I said stupidly.

"Señorita." He took my hand and kissed it before I could pull away. "I am Gudesto Gonzalez, a soldier of his excellency Alfonso, king of Castile, Leon, and Asturias. I have completed my negotiations here, but I am deeply saddened to learn you are still a prisoner." His deep baritone was hypnotic, reminding me of my Uncle Ross who used to read to me.

I finally recovered my hand from his thick, square paw. "I am saddened too. I must get out of here soon."

Gudesto nodded, gray-green eyes sparkling under heavy lids. "While I seem to be powerless to free my comrades from the barbarian Mu'tamin's dungeons, I can offer you safe passage from this hellhole to a civilized world. Return to Burgos with me and you will be treated with dignity and respect, not as some Moorish whore locked away from the world."

I straightened. Freedom stood before me, a polite, armed man with a Roman nose and bronze leggings, breathing heavily in the heat of the day. The only way I could find my way back to Zaragoza, the real Zaragoza, was to get *out* of here. While Gudesto, all copper and bronze and brown, seemed to be formed from the very soil of Spain, when he wasn't playing soldier he probably spent his days as a computer geek in some Madrid office tower. "Once we leave, I am free to go wherever I want, correct?"

"Certainly. You would be the prisoner of no man."

I ran back to my room, grabbed my fanny pack and stuffed another bag with my own clothes. At the door I expected Abu to stop me, but Gudesto fairly bristled with steel. "*Gracias*, Abu, for the charcoal." I shook his hand, then like a dog suddenly off a leash, my heart soared as I followed the cloak ahead of me. "Anna, I'm coming," I said under my breath. At each doorway Gudesto stepped aside to let me go through first, then resumed the lead, clearly confident I was behind him.

"Where are we going?" I finally asked after following him through a confusing maze of rooms, courtyards, and stairs.

"To the stables by an indirect route. I would not want your captors to stop your flight to freedom." Just as he spoke, we turned a corner and nearly bumped into Luis leaning against an iron grille, gnawing on a hunk of brown bread.

Gudesto roared, thrust me behind him, then drew his sword. Luis finished chewing, then wiped his sleeve across his face.

"Stealing from your host, Gudesto?" Luis rubbed his chin. "Mu'tamin and Rodrigo may be less inclined to release your men."

"Draw your sword, coward." This made no sense. Why would these two men, both playing Christian soldiers, be on different sides in this bizarre charade?

Luis belched delicately, then put his hands on his narrow hips. "I would hate to widow poor Marisella before she even weds you."

"She will not have me now that you—" Gudesto bit off his sentence, waving his sword menacingly, face dark with anger. "I will have this woman as compensation."

My heart flipped. "First, that's not what you told me. Second, screw you." The guy probably already had a 401k plan and stock options up the wazoo, yet he thought he would add *me* as compensation?

Luis's relaxed smile softened his ferocious eyebrows. "I am not surprised. Marisella told me Gudesto lies to women."

Now thoroughly confused, I began stepping away from Gudesto. "I don't really understand—" The large man grabbed me by the hair, pulling me close enough to pin me to his side with a hammerlock hold. "Hey!" I shouted, head throbbing, but Gudesto's booming voice drowned out my own.

"You ruined Marisella. Now I will ruin this woman in return."

I pulled and clawed at Gudesto's arm, but he was too strong. Luis laughed. "To what end? She is nothing to me."

"She is, or she would not still be alive." This ridiculous discussion faded as I suddenly remembered my self-defense. Behind Gudesto, bent over his spread legs, I was powerless. I took two deep breaths, then swung my leg around in front of his, raised my arm, then slammed my elbow into the Gonzalez family jewels.

Without a sound, Gudesto doubled over. I stood slightly, then smashed an elbow into his face, sending him staggering back with both hands clutching his groin. Panting, I stepped out of sword reach, pleased that all those hours of watching Buffy and Sydney Bristol and Xena kick ass had finally paid off.

"Holy Bullocks," Fadri said. He, Enzo, and four other men had appeared behind Luis and stood gaping at me and my white-faced victim.

Luis's blue eyes sparkled as he barely suppressed a smile. "Men, watch yourselves with this one."

"Damn right," I sputtered, then flushed as all five men stared at me.

Gudesto grunted softly, staggered to his feet, then swung his sword straight for Luis's head. I gasped and fell back as the lithe man ducked and whirled, sword still in his scabbard, but a dagger now in his hand. Within seconds he had Gudesto against the wall, his dagger pressed against the larger man's throat.

"Do not be stupid, old friend. We are five swords to your one. And even if you kill us all, your bullocks will never survive another encounter with our beautiful Kate."

The men snickered and Gudesto's face flushed an alarming red. When he glared at me, an odd flicker of fear spread up my spine as the man's eyes burned with fury. What if he was one of those guys to carry a grudge about the whole knee-in-the-gonad thing? "This is not over, Navarro."

"It will not be over until one of us is dead." Luis sighed. "Enzo, I believe Señor Gonzalez here needs an escort to his horse. I will return our guest to the harem." With a furious glare, Gudesto whirled, his escorts following him down the hallway. Luis sheathed his dagger then took firm hold of my elbow. I tried to pull away but he held too tightly as we walked.

"You should not be so gullible, Kate," Luis said softly. "Once clear of the palace, he would have...abused you, then left you to die."

I said nothing, uncomfortable he might be right. Gudesto had been so calm, so reasonable, so helpful. A minute later, I stopped. "Who are you, really?"

Luis froze, tightening his grip. "Luis Navarro."

I shook my head. "Not who you are pretending to be." His eyes widened and I pressed further. "Are you a plumber from Madrid who likes to dress up like a knight? Are you a schoolteacher from Valencia on summer break?"

His blue eyes turned to icy pools as he released me and stepped back. "I am Luis Navarro from Castile. I am Rodrigo Díaz's first lieutenant. That is it."

I sighed, slumping against the wall. "My god, I can't take much more of this." My knees felt weak as noodles.

"A walk on the roof, perhaps?" he asked, hands casually clasped behind his back. I nodded. I was not meant to live in a cage. Back at the harem, he barked a command in Arabic to a relieved Abu, who returned quickly with a blue veil, which he and Suley began draping around my head.

"Women must be veiled outside the harem," Luis said as I made a face.

When Abu finished tucking the final drape, I batted my eyelashes at all three men. Luis laughed. Suley and Abu covered their smiles in alarm. Luis's eyes sparkled, as did his smile, the first real smile I'd seen on his attractive but deadly serious face. "I feel ridiculous," I said.

"Come, you look lovely." He held out his arm, and feeling even more ridiculous, I took it. We walked in silence for a minute, but as we rounded a corner I nearly ran into a woman dressed in a flowing robe, her glowing copper skin taking my breath away. As she tossed back waist-length auburn hair, the woman's crimson robe fluttered open to reveal a chemise so thin I even blushed. The woman's nose was long and narrow, almost severe, but she bore it with grace and confidence.

"Al-zarca," she cooed suggestively at Luis, hardly giving me a glance. Luis bowed, kissed her slender hand, then pulled me down the hallway, away from the luscious sandalwood surrounding the Arab woman.

"Why is that woman outside the harem? And why wasn't she veiled?"

"That was Walladah, the daughter of al-Mu'tamin. As the princess of Zaragoza, she does what she wants, goes where she wants, wears what she wants."

"Al-zarca?"

Luis flushed. "Never mind."

I would have pressed, but we reached the staircase and I could smell the fresher air above, so I bounded up the stairs. With a surprised yelp, Luis followed and we ended up racing each other. I won, leaping out onto the sand-covered roof, reaching for the cloudy but endless sky above me. Perhaps it was because I'd been inside for days, but the light in this strange city had a clear, sharp quality I'd never seen. Colors seemed brighter, the world more intense.

Two teenaged boys in Arabic dress huddled over the roof's short wall; they looked up in alarm, then dashed toward the far staircase and disappeared. I ran to the wall, skin tingling as the breeze brought me to life again. Panting slightly, Luis joined me.

The hills behind the palace rose up toward pure white clouds; the hills themselves were dotted with sheep, as if wooly wisps of clouds had settled onto the earth. Laundry fluttered from ropes strung across rooftops, smoke billowed from a chimney somewhere below us. Part of the palace walls were covered with fragile wooden scaffolding so rickety OSHA would never approve. Men of every shade of brown teetered on the scaffolding painting the wall a blinding white. I spun in circles, seeing at least ten different scenes to paint, but not seeing one telephone pole or power line or high rise.

From here I could see the palace formed a rectangle with one wall slightly askew, just like the Palacio de la Aljafería. Towers ran along three sides of the palace, just like the Aljafería. We stood on the rampart, which at each corner jutted out into a diamond bastion, just like the Aljafería. I blinked twice. Don't panic. Bastions were a common Spanish architectural feature. Hills grew into craggy cobalt mountains to the north, the distant sky shimmering almost turquoise in the clear air. A stone aqueduct on graceful arches snaked up from the river, likely having once delivered water to the palace centuries ago. I gasped at the palace gates below. Four human heads, impaled on stakes.

"Are those real heads?"

Luis nodded. "One man tried to cheat Mu'tamin at the Games. Another is a Christian who insulted the prophet Muhammad. The third head is a man who dared make love to one of Mu'tamin's harem."

The long black hair on the fourth head stirred in the breeze. "And the fourth?" I already knew the answer.

"I believe her name was Chamin."

"I think I need to sit down." Luis led me to the low wall, where I sank gratefully, turning away from the gruesome heads to look toward the river. My heart nearly stopped. The river snaked through the city, hooking sharply to the left, just as I'd seen the Ebro do when Carlos had taken Anna and me to the Aljafería's roof.

Luis pointed to the north. "The Rio Ebro. The Moors call it '*nahru ibruh.*'" Small painted wooden boats bobbed in the river, avoiding rafts of floating logs tied together.

I brushed at the stone beside me, where the Moorish boys had huddled just minutes earlier, obviously carving Arabic numbers into the coarse, soft blocks.

"What's this?" I asked.

"Today's date, in Arabic. June 15, 463."

I stared at the carved date. "463?" I squeaked, heart thudding so loudly it drowned out the donkeys braying in the street below.

"No, no." Luis laughed, then touched my arm. "The Moors use a different calendar than we do. The year their calendar begins is 622 by our calendar. So you add 463 to 622, and get 1085."

The roaring in my head grew louder. My breath froze in my chest—nothing moved in, nothing moved out.

"I made the same mistake the first time I saw an Arabic date," Luis said. "Nearly stopped my heart."

Pain shot up my fingers as I dug my nails into the clay wall. Pain would stop me from blacking out. Holy, holy shit. It was true. Jesus. I squeezed my eyes tight, gasping for breath. That nagging idea I'd been pushing back for the last few days roared through my head like a cyclone. Sour, bitter, sharpness filled my mouth. I gagged violently but nothing came up. The moaning in my ears was my own voice. Still gripping the wall, I rocked back and forth.

"Kate?" Luis sounded far away.

My god. It was impossible, but true. I'd become separated from my lover, my soon-to-be son, my family, my dog, my friends, my life, not by nine hundred miles, but by over nine hundred years. I sank to my knees, gasps racking my chest.

"Kate!"

What was I going to do? My head began to tingle, and the roof spun around me. Only a pair of awkward but determined arms around me broke my fall to the sandy roof. I clutched at my chest, too shocked to even cry. This just could not be real. Images flashed behind my closed eyes and I knew that it had to be real. The graffiti above the cave ledge. Roberto, the janitor from the orphanage, with his garlic breath and his ominous words, "No go cave."

I don't know how long I lost myself in shock, gasping, moaning, even finally tearing up. Hell, I never cried, ever. Finally I stopped, my breath coming in ragged gasps. When I pulled off the stupid veil and blew my nose, Luis released me and leaned back against the wall. My breath still came in shudders, but I had no more tears. I'd gone hollow, my bones, internal organs, blood all fused into one twisted knot of pain.

"1085," I finally said.

"All year long, Kate."

"You really are El Cid's first lieutenant."

"Of course."

"This really is the Aljafería."

"Yes."

"Nuño Súarez really is your best friend."

"Yes."

"He really will be executed, tortured, or ransomed."

A brief pause. "Yes. King Alfonso has not paid a ransom yet, so Mu'tamin has begun the torture. Gudesto Gonzalez takes one of the prisoner's fingers to Alfonso in Burgos."

"How horrible."

"Not really. The man could not handle a sword with five fingers. One less will make no difference."

I took several deep breaths, then really looked at him. He wasn't a hallucination. His smooth, firm jaw was real, as were his bitten-off fingernails, black eyebrows, thick black lashes, thin white scars on his cheek and nose. His strength, his skills with sharp objects. All real.

"Kate, I need to know who you are."

I blew my nose again, then took a few deep breaths. Anna was much better at white lies than I was, so I'd better stick as close to the truth as possible. "My name really is Kate Vincent. I live in America... west of here. I live with...Anna." I swallowed hard.

"Where were you going when I found you?"

"I...I was going...on a journey."

A man's exasperation looked the same in the eleventh century as in the twenty-first. "Yes, I know. To where?"

The graffiti at the Mirabueno cave flooded back. *If you are lost, only at Altamira can you find your way home.* Had the janitor fallen back in time, then found his way back to the present through Altamira? I searched my memory. Hadn't someone discovered prehistoric drawings in a cave at Altamira? That was it. "We came to Spain to see the cave at Altamira."

"Spain?"

Christ, it wasn't even a country yet. "Here, to the Iberian peninsula." Where the hell was Altamira? I shifted against the stone, watching a flock of pigeons land before us and begin pecking at insects in the sand. They were identical to the pigeons in Wilson Park near our house, down to the coy bobbing of the head, the gentle cooing, the fragile pink feathers ringing their necks.

"I do not know this Altamira, but I have heard that there is a cave with paintings near Santillana del Mar. But Kate, this is on the northern coast. How did you come to be at Mirabueno?"

I made up some drivel about a guide bringing us across the Pyrenees, then our group being attacked and me getting lost.

"The guide should have taken you west as soon as you cleared the Pyrenees."

"He was a bad guide. I knew it from the start."

"Where did you lose your clothes?"

"I didn't. Those were my clothes. That's how we dress in... America."

Luis's eyes widened. "Oh."

The pigeons took off in an alarming flapping of wings as I picked up a handful of warm sand, letting it run through my fingers.

"Mu'tamin misses the sea," Luis said, "so a whole caravan of ox carted the sand in from Tarragona." A strange look crossed his face. "The Moors do like their comforts."

I could not control time. I could not just wake up and find myself where I belonged. Life had flung me over nine hundred and twenty years back in time, ripping me from everything I'd known. And Anna. Oh my god. She'd have no idea where I went or what had happened to me. She'd be furious for a few weeks, then desperately worried, then alone. "I'd like to go back to my room," I said quietly. As Luis escorted me back, parts of our route felt familiar, parts foreign. Carlos, the guide, had said the palace had been renovated. Because the floor plan wasn't exactly the same in this palace as in the Palacio de la Aljafería, I'd been able to deny my nagging suspicions.

At the harem door, Luis bowed slightly and left me. Once inside my room, I unzipped my pack. Hands sweating, I pulled out the Lion King key chain, bending the familiar plastic. I huddled over the flashlight, squeezing my eyes shut as the tiny light danced across my lap. I ran my fingers over the hard, cool bubbles encasing the Benadryl, then pulled out the postcard of Aljafería, wiping my eyes. I re-read my note from Paloma de Palma, then unfolded Arturo's drawing, shivering. A complete Anna, a complete Max, but only my body. And now all of me was missing in action. Vanished. Disappeared.

I put everything back, zipped up the bag, lay on the divan, pressed the pack to my belly, curled myself around it. I tuned out the laughter and children's yelling in the courtyard, hearing only the fountains, their splashing, splattering coming nearer, growing louder, rushing past me, until I buried my head under the pillow. What on earth was going to happen to me now?

CHAPTER FIVE

I awoke to shouting in Arabic—two children fought over something, their shrill voices bouncing off the courtyard walls. Women laughed nearby. The smell of fresh bread drifted past me. I rolled onto my back. 1085. I closed my eyes. I missed Anna. I missed my friends Laura and Deb. I missed my dog. I missed my squeezed-out tubes of paint. I wanted my life back.

I rubbed my forehead, struggling to remember the Spanish history lectures Anna had given me. 1085. Christians fighting Christians. Moors fighting Moors. Everyone struggling for land, for power.

El Cid. I replayed the Charlton Heston-Sophia Loren movie Anna had insisted we watch at least once a year even though it was historically inaccurate, but I could remember little more than Loren's lips and dark eyes.

Burying my nose in the lavender-scented pillow didn't change things. Neither did lying in bed. As I sat up and my own body odor overpowered the scent of bread, I scratched my head, realizing for the first time just how filthy I was. I needed a bath. I slipped through the courtyard and peeked into the bath. Only a small black woman, naked from the waist up, stood in the room folding towels. She looked up at me, but said nothing.

"You, bath?"

I whirled around. From the doorway, the young mother of the gazelle owners smiled, two dimples appearing in a round face framed by those waves of black curly hair. "My name Liana. Spanish not good. Bath good. Come." Her accent seemed French. Before I could protest, she hustled me into the warm room, into the care of the black woman.

"Ali wash you."

"No, that's not nec—" With two quick tugs, Ali efficiently stripped off my clothes. Naked, I could feel a blush as bright as Hamara's creeping up my neck. Then Liana, bless her heart, did what any sensitive woman would do in that situation—she stripped off her own clothes.

"Ali wash us both," she said, hazel eyes sparkling.

I stunk, there was no denying that, but I could still wash myself. Unfortunately Ali had other ideas. She pushed me toward a low stone bench, forcing me onto my stomach.

"I can—ouch!" The wet sponge scraped down my back and across my buttocks, then up my sides and under my arms. Ali flipped me over, dipped the sponge in a bucket of slightly sulfuric water. Around my neck, across my breasts, and even though I squeaked in protest, she vigorously scrubbed between my legs.

Liana sat companionably on the floor next to my head as my skin screamed in pain. "We thought you new wife," she said, hands puncturing the air. "But Abu say no. This good. His Excellency no need more wives."

"No, I definitely am not—oof." The washerwoman seemed determined to remove every one of my skin cells. She sat me up, poured the bucket of warm water over my head, then massaged soap into my scalp. I grunted at the rough treatment, rolling my eyes at Liana. She rewarded me with a delighted chuckle. I covered my face as Ali tugged, massaged, rinsed, and squeezed, not stopping until my hair squeaked. Then she led me into a deep bath in the corner of the room, where, body tingling, I sank gratefully into the warm water.

After similar treatment, Liana joined me. I tried not to stare as she lowered herself into the water across from me. "Are you one of Mu'tamin's wives?" I asked.

"No, wife of Musta'in. He is son of al-Mu'tamin." Her olive face glowed above the nearly steaming water. "You long way from home."

"Yes." I lay back, resting my head on the hard edge of the bath, letting my body float.

"Me, too."

I sat up again. "Where are you from?" I rubbed at my heel, which ached slightly.

"Born in village outside Paris." I felt my eyes widen and I sat up. "Raised on parents' horse farm. I help with horses, but then parents must sell me to harem dealer when still young. Have lived here ever since."

"That's terrible." And I thought I'd had poor parents.

"No, no, parents need money," Liana said as she rinsed her hair. "Our best horses get sick and die. Need to buy more."

"Children are more important than horses," I sputtered.

"Not our horses. We raise best in France. Is good. I happy here."

I frowned into the murky water, white with minerals. Liana floated close. "Not sad. Parents need money. Is good." She told me more about her life and her children. She'd been ripped from her life just as I had. How could she possibly be happy? As we talked, I let my feet rise to the surface and I stared at my toes. They were the very same toes I'd had a week ago—short and stubby. How could I be transported back in time and still be exactly the same? "You speak Arabic very well."

She shrugged, watching water droplets roll off her arm. "It take time, but you learn too."

"No, I won't be here long enough to—"

"We start now." The woman glowed with determination. She touched my hair. "*Sa'rah*."

"No, I—"

"*Sa'rah*."

I dutifully repeated the word for hair. I was going to find my way home. I did not need this language. She touched my nose. "*Anafah*," then my foot, "*rijlani*." She made me repeat every word twice, then worked her way around my body, until finally giggling and touching my breast. "*Taddu*. And this is *bizz*."

I yelped when she touched my nipple and we both laughed, deep, hearty laughs that roiled the bathwater. My first real laugh in the eleventh century. I leaned back and said, "*bizz*," still chuckling.

She touched my eyelashes. "Your eyes require combs."

I felt a blush start up my neck.

"You and Luis lovers?"

"What?" I sat up, nearly swallowing bathwater.

"You and Luis?" She made a gesture Anna would have called obscene.

"No, no. Why?"

Rising slightly, Liana brushed wild, unruly wisps off her face, and I did my best to look directly into her eyes, instead of lower. "I hear secret door many nights now. Passageway leads to room of Luis."

"What secret door?" Then I remembered Carlos's words about palace intrigue and secret lovers and hidden passageways.

She pointed toward the far wall tiled in blue and green waves. "Push center of bottom wave, door opens." I stared at the undulating pattern of the tiles, memorizing the spot for future reference.

"You hear the door?"

"My room next to bath. Hear every night this week."

Well, well, well. My friend Luis was quite the ladies' man after all, just as his men had teased. Ali helped us from the bath, then briskly toweled each of us off, once again being a little too familiar with my body. Then she wrapped a thick towel around each of us and ushered us into a small steam room, lowering us onto reclining benches. Carlos had said the Moors were engineering wizards. I exhaled slowly, agreeing. Hot bath, steam room, running water, all in 1085. By this time my muscles had gone limp. Ali rubbed oil all over me, filling my nose with a rich vanilla so like Anna's shampoo an ache burned in my heart. The black woman tucked the towel back around me and left.

"I met Walladah yesterday," I said. "She seems interesting."

"Walladah...yes."

I raised my head. Liana's round face was as flushed and rosy as my own felt, but her hazel eyes were serious. "What?" I asked.

"Walladah...she spoiled child. She go where she want."

"Mmmm," I said, my eyes slamming shut. I could handle a spoiled child. I wanted to go home. I wanted to give Arturo a home. I wanted to hold Anna in my arms. I imagined myself at the bottom of a deep, dry well. Every piece of information I gathered, every contact I made, every meal I ate, every day I survived, was a rock on which I could stand. I would pile up those rocks, and some day, somehow, if I stayed focused and lucky, that pile would reach high enough that I could step out into the sunshine, finding myself before the entrance to the cave at Santillana del Mar, the cave that would take me home.

❖

Luis came for me that afternoon. "I have decided you need more exercise. Perhaps that is why you were so upset yesterday. Another walk?"

I raced for my veil, wrapping it wildly around my head as I returned to the harem entrance. Luis winced and reached for the veil.

"This looks like one of the harem monkeys dressed you." Hands sure and firm, he wrapped and tucked until the soft fabric lightly brushed my cheeks. He leaned closer. "You do not smell of monkey, however. More like...could it be...soap?"

"Ha. Very funny. Maybe you should try it." He smelled as if he'd been riding a horse and camping outside for days, which obviously hadn't deterred some woman from sneaking into his room. But it certainly would have stopped me. That, and of course, the whole man thing. While I found androgyny appealing, I certainly wasn't going to act on that interest.

Luis wrinkled his nose. "Everyone but the Moors know that bathing isn't healthy."

I shook my head, then noticed the path we took felt familiar. "Why the roof again? I'd like to walk around the grounds."

"Not just yet," Luis said tightly.

"You don't trust me."

I couldn't read the look in his eyes, so I shrugged and gave up. At least I could see more of the sky than in the harem. As we walked along the sandy roof, a slight breeze fluttering my veil, I tried the direct approach. "Luis, when I am released, which I expect you will arrange soon, I need to continue my travels to the cave at Santillana del Mar."

"Do you expect to find your friend Anna there?"

I sighed. "No, I'm sure she has returned to America by now."

"Santillana is many days from here, through rugged country."

Luis and I stopped in the sliver of shade thrown by a tower. "How long a ride?"

"Two weeks' hard ride, but plenty of rabbits to eat along the way."

I was no horsewoman. I wasn't a survivalist. My best friend Laura always ribbed me about starving to death if there weren't a Taco Bell within walking distance. An accomplished winter camper, Laura knew how to survive on freeze-dried hiking food, how to filter water, how to avoid eating poisonous berries. But I doubt even she could snare a rabbit, kill it, skin it, cook it, then actually have an appetite left. "I don't know that area. I'm not too good on a horse."

"That much is certain."

"I would need a guide. Could you take me to Santillana?"

"Much as I would like to be your guide, I cannot return until Alfonso lifts the exile. Even then, Ordóñez will seek my head, and Gudesto and I, well, we go back a long time."

"I don't understand."

Luis stopped, his short black hair turning to velvet in the shade of another tower, then dropped to his knees, where he traced an outline of the Iberian Peninsula in the sand. He drilled a depression in the northeast. "This is Zaragoza." Then he made another mark along the northern coast. "This is Santillana."

The two spots didn't look that far apart. But then he drew a jagged diagonal line between the two. "This is the frontier." He made stripes on the much smaller Santillana side. "This is Christian land—Castile, León, Asturias. Here is Burgos in Castile, where King Alfonso lives. Here, along the Ebro just inside La Rioja, is where Count Ordóñez lives."

"Oh."

"If I return to Castile, León, or Asturias, Alfonso will throw me in the dungeon below his castle and conveniently lose the key. If Count Ordóñez found me anywhere on his land, which stretches through La Rioja all the way up to Santillana, he would let Gudesto Gonzalez personally peel the skin from my face, head, and body while I still live."

"An enemy then?"

"Rodrigo and I raided two of Ordóñez's castles just after the exile. He lost a great deal of money and is sure the devil possesses both of us. Rodrigo also defeated him in battle years ago. And Gudesto, well..."

"Marisella?"

Luis sighed, rubbing his fine brow. "It was not really my fault. We sat together at a banquet, and she found me...intriguing. That night when she came to my—" He blushed, a man unable to turn down a free box of chocolates. Chocolate. Oh god, was there chocolate here, at this time? Where had it come from?

"Luis, have you ever eaten chocolate?"

"What?"

I described chocolate but when Luis wrinkled his nose, my heart sank. No chocolate. And no Luis as my guide. I sighed. Luis would have been the perfect guide—strong, brave, competent, and so far, polite.

Luis was only one man. Surely I could find someone else who could help me. I was not giving up. The beautiful Walladah, perhaps. We passed the gruesome heads below, and I turned away. "So, Luis, how did you come to be here?"

Blush now faded, the man hesitated. "It is a long story. You do not—"

I stared at the date carved in the wall, and my body tensed as reality hit me again right between the eyes. No wonder Roberto had tried to warn me. He knew where I might end up.

By the time I snapped out of my self-pity, Luis's face had softened. "My family loved stories, so I will tell you a story," Luis said, rubbing his face briskly. "I come from Anguiano, a small town in Castile on the edge of the Moor-Christian frontier. My life was nothing until I turned sixteen, and I fell in love." He blushed again, then looked away. "One Saturday morning, when I should have been helping my father with chores, I met her at a hidden waterfall. She was beautiful—thick, chestnut hair, green eyes, skin like—" He smiled ruefully. "Perhaps I am still a little in love with her." I nodded, desperate for something to fill my head. "We spent the day...kissing." Another blush spread up his neck as I leered. "Kissing, just kissing. Mid-afternoon I finally headed home, ready to face the wrath of my father." When his throat began working furiously, I knew I didn't want to hear the rest of the story.

His eyes narrowed. "In those days the border skirmishes between the Moors and Christians were almost constant. That day a band of Moors came through. They burned our barn, stole our cattle and sheep, and...murdered my entire family." Luis's jaw tightened, a tiny muscle jumping in his high cheekbone. "I found all their bodies, or what was left of them. Mama. Papa. Tío Mingo. Tía Solana. My brother Miguel... my sister..." Luis studied his hands, covered with thick calluses where his fingers gripped his sword. "I dug a long grave between the house and what was left of the barn, lighting a torch so I could dig through the night. By the time the first sun hit our wheat field, I had buried my family."

"Oh, Luis." I swallowed hard.

"I packed a bag, saddled my horse, and rode away. Eventually I met Nuño, and a few others. Together we searched until we found a great knight who could help me vanquish the Moors from all of Iberia."

"Rodrigo Díaz."

Luis traced a cross in the sand. "I pledged my lifelong loyalty to Rodrigo."

"And now here you sit in a Moorish palace surrounded by Moors, speaking their language."

Luis's eyes darkened and I breathed in his sense of betrayal and confusion. "For four years we have been exiled from Castile. The Moors were the only ones who would hire us; everyone else feared the wrath of Alfonso."

"And Nuño?"

"Rodrigo had sent him on an errand to Santiago, so he did not hear of the exile until we were long gone from Castile. While he waits for our exile to lift, he has been fighting for any Castilian lord that will have him. On this most recent raid I had no idea Nuño was working for Ordóñez. I did not intend to capture him, but the moron slept so soundly that we were in the castle before he awoke, and I had no choice."

"What will happen to him?" I couldn't imagine throwing my best friend into a dungeon.

Luis's shoulders stiffened. "As long as I draw breath, no harm will come to him. Nuño has saved my life a dozen times. He is my family now."

I struggled to fit all the puzzle pieces together. "Why was Gudesto Gonzalez here?"

"Under a flag of truce, he came to negotiate for the release of Nuño and the others. But he has tucked his tail between his legs and returned to Castile."

Luis took my hand, holding it between his warm palms, which felt nice, but weird. "And what of you? I do not know how to keep you safe. Neither Rodrigo nor Mu'tamin has use for a woman unless he can sell her or bed her."

"I don't like either of those options."

"I did not think you would."

A shout from the west city gate drew us to our feet in time to see a lone rider approaching down the road along the Ebro, a red and black cape billowing behind him.

"A messenger from King Alfonso. I must return you to the harem. Come."

"Who's that?" I pointed to a black Moor approaching from the opposite direction, gold robe and turban flying behind him.

"A messenger from al-Hayib. Saint's Blood." Luis gave a low growl after the curse.

"Busy day," I said.

Luis steered me toward the stairs. "Imagine a city being squeezed dry from both sides. That is Zaragoza."

"I don't understand."

"King Alfonso wants to capture Zaragoza as another jewel in his crown. Al-Hayib, Mu'tamin's brother, wants Zaragoza because he hates Mu'tamin." We hurried down the cool staircase.

"What will Mu'tamin do?"

"If Ordóñez will not pay the ransom, Mu'tamin might sweeten the pot by adding a few slaves to the deal in order to delay Ordóñez from attacking from the west. At the same time he'll probably have to send more harem women to al-Hayib to delay an attack from the east." Luis's boots clattered against the marble floor; my slippers made quiet shooshing sounds.

"Neither option would involve a woman found wandering through the countryside, would it?"

"Both would," Luis said, his voice low. Goose bumps rose on my arms.

The door to the harem stood unguarded and we entered into chaos. Children's screams filled the courtyard as Abu and Suley chased a small black puppy, who in turn was gleefully chasing the young gazelle. The terrified creature leapt over plants, knocked over trays of food, a glass water pipe, a lute leaning against a cushion, but ended up cornered, where the little puppy immediately chomped down on the gazelle's slender back leg.

"Radi! Radi!" Liana's two young children cried, tears streaming down their faces. Luis pushed his way through the women and children and grabbed the puppy, handing it to Abu. The gazelle lay on the floor in shock, its legbone puncturing the skin. Luis reached for the animal's neck as if to break it.

I grabbed his arm. "No! This break might be fixed." I knelt by the trembling animal. I'd never done this before, but had taken a first aid course, and couldn't bear to lose one of the few friends I had. "Hold her down by her shoulders. No, there."

"But it will not heal—"

"Quiet!" I snapped as I positioned myself over the broken leg. Before I could talk myself out of it, I popped the bone back into place, then ripped off a piece of my veil and wrapped it tightly around the wound. The animal was so light I didn't think she needed a splint. I tied off the veil, then gathered the animal in my arms.

Liana's son sniffed loudly, wiping his nose on his dark bare arm. I knelt down, my heart stopping at the sight of his round brown eyes, so like Arturo's. I handed Radi to him. "Luis, tell him they must keep the animal quiet. She is not to run for at least a week. I will wash the wound every day and change its bandages." Luis stared at me, mouth open. "Luis!"

He rattled something off in Arabic, and the boy nodded, then softly said, "*Shukran.*"

"You're welcome." The boy ran off, Radi clutched to his chest.

Luis stood before me. "You can heal animals?"

I shrugged. It was just basic first aid. Anna had always given me a hard time about wasting time on abandoned baby rabbits and birds with broken wings, but it always felt so good to try to help them, even when they were beyond saving.

"Luis!" The one-eyed man, Enzo, bellowed at the entrance to the harem. "We need you in Mu'tamin's chambers. And bring the woman!"

❖

Al-Mu'tamin could have been an actor with his sculpted face, bald head, and ebony skin. Deep wrinkles around his eyes revealed his age, and his hard life. A permanent dark callus marked his forehead, the result of years of pressing against the ground in prayer. His spotless white robes draped his knees as he sat cross-legged on a massive green oriental rug. A handful of white slaves lined the wall behind him, one lighting sandalwood and musk candles.

The throne courtyard was twice the size of the harem's, and lined with gold-trimmed benches, porcelain vases, thick tapestry cushions. Solid gold stags emerged from the oval fountain. Red and blue parrots trilled, some in cages, others loose on the floor, pecking at bits of dropped food. A young Moor with a receding hairline, as dark as Mu'tamin and dressed as formally, sat by his side, his face buried in his book; this was likely Liana's husband, Musta'in. His beard wasn't as white as his father's, but it was trimmed just as neatly.

Rodrigo sat glowering and grizzled in a massive oak chair that looked out of place in such a delicate room. Luis left me at the entrance and stood behind Rodrigo with Enzo and Fadri, the Blond Moron. Tension pulsed between the white mercenary Christians and al-Mu'tamin's men, who ranged from a deep black to a tawny gold. Anna had said the Moors came from Africa in 711. Three hundred years must have allowed enough intermarrying to diversify the spectrum of Moorish skin. Most of the slaves were white Slavs from the north, and a few were Africans, like Abu and Suley.

The Christian messenger strutted before Mu'tamin, dusty cape dragging on the ground, mail rattling. "Count Ordóñez is incensed at the lack of hospitality shown Señor Gonzalez. He also demands you return his men at once."

When the man scratched his beard, I shuddered to think what might be living in there. My head spun and I wished I had a program to keep this all straight. This Christian wanted the soldiers, whom Luis had captured on behalf of the Moor sitting at the center of the room.

"Ordóñez has not paid my ransom. He runs out of time." Mu'tamin's withered hands, knotted with arthritis, rested calmly on his knees. Servants quietly served dates and wine.

"It is you who are out of time." As the messenger added to his list of threats, I noticed Walladah lounging in one corner of the room, robe now discreetly closed with a wide beaded gold belt. She watched with intense interest, her generous lips parted. She and I were the only women in the room.

Suddenly a man in flowing white robes pushed past me, knocking me against a pillar. I grunted softly, but didn't want to draw attention to myself.

The man shoved aside the messengers and dropped to one knee. "Your excellency, I bring most disturbing news that al-Baroun has just been found behind the shop of the weaver." The man dropped his head. "Allah protect me, he was stabbed in the chest, many many times."

The Moors in the room inhaled in unison, then exploded in angry shouts directed at Rodrigo and the Christians. *"Alqahbat! Ablah rum!"* The Christians responded with their own colorful curses. Luis said nothing.

I could barely hear the rest of the man's words. "...dead...much blood..."

"We did not kill the stinking barbarian," Enzo growled. Accusations filled the courtyard as angry men moved toward each other.

"You Moors stole five horses yesterday," a man next to Enzo snarled.

"And beat up Tomás last night," another cried, and I moved out of the way as fleeing servants stumbled over each other.

Rodrigo and Mu'tamin shouted orders, but no one responded as weeks of tension sought release. Only when Luis whirled to face his men, sword drawn, and Mu'tamin's supreme commander followed suit, did the room quiet. "Al-Mu'tamin pays us," Luis said evenly. "We do *not* fight those who pay us." The Moor shouted what must have been something similar to his men.

"You want to fight these Moors?" Luis shifted his weight, his sword at the ready. "You fight me first."

Each mercenary looked at the floor, shook his head, and shuffled back a step. I marveled at Luis's loyalty, given his tragic background. It would take years to understand this complex man, but since I was headed for Santillana, that would not come to pass.

"Abdu," Mu'tamin barked. "Speak to all your men. No fighting with the Christians."

Rodrigo turned to Luis, who nodded. "I will do the same," Luis said.

"Al-Mu'tamin," the Moorish messenger stepped forward, arrogant and clean. "The loss of your official and this squabble with your mercenary soldiers is regrettable, but my lord Hayib demands his tribute or he will attack." Christians and Moors returned to their own sides of the room, and Luis sheathed his sword. Okay. I checked my mental notes. Al-Hayib was al-Mu'tamin's hated brother, and he wanted control of Zaragoza.

"Al-Hayib is weak," Rodrigo said with an ugly sneer. Charlton Heston had clearly played El Cid too generously in the movie. I closed my eyes as a wave of loneliness swept over me. Anna. I was so tired of being in the wrong time. Why couldn't I just click my heels together three times and say "there's no place like home?"

The Moorish messenger ignored Rodrigo. "My esteemed lord Hayib knows you have sent the bulk of your men to defend Toledo."

"Are you threatening me?" Mu'tamin demanded.

"We demand ten more harem women, preferably white, and ten thousand dirhem by the end of the week, or you lose Zaragoza."

"Ridiculous!" Rodrigo stormed.

"Al-Hayib's harem grows small. The women tend to...do themselves harm."

"You are bluffing," Rodrigo said.

Mu'tamin held up his hand at Rodrigo's protest. "We will pay my weak brother, but may Allah only increase his unhappiness." He looked past the messengers, then straight at me. "My swaggering brother may have *her,* among others."

My heart raced as everyone in the room turned, even Musta'in, the bookworm beside the emir. Both messengers approached me, clearly assessing my figure. I was too angry to be afraid. Ordóñez's thug tried to lift my veil but I slapped his hand away. His breath nearly gagged me when he stepped closer.

"Count Ordóñez appreciates beautiful women, and always has need of...servants." He fingered my hair, so I slapped his hand again. "I will take her. Perhaps the Count will agree to pay a portion of the ransom in exchange." He grabbed my wrist, twisting cruelly. "And perhaps we can teach her a few manners while she is our guest."

I looked at Luis, but his face was blank.

"No, I am taking her for al-Hayib," the gold-robed Moor said, grabbing my other wrist. "Of course she is a virgin."

"That is certainly none of your—"

"She is a virgin!" Mu'tamin shouted as I struggled against the messenger's grip.

"Our doctors have taught me how to check," the Moorish messenger said, pulling me closer.

"I will decide," Mu'tamin roared, and suddenly the room erupted in argument as the two men pulled at my arms.

Furious, I bit the Moor's hand and the Christian dropped my arm in alarm. "Shut up!" I yelled. "No one is taking me anywhere." The veil caught in my mouth so I ripped it off. The Moors in the room gasped. I pushed past the flunkies and stood before Mu'tamin and Rodrigo. "Look, you stupid assholes. I am not some pawn on a chessboard. You don't own me. You can't just use me to pay your stupid petty debts. It's a violation of my rights as a human being and as a woman." My chest heaved with fury. Walladah sat up, interested in my presence for the first time. "Let me go, or…or…" I struggled for the words. "Or you can all just sit on your swords and spin, for all I care."

The men were absolutely silent, the only sound a soft fluttering of the caged birds. I glared at the two leaders, fists rigid at my sides. The look on Luis's face was an odd mix of fear and pride. Mu'tamin and Rodrigo looked at me as if I'd grown a second head. Welcome to Feminism 101, boys.

Mu'tamin finally frowned, then leaned forward. "You play chess? I always seek new players." Christ. I'd just told them to impale themselves, and this guy wanted to talk about chess?

Rodrigo snorted. "Games are a waste of time. You are a woman. You belong to me because my First Lieutenant found you. You will go to al-Hayib's."

Luis leaned forward and whispered something in Rodrigo's ear.

One bushy gray eyebrow raised. "How do you know?" Luis bent forward again. Rodrigo stood. "You are sure?"

"Yes, my lord." Luis threw me a desperate look.

Rodrigo rose from the chair, then gripped my wrist with his massive hand, pinching my skin as he pulled me toward the door. "We will see," he said. "We will see."

CHAPTER SIX

Rodrigo half-dragged me out the palace doors and down a brick walkway to the stables. Once inside, sweet hay and sour manure filled my head. We stopped before a stall and Rodrigo released my wrist. "Luis tells me you heal animals."

I stood before a massive white stallion with a silver gray tail, sunken black eyes, and labored breath. Watery fluid ran from his eyes and nostrils. The horse stood with his forelegs wide apart, his back hunched. This was one sick horse.

Rodrigo nearly rung his hands at my side. "The stablemaster of al-Mu'tamin died of old age one month ago. Two weeks ago my Babieca took ill, but that fool over there knows nothing of healing horses."

A young man stepped from the shadows, his dark face flushed but proud. It was the Moor who'd fainted at the sight of my bare knees. "Ibn Yusef died before I could learn all he knew," the boy said, accent so thick I could barely understand his Spanish. Despite Rodrigo's anger, the boy showed no sign of fainting.

"You must cure my horse," Rodrigo said to me, turning his back on the boy.

"May I see a few more horses first?" I asked.

"But Babieca is the only one—"

"I need to see some of the others." Anything to give me more time to think. I entered the stalls of fifteen other Arabians, all as solid and incredibly long-legged as Babieca. These horses carried men weighed down with chain mail, swords, shields, and lances, not to mention the horse's own mail and tack. I ran my hands along each horse's neck, ribcage and rump, then pretended to check eyes and mouth, finally tapping their manure with the toe of my ridiculously flimsy slippers. At one stall, sharp kicks from inside rattled the closed door. The young man shook his head and steered me past the furious grunting. "Evil horse," he said. "But he makes good foals, so al-Mu'tamin keeps." Before we finished, we found another ill horse, Rosario, who looked as bad as Babieca.

We returned to Babieca, whose eyes flickered briefly toward me, but resumed their empty stare. I rubbed his jaw. While I had disliked riding horses, I hated to see them so miserable. Inside the stall, I pretended to examine Babieca, trying not to flinch every time the massive animal moved. No cuts, bruises, or other marks. No signs of loose stool. I stepped back.

"Well? What is it?" Rodrigo demanded, hands on leather-covered hips.

"How long have you owned him?"

"Since he was a foal. He's been with me since I left Castile." An odd look passed over the man's rough features. "Alfonso forced me to abandon my lands, my wife, my daughters, but he could not deny me Babieca."

I asked a few more questions about the horse's history, then considered my options. I could become an unhappy member of al-Hayib's harem, likely being raped repeatedly until I threw myself from the highest tower available. Or I could remain here, impersonating a vet until Rodrigo found me out and sent me to Ordóñez or added my head to the decorations already adorning the palace gates. Then I remembered my last visit to the vet with Max and clutched at that remote straw. "Babieca has round worms. Normally they aren't serious, but he must be carrying a huge load."

"No." The boy pushed past me and kicked through the straw for a chunk of manure, which he broke apart to show that no worms riddled the feces.

I struggled to explain. "Round worms are very, very small. They attach themselves to the intestine wall." I pointed to my own intestinal region, then to Babieca's. "The worms feed off the animal, slowly weakening it."

The boy pursed his lips, then ran for a jar of a thick, brown liquid, then started rattling on in Arabic so I had no idea of the contents until I opened it. Molasses. "This is good. But for round worms, we must treat Babieca with garlic."

"Garlic?" Rodrigo and the boy said together.

"Garlic in a bran mash for four days, with carrots, the stringier the better."

Rodrigo's brown eyes bore into me. "This must work." No kidding. It had worked for Max the black lab. Would it work for Babieca the horse? Rodrigo gave Babieca a rough pat, then surprised me when he said, "I will go to the kitchen for garlic and carrots. You tell Hamara exactly what to do."

We watched Rodrigo's broad back disappear through the archway leading back to the palace. I needed this boy on my side, for Babieca's care would fall to him. I touched my chest. "My name is Kate."

He nodded, then touched his own chest. "Hamara."

I smiled. "You seem at home around horses."

The young man stroked Babieca's nose, then scratched under the horse's chin. "Horses are easy to understand. Much easier than...well, than..." He blushed then dropped his gaze.

I nodded. "I know. Sometimes I find women hard to understand as well."

While we waited, Hamara and I looked at Rosario again, and because I didn't have a clue, obviously, I recommended the same garlic diet. Man, I was skating on thin ice here. Soon Hamara and I were talking a weird mix of Arabic and Spanish, touching the relevant spots on the horses when our vocabularies failed us. Hamara was sharp, and I learned a lot just by listening to him.

A third horse was bothered by flies on her backside, so we looked through the old man's bottles until we found a vile-smelling oil, which I assumed would work like castor oil, something I'd read about in our holistic dog book. I showed Hamara how to rub it around the horse's anus to discourage flies from landing; the pungent oil made my eyes water.

"This is a cozy scene." Luis stood at the stall entrance carrying a basket filled with carrots and garlic.

I straightened my back, brushing the hair from my face with the back of my wrist, throwing Hamara a wink. "You're just jealous."

"Of Hamara?"

"No, of the horse."

Luis threw back his head with delight, and even Hamara chuckled. I raised my oily hands. "Care to bend over?" Luis's laugh turned into a coughing fit at my suggestion. I wiped my hands on a rag, then showed the young man how to heat the garlic into a mash and shred the carrots.

Luis waited, watching me closely. When I finished, he motioned toward the stable exit. "I am to escort you back to the harem."

"I will not be cut in half, one half given to Ordóñez, the other to al-Hayib?"

He smiled, resting his lanky frame against the stall door. "Not until Babieca recovers...or dies."

That was just great, since I had no chance in hell of curing the horse. We said good-bye to Hamara, then Luis and I walked under the massive archway connecting the stables with the palace. "Thank you for my reprieve," I said quietly.

"I was only thinking of Babieca," Luis responded.

"Yeah, right." The walkway was lined with a forest of marble columns topped by more intricate carvings. I ran a hand along the cool marble, marveling at the smoothness obtained by hand, not by machine. My Goddess, had it only been a day since I'd accepted the truth about my situation?

Luis sniffed delicately. "I would recommend another bath."

"Why, Luis, I thought Christians didn't believe in bathing."

We headed for the stairs. "While it is true that Saint Benedict considered an unwashed body a temple of piety," he stopped and wrinkled up his nose, "perhaps we should make an exception in your case. Your hair smells of horses, your hands of foul oil, and there is something dark green on your neck and cheek."

"I thought you'd never notice." What an irritating man; he brought out the flirt in me. "But Luis, what do you care? You never bathe." I'd figured out by now that Christians soldiers like Luis rarely even took their clothes off, but just lived in them for weeks on end.

He chuckled. "I suggest a bath not for my sake, but for our Saracen hosts. At the end of the week al-Mu'tamin holds another huge banquet, and Rodrigo may want you to attend. He measures people by watching them."

"I'd rather not. A joint Christian-Muslim party isn't my idea of a good time."

Luis shrugged as he dropped me off at the harem. "Depends on El Cid's mood. We'll just—"

"Señor!" One of Luis's lance corporals jogged toward us. "Ten men from the west camp claim one of Abdu's men cheated them. The food rations for next week have gone bad. Chavez and Villanueva are missing, and nearly everyone in my lance has some sort of rash on their—" He suddenly noticed me. "—on their bodies. Perhaps one of the...Moorish women?"

Luis sighed, and took one of my hands between his own. "I spend my days breaking up silly fights and dealing with rashes."

"You'd make a good mother," I said with a chuckle, then stopped, hoping I hadn't insulted him. "I mean father."

Something in those blue eyes flickered then disappeared. He smiled wryly. "I will be man enough to take that as a compliment. Let us go, Jose. Hamara may have something for that rash."

After Luis disappeared down the corridor, lit with torches, Suley and Abu each raised a fist in the greeting I'd taught them. "Free Malcolm X," they both said in English, thick accents reshaping the words so they sounded like "Free May Come Next."

I returned the salute, wondering if I was screwing up history by teaching them the future. "Free May Come Next," I recited, and hoped they were right. The courtyard was silent; voices, laughter, and steam came from the baths. I shooed two curious gray monkeys from my room, then instead of stripping naked in front of twenty strangers to bathe, I curled up on my sofa, pulling the robe up to my neck, snuggling down in the warmth and inhaling the rich scent of brown oil, horses, and whatever green had dried on my neck.

I relived yesterday over and over again. I wanted to cry each time I reached the image of the date carved in the brown wall but found no tears. Somehow, in the hours since that moment, every cell in my body had come to attention, every muscle had tightened, every sense heightened. I had no time or energy to mourn.

❖

Over the next week I missed my life, and Anna, with a desperation I didn't know was possible. How did a person find her footing after every single detail in her life had changed? Each day was an exhausting marathon punctuated only by plentiful food and Luis's visits.

Meanwhile, little Radi healed nicely, finally trusting me enough not to shiver every time I touched her. I showed the young owners of the errant puppy how to train him to stay. With all the harem gathered around, murmuring in Arabic, I showed the girl how to "alpha wolf" the naughty puppy by rolling him on his back, grasping the loose skin under his neck, and shaking him gently. "Bad dog," I said firmly, my tone easily understood in any language. The puppy's tail curled up between his legs, his eyes wide, ears back, just as Max had done when I'd flipped him as a puppy. My demonstration was so popular that later in the day kids took turns sitting atop one another, grabbing each other's tunic and giggling, in English, "Bad dog."

The women started to relax around me. Rhame, the oldest of Mu'tamin's wives, smiled now and then, and both Shajar and Fatin tried to communicate with me, but neither spoke enough Spanish for us to get very far. The beautiful Aisha, her blond hair falling in spiraling ringlets down her back, loved to touch my hair, then run away, giggling. Ladgha tended my swollen finger the day a bee stung me while I sat on the toilet. She plastered it with cool mud and made me hold it in the air for hours until the mud dried, caked up, and finally fell off.

The women warmed even more the day I, too, fell victim to the harem thieves. I had just left the *mirhadun* and begun crossing the courtyard when the two monkeys scampered from my room, one of them dragging my fanny pack in its thieving paws.

"No!" I shouted as I broke into a run. "Come back, you little rodents." Screaming now, the little brats leapt with my precious bundle into an orange tree, setting it swinging wildly, then hopped down and pounced in the middle of Rhame, Fatin, and Shajar as they sat talking. When Rhame plucked the pack free as the monkey ran by, he immediately sat down, eyes wide at losing his treasure.

"*Shukran*," I said softly as Rhame returned the pack, clearly curious but too polite to ask about it. She smiled and spoke in Arabic. I'd begun picking up some vocabulary, enough to figure out the monkey had stolen her hairbrush last week.

"And my slipper yesterday," Fatin said.

"And the heart of my little boy," Shajar added wistfully.

I thanked them again, weak with pleasure at finally connecting, at drowning a bit of my loneliness. I made a mental note to be nicer to the monkeys.

I visited Babieca every day, but only when Luis came to escort me. When he grew too busy, he sent Enzo instead, and I soon grew used to the gruffer but still kind man. Babieca showed no improvement, and Rosario had worsened. I never saw Rodrigo there, but Hamara said he came at least twice a day.

One day Liana noticed me rubbing my sore heel, which burned constantly. After quizzing me, she sent Suley off with a list. When he returned, she mashed up pungent leaves and mixed the pulp with warm animal fat, then reached for my foot.

"We use this on horses when ache," she said briskly as she smeared the foul-smelling poultice around my heel. "Do this once a day for a week."

I wrinkled up my nose. "I reek. No one will come near me."

Liana winked. "Luis will."

"You said he has a lover in the harem," I replied, wincing as she pressed hard against my heel.

"Yes, but I have seen the way he looks at you."

"Don't be ridiculous," I snapped, irritated not with Liana, but with the odd, weak pounding the words set off in my chest. I was a lesbian, and not even time travel was going to change that. True, my Spanish Johnny Depp was beautiful, but he was still a man.

I quizzed both Hamara and Liana about Santillana and the Altamira cave, but they knew nothing. I helped Liana with her children. Little Hazm was my serious and silent shadow, sticking close should Radi need more emergency help. Tayani, the girl, was constantly sneaking out of the harem when Suley and Abu weren't looking, only to be returned by an angry servant or a bemused Christian soldier, tiny Tayani swinging gleefully from the man's scabbard belt. I envied the girl's freedom, not only of body, but of spirit.

The harem was a safe, relatively calm place where I could get my bearings in the eleventh century. I found myself observing all the women with their children, wondering what sort of parent I would be to Arturo. Patient? Fun? Anxious? Overly-strict?

After days of too much thought and not enough action, of not seeing the city, the mountains, or more of the sky than the walk to the stables revealed, I started to chafe. So when an unfamiliar servant came for me one day, I went eagerly. The short man led me into al-Mu'tamin's chambers, where the ruler lounged on a cushion, heavy embroidered ivory robes gathered around him, slender feet in leather sandals.

"Ah, my lovely guest." Mu'tamin waved me down next to him. "While the sun envies your beauty and the mirror longs for your face, let us see if Allah has given you a brain as well."

His Spanish was excellent, but he often slid into the mix of Spanish and Arabic that most everyone in the palace spoke. He tapped his black and white marble board, then dumped the pieces out of a blue velvet bag. "Let us play." Not one piece looked familiar. No king, no queen, knight, or bishop. The pieces—smooth, cool, and intricately carved—were slender obliques, carved towers, small orbs. "*Shah*," he said, pointing to the king, then to the queen next. "*Raynah*." I touched the pawn. "*Baydaq*," Mu'tamin said, setting up the last pawn. He studied the board. "You are a valuable woman," he said as he finally moved a pawn forward with a gnarled hand. "Much like this piece on the board."

"What?" I shivered. I knew the basics of chess, not the strategies.

"It would seem that both Ordóñez and my ridiculous brother al-Hayib want you for themselves."

I moved a pawn, too rattled to care if it was the right one. "I told you. I'm not a pawn."

"May Allah forgive them their weakness of mind, but both men want you, one as a slave, the other as a harem member." Another pawn moved.

"That's ridiculous. I'm nothing to either of them." Al-Mu'tamin's eyes burned deep in their sockets like glowing coals, crow's feet running from the corners. All I needed was for al-Mu'tamin himself to be interested in me, but I didn't sense that from him. Thank goddess he didn't like mouthy women.

"Oh, but you are." He moved his knight forward. "Allah has made my loveliest captive a prize for those fools who would try to take over Zaragoza. Pale-skinned women are highly desired in harems or as slaves."

"Me as a pawn? That's the dumbest thing I've ever heard." I moved my rook, torn between staying to get more information and fleeing to avoid those intense eyes.

Mu'tamin pursed his lips. "You speak the truth. But a pawn is nothing more than a reason for men to fight, and both Ordóñez and my brother would like nothing more. You, as a woman, are of course unimportant."

"Of course," I responded dryly, and was rewarded by Mu'tamin's amused smile.

"But in this land, we are forever struggling to retain what we possess. With the blessing and grace of Allah, Zaragoza will not fall to either King Alfonso or Hayib, although each pile of lizard dung underestimates both my men and Rodrigo's."

"Now I'm totally confused." I shifted on the floor, wishing chairs were part of the decor.

"Zaragoza is a jewel trapped on the border between the two worlds. Christians believe it should be their land. We Moors believe it should be ours."

"Why tell me this if Rodrigo and you think I might be a spy?"

Mu'tamin smiled. "If you are a spy, you already know this." He moved another piece, and I saw the certain death of my king.

"So what are you going to do with me?" I asked. God, I hated this powerlessness. The image of the harem woman's head on the spike continued to haunt me.

Mu'tamin looked at the board, not me. "For now, I will let Ordóñez and al-Hayib each make camel's asses of themselves. No woman is worth what you've become to them."

"Gee, thanks."

Mu'tamin moved his king forward, sliding straight down into my territory. "I think highly of women, despite what you may think. My daughter is brilliant. My wives have all been beautiful..."

"But not brilliant."

Mu'tamin winked at me. "Allah be praised, Walladah takes after her father." He moved another piece, sighing heavily.

"And your son? He doesn't seem very interested in life." I sacrificed a knight, but couldn't see any way around it.

The man who easily had people killed and decapitated and stuck up on posts suddenly seemed nothing more than a middle-aged father worried about his children's future. "Musta'in is a scholar, and will continue my studies in mathematics. But we Moors have been fighting each other for sixty years. Zaragoza needs a strong hand."

That's when I noticed that Mu'tamin's hand trembled. He drew back quickly, but there was no mistaking the tremor. Casually, as the game progressed, I snuck closer looks at his face. The shadows in the room did nothing to hide the yellow tint to his skin, the bags under his eyes, the thinness around his shoulders, his bloated abdomen.

My Uncle Kevin had that same look the months before he died of liver cancer. I inhaled slowly, and smelled it—the smell of flesh not right. Mu'tamin slid his king close to mine, closing off all escape. "Your king has died," he said. *Shah-mat.* Checkmate.

I sat up straighter. "Lord Mu'tamin, I'm a prisoner in your harem, not a guest. I can't leave without Luis or Enzo watching my every move. Why do you continue to treat me this way?"

"You tell me."

My hands started to sweat. I was the type who felt guilty when a squad car passed, even if I had done nothing wrong. "Because you don't trust me."

Mu'tamin took my king. "What would happen if I turned you over to Ordóñez or my brother? Would there be peace for a month or two?"

Wisps of sandalwood suddenly filled my head and I turned. Walladah and her gaggle of servants marched toward us. Her violet robe rustled as she passed so closely I could have reached out and touched the flaxen silk scarf fluttering down her back.

"Father." The princess threw me a coy, sideways glance. "Once again, my beloved brother has made a mess of things. He fired Abdul the cook because the poor man could not recite the Greek alphabet."

Al-Mu'tamin sagged into his cushion, suddenly an old man. "I will not change my mind. Your brother must learn to manage people."

Walladah huffed, then turned toward me, face curious and open. "You may be sorry at the next meal, Father. Abdul was the only one who could cook goat meat tender enough for you. Besides, my brother should not terrorize the people who work so hard for us." I blushed as her thick-lashed gaze lingered on me, liking her politics but suddenly wishing I wore baggy clothes. "And who is this, Father? A new wife?" She toyed with the gold tasseled braid cinching her narrow waist, mesmerizing me as she slowly slid the tassel across her open palm. I swallowed, not used to feeling like the awkward teenager awed by the most popular girl in school.

Mu'tamin straightened, then began packing up the chess pieces. "No, she is my pawn. Possibly a spy."

One fine eyebrow arched slightly. "How interesting."

I finally found my voice. "I am a traveler unfairly imprisoned here. I demand my freedom."

"No," Mu'tamin said simply.

"A *demanding* woman," Walladah cooed. "Even more interesting..."

"I must go now," I said.

Mu'tamin nodded to his servant. "Come back tomorrow and we will play again. Next time do not let me win. I can win perfectly well on my own."

Mu'tamin's servant nearly jogged to keep up with me as I hurried back to the harem, where I would have slammed my door if I'd had one. While taking baths and pretending to heal horses and worrying about Anna and Arturo, I'd unknowingly become a pawn in a stupid male power struggle. I had to get to Santillana myself, and soon, very soon. An escape plan grew in my head as I lay awake long after darkness fell and Abu extinguished the torches. It involved finding the right clothes for a disguise and forcing myself to climb back onto a horse—not something I relished, but clearly no one was going to rescue me but myself.

❖

I needed to wait for the right opportunity to implement my plan, so I was still stuck in the harem. Nervous about Babieca's health, desperate for distraction, I begged for more cloth from Zaydun, and when I showed Abu how I could stretch out the fabric if I had a wood frame, the guy came through. I began lacing my cloth canvases onto rough frames, and soon I had a plethora of drawings propped up along the wall of my room. I drew Radi. I drew the courtyard's fountains and lush ferns. My fingers were constantly gray, and I soon gave up trying to keep my filmy skirt clean. At night I would raid the braziers in the warming kitchen, picking out the long, narrow bits of charcoaled wood.

I had just finished the shading on a drawing of the courtyard when Zaydun and Luis arrived. "*Jamal*," Zaydun breathed. She reached out tentatively toward the canvas, almost as if she expected the image to disappear when she touched it.

Luis stared, transfixed, then walked around behind the drawing, then back around to face it. He looked at me, then back at the drawing. "You drew this?"

I nodded, unable to decipher his look, an odd mixture of admiration and something that could have been awe or fear. I blushed a bit at the warmth spreading through my chest as he continued to stare at me. "So," I said, "did you come for a reason, or just to gaze deeply into my eyes?"

"Oh." Luis snapped out of it. "I have come to help you set up your shop." He reached for my veil and tossed it toward me.

"My shop?" We left Zaydun still enraptured with my drawing, which felt odd, because it wasn't *that* good.

"Rodrigo wants you to have a shop where you can cure animals from the city. It will bring in much needed income for us." My throat tightened. Shit. Out beside the stables Luis pointed to an old, run-down shack with its door off, the windows filled with cobwebs. "This is perfect. Near the palace entrance, near the main road, so many townspeople and farmers could bring their animals to you." He yanked the door off its rusty iron hinges and flung it aside. "We will clean this up and it will be just fine." He stopped at the look on my face. "Surely you are not afraid of a few cobwebs."

When I sank down onto the stone steps leading up to the shack, Luis joined me. "You have the look of a woman carrying a heavy burden."

I rested my chin in my hands. When Anna and I were dating, she'd somehow gotten the impression I could read Latin, I suppose from me smarting off about one thing or another. Two years later she'd brought home photocopies of a fifteenth century Cordoban manuscript, written in Latin, eager to translate it together. "I don't know Latin," I sputtered. Incredulous, she refused to speak to me for two days, only scribbling furious notes with words like "betrayed" and "hoodwinked" and "pretender." We finally recovered, but in weak moments I suspected the needle on her Kate Love-O-Meter didn't rise as high as it once had.

Once again I had to confess my ignorance. "Remember the other day, when I either had the choice to be carted off to al-Hayib's harem or stay and cure Babieca?"

He nodded, brows fierce. "I am not going to like this, am I?"

I shook my head, wishing my stomach would stop cramping. "I don't know how to cure animals. I just said that to buy more time, to avoid being sent away."

"And the garlic and carrot mash?"

"It cured my dog."

Luis leapt to his feet, sword clattering. "Kate, Babieca is not a dog."

"No kidding."

He began pacing. "This is my fault. I told Rodrigo you could cure animals. I put you in that position. But it was all I could think of to keep you here."

Why that would be important, I didn't ask, too amazed he wasn't angry. "Luis, if Babieca lives, it will be just dumb luck. I don't know how to cure horses, or sheep, or pigs, or goats, or chickens, or dogs." Or read Latin.

Luis dropped to his knee in the rocky ground at my feet, grabbing my hand. "I am afraid your life is still in great danger. What can I do?"

I squeezed his hand gratefully, then released him. "Not much." Then it hit me. A shop meant more time out of the harem and contact with more people, which had to increase my chances of reaching Santillana.

Luis sighed, then stood, a man used to fighting battles and solving impossible problems. "Come, let us clean out this mess so it will at least look as if you are ready to heal animals."

❖

I spent the next week in my shop, setting it up to look authentic should Rodrigo stop by. But most of the time the light was perfect for painting, and after Zaydun found me a small jar of tree resin and a handful of camel-bristled brushes, I became a mad chemist, forced to make my own paints because nothing came pre-mixed in a squeeze tube in 1085. I tried mixing a satisfying paint with the resin, but failed, so she next brought eggs, showing me how her father had mixed eggs as a paint base. Elderly Zaydun had more freedom than the others, so she brought some roots from the kitchen, which I ground into a powder and added to the egg base for magenta. Liana gave me a malachite pin that had broken, so I crushed that and ended up with a green paint. A few more experiments, and I began painting like a madwoman. Zaydun found an old linen sheet that I ripped up into canvases, so I gave her my first real painting, of the fountain in the courtyard's center. Her eyes shone as she took it from me.

I found myself thinking about Anna as I painted, wondering how she was, if she missed me. I remembered the book we'd once read together called *The Two-Step*, about how a relationship is a dance between two people. In that dance, one person is the seeker, the other is the sought. We'd laughed, not even having to say it out loud—I'd always been pursuing Anna, while she played distant, cool, hard to catch. Now I'd run away, sort of, though not by choice. Would Anna switch roles and start seeking me? Or would she just find herself a new seeker to pursue her? Loneliness ran from my heart, down my arm, through my brush, and onto my paintings.

Painting felt like a lifeline, a thin thread connecting me with the twenty-first century. I painted then, and I painted now, so I had to be the same person, right? But homesickness washed over me as I worked, flooding me with memories of my friends, Laura, my book group, the people at work, Max when he was a puppy, Anna, previous lovers, my parents, even the last meal I'd had before falling back in time. That week my brain played the DVD called "Kate's Life," and while I guess it was a good show, it only served to highlight how truly foreign I felt in this land, in this time.

The oddest things set me off. One day when I returned to my room, Zaydun had placed a small stack of clean clothes on my bed, and suddenly I was back in Chicago. Anna had been sitting on our bed folding our laundry, neatly stacking it, when I burst into the room, suddenly in love with the way the afternoon sun filtered through her hair. Wanting to show her how sexy she was doing even mundane tasks, I took her in my arms and rolled her across the bed. Anna shrieked and pulled me to my feet, scolding about the laundry. But when I quickly moved the stacks, she relaxed and I successfully distracted her from household chores.

Each day in that harem I tried to shake off my melancholy, but it wasn't easy, since Babieca seemed no better, no worse. Rosario, however, looked more and more depressed every time I visited. Hamara and I would stand outside the stall and watch her wheezing sides, her flared nostrils, her sweating flanks. Not good. Not good at all.

CHAPTER SEVEN

My escape plan required clothing, and since Luis was one of the few soldiers living in the palace—most men preferred getting rooms in Zaragoza, or camping at the edges of the forest pressing up against the city—I would *borrow* some of Luis's clothes. The quickest way to gain my freedom in this oppressive society would be to dress as a man. I tried getting a sense of his schedule, but he just shrugged, giving me that half-smile that said his time belonged to Rodrigo, so he himself did not know his schedule. Then he effectively changed the topic by looking down at my now-gray threads and frayed slippers. "You will be expected to appear at the banquet tonight. Perhaps Liana could find you something a little less...gray?"

The banquet! Getting into his room would be a challenge, but if he could be diverted during the banquet, that would be my chance. I spent the rest of the morning excited about my plan, but just thinking wasn't enough. I needed to *do* something. This waiting and watching was driving me crazy. By the afternoon images plagued me: Anna and I cuddling before the fire, Anna complaining about my low income, Anna forgetting our anniversary, Anna showing the boy next door how to ride a bike, Laura at the coffeehouse, listening as I talked about Anna. God, I missed Laura and her wild laugh. I missed Max's warm doggy smell. I missed the comfort of Anna that came from five years together, most of which had been good years. Truth be told, however, I didn't miss her harsh disappointment the day I washed my red painting shirt with her white chinos, or the evening she blamed me when Max brought home a dead rabbit and dropped it on the front step. But I missed her smell and her hands and how she'd suddenly grab my waist and tell me she loved me.

And what about Arturo? Poor kid. It wasn't his fault he was an orphan. It wasn't his fault I fell back in time, so he would have only one parent. As a child I'd thought if I'd been smarter or funnier or more athletic, my parents would have opened the circle of their busy lives and let me in. But they palmed me off to babysitters, neighbors, camps, chaperoned church trips, and when I was old enough, to a medium pepperoni and black olive delivered pizza and an empty house. I knew how it felt to be unwanted, and I didn't want Arturo to go through that hell. No, I was going to get my ass back to the future, just like Michael J. Fox, and I would adopt Arturo.

When I finally forced myself up from the warm divan, the harem throbbed with activity and anticipation. I waited until most of the women had bathed before I let Ali have her way with me in the late afternoon. I'd come to crave that languid heaviness that overcame me after every bath, as close to an afterglow as one could get without sex, and I resolved to find some way to afford spa visits when I returned to the future.

"You need new clothes for the banquet," Liana said as she saw me shuffle back from the bath in my grimy harem-wear.

"You've been talking to Luis."

"Nonsense. I have eyes. Come." She darted into a clothes-filled room I had assumed was someone's bedroom. "Al-Mu'tamin pay women in city to sew for us." She began holding up diaphanous silks to my face, stopping with a deep emerald green.

"Perfect for eyes." She wrapped three layers of filmy green skirts around my waist, each a slightly different shade. Over this she fastened a wide, heavy belt encrusted with what I assumed were fake emeralds and rubies, with shimmering pearls sewn around the edges.

"Off," she commanded, and pulled my tunic over my head. My nipples tightened when exposed, so I jammed my hands awkwardly under my arms as Liana dug through another pile.

"Put on." She slipped the green bodice over my arms and fastened the hooks in the back. The bodice, a brocade embroidered with gold and silver, covered my nipples, the top half of my ribcage, and not much more. Liana stepped back to examine her creation.

I made a face. "I don't think—"

"Off," Liana said, whirling me around to unfasten me.

"Good," I said. "Perhaps something with a little more...fabric."

Liana stuffed silk scarves into two small pockets in the bodice, then put it back on me. I inhaled sharply as Liana tugged it closed. I looked down at my chest. "Good heavens."

Without embarrassment, Liana adjusted my breasts until she was happy. "Very pretty." Then she found a long, matching brocade robe, sleeveless, which she slipped on my shoulders. It did nothing to hide my swelling breasts.

"I cannot wear this," I said.

Liana began brushing my hair vigorously.

"Liana." My head hurt. I had *never* worn such a politically incorrect outfit in my entire life, not even for a Halloween gag.

She ignored me, pinning a green cap on my head, the attached veil falling down my back.

"I cannot wear this." Forget butch. Forget femme. This was a blatant slut suit, and I wasn't wearing it outside of this room. But damn, I did look fine, even though Laura and my other friends would have fallen over from laughter. Anna would have raised an eyebrow but smiled.

Liana held me by the arms. "Al-Mu'tamin choose eight women from Zaragoza to send to his brother Hayib. To not be on list, we must be prettiest women at party."

She began dressing in a fragile peach skirt.

"Al-Mu'tamin will not send you away. You bore him two grandchildren with Musta'in."

She draped a delicate gold chain several times around her waist, then sighed. "Musta'in goes through women as quickly as he does books. He became bored with me when I swelled with little Tayani."

I helped her with her cap. "Why would Musta'in send his own children away?"

"He wouldn't," Liana said, her voice small. "He send his first wife away but keep his daughter, Noor, until she marry official in Valencia. He send second wife away because no give children. If he send me away, my children stay here. Hazm is only heir."

"Oh, Liana." She smiled bravely, then whirled in place, a delicate peach blossom, rosy and warm. Now, however, I could recognize the shiver of fear just behind that smile. "You are stunning," I said, then sighed. "I hate that we must use our bodies to keep children or gain freedom."

Liana slipped a gold band on each finger, then handed me a bowl of rings. "Smart women use every resource. Men only see body; we know we much more."

I picked out a single massive emerald and slipped it on my right hand.

"Be brave," Liana said, an odd thing to say before a party, then gave me a quick hug. I did need courage, but not for the reason she thought. Tonight I would take my first step toward freeing myself from this prison.

❖

The women, dressed in silk skirts and velvet robes and gold slippers, buzzed with excitement as they gathered at the harem's entrance, clouds of myrrh and sandalwood hovering above them. Suley began leading them out, but when I brought up the rear, Abu stopped me. "Luis Navarro say you stay here. He come for you."

I put my hands on my hips.

"Sorry I am late, Abu." I could hear Luis's boots in the hall. Abu bowed to me, then hurried after the other women. Luis jogged into the doorway. "I am sorry to be delayed—" The man's mouth dropped open and I smiled at the sharp intake of breath. "Holy Mother of God," he breathed.

I hated that my heart beat faster as Luis struggled to find his voice. Damn, why did he have to be a man? Why couldn't he have been a woman instead, so at least flirting would have felt more normal? I stared down at my skirts. "Liana dressed me up."

Luis swallowed twice. "Holy Mother of God."

"You said that already. Shall we go?" Even though I knew that women in history had passed as men so they could fight, I would never be so lucky as to find one of those women. And why on earth was I even thinking this because I had Anna, or would have when I got home. Besides, Luis was too fast and too strong and too much of a guy to ever be a woman.

"You are…you…shimmer like a pearl."

I held out my skirts and was actually on the verge of twirling, but stopped myself in time. Lesbians don't twirl. "I thought I looked more like an emerald."

Luis took my hand and tucked it under his arm, serious blue eyes blazing. "An emerald dazzles but is soon forgotten. A pearl haunts your dreams forever, its beauty too unbearable to forget."

"Why, Luis. The Moors are rubbing off on you. I swear you are becoming poetic." I draped my veil across my face, tucking the end into the cap.

He shook his head. "Cannot happen. I have instructed my men to run me through with my broadsword if I ever begin spouting poetry." Recovered, Luis slipped into our friendship again, but I couldn't resist pressing my breast against his arm as we walked. Because he had a sweetie to take care of things, I could have a little fun with him. Still, breast-pressing a guy was not my usual style. Must have been the ridiculous outfit I wore. Dress like a Barbie doll and you were bound to become one.

We could hear the party in the massive banquet room in Mu'tamin's quarters before we reached the door—loud laughing, shouts, and music. Once inside, my senses were assaulted. Eight long, low tables nearly groaned under the weight of trays of lamb, beef, and goat meat. Pomegranates, limes, grapes, oranges, figs, dates filled every open space on the tables. Bowls of steaming brown rice and huge hunks of dark, seed-filled bread somehow fit onto the tables as well. Their indoor plumbing was a bit rustic for me, and the whole women-in-harems thing stunk, but these Moors knew how to eat. My mouth began to water.

A Moorish band played in the corner: two flutes, a drum, four lutes, and two small round guitars. Many of the guests, a mixture of Moors from the city and Rodrigo's soldiers, were already seated. My harem companions had gathered at the end of one table, too shy to mingle, but Liana had planted herself right behind Musta'in, who didn't seem to notice.

Luis was dressed much as the other soldiers—black leggings, clean brown boots. His red blouse, full in the sleeves and with a tailored hem, stood out among the brown, green and tan blouses, but most of the red was covered by his smooth black leather tunic. Every man, Christian or Arab, wore a sword, and Luis's shone in the bright torchlight. I studied Luis as he found us two seats along the first table with his men. As usual, he was the only clean-shaven soldier there, clearly feeling no need to hide behind whiskers. And he smelled better than usual.

"You bathed," I whispered.

Flushing, Luis made a face. "Let us not speak of that hideous experience."

Laughing, when I sat down I nearly rolled off the plump pillow, but Luis caught me. "Thank you," I said. "I nearly fell out."

Luis seated himself beside me. "You mean you nearly fell over."

"Yes," I whispered, eyes dropping to my bodice. "But I also nearly fell *out*."

Luis laughed so hard he did fall off his cushion.

Rodrigo sat at the head table with al-Mu'tamin. Luis introduced me to his corporals, the last one a young man with one intense brown eye, a black patch over the other, and a ready laugh.

"Kate, this is Alvar Fáñez, just returned from a journey to Barcelona."

The young man bowed at the introduction, probably so he could get a birds-eye view down my flimsy blouse. I tried to be angry, but couldn't help smiling at his open look of delight, at his well-manicured moustache.

"So this is who El Picador has been hiding up in that harem. I know now that he is a terribly selfish man."

I pulled my hand away, laughing in spite of myself. Alvar Fáñez. I knew that name, but I couldn't remember why. "Have we met before?"

The man clutched at my hands again, pressing his warm lips against them. "Every night in my dreams." The men at the table groaned, and Luis hustled the hustler to an open spot at the table. Food, laughter, and conversation flowed as freely as the wine as Luis and his men drained carafe after carafe of sweet wine. Moors and Christians argued good-naturedly about bathing and harems and where the best mules could be bought. I learned so much about Majorcan mules I could have selected one myself. "I thought Islam forbids alcohol," I whispered to Luis.

"As al-Mu'tamin says, Zaragoza is a long camel ride from Mecca."

While the diners milled about and I stuffed my face with incredible sugared dates and spiced lamb and a glass of really intense wine, I watched Luis and the women, hoping to discover the identity of his mysterious lover, but Luis spent the entire meal at my side. Most people ignored me, but one Moor in a crimson robe did look straight at me, then dart away when I met his glance. I hadn't seen enough of his face to recognize him, but he seemed uncomfortable, keeping his back turned to me the rest of the meal.

At one point our table grew silent when Alvar leaned forward.

"Word is that Alfonso will take Toledo." Luis stopped chewing. "And we all know if Alfonso takes Toledo, he will come for Zaragoza next." Alvar's friendly face had turned to stone as he glared at Luis.

After a long pause, Luis bit off another hunk of goat meat, speaking between chews. "And if Alfonso attacks Zaragoza, we will defend her. This is Rodrigo's command."

Alvar clenched both fists, his face growing dark. "It is one thing to conduct raids on the Christian nobles, but to fight the king who rules us—"

Luis quietly reached across the table, gripping Alvar's wrist. "The day we left Castile, we all swore an oath to Rodrigo Díaz. This is the oath you will honor. He pays well for our loyalty."

"Alfonso is our *king*."

"I know." Luis slowly released the younger man and sat back down. While the rest of the banquet rang with laughter and song, our table sat tight and tense. A few of the men picked at their food, but no one spoke. It was impossible to tell who supported Alvar, who supported Luis. My ears rang with the tense silence, and the awkward moment made my teeth hurt.

"Well," I said, "if Alvar won't fight, I'll wear his armor and go in his place. Anything to get out of the harem." I smiled as chuckles rippled down the table. A few laughed out loud at the image; only I knew how closely the joke mirrored my own plan.

Alvar relaxed enough to reward me with a grin. "I would be delighted to lend you my mail. It would be far too tight in all the right places." Even Luis laughed at that, and the party mood returned.

After we'd eaten all the food within reach, and then some, I leaned back, stretching out my full belly, only to find Walladah, seated at the table on the raised platform, staring directly at me. She smoothed her russet silk dress down over trousers, then caressed the chain of heavy copper coins draped around her neck. She looked slyly from side to side, then blew me a kiss. I looked down at the table, ears burning.

A few minutes later Luis tapped my arm. "I see her most royal highness has noticed you."

"You saw, huh?"

"Walladah is like a hawk in a tree, nothing moving but the eyes, as she seeks her prey."

"That's a little harsh, don't you think?"

"Be careful with Walladah. She is different." Luis refilled my wine glass. Behind me Enzo and a Moor stood arguing about whose sword was the better built—something about the way the hilts were attached.

"I like different women. I find them fascinating."

"No, you do not understand." Luis frowned into his glass, having drunk enough that his cheeks were as flushed as the wine. "She is a woman who enjoys both men and..." He rubbed the bridge of his nose.

I patted his arm. "Relax. She might just be my kind of woman."

"There is a danger, Kate. If you are alone with her, she might..."

I leaned close enough to smell Luis's musk, mingled with the jasmine Liana had dabbed between my exposed breasts, and noticed Luis struggled, without much success, to keep his gaze on my face. I was damned tired of living in the harem, so the least I could do was peek out from the closet as well, even though it could be a stupid thing to do. I just felt I could trust Luis. "I love women, Luis. I love *women*—their bodies, their—"

"Do you mean—"

"That's exactly what I mean."

He froze, his shoulder touching mine, then the color drained from his face and he gripped the edge of the table to steady himself. Perhaps too much wine? Or too much honesty? At the far table, the harem women rose up and began dancing, a whirl of spinning rainbows pulling soldiers to their feet.

"I'm sorry. I didn't mean to shock you." Not true, of course, but I also didn't want to lose his friendship. He and Liana were all I had. Liana's smiling face whirled among the dancers.

Luis threw back the rest of his wine and poured more. "Kate, it is no matter to me who you bed or wed. I just want you to know that Walladah cares only for herself. She respects marriage and the sword, but nothing else."

"Because I am neither married nor carry a sword, I am in danger from this woman?"

Before Luis could respond, al-Mu'tamin clapped his hands, paler than at our chess game, then motioned for us to join him in the adjoining courtyard. "*Buw aytat, buw aytat!*"

It was time to put my plan into action before Luis got so drunk he staggered back to his room, the last place I wanted him. As we stood, I whispered to Luis, "I'm not feeling well. Could you take me back?"

"Mu'tamin has called for a few lines of poetry. It would be an insult to leave now." Luis picked up our cushions and I grabbed the wine glasses. Damn.

"But—"

"I cannot take you back now. Mu'tamin notices everything."

"Now the torture really begins," Alvar grumbled, and the soldiers within earshot all agreed.

"Hush, gentlemen," Luis scolded. The cool night air felt good after the muggy air in the banquet room.

The black sky, sprinkled with stars, spanned the courtyard like a work of art. Servants set up torches around the outside of the courtyard, but not enough to ruin the magic. I nearly bumped into the Moor in the crimson robe, but Luis moved me away in time. We sat down, leaning against one of the marble pillars.

The emir stood before the group, waving his arm across the crowd. "My son, the brilliant al-Musta'in, will begin." He coughed slightly, then collapsed on a waiting cushion, black eyes bleary, skin paper thin. No, this was not a well man.

Tossing back the long end of his turban, Musta'in began to recite while Luis translated softly, his breath tickling my ear. "For women are as aromatic herbs, which if not well-tended soon lose their fragrance; they are as edifices which, if not constantly cared for, quickly fall into ruin."

I put my mouth against Luis's ear. "I think I'm going to be sick."

"Therefore, it has been said that manly beauty is of higher excellence, since it can endure onslaughts the merest fraction of which would transform the loveliness of a woman's face beyond recognition: such enemies as the burning heat of the noonday, the scorching wind of the desert, every air of heaven, and all the changing moods of the season."

Applause accompanied Musta'in's slight bow. "See why we keep you tucked away in that harem?" Luis whispered. I took great satisfaction in his surprised 'oof' when I jabbed him in the ribs. When my plan worked, these bozos would see just how fragile women were.

Another Moor stood, reciting a ridiculous poem about lost love, something about a dove killed by an arrow. I kept checking my wrist, but of course I'd taken my watch off days ago. Time. I was burning up valuable time listening to ridiculous poetry.

Another Moor spoke a poem about the beauty of flowers, a rambling thing that so bored us Luis finally stopped translating. Enzo snored quietly behind me until Luis reached back and tugged on his beard.

"Let us hear from the soldiers," one Moor cried after a particularly painful poem about the beauty of geometry. The Christians, roused by the applause, looked at each other in discomfort. Finally, at a nod from Luis, a tall man, a graying beard draped down his chest, stood and pulled a piece of paper from his tunic. He cleared his throat, then began a bloody war poem about arrows turning men into sieves and swords putting out men's lights and valiant warriors for whom dying was a virtue.

Polite applause from the Moors and wild clapping and lusty cheers from the Christians followed the tall man, now beet red, as he sat back down.

"Lovely sentiments," I whispered. "Can we go now, Luis?"

"And now the woman!" someone roared. "Let us hear from the Christian woman."

A Moor ran over, laughing, and yanked me to my feet. I started to sputter a protest, but it died in the silence. Mu'tamin's eyes were hard, Rodrigo's not much better. My hands trembled as I smoothed out my skirts, searching frantically for a poem. I quickly rejected *Green Eggs and Ham* given the dietary constraints of the Muslims. Thank god Lewis Carroll's "Jabberwocky" popped into my head, an interpretive reading I'd done in college. I swallowed a few times, then began in English. "Twas brillig and the slithy toves did gyre and gimble in the wabe—"

Al-Musta'in tried to translate, but immediately ran into trouble, his eyes wide with outrage at not knowing everything. "No translating," I said. "Just listen."

The poem was the story of a hunt told in nonsense words, so language was irrelevant. After the first stanza, I relaxed, leaning forward, using my voice and body to capture the story of a prince sent into the forest to hunt the horrible jabberwocky.

Somehow, it worked. The Moors were enthralled with the language itself, but even Luis and his men listened intently, sensing a battle. I nearly forgot the last stanza when I noticed Walladah's flushed face and intent gaze, but I recovered, finishing with a flourish of my arms. Al-

Mu'tamin nodded vigorously, wearing almost a smile. Wild applause followed, and I dropped gratefully onto my cushion.

"I will tell the next story," an older Moor said. "I will use the soldiers' tongue so all can understand." I leaned back against the column, breathing deeply to still my racing heart. I hated public speaking, even in the eleventh century.

The man's voice was smooth, his face open and friendly. "Once a nightingale loved a rose, and the rose, awakened by the bird's passionate song, trembled on her stem. It was a white rose, like all the roses at that time—white, innocent, and virginal."

I rolled my eyes at Luis and he quickly covered his smile.

"As the rose listened, something in its rose heart stirred. The nightingale came near and whispered, 'I love you, rose.' The heart of the rose blushed, and pink roses were born. The bird came closer, and although Allah had never intended that the rose know earthly love, the rose opened its petals and the nightingale stole its virginity." Rude hoots from the soldiers broke out, which Luis halted immediately with a scowl. "The next day the shamed rose turned red, giving birth to red roses, and although the nightingale still returns every night asking for love, the rose refuses, for Allah never meant rose and bird to mate. The rose trembles at the nightingale's song, but its petals remain closed forever."

More applause, then Mu'tamin stood. "Let us break for more food and wine, then we will continue." The music started again, and Liana and her friends began to dance in the starlit courtyard. This party would continue all night.

As I turned to Luis, Rodrigo stepped between us. "Babieca is no better," he murmured, more threatening than if he'd yelled at me.

"I know." I met his gaze.

"Rosario died this afternoon," Rodrigo said.

My throat tightened. "Luis, could you take me back now?" Luis nodded and we headed toward the main walkway. Damn, what a mess. Tonight just had to work. "Will you return to the party?" I asked.

Away from the crowd and his men, Luis allowed himself a grimace. "Rodrigo expects me to, even though he will start snoring soon. I must stay at least until Mu'tamin has recited his latest poems, which he usually does last. I am sorry about Rosario."

I waved my hand. No time to worry about that now. Luis would be away from his room for a few more hours. Perfect. I walked faster, my skirts swirling like grass around me. "So are you the nightingale in the story?"

"No, and slow down. Why must you always walk so fast?" How could I explain the pace of life in the twenty-first century? I slowed some, but couldn't wait to reach the harem.

"What about Marisella?" I teased.

"I hate to be so blunt about a young woman's virtue, but Marisella was no white rose when she came to me."

"Well, if you aren't the nightingale, are you the rose?"

Luis looked momentarily startled, then grinned such a rakish grin it was no wonder poor Marisella had fallen for his charms. "Hardly."

"You didn't recite anything," I continued to tease as we ambled through the columns, the carved ceilings deeply shadowed by the occasional torch.

"No, I choose not to."

"If you did, what would you recite?"

Luis brushed his fingertips against the clipped bushes lining the walkway. "No poem, but I do remember something my mother used to say. 'Even in a golden cage, the nightingale yearns for its native land.'"

I blinked back sudden tears. So true, so true. God, how I wanted to be home, to be in my own house. Nothing more was said until we reached Abu at the harem entrance. "Thank you. Now you can return to the party and woo the prettiest young woman there, or perhaps one woman in particular?" I winked, but he revealed nothing.

"The prettiest is no longer there," he said, his voice husky as he bowed deeply and kissed my hand.

"Don't be ridiculous. You've ignored her all evening. Go to her."

Smiling at Luis's attempt to look confused, I hurried to my room, waiting until Luis's footsteps had faded to nothing. From under my sofa I pulled out the silk bag I'd taken from the clothing room, struggled to lift my voluminous skirts, then tied the bag around my waist with a silk scarf. I slipped into the bath, pulled the lit torch from its iron holder and began feeling along the wall, near the center of the lowest wave in the tiled design that Liana had described the first day I'd used the bath. When I felt a small depression I pressed it with my thumb and pushed. A small section of the wall moved back and I shoved, hoping Abu couldn't hear the stone grinding on stone. The torch revealed rough red clay walls, a small landing, then stairs spiraling down. I crawled inside, my nose twitching at the dust, pushed the wall closed, held the torch before me, and headed down the stairs.

❖

Once inside Luis's room, I pushed the secret door shut, then held the torch high. As Luis had explained to me on one of our walks, his room was one of the few palace rooms with a locking door, with a door at all, actually. Formerly the emir's treasury, it had been empty when Luis and company had arrived, since Mu'tamin had moved his expanding wealth to a larger room in the palace.

I stepped farther out into the room, shining my torch on the door, outfitted with a bar latch. Much easier to make love if a locked door keeps away visitors, eh Luis? Light filtered through the ivory grill covering the round window. Round window? My gasp sounded harsh in the quiet room. I'd been here before, over nine hundred and twenty years in the future.

Luis's clothes lay stacked in one corner, so I searched for and found a pair of coarse black leggings, then a dark green linen blouse. Neither was clean, but at this point I didn't care. A scarred leather tunic lay on the floor.

As I searched for a spare pair of boots, I found a small bundle of rags, similar to the ones Liana had given me last week when my period had started. I smiled, shaking my head. Luis was something else. How many men in the twenty-first century would keep a box of tampons on hand should a visiting woman need them?

Finally I found a pair of boots, a little big, but wearable. I considered taking the dagger I found hidden under the clothes, then put it back. No clue *how* to use it. No will *to* use it.

A helmet rested in the corner. I hesitated, then stuffed the cold metal into the bag with the rest of the clothes. Even when I cut my hair, the helmet would do much to hide my sex. I counted on the same phenomenon my first lover Karen experienced whenever she entered a women's bathroom. Usually some unobservant woman would take in Karen's buzz cut, slender hips, and jean jacket, then start sputtering, wide-eyed, that this was the *women's* restroom. The poor women never seemed to notice Karen's definitely female chest. If I could create the illusion of being male, I could pull this off.

I scooted back to the secret door, but could find no way to open it. Shit. I had to get back to the harem without being seen. Why had I closed the stupid door? I groaned. Five years with Anna had trained me to close doors behind me, turn off lights, and never soak dishes in the sink. I dug at the door's edges, but all I did was rub my fingertips raw. I held the torch close, searching for a release mechanism. Nothing. Damn it. I would have to go back through the palace. I tied the heavy bag around my waist again, shifting it over my backside. The helmet bumped against my calves with every step, but my skirt camouflaged the bag well.

I lifted the latch, relieved Luis hadn't locked it from the outside, then slipped into the empty hall. Sounds of the party came from far away. Struggling to get my bearings, I finally recognized the corner staircase and hurried toward it, wincing as the helmet bashed against my calves. Hang on, Arturo, I chanted as I reached the stairs and started climbing. This will work.

I reached the top of the stairs. Only a few more turns and I'd reach the harem with the clothes I needed for my escape.

I never saw his face, only heard a soft whooshing, saw a brief flash of crimson as someone grabbed me from behind, clamped one hand down over my mouth and used the other to smoothly pin both my arms back.

My muffled shouts echoed down the hall as I struggled. I kicked, but my skirts and the damn helmet got in the way. Heart pounding, I struggled to bite, but the man's sweaty hand was too tight. I kicked as he dragged me back toward the stairs. One of my elbows connected with his rib cage; he let go of my mouth long enough to grab my hair, yanking it so hard that tears stung my eyes and I couldn't have shouted. He crushed my mouth again. Instead of being subdued, I fought harder, but could not break free. He swung me in front of him as we reached the stairs. Somehow, over my own muffled shouts, I heard running boots.

"Stop struggling!" came a shout from the far end of the hallway behind us. Surprised, I did stop, and my captor suddenly slammed against me, then let go. Falling, sliding, he landed face down on the landing below, a dagger buried to the hilt in his back.

"Kate!" Luis's breath was ragged as he reached me.

My first impulse was to fling my arms around Luis's neck—it must have been the influence of my ultra-feminine clothes—but if he discovered the bag, somehow miraculously still under my skirt, I was sunk. I backed up against the wall, chest heaving. "Jesus, Luis. You killed him!"

"Yes, I did," Luis said way too calmly. "He must be one of al-Hayib's men. He was kidnapping you."

I stared at the dead body, the trail of smeared blood on the steps. "Why did you have to kill him? Couldn't you have knocked him down or something?"

Luis flung up his hands, incredulous. "Once down the stairs, he would have disappeared with you. I may never have found you."

My arms and knees trembled, and I began shivering violently. "Why are you so quick to kill? You kill Christians! You kill Moors!" I was shouting now, my voice shrill in the echoing hallway.

Luis brought his face inches from mine. "I do not expect gratitude. But do not berate me for saving your life, or I may not be so quick to do it next time."

My knees buckled and Luis caught me. I pushed him away, then leaned against the rough stucco wall. "Killing comes too easily to you." My voice rasped as I tried not to stare at the crimson pool spreading beneath the body.

"I kill when I must," Luis responded, eyes blazing, jaw set. Muscles twitched along his fine jaw, but he said nothing more. His furious glare would have set me trembling if my knees weren't already rattling like a weak lamb's. Then he stepped back. Free, I staggered toward the harem. Luis followed, but did not try to help me again.

At the harem's entrance, Abu stepped out, confused, as Luis cursed him in Arabic, cuffing his ear for letting me escape. I would apologize to Abu later, but for now, all I could do was drag myself to my room and collapse on the divan, curling up into a tight ball, tucking the helmet behind my quaking knees. Still shaking, I squeezed my eyes shut. Seconds later musk filled my head as someone covered me with a robe, tucking it around my feet. Sleep came and went all night. Each time I roused, I smelled Luis's familiar scent. Once, in the dead of night, when my eyes flew open, moonlight revealed Luis, his back to me, sitting bolt upright guarding my doorway. Luis Navarro, El Cid's first lieutenant. No. That wasn't right. I could hear Anna's voice in my head. In her stories about El Cid, Alvar Fáñez was El Cid's first lieutenant, not Luis Navarro. Alvar Fáñez helped El Cid take Valencia. But if history recorded Fáñez as El Cid's first lieutenant, what the hell had happened to Luis Navarro?

CHAPTER EIGHT

When I awoke, Luis was gone. A steady rain beat down into the courtyard, the smell of wetness so familiar my heart ached. I closed my eyes. Before Anna and I had left Chicago, a steady rain had streaked the windows, separating us from the rest of the world. I lit candles, poured wine, and tried to lure Anna from her office. Too engrossed in her research about the settlement patterns of medieval Spain, she'd waved me away. I wished now that I'd insisted. I wished I'd figured out why settlement patterns attracted her more than I did. Maybe if I'd been more supportive, maybe if I'd been more patient.

Eyes still closed, I rolled to the edge of the divan, inhaled the rain, and noticed an undercurrent of sweetness. I opened my eyes. A fragile white rose lay next to me. I smiled, then drew the soft petals across my cheek. Luis? One of his men? One of the Moors?

"Kate?" Liana stood in my doorway, hair tamed by a cap and veil, face pale in the gray day. "Abu said you had a bad night, so I brought you juice."

I pulled on my robe and took the cool mug gratefully, practically guzzling the tangy apricot juice. Liana sat on the bed, hugging her knees, not letting on if she knew what had happened the night before. "I know who Luis's lover is."

I stopped drinking. "You saw her?"

Liana's hazel eyes darkened. "I could not sleep after party, so got up. Saw Aisha slip through secret doorway."

I struggled to sort out the women I'd come to know. A sick feeling landed in my stomach. "Aisha. Isn't she the young blond woman? Mu'tamin's new virgin?" Liana nodded, eyes wide. "Jesus." I dropped onto the divan, the rose still in my hand.

"Your friend Luis make bad choice. If Mu'tamin find out…" Liana shuddered, then drew her finger across her throat.

I tried to picture Luis and Aisha together, but couldn't. Aisha was too young. She could never match his mind. And how could Luis, always so cool and in control, so hung up on following the rules, how could he be so stupid? I flung myself back on a tapestry cushion as a brilliant green parrot flew into my room. "Luis isn't the only one in trouble." I explained about Babieca and King Alfonso and al-Hayib.

Liana's brows knit together, her face suddenly angry. "Why did you not tell me?"

I sighed. "You've had enough to worry about. Being sent to al-Hayib's is a possibility for you as well."

Liana leaned forward and slapped my knee. "You not thinking. Forget about Hayib. I grow up with horses. I know how to cure sickness. Tell me symptoms."

I *hadn't* been thinking. Something started bouncing around inside me, struggling to get out. Hope, perhaps? "Labored breathing, watery eyes and nose, no appetite, but drinks water." I hugged my knees with excitement.

"Legs cold?"

"No, I'm fine, thanks. I—"

"The horse!" Liana slapped me again, smiling this time.

"Yes, I guess they were." I explained my rough stab at treatment.

"Garlic good," she nodded. "Horse have..." Her Spanish failing, she tapped her chest. "Sick in here. Sick breathing." Pneumonia. "Must make steam bag." She described how to fill a sack half-full of bran, then pour in boiling water and a spoonful of eucalyptus oil. The soaked bran would begin to steam. "Tie the bag around Babieca's head so he can breathe it. Wrap legs with cloth. Do three times a day."

I clutched at Liana's hands. "Will this work?"

Eyes shining, she returned my squeeze. "Four, five days, horse all better." She squealed in surprise when I flung my arms around her.

"You might have just saved my life," I whispered.

"I am honored," Liana said. Hazm and Tayani began fighting in the courtyard, so Liana slipped away with a wink.

After Liana left, I splashed off my face and put on another robe. The air was warm, but the rain, now drifting in a mist into my room, sent chills down my bare arms. I found a vase for the rose, then after an hour, joined the rest of the harem in one of the larger rooms for breakfast.

Aisha sat at the far end of the table, dark blue eyes sparkling, a dimple in each cheek as she laughed with the young women around her. I tried out a few Arabic phrases on Zaydun, who cackled at my attempts. Eating slowly, I surveyed the remaining food. Fruit would be my best bet for my long journey. After the others had left, but before Ali cleaned up, I filled my skirt with oranges, a few scraps of cheese, dried meat, then hurried back to my room. Tonight was the night. Even if Liana's cure worked miracles, I couldn't wait around to find out.

After I stashed the food, I begged Suley to take me to the stables. He hesitated, then folded his thick arms. "More stories."

"Absolutely," I said, and told him all about Mohammed Ali—moves like a butterfly, stings like a bee—on the walk to the stables. "Hamara!" I called as we neared the stable entrance. The young Moor turned, sorrow flooding his face. It crossed my mind to wonder why, but right now Babieca's treatment was all that mattered. Hamara nodded, growing excited as I explained.

"I do three times a day."

"And wrap his legs."

"I do," he said, already looking for an empty sack. "No worry, Kate. It is too late for Rosario, but we fix Babieca." With Hamara's positive energy, it just might happen.

I languished in the damned harem all afternoon, alternating between fury at being a prisoner and terror at my plan. Two weeks on oranges, dried apricots, and dried goat meat would get old fast. What if it took me longer? Without a map, I could wander forever through the forested mountains between here and Santillana. Luis and his men survived on rabbit during their campaigns, an option I lacked. I closed my eyes and imagined the map in Mu'tamin's quarters. Follow the Ebro to the northwest until it ends, then go straight north until I hit the coast, then follow the coast east a few miles, and voilà—Santillana del Mar and its cave. I would no longer be a pawn in Mu'tamin's game or El Cid's hostage. I would be home. Anna. Arturo. Laura. Max.

Finally I pulled out my paints, stretched a new canvas, then stood in my doorway for inspiration. Shajar and her friends lounged in the far corner. She wasn't the most beautiful woman in the harem, but my gaze returned often to her almond eyes, crooked nose, plump arms.

I stepped back into my room and began to paint Shajar. I would keep this canvas private because of the Moors' dislike for human figures in art, but I needed new challenges. I sketched a rough outline with charcoal, one of Shajar's arms thrown back across the stack of pillows, the other draped along her lush waist and hips. I drew in a few of the other women, but would keep them part of the background so the painting's focus remained Shajar. When I began adding color, the subtle creams and burnt umbers, a pale viridian, Shajar came alive, a round, happy, sensual woman, the center of attention. Pleased with myself, I worked through the afternoon.

At one point angry shouts in Arabic broke out somewhere else in the palace, and soon a pair of the emir's eunuchs stormed into the harem. My heart raced as they disappeared down the central hallway. They returned moments later with a terrified Aisha between them, tears streaming down her cheeks. Oh God. Luis and Aisha had been discovered. I considered delaying my escape, but there was nothing I could do to help. I hated to leave without thanking Luis for all he had done to make my imprisonment bearable, but a thank you might tip him off, so I just sent him a mental thanks, hoping he would understand. Surely he'd figure out a way to escape Mu'tamin's wrath. I smiled at the white rose, hid the painting under my divan, then napped until dusk.

❖

The constant rain filled the harem with its incessant pounding as I stripped, bound my breasts with a scarf, then slipped on Luis's black leggings and green blouse. The leather tunic was heavier than I expected, but warmed me in the cool evening air. I tightened the wide belt around my waist, then stuffed my foodstores and fanny pack into the bag. I tucked my hair up and jammed the helmet over my head, wincing as the cold metal touched my skin. I would cut my hair later with a knife I'd spied in the stables. The helmet came down to my eyebrows, around my cheeks, then along my jaw.

I looked into the courtyard. Suley was gone, Abu rested on a bench, head on his chest. I raised my fist in a silent salute, then skirted the courtyard, grateful the rain muffled my footsteps. Luck shone on me—the baths were empty, so I was able to slip through the secret door, close it behind me, and hurry down the tight stairway. Now came the tricky part. Ear against the wall, I heard nothing from Luis's room, so I waited, softly humming a few bars of "I Heard it Through the

Grapevine," then opened the door a crack. More good luck—Luis was gone.

I pulled the bag behind me, slid the secret door shut, and lay the white rose on Luis's bed. Trying to mentally shift my center of gravity up from my hips, I stood tall, imagining myself already outside the city walls, took a deep breath, and entered the hallway. The rain must have depressed the entire palace, for I met only one servant. I scowled darkly like a highly ranked soldier and the poor man scurried away. So far, so good.

Heart racing, I nearly jogged across the walkway to the stables. One lone torch lit the entrance. Smells of wet straw and earth and horse urine hit me as I headed for Babieca's stall. I stroked his long, velvet muzzle, noting that Hamara had wrapped green rags around the horse's legs, and they felt much warmer to the touch. I leaned closer. "Be well, Babieca."

On my way to the tack wall, I passed one of the aisles leading deeper into the stable and stopped. There, tied to a post, stood a massive brown stallion, already bridled and saddled. Ridiculous luck, but clearly I was meant to escape. I rubbed the horse's nose, then began untying the leather reins.

"What are you doing?"

With a gasp, I whirled to face Luis, who stood with one hand on his sword hilt, the other hitched casually into his scabbard belt. I looked down, my heart pounding, then I lowered my voice. "Rodrigo asked me to take a message to Ordóñez."

"Wearing my clothes? Wearing my helmet?"

I cursed under my breath, then yelled as Luis grabbed the helmet and pulled it off, releasing my hair. Luis flung the helmet down in disgust, voice trembling with rage. "What in God's name do you think you are doing?"

I held firm to the horse's reins. "Leaving. Don't try to stop me. I—"

"Me stop you? You will get no farther than Mirabueno before you are caught, raped, and sold into slavery. Look at you!" He yanked the tunic up around my waist. "You have *hips*. The clothes of men cannot disguise that." I struggled as he reached around and grabbed my buttock. "You have the ass of a woman."

Furious, I pushed him away. "Not all women have round asses, you jerk. Now let me leave."

Luis grabbed me and slammed me against the nearest stall door. "Do you know what happens to women who impersonate men?" With his face only inches from mine, I squirmed as his furious fingers dug into my arms. "A woman in Toledo dressed as a man and was flogged to death when discovered. Two women in Barcelona were caught being... intimate. The woman in the skirt was beaten but released. The woman with the male dress and...equipment was stoned to death." He shook me so hard my teeth hurt. I tried to knee him, but he neatly sidestepped, pressing against me. "I will not let you do this."

"Woman troubles, Luis?" Nuño Súarez, Luis's friend and one of Mu'tamin's prisoners, stepped out from the aisle. When he moved around to the front of the horse, I could see he was a man obviously dressed to ride, his leather hood pulled over curly dark hair, an oilskin poncho flung over his shoulders.

"I seem to have more than my share." Luis's voice still shook. He turned back to me. "You are going nowhere."

Unbidden, the thought popped into my head that Luis was downright beautiful when he was angry. I struggled again, but Luis's iron grip pinned me to the wooden door. He opened the stall and flung me to the ground inside. I yelled as the dry straw poked my back and legs. I leapt to my feet but Luis had locked the door, so I pounded on the wooden slats. "You *asshole*. Let me out!"

"Nuño, my friend. I must ask you to delay your escape a moment. Could you see she stays put while I fetch her own clothes?"

I stormed around my cage. The wooden walls of the sides and back met a wooden ceiling coated in cobwebs. The door's slats were too close together. There was a two foot gap above the door, which did me no good while Nuño stood guard. I pressed against the door. "Nuño, let me out. Take me with you. Surely they treat women better in Burgos."

The tall man peered at me through a slat, his face rough but kind. "Have you been so mistreated?"

"I've been a prisoner."

Nuño snorted. "So have I. Only I have lived the last weeks in a damp, moldy dungeon fighting with the rats for my food. You have lived in your own room with plenty of the best food."

I leaned my forehead against the worn door. "Yes, I know. I'm sorry. But I need to get out of here. Luis doesn't care at all. He—"

"Luis cares a great deal. He is a...a man of deep, deep passion." Nuño's voice was strangely thick, and for a second I wondered if Nuño felt more than friendship for Luis.

"He doesn't show it. All he does is boss me around and tell me what I cannot do."

Nuño looked back at me, rubbing his beard. "Yes, well, that is likely the training. Do not judge Luis so harshly."

"What training?"

Nuño's eyes darted away, then he fell silent, refusing to answer any more questions.

Luis returned with a bundle, which he tossed over the stable door. "Change," he commanded. "Nuño, ride swiftly. The rain will delay a search party."

The two men clasped each other's forearms for a second, then Nuño untied the horse.

"Why will you let him escape and not me?" I spat out between clenched teeth.

"Change your clothes, woman. I must get you back before they notice you are missing." With a nod to me, Nuño led the horse from the stable and mounted. Horseshoes clopped on the brick path, then faded. The tremor in Luis's voice had been replaced by iron as he turned back to me. "Change or I will change you myself."

I glared at him through the slats, my fists clenched. "Try it and you'll be singing soprano." I breathed through my nostrils, searching for options. There were none. "Turn your back." I clipped off each word, mad enough to spit.

Luis turned, then I did the same, tears stinging my eyes as I stripped off the solid, practical clothes and put on the silky, diaphanous crap that imprisoned women just as much as the harem did.

I turned to face a pair of blue eyes. "Damn it! You said you would turn around."

"I lied." He opened the door and grabbed my wrist. As he dragged me toward the archway, I made one last desperate attempt, tackling him to the ground. I scrambled to my feet but he pulled me down. I clawed at his face, but only succeeded in ripping out the shoulder of his tunic to reveal a small tattoo.

Luis rolled over on top of me, his weight pressing my tailbone into the hard-packed stable floor. With my hands pinned over my head, I couldn't move. Luis's chest heaved against mine as we both struggled for breath.

His perfect slender face, his full mouth, his almond-shaped eyes, hovered inches above mine, and a sudden warmth spread across my belly. Something hard pressed against my inner thigh. Jesus, what was happening? I could barely control the urge to arch toward those lips. Time froze as I could feel both our hearts racing.

Luis's cheek twitched, his eyes flickering between my eyes and my mouth. I held my breath, knowing if he'd been a woman, I wouldn't have even hesitated. Crap. What did that say about me and fidelity? About me and Anna? About me, the lesbian, and the fact that Luis was, well, a guy? Finally, with a low moan, he rolled off me.

We lay there, side by side. Pressure filled my head as I realized what I'd almost done. Shit. This century was totally screwing me up.

Luis's voice broke as he said my name. "Kate, they began to torture Nuño yesterday. I could not bear it, so I helped him escape. To be safe, Nuño must leave. To be safe, you must stay."

I swallowed hard. "I have to leave..." I struggled for an image of Anna's face, but nothing came. A few cold tears ran down into my ear.

Luis rolled over, then pulled me to my feet, brushing dirt from my arms and skirt. "Come, you must get back," he said, his voice tight.

I sniffed, wiping my face on the veil. "You really are not going to help me, are you?"

"Not this way, no."

I gave him my coldest look, shrugging him off as he reached for my arm. "I will escape without your help." What I didn't say was by now I'd figured out how stupid my plan had been. I'd just come close to galloping out into the dark, snarled forests of eleventh century Spain without a compass. Wow. Had that even been invented yet? No map, no real food, and nothing but my pigheadedness. Brilliant plan, Kate.

As we walked back the too-familiar path, side-by-side but not speaking, I shivered in the cool air, my skin clammy and sticky. My ridiculous situation had to be *someone's* fault, since I hadn't asked for any of this. A sudden fury pulsed through my veins, so at the top of the stairs, I turned to Luis, fists clenched, voice low. "Nuño is your friend, so you do what is right for him. You say I am your friend, but you do what is right for *you*. Let me remove one burden from your life. I am no longer your friend." His eyes narrowed, but jaw tight, he said nothing.

Just before we reached the harem entrance, Walladah and two tall black servants appeared from another hallway. Breathtaking in a deep magenta robe, the woman approached me without looking once at Luis. From her voluminous sleeve she produced a pink rose.

"For you," she said in a smooth, silky voice.

I took the rose, smiling through my fury. "So it was you."

She moved closer, bringing along a cloud of spicy perfume. "That nightingale and rose story always saddens me. Allah did not mean for the nightingale and rose to be together." Her smile was warm and open. "But perhaps two roses could be happy together."

Luis's jaw dropped as a spreading heat warmed my face.

"Ah, al-zarca, the blue-eyed one," Walladah said, finally turning her gaze on him. "How is my favorite nightingale?"

"Fine, your highness. But I must return Kate to her room."

Walladah shook her head. "No, not tonight. Father has given me permission to invite her to my quarters for dinner. I told him perhaps I could trick her into confessing to being a spy." She winked at me, and I sighed. Things were looking up.

"She is no spy," Luis said impatiently. "But she must be guarded. She—"

"Do not worry, my great warrior. My servants will be able to handle any problems." The woman took my hand in her own warm, smooth one. "Shall we go?"

I lifted the rose, inhaled, then with a dagger-sharp glare at Luis, I nodded. "I would be delighted."

❖

I picked straw from my hair while Walladah ordered servants around her extravagant quarters as they prepared our meal. A series of four connected rooms, Walladah's walls glittered with gold-infused tiles, and carved columns supported red and white arches. I stood by the window in the largest room, her massive bed dwarfed by the tall window, huge oriental rugs, and gigantic Ficus trees.

Maybe Walladah could help. I had to get to Santillana.

The rain had stopped, leaving the night clean and bright with stars, meaning Nuño would likely ride all night. I bore him no ill will, since torture in a dungeon could blind one to the troubles of a stranger, and I supposed my being held in a harem had blinded me to Nuño's troubles.

Walladah led me to a low table pushed against a creamy wall covered in red oriental tapestries, where she poured us each a goblet of wine. It was late, but I was wide awake. I hated people who made friends just to serve themselves, but in this time, in this place, I had no choice.

Walladah's Spanish was excellent. She asked about my life, and I told her what I could, leaving out all mention of computers, cars, trains, planes, microwave ovens, and television. Nearly crying with relief, I told her of Arturo and my need to meet him in Santillana.

"Such a long way," she said, her smooth, coffee face betraying nothing.

I told her about treating the gazelle and about my painting. Her encouraging nod kept me running off at the mouth for nearly an hour until I began to ask her questions. She told me of growing up in the Aljafería, of traveling to the ocean, of her hatred for her uncle Hayib.

"So no husband or children?" I pried.

"Absolutely not. Why shop at only one stall when the wares of the entire market can be yours?"

"Why indeed," I said with a smile. "Anyone special?"

She shook her head wistfully, her hair gleaming with deep gold shadows. "No, I am bored with the men—" She looked at me through long pale lashes. "—and the women of the city. I seek new challenges."

"I see." Curiosity made me nosy. "How about Luis? Has he ever been...special?"

Walladah grinned, then waggled her eyebrows. "Several years ago Luis was *very* special." She gave a lusty growl, setting off such a weird sort of jealousy in me that I resolved to get a grip on myself before I totally lost it. "Stars exploded in the heavens the nights Luis visited." She sighed, loosening the neck of her robe. "But alas, he proved too modest for my tastes. I have never met a man so determined to keep his clothes on during love." She snickered. "And he would only make love in total darkness."

I nodded, suddenly uncomfortable to know such intimate details about Luis, even if he was no longer my friend. I asked Walladah about

Zaragoza's struggle against both the Christians and her uncle. Snorting, she removed her head scarf and undid her four thick braids, releasing a cascade of glistening waves. After Walladah gave a long, enthusiastic, detailed answer to my question, she leaned back and stretched out her legs, revealing two slender ankles ringed with gold chains. "Teach me your poem, Kate."

We laughed and giggled for another hour as I tried to help her get those luscious lips around words like *frabjous* and *brillig* and *jabberwocky*. Luis's and Liana's warnings seemed groundless. I'd been prepared for a volatile, petulant child but was delighted to find a mature woman. One of my lovers before Anna had been a spoiled brat, but I'd stayed with Sarah months longer than I should have because her androgyny intrigued me. In some settings she appeared to be a young man; in others the curve of her cheek, the swell of her lips, made her all woman. Sarah had been tough and swaggering, but in my arms she was both that *and* soft and yielding. Too bad she'd been so impossible.

Walladah and I gave up halfway through the poem, leaning back against the wall, the table between us. "Walladah, about Santillana." She rolled her head toward me, eyes blazing with wine, gaze fixed on my chest. "You have the freedom to leave the palace. Why not go on a journey?" Elbows on the table, I leaned toward her, my breasts now pressing against my robe. "We could have a great adventure traveling to Santillana...together." I lowered my eyes demurely. God, what a trollop I'd become.

"Hmmm, a journey." She undid her sash, letting the robe reveal a layered ivory dress, then looked at my chest again. I felt like a trader on the floor of the Chicago Grain Exchange, trying to sell a bushel of corn for whatever I could get. "It *would* be cooler in the mountains."

My pulse quickened. Finally I was getting somewhere. But then Walladah shoved the table away, scooting her hip right next to mine. She took my hand, then kissed my cheek, her hair cascading into my lap.

"Perhaps we might go to Santillana some day soon. But for now, my love, let us retire. It is time for the two pink roses to know each other, to become red roses." Her breath tickled my ear.

I laughed nervously, looking past her at the bed. Let's see. I had two options. One was to cheat on Anna by making love to a beautiful, exotic, sexy woman in a soft bed larger than my entire room, waking to servants waiting on me hand and foot, enjoying a quiet morning away from the chaos of the harem. The other choice was to return to my hard divan in a cold room moist from the constant rain.

I had something she wanted; she had something I wanted. If I was going to barter myself for my freedom, I wouldn't go cheaply. And all calculation aside, I just didn't know if I could do it, even if she was beautiful.

I kissed her cheek, surprising myself. "Much as I would love to, Walladah, I think not. Let's get to know one another first. It will make everything so much better." I stood.

Walladah leapt to her feet, smooth forehead wrinkled into a frown. "You are not staying?"

I expelled my breath slowly. "No, but I would love to see you tomorrow." Her rich lips parted in surprise, then a darkness flashed through her eyes. With a tight smile, she clapped her hands, harshly ordering the servant who appeared to escort me back.

I tried to fill my own smile with promise as I left. When she agreed to take me to Santillana del Mar, then, and only then, would I think about what might come next.

CHAPTER NINE

The red rose came mid-morning, delivered by a servant, who also handed me a note. "You are forgiven," the note read. I snickered. Perhaps this woman *was* a bit spoiled. The note then invited me for a walk along the Ebro. A chance to get outside.

I flew to the clothing room, pulled on a pair of blue-green billowing trousers, an ivory white shift that this time covered everything, but snugly, and a blue-green robe. I grabbed an ivory veil in case Walladah thought it would be best. On my way back to my room, I heard heart-wrenching sobs coming from Liana's room. Inside, Liana rocked on the floor, her face splotchy from crying. Hazm and Tayani tugged on her light blue veil. "*Umm, Umm,*" they whimpered, Arabic for mother.

I knelt before Liana and she flung her arms around my neck, her sobs finally slowing to ragged deep breaths. "I am to be sent to al-Hayib's," she whispered.

"No!"

She squeezed me harder. "My children. Kate, will you watch over them?"

I felt sick. This was so unfair. "Liana, I can barely talk to them." Liana sat back on her heels, sniffing, rubbing her red eyes as my brain raced. "What about Zaydun? Or Shajar or Fatin? Couldn't one of them take care of the children?" And what if Liana's potion saved Babieca? I was the one who should be sent to al-Hayib's, not Liana.

"Their own children will always come first. You have no one. You will be a great mother." She bent over the children, crooning soothing sounds. I literally slapped my forehead. This could not be happening. I was headed for the Altamira cave and my future. I couldn't bring Hazm and Tayani with me. The children's shining black heads burrowed into Liana's chest, clinging to her as I'd cling to a log in a swollen river. Besides, my one baby-sitting experience had nearly ended in tragedy.

While I'd been yakking on the phone, little Lucy had filled the tub and fallen in. Only the loud splash and my sprint up the stairs saved her. I shook for days.

"Liana." I touched her wonderful cloud of hair and she looked up. "I will do my best to care for your children until you are able to return." If she returned.

Eyes red, lips puffy, she nodded. "*Shukran*," she said.

"You're welcome." Coward, coward. I just needed to tell Mu'tamin or Rodrigo that Liana knew horses. I should offer to go in her place.

Liana murmured something to the children, and they both gave me a kiss on the cheek, eyes wide and serious. Then they ran from the room. Liana sighed. "Aisha goes as well."

"What will happen to Luis? I saw him last night, but...we didn't discuss that matter."

"That Luis still lives is amazing."

When Walladah's servant came for me an hour later, I sat on a bench against the courtyard wall, the same spot where Carlos had shared his pear with me, a scene that would not actually occur for over nine hundred and twenty years. I half-heartedly picked at a pomegranate, then tossed the rest to one of the monkeys scampering past. The other monkeys screamed in hot pursuit.

After washing the ruby stains from my fingers, I followed the servant to Walladah's quarters. Why had I promised Liana something I likely could not do? And why was I such a coward? Because I knew al-Hayib's harem would be a worse prison that this and would take me farther from my goal.

At Walladah's I looked for signs of a spoiled child bent on punishing me, but saw none. Instead I admired her proud bearing, her ivory woven long jacket and black billowing trousers. Anna would have enjoyed Walladah's fashion sense. The Moorish princess took my arm, and we walked toward the stairs, an entourage of seven servants loaded down with baskets at our heels. When I reached for my veil, Walladah stopped me. "I would hate to hide such a beautiful face under that veil."

I flashed her a smile of relief. "Won't I get in trouble?"

She shrugged wide, fine shoulders. "I am Walladah. This is my city."

We first detoured to the stables, where I looked in on Babieca.

Hamara's tired face flushed to see Walladah with me, but he managed to give me an update. "I have been giving him steam bags three times a day. Come, look. I think he is a little better." I held my breath as we neared the stall. My breath caught at the horse's dull coat and wheezing breath, but he did raise his head to sniff my hand. "You are great healer," Hamara crowed. Guilt twisted my insides. Liana was the hero, yet she was being sent to al-Hayib's. If Rodrigo knew I had lied, my fate would be the same.

Outside the palace gates I inhaled deeply—horse manure, baking bread, spoiled fruit, body odor, wood smoke, and cinnamon. God, it felt good to get out of that damned harem. A flock of wide-eyed wooly sheep clattered past, baaing as the shepherd urged them on with a soft 'shooshing.' Walladah and I waited, laughing at the bobbing ears, until the sheep passed, then Walladah took me to the market, an open square crowded with carts laden with muskmelons, chickens and eggs, and rugs on the ground displaying iron pots and bolts of shimmering fabrics.

We passed a dozen public bath houses, two huge mosques, a synagogue, and one small Catholic church. At the end of what seemed the main street, Walladah steered me left toward the Ebro, where gangs of kids played on the muddy banks below. The water was so clear I could see dark fish zipping upstream. I sat down on the rough grass and refused to move for an hour, soaking up the quacking ducks, the smell of fish, the water rushing over rocks downstream, the hawks circling the foothills across the river.

Walladah's servants laid out a meal. As I sipped wine and ate thick slices of bread coated with a spicy honey, children threw rocks in the river, laughing at the satisfying "thu-dunk." Whatever it took, I must get both myself and Liana's children out of the harem.

Walladah read me poems from a thin calfskin book. The illustrations seemed to shimmer with light, and my eyes stung to see a book again, even if I couldn't read a word of it. She explained the huge floating flour mill upstream, its paddles splashing rhythmically as the rushing water ground millet and wheat into flour. Two millers, faces and aprons powdered with flour, used long poles to push logs away from the rapids churned up by the wheel.

Finally Walladah pulled me to my feet. The servants packed up the food. "Come, one more thing to show you." A short walk brought us down a narrow street lined with two-story buildings crammed together so tightly they formed a continuous wall of red and white and tan. Walladah led me through an elaborate wrought iron gate; we entered a small courtyard. Pink, white, red, yellow, burgundy, peach roses climbed the walls and carpeted the brown-tiled floor. The scent lifted me off the ground.

Walladah ordered her servants to remain in the courtyard, while she took my hand and led me up a slender wooden staircase. We walked along the narrow balcony, also filled with roses, then into a small bedroom lit by large windows facing the street. Walladah closed and latched the door behind us. Not until I heard the wooden latch fall into place did I understand. I turned to face her.

She smiled that magnetic smile, her palms open to the room. "More privacy." She reached me in two smooth steps, pulling me close, snuggling our hips together with her strong arms. "Kate, my rose, we know each other better now."

Her kiss would have landed on my lips if I hadn't shifted my head at the last minute, sending the kiss across my cheek. Not yet. Too soon. My heart pounded as I hugged her to buy time. What was wrong with me? Since when had I become so virginal? Anna would understand, if I ever made it back...when I made it back. My brain searched for a polite way out of this. Nothing came. Walladah was my best chance to get to Santillana.

She murmured Arabic in my ear, nuzzling my neck, then taking my ear lobe into her warm mouth. Jesus, I felt like a stone statue, nothing alive except my pounding heart threatening to leap from my chest. Wrong, my mind screamed. I grabbed Walladah's arms and stepped back. "Walladah, you are a beautiful woman. We will be together. But I—" What was the Arabic word Liana had taught me? "*Hayidatun.*" I had finished my period last week, but Walladah couldn't know that.

Walladah frowned. "No matter. You can wash."

"No. I bleed heavily. Very messy." Distaste graced her fine features. The stubborn set to the jaw could have been Anna, and I blinked rapidly. When faced with something she didn't like, Anna worked to change it, and that often included me. She'd change history, if she could, to ensure Walladah's descendants ruled all of Spain. I considered the hard glint in Walladah's eyes and thought perhaps the world was safer because I'd fallen back in time and not Anna. "Oh, yes, much blood. The blood of an entire village. Never stops." Relief weakened my limbs as Walladah looked ready to lose her picnic lunch.

She stepped back, nose actually wrinkling. "Perhaps we should wait."

"Excellent idea, though it will be torture." I moved closer, biting off a smile as she whirled and slammed open the latch.

"We must return to the palace," she said. Pleased with myself, I enjoyed the walk back, happily stepping around fresh horse manure, helping a young woman who'd dropped a basket of oranges.

As we entered the palace and walked through the massive courtyard, a familiar brown tunic walked toward us. Head bent, Luis did not see us until almost upon us. Tension gripped his forehead, and his skin was sallow, his jaw tight, his eyes in such pain my own began to burn.

"Al-zarca," Walladah crooned coyly.

"Walladah." Luis did not look at me.

"I am so sorry to hear about little Aisha being sent away. I do hope my uncle takes good care of her."

Luis threw me a look I couldn't interpret. "Aisha is of no concern to me," he said.

Walladah patted Luis's arm. "Are we still denying we stole the flower of my papa's next concubine?"

Luis's jaw twitched and he tossed off Walladah's hand, a rude act for him. "I have not laid a finger on Aisha."

"Oh, Luis, I remember well when you laid a finger on me." The woman's cruel streak suddenly surfaced. "You did not steal my flower, but instead my heart. Bad boy." Suddenly I wanted to punch her flat stomach.

"Princess Walladah!" A tall eunuch strode across the courtyard, bowed respectfully, then continued in Arabic too rapid for me to follow.

Walladah frowned, then gave me a regretful smile. "My father wishes to see me. Luis will escort you back. I will see you *tonight*." In a flash of whirling robes and flowing hair, she was gone.

"Luis, you look terrible."

"I feel terrible. Come."

"What will Mu'tamin do to you?" I hurried to match his long strides.

"Nothing yet. Rodrigo has argued on behalf of my innocence. Mu'tamin is still not entirely sure I am the one. If he kills me, the true lover may still remain to prey on his prizes."

"Aisha is very beautiful."

"She is a child. I never touched her." We climbed the steps. "Walladah is also beautiful," he said thickly.

"She is also something of a child herself. And I have never touched her. But I am handling her." And she might get me to Santillana, something Luis could not do.

Luis stopped. "You must be careful."

I snorted. "She's spoiled, not dangerous."

Luis pulled me into a shadowy alcove, his fingers once again digging into my arms. Plaster pricked my back through my robe. "This whole *palace* is dangerous. Do not be blinded by its beauty. I have learned how quickly life can sour here." I shook my head, squirming a little, but Luis just pressed closer. "Walladah can make anything happen." His fingers tightened. "Anything."

"But—"

"You cannot trust her."

"You're wrong. She—"

"Kate, I..." He stopped. My breath caught in my throat as I saw the look in his eyes. We stood, the same height, faces inches apart. Luis moved closer.

"No, Luis, don't."

He did anyway. The kiss was soft and gentle at first, and might have remained only that if my body hadn't totally betrayed me. My mouth slid open, drawing him deeper into a searing, greedy kiss that sent white-hot flashes down every limb. I willed my hands to push him away, but instead they slid around his neck, pulling him closer. Luis moaned, and all strength left my legs. His burning lips consumed mine, then bit my neck, then sweeping lower.

I finally broke free, staggering a few steps away, gasping for breath, holding my knees rigid so I wouldn't collapse. Luis leaned back, chest heaving. My hands shook as our eyes locked, and I knew I must leave. But my feet wouldn't respond. I licked my lips.

"Kate," Luis whispered.

Using every ounce of strength I had, I tore myself from the alcove and ran for the safety of my room. Luis did not follow.

Once there, I huddled on the floor in the corner, shivering under my blanket, still feeling Luis's passion on my swollen lips, while children played with the monkeys in the courtyard. I clutched my stomach against the churning, then held myself to stem the wild throbbing.

Fury raced through me. How dare he kiss me. How dare I kiss him back. No one's kiss—*ever*—had so unnerved me. What if I were really straight? The thought hollowed out my entire chest; I held my breath. Maybe I could black out and make it all go away. After sixty seconds I gasped involuntarily.

This just was *not* me. It had to be the pressures of life in this century. How could the person I was get so turned upside down?

I pulled the blanket tighter up under my chin, wishing I could call Laura and ask her why I was feeling so insane. She'd laugh, shake her head, and say, "Hey, I think Johnny Depp makes a damn sexy pirate, but you won't find me climbing into bed with him." No kidding.

When our friends Lisa and Chloe had separated, Chloe stunned us by marrying Phil. She tried to explain, but we just couldn't listen, so the friendship faded fast. We eventually learned enough about bisexuality to understand Chloe, but bisexuality wasn't me. I knew it wasn't.

Loneliness racked my body. A month away from Anna and my mind and body were so muddled I didn't know myself anymore. Not only had I come close to cheating on her, but I had nearly done so with a man. What did it mean for my relationship with Anna that this guy, a *guy* for Christ's sake, could melt my knees. Damn it! Why did Luis have to be a man? Why couldn't I feel this way when Walladah touched me? A moan escaped my lips. Why couldn't I feel this way when *Anna* touched me?

❖

Late that afternoon, after a glass of juice and a few pieces of cheese, I pulled myself together enough to sit with Liana and the others in the courtyard. I braided Tayani's hair, then looped each braid into a zany circle. She giggled when I held up the gold handled mirror. Liana knelt next to Hazm, watching him draw what appeared to be a camel, and I remembered the smell of Arturo and his small pile of crayons. It exhausted me to be so close to tears all the time.

While I fussed over Tayani's hair, Rhame had stood whispering to a palace servant. She returned, grim-faced, to our group lounging around the fountain. I caught some of it; Liana translated the rest. More rumors were flying of harem members being sent to al-Hayib, who apparently ran the Harem from Hell.

I sighed, hugging Tayani to my chest. As tension pulsed through the courtyard, the irritating monkeys started fighting over something near my room. When Shajar hurried over to break up the fight, my heart nearly stopped to see the monkeys fought over a painting. Those damned monkeys raided my room again. I jumped to my feet. Please let it be the painting of the lion fountain in Mu'tamin's quarters. Or the study of arches.

Before I could reach her, Shajar grabbed the canvas from the naughty monkeys and unrolled it. Her lithe body went rigid, she gasped, screamed something in Arabic, then collapsed in a heap on the floor. We rushed toward her, and I pushed through the women, frantic to retrieve the painting. But Zaydun found it first, unfurling it for all to see.

Stunned gasps filled the harem. One woman started wailing. The others turned on me, screaming, and I was forced to cover my head with my arms as they began flailing at me, yanking at my hair, slapping me, pinching my flesh. "What!" I cried. "What did I do?"

Liana waded through the crowd, followed by Abu and Suley, who began pulling the women off me. Liana reached for me. "They say you steal Shajar's soul. You take it from her body and put on this linen."

"I didn't!" I waved at the painting. "It is just a painting. Tell them. Just like my other drawings of the courtyard and the fountains."

Liana translated, but the women, trembling in terror or anger, didn't buy it. Rhame attached her veil, glared coldly at me, then grabbed the painting from Zaydun. "Mu'tamin," is all she said to Abu, and they left the harem together.

"But it's just a painting!" I called lamely.

Liana's eyes were huge. "But Shajar is alive in the painting. She is real."

Then it hit me. The drawings I'd seen scattered throughout the palace were all two dimensional, with no sense of depth. In the one filled with soldiers, the men were all the same size, whether they were close or farther away. My paintings, no matter how crude, used modern shading and perspective to create depth. No wonder people kept looking at the backside of the paintings. To them, a painting with perspective looked as if you could enter it, step through it. And the painting of Shajar showed a round, fleshy, three-dimensional woman. I rubbed my eyes. What a total nimrod.

Shajar stirred at our feet. One woman rushed to get her a drink from the fountain. Another helped her sit up. But when Shajar saw me standing there, she fainted again. Her flare for drama only made things worse. As I tried to explain perspective, an unfamiliar woman entered the harem, and without any hesitation, tapped me on the arm. "Walladah say 'come now.'"

I shook my head. "No, I have big troubles here. I will come another evening."

The woman's eyes widened. "I must bring. Walladah say."

I shook my head again but stopped when Liana reached for my arm. "Do not anger the princess." She looked over at Shajar. "It might be better if you leave for few hours."

Wearily I nodded. Rodrigo was ready to ship me off to Burgos. And now I had stolen the soul of Mu'tamin's favorite wife. I was totally screwed. What other shit could I step in? I certainly had no energy for an elaborate courtship dance with Walladah. And after seeing her taunt Luis earlier, her company held no charm for me tonight.

Once in her quarters, I did admire her physical beauty, but I knew it hid a cruel streak. How could I summon enough attraction to do what needed to be done? Walladah's charming manners gave no hint of my earlier rejection. She sat me at the table, and after an hour I'd eaten too many dates, rice, and meat. But at least Shajar's screams had stopped ringing in my ears.

"Let us talk more about Santillana," she said.

I sat up straighter. "Yes, let's."

She described how we could put together a caravan of horses and donkeys. We would sleep in tents, eat the finest food, and perhaps bring the hawks for hunting. The grander the scenario she painted, the further my hopes fell. Walladah had no interest in a trip; she just knew the idea would tie me to her.

I wiped my mouth on the silky napkin, then rose, adjusting my skirts. "Walladah, I'm tired. I've had a difficult day. Perhaps we can discuss this later."

On her feet, Walladah spun me around and pushed me up against the wall. I grunted. I needed to develop faster reflexes; too many people took me by surprise.

Walladah leaned closer, her full breasts pressed against mine. "I checked with Ali. She washed your bleeding rags last week. You lied to me this morning." She smiled. "I admire that in a woman."

When she kissed me, I pushed away, but she captured my wrists and forced my mouth open, her tongue nearly consuming mine. With a huge push, I twisted and broke free, staggering five feet away.

"No thanks, Walladah." I stood straight, despite my exhaustion. "You are beautiful, but no one can force me to do this."

Walladah's eyes blazed. "You enjoy the pleasure of a woman?"

"Yes, but—"

"I am the most desired woman in Zaragoza, in all of al-Andaluz."

I coughed to hide my smile. "I do not doubt that. But Walladah, I must feel something first."

"You feel nothing for me?" I shook my head. Slowly, painfully slowly, Walladah opened her robe, revealing creamy satin breasts, rose-tinged nipples, and an encitingly-narrow waist. I dared not look lower. "I ask you again. You feel absolutely nothing at all?"

I drew in a ragged breath, as furious as the heat rushing through my body. Christ. How could I not feel something? Her claim of most desirable woman in all of al-Andaluz might not have been overstated. "No, Walladah, I do not." Her mouth dropped open, too stunned to speak. Before she could recover, I whirled and marched unescorted from the room. I ran down the hall and around the corner, stopping at the top of the stairs. Heart pounding, I sat down on the cool marble step. Now I'd done it. I rested my forehead against my knees, shivering in the unlit staircase. I'd stolen the soul of al-Mu'tamin's wife, and wounded the pride of his daughter, all within a few hours' time.

Life in the twenty-first century had never been this complex. I walked a field of foreign land mines, setting them off one by one. Groaning, I shuffled to the stables, my legs heavy. No one stopped me. I could have saddled any horse, mounted, and ridden away, and no one would have found my bones for years. Babieca whinnied as I approached and actually nuzzled my hand, looking for a treat. His eyes were clear, his breath almost normal. Thank you, Liana. Thank you,

Hamara. Thank you, Goddess of the Horses—at least one thing went right today. I exhaled deeply, releasing tension building since Rodrigo had brought me to Babieca.

Shaky and exhausted, I returned to the harem cautiously, but all had quieted down. No one rested in the courtyard, but I could hear voices in the rooms down the hall. I sat on my divan, trying to steady my breathing. I felt that my odds of reaching the cave at Santillana had never been lower.

CHAPTER TEN

The next morning totally erased the six weeks I'd spent developing good will and friendships in the harem. Neither Suley nor Abu returned my daily salute as I headed for the *mirhadun*. Instead, their black eyes focused on the opposite wall. Zaydun didn't respond to my greeting. At the morning meal, no one sat next to me, as if I carried the plague. Even Liana scurried Hazm and Tayani to the other table without meeting my eyes.

When I tried to enter the bath, Ali blocked the way, eyes focused on the wall behind me. So, my punishment would be isolation and an unclean body—but who was punishing me—Walladah or Mu'tamin? I tried to get Suley or Abu to take a message to Luis but neither responded.

One of Mu'tamin's eunuchs came for me. Spirits sagging, I followed the short white man back to Mu'tamin's quarters and was led directly into his bedroom, where an even-stronger smell of illness hung in the air. Mu'tamin's yellow cheeks sunk into massive hollows below his eyes, and his hands looked too large for his arms. Despite his condition, Mu'tamin rose from the gilded chair, his arms trembling with the effort.

I curtsied when the eunuch yanked on my arm. "My lord," I murmured.

Mu'tamin's eyes burned into mine. He flung the portrait of Shajar at my feet. "My wife grieves herself into the grave. You have stolen her soul. I want it back."

My brain felt muddled. "My lord, it is a simple painting. I have not stolen—"

"Shajar may die." I nearly rolled my eyes. Shajar was a self-centered, overly-dramatic brat. How could I fight such powerful superstition?

The feeble man actually growled at me. "Rodrigo says Babieca lives, so your healing talents are useful. Yet I want to order your head hacked from your neck and stuck on a post for my beloved's comfort."

Shit. My brain spun. "Ahh, bring the painting to Shajar's side. Douse it with lamp oil. Burn the painting, all the while telling Shajar her soul is returning to her body."

Mu'tamin scowled. "We will do as you say. But if it does not work, you will be killed."

Wearily, I nodded, and followed the eunuch back to the harem, where I languished in my room, hot and sweaty in the breezeless day. No one spoke with me. I didn't dare even pick up a charcoal, let alone paint. In the late morning another servant I didn't recognize appeared in my doorway. "Come, horses," he said. I moaned. Had Babieca grown worse? Grateful for the activity, I followed his stiff back to the stable.

"How's our patient?" I asked Hamara, who stood waxing a saddle. The boy's red-rimmed eyes were bloodshot, his face pale as snow. "Hamara, what's wrong?"

The boy shook his head. "Nothing. What do you want?"

I stepped away from the strange servant behind me. "What is wrong?" I whispered.

Hamara's shoulders sagged. "I am sad," he said.

"Because of me?"

Hamara's pale red brows pulled together. "No, I am sad because... of someone else." He wiped his eyes and rubbed the saddle even harder. I would get nothing more out of him.

"Where is Babieca?" I asked.

"I will take you to him," the servant said, stepping forward. Hamara shrugged, lost in a pain he wouldn't share, so I followed the servant into a darker region of the stables. Why had they moved Babieca down here?

The servant opened a stall door. "He is in here." When I peered into the dark stall, a hand shoved me inside. The door slammed and locked behind me as hooves whooshed past my head and I flung myself against the nearest wall. This wasn't Babieca! The massive black horse reared again, screaming in fury. Then he lunged at me, teeth bared. Heart racing, I grasped my skirts in sweating palms. If I tripped, I was dead.

"Hamara!" Mu'tamin's wild stud raked the wall. "Hamara!" The horse switched tactics, whirling and kicking blindly with his back legs, one grazing my arm.

"Shit!" I bounced from wall to wall, working my way back to the door, but I stumbled twice, ducking as hooves whistled overhead. The smell of horse sweat and fury threatened to pull me under like a rip tide. Furious teeth chomped down on my sleeve, just missing my arm, then flung me against the door. Gasping, I threw my veil into the nearest corner. The horse attacked it while I scrambled up the door's slats, slid through the two-foot opening at the top, and dropped six feet to the ground. I whirled around, but no servant stood by. I ran to the stable's entrance, but even Hamara was gone. My hands shook, my arm was scraped and bleeding, and I'd have a hell of a bruise in the morning, but nothing seemed broken.

Furious, I stomped across the walkway and into the palace. But before I could reach Luis's room, two eunuchs stopped me. "Harem," one said.

"Fuck you," I snarled in English. But the two men dragged me back, with me yelling the whole way in case Luis was within earshot. They hauled me past the wide-eyed harem women, then tossed me into my room. I scrambled to my feet and ran after them, cursing vividly in English, but Suley and Abu barred my way again. I threw myself at the black sentries, both men restraining me. Through my fury and pain I heard one of them whispering "no, no, Kate, no." My friends had rock-hard grips, so I stopped struggling and they let me go. Defiant, I refused to return to my room, but instead sat on Carlos's bench, gripping the stone. Walladah. This had to be her doing, since Mu'tamin would have simply chopped off my head. I groaned. Why had I expected this world to function with the logic of my own?

No one spoke to me, and Liana wasn't in the courtyard. My heart ached to think she might have been sent to Hayib's already. Only Radi the gazelle approached me, sniffing my slippered feet, letting me rub her tiny ears and check her healed break.

Would this blow over? Walladah couldn't have so strong a hold that my friends could keep this up forever, but then goose bumps rose on my arms. The scene in the stable had been meant as more than a scare.

When the harem filled the sunny courtyard for noon meal, I

stubbornly joined them on the central platform. Hazm ran toward me, but Liana, still here, cut him off, scolding him until his tender lower lip trembled.

Instead of bringing out trays of food for us to fill our plates, the servants brought us each a plate already filled. Despite my outward stubbornness, my head hurt, my arm throbbed, and I considered for the first time that I might actually be in real danger. I couldn't call nine-one-one; I couldn't reach Luis. Laura and Anna and all my friends would not be born for almost nine hundred years, so there was nothing they could do to help. My bowels cramped as I stared at my plate of food, then I leapt to my feet and ran for the *mirhadun*. Weak and worn down, I sat there until the nausea left me. Hollowed out, I finally returned to my meal. I'd left my plate at the edge of the platform, but now one of the blasted parrots stood next to it, happily pecking at my rice.

"Shoo!" I hissed, waving my arms. The green and blue parrot flew to a nearby Ficus tree, squawking and babbling on in Arabic. I recognized enough curse words to understand why a few women snickered. I scooped up a handful of rice to eat just as the parrot fell silent and landed with a soft thud on the floor.

"Pluma!" a child cried.

I reached the bird first, hoping he was still alive, but he hung limp and warm in my hand, his beak twisted into a horrible grin. He'd been eating my food. I stared back at my plate, breathing hard, then met Liana's eyes across the courtyard; her barely perceptible nod motioned me toward her room. Sobbing, the young boy took the parrot's body and ran for his mother.

I waited until things quieted down, then I snuck into Liana's room. She clutched my hands. "None of us can help you. Walladah will kill us or our children if we do. And everyone is afraid of you because you stole Shajar's soul."

"I didn't steal her soul. How is she?"

"Up and eating again, pale, but she will be fine."

"Walladah's trying to kill me." The words sounded so melodramatic, but saying them out loud made them terribly real. "What do I do?"

"Get away." Liana's cold hands chilled mine; even her rosy face was pale.

"I can't get into the bath. There are always women in there. I think they're guarding that secret door."

Liana took a deep breath. "My life worth little now I go to al-Hayib, so I tell you this. All other secret passageways will be closed to you, since we all fear Walladah. Too many people disappear because of her." She squeezed my hands. "There used to be secret passageway in your room, but all who knew how to open have died. None of us even know where it might go."

I hugged Liana. "Stay safe," I whispered into her hair, then hurried to my room.

By dusk I still hadn't found the trigger, even though I'd been over every inch of the walls I could reach, and my fingertips burned from scraping against the rough stucco. I held my oil lamp close to every crack, every depression, but no luck. The courtyard was silent. Even the oil lamps that usually burned all night were dark and cold. Frantic now, I pounded the wall.

"Open up, damn it!" When I slapped my palms flat against the cool walls, I glared down at the floor. That's when I noticed the flaw. The patterned floor was perfectly symmetrical except for one small light blue tile near the back wall. It had been placed in the mud slightly askew. I pushed at the tile; an opening in the floor appeared as the door swung down into darkness. Holy Frijoles. Carlos the guide had pointed out a room with a passageway in the floor. This was it. Hands shaking, I draped a robe across my bed, stuffing it with clothes. Then oil lamp in hand, I started down the narrow staircase, stopping to push the door back up into place. I froze as it clicked, then lowered myself onto the top stair, trying to slow my pounding heart in the weak light of my lamp as heavy footsteps approached overhead. Something slammed down on my bed. Over and over again, the hacking continued. Slowly, carefully, I headed down the narrow steps. In seconds the men in my room would discover that all they'd murdered was a bed.

At the bottom, I pushed against the door. It gave an inch. I listened, but heard nothing, so I pushed the door all the way open and crawled out into a wide hallway lit with torches. Where was I? I ran to the nearest corner, recognized that I was near the main courtyard, then headed down the hall. I heard distant shouts upstairs and ran faster, my stupid slippers useless on the slick tile. At Luis's door, I slid to a stop. "Luis," I hissed, banging on the door. "Luis!" Oh goddess, please be there. I had no back-up plan. "Luis, it's me."

Relief roared in my ears as Luis opened the door. I stepped in and shut the door behind me, dropping the heavy wooden latch. "Walladah is trying to have me killed." I struggled for breath. "She's failed three times. I doubt she'll fail again."

Luis winced as he scanned his room. Bless him for not saying "I told you so." A bed and a small table—nowhere to hide. "Here." Luis opened the secret door. "Hide in here."

"They probably know about it."

Luis shook his head as he helped me inside. "Mu'tamin's servants would have destroyed the passageway after Aisha if they'd known. And we must hope the women of the harem say nothing." I huddled on the cold floor, arms tight around my knees, as he shut me up in the passageway.

The pounding rattled the hinges until Luis opened the door, arguing roughly in Arabic. Sounds of angry voices filled the room, then his door closed and the latch dropped. When my small secret door creaked open, I crawled out, and Luis helped me to my feet. He fingered my torn bodice, touched my scrapped arm. "You have been hurt."

I nodded wearily as Luis led me to his bed. "Love bite from an angry horse." I dropped down, grateful. "Walladah does not like rejection. But I could not do it. Felt too wrong." I shivered; Luis draped something over me, then used a small bowl of water to gently wash my face and hands, apparently filthy from three near-death encounters. "You were right, Luis."

"I will gloat over that later. First, we need a plan. Walladah will not stop until you are dead."

"Help me steal a horse and I will ride to Santillana."

"The arms of Walladah are long. One man made it all the way to the Pyrenees before he lost his head."

I looked into his face, strangely calm in the flickering oil light. "What did you do? You were Walladah's lover."

Luis smiled wryly. "Yes, I was. She is a stunning woman..." He pursed his lips.

I touched his arm. "Let's skip the wonderful memories. How did you get out of her clutches?"

He rubbed his face. "I started practicing my knife on the grounds outside her quarters. I set up a wooden stump, draped it with a veil that fluttered in the wind, then threw the knife for hours on end."

"Could you see the stump under the veil?"

"No, but I hit the stump every time."

I sighed. "Impressive. You did say she respected the knife. But I don't think my knife-throwing skills will worry her in the least."

"No, probably not."

"Why didn't she just have you killed like the others?"

"I had been...her favorite. Perhaps because of that, she spared me. I have never asked." Luis looked at his hands and cleared his throat. "There is one other option."

I had calmed down enough that I could feel the warmth from Luis's body along my side and thigh. "What's that?"

Luis took a deep breath. "Marriage."

I snorted. "She'll sleep with anyone, man or woman. She has power. Why should she respect marriage?"

"Her mother was married to al-Mu'tamin, so Walladah considers herself a legitimate heir. Her half-brother al-Musta'in is a bastard born to one of Mu'tamin's concubines, but because he is male, he will eventually rule Zaragoza, not Walladah."

"So she's angry her mother, the legal wife, was less important than a concubine." Luis nodded. "Okay, that makes sense. But who am I supposed to marry?"

Luis's gaze was direct. "Me."

My pulse thudded in my ears. "Oh."

Luis stood and began pacing the small room. "Mu'tamin no longer trusts me, but if a woman were to come forth and claim me as her lover, then he might believe I had nothing to do with Aisha."

"Did you?"

Luis waved impatiently. "No, she used the passageway to leave the harem to meet her lover. I just kept my mouth shut." Luis pulled me to my feet. I avoided looking at his lips to keep my head clear. "Kate, if you marry, Walladah will give up. It is a game to her, and she respects the rules she has set up. If married, you need not fear a knife in your back one night."

"And you?"

"And I would hopefully be absolved of responsibility in Aisha's deflowering."

"And us?"

Luis looked down, suddenly shy. "If you want, we need not... consummate the marriage."

"That would help," I said.

Hands on his hips, Luis looked out the window. "Then it shall be so." His terse, clipped words didn't entirely ease my mind, but it did relax it a bit. If I could not feel safe with Luis, I had no haven in this time. Besides, the idea of marrying a man was almost too massive to fit into my head. Throat dry, temples throbbing, I looked deep into his sensitive eyes. Would I be a lesbian still? What was I? My skin crawled. This would turn my self-concept so topsy-turvy I could never trust myself again. No, it would be a marriage of convenience, nothing more.

I breathed deeply. My life was in real danger for the first time. Luis was right. At least in the immediate short term, marriage seemed my only option. But I was still me. Six weeks in flimsy skirts and slippers, six weeks of languishing in the harem couldn't change that. I could approach this like a wilting flower, throwing myself in my hero's arms like a desperate character in a bad romance novel. Or I could approach it as I had most other things in my life—directly. If I made my own choices, I could survive anything, even marriage to a man whose kisses melted my joints, but whom I did not love. What that marriage meant for me and Anna, I would figure out later.

I would do this my way, or Walladah could just go ahead and kill me. "I will marry you, Luis."

He studied my face for a moment, then nodded. "It is the only plan to succeed. I will go speak to Rodrigo. Lock the door when I leave."

I did so, then wandered to the round window, leaning my elbows on the narrow ledge. The moon waned in the west. Oil lamps lit the streets below. I counted rooftops. I sniffed and tried to identify the smells. I traced the edges of the blocks around the window. Anything not to think. A soldier ran into the city, returning ten minutes later. Shortly after, Luis knocked on the door. "Rodrigo has agreed. The priest is with his mistress in the country but will be back tomorrow." Luis nodded brusquely. "You will be safe here until then. I will be right outside."

"Luis, we can make you a bed in here. I could pile up your clothes."

Luis shook his head, a lock of hair falling into his eyes, then smiled, closing the door behind him. As I dropped the latch. I could hear him settle his back against the door. Mind spinning, I crawled into bed and pulled the blanket to my chin. The wool scratched through my clothes, but I was too exhausted to care.

I was also too exhausted to sleep. The window-shaped moonlight worked its way across the wall, slowly, painfully, hour by hour. Tomorrow night I would not sleep alone. But at least I would still be alive, my new daily goal.

CHAPTER ELEVEN

The loud knock jarred me from a troubling dream where I'd held Luis in my arms, and he became first a black-haired woman, then a madman with a knife to my throat, then Arturo, then a confusing collage of faces from my past, both male and female. When I sat up, groggy, and shocked to realize Luis had replaced Anna in my dreams, it hit me how little Anna had been in my thoughts lately.

When I opened the door, Zaydun and Ali bustled into the room carrying baskets and buckets of water and closed the door, leaving Luis out in the hall. "You wedding. We prepare."

Ali once again stripped me like a pro. My teeth chattered as she sponged me down.

"But what about Walladah?"

"You wedding, al-Mu'tamin say so. Walladah no can hurt." Zaydun poured a deep red powder into a small white bowl, added a few drops of water, then stirred vigorously.

Ali toweled me off, then wrapped the towel around me. I yelped as she began brushing my hair, tugging out the stubborn snarls. "Ouch! And what's that red stuff?"

Ali tied back my hair and sat me on the ground before Zaydun. The old woman dipped her finger in the brick-red mixture and began tracing a design on my face. "*Hunayna* make beautiful for wedding," Zaydun said.

"Where is Liana?"

"With children. She say good-bye." She drew the cool henna mixture along the backs of my hands and up my arms. My eyes stung to think about Liana. She shouldn't be leaving. She cured my sore heel. She saved Babieca. Why didn't I just tell someone that? Because I was a dried up sponge, all the courage squeezed out of me. I watched, fascinated, while Zaydun drew an elaborate maze on my chest that draped from shoulder to shoulder, then circled each breast, ending right at each nipple. Great. A road map.

The henna dried quickly, then Ali slipped a thin white silk slip over my head, small enough that it fit too snugly across my chest and hips. Next came a soft green muslin robe with white embroidery up the sleeves and down the front. I stood in the middle of the room, arms out, feeling like a mannequin at Bloomingdale's. Around my neck Ali fastened an ivory cloak, lined in green silk, that swept to the ground. They laced white leather boots tightly around my ankles. Zaydun let down my hair and topped my head with a small green cap, then fastened the gauzy veil across my face. Zaydun held up a hand mirror; a stranger stared back at me. Zaydun unlatched the door, and the two women left as quickly as they'd come, Zaydun commanding me to, "Lock door. You wait."

Shaking, I walked to the window, unnerved by the cloak fluttering behind me. Now I really did feel like some character in a bad romance. Down in the courtyard, ten women mounted horses. The shortest, heavily veiled and cloaked in blue, would be Liana. Heaviness dragged at my heart and limbs as I leaned out the window, hoping she would look up.

The horses began filing out of the courtyard, but just as she reached the palace gates, Liana turned. She fixed her gaze on the windowless wall that held the harem and saw me. The horse danced in place as we stared at one another, both veiled but for our eyes. She lightly touched her chest, then extended her hand toward me. I did the same, then hated myself. Damn it. This just could not go down this way.

I leaned farther out the window and cried out in Arabic, "Stop!" No matter what Rodrigo did to me, I couldn't let Liana suffer because I was afraid. "Stop, Lord Mu'tamin say no go." My ridiculous Arabic was enough to stop the man leading the women. "Wait. No go. Mu'tamin say no go."

I flung the door open and raced down the hall. Servants stared as I flew around the corner, through the central courtyard, past the main kitchen where chickens squawked as I scattered them. Finally I stopped at Mu'tamin's quarters, where only one eunuch guarded the door. I touched my chest. "Me see my lord Mu'tamin. Very urgent. Most necessary." The man frowned but couldn't stop me as I pushed past.

Mu'tamin sat at his desk, hunched over, but alert. He raised his head as I dropped to my knees, switching to Spanish. "My lord, I must confess something."

His bleary eyes, the whites nearly yellow, no longer terrified me. "Muhammad docs not ask confession of his believers."

I shook my head. "Both you and Rodrigo believe I cure animals. I don't. I lied so you wouldn't send me to King Alfonso or al-Hayib."

Mu'tamin stroked his chin, mouth pensive. "Yet Babieca lives."

"Only because of a woman in your harem named Liana. She is the mother of your two grandchildren, Hazm and Tayani. She is one of Musta'in's wives. She saved Babieca."

Mu'tamin frowned. "A harem woman healed the horse?" He rubbed his chin even more vigorously. His harem women had one skill only.

"Liana was raised on her parents' farm in France. You bought her from traders ten years ago. She knows much about animals. While she could of course never replace your stable master—" I was getting the hang of this male kiss-ass thing, "she could keep your horses healthy."

Mu'tamin straightened, leaning forward against the low desk. "I will take this information under consideration. Rodrigo will be unhappy to learn he has kept you here when you really made no contribution."

"You'd better think fast, my lord, for as we speak your man leaves with Liana and the others for al-Hayib's."

A weary groan escaped the thin, compressed lips. "My stupid brother will no doubt waste her talents." His dark eyes bore into me as a servant entered with a cup of spicy tea and a plate of couscous. Mu'tamin scooped up a handful, chewed thoughtfully, then took a sip of tea. "If I allow the woman to remain, I expect something in return."

I kept my face calm, but inside I winced. How far would I have to go to keep Liana, Hazm, and Tayani together? I sat up straight and nodded, even if it meant taking my turn as a member of al-Mu'tamin's harem.

Mu'tamin picked something from his teeth. "I have seen the painting of Shajar. Your skill is a gift from Allah, one I can use. My brother Hayib comes to Zaragoza in a few days. Paint him as you have Shajar, and this horse healer may remain in my harem."

Relief flowed down my arms, tingling my hands. Mu'tamin's request was not for sentimental reasons, but that wasn't my business. "I will paint your brother."

With a weak clap, he summoned a servant, muttered an order in Arabic, and watched as the man dashed from the room to do his bidding. "It is done. The woman stays."

I bowed my head gratefully. "*Shukran*, my lord."

The leader coughed slightly. "You have the appearance of a bride."

I leapt to my feet. "Yes, my lord. I marry Luis Navarro," I stammered. "He had nothing to do with Aisha, my lord. He spent all his nights with me."

Mu'tamin dismissed me with a feeble wave. "I came to that same conclusion. I have heard rumors you are also experiencing difficulties with my daughter." He sighed. "My children frighten me. What will become of Zaragoza when I am gone?"

I licked my lips. "Your children love this city. One way or another, they will defend it."

The old man smiled wryly. "You lie just as you play chess."

"How is that, my lord?"

"Badly. Now be off to your wedding. I am tired."

❖

An hour later, still languishing in Luis's room, I rubbed my throbbing temples. Life without aspirin was torture, all the more reason any reasonable woman would struggle as I did to return to the twenty-first century. When Luis finally knocked on the door, the headache had spread to my neck. He wore his red blouse and black tunic, the ones I hadn't stolen. I tried to smile but could not. Behind him Enzo and Fadri shifted from foot to foot, both actually clean and in fresh leather tunics studded with metal. Each gave me a nervous nod, then looked away.

Luis gazed at nothing but my eyes, then held out his arm. The walk to the small Christian church in Zaragoza was a short one. At one point Luis sighed heavily. I looked over.

"I wish Nuño were here," he whispered. I stared straight ahead, trying to sort out the cultural morass into which I'd sunk. I was an agnostic lesbian marrying a Christian man while dressed in a Moorish wedding dress. No TV network could ever dream up a reality show as bizarre as my life. The headache settled behind my eyes.

Once inside, a dour Father Manolo led us into his office, a dismal cold room, where Luis signed the official marriage license. As a woman, I of course had no rights to sign anything, which made me clench my jaw so tightly my teeth hurt. Enzo and Fadri scrawled their names as witnesses, then the priest led us into the sanctuary, positioning us just so.

The ceremony was in Latin, so I had no clue what was said. Luis and I stood side-by-side, just close enough that I felt his entire body trembling like a lamb on unsteady legs. When the priest nodded to Luis, and Luis took my hand, his tremors spread through my body as well. Our hands were both cold and clammy. Luis's breathing was so quick and shallow I feared he'd hyperventilate and collapse.

The priest waved his hands over us, blew incense toward us, then intoned something, after which Luis repeated his words. The priest then turned to me, intoning something, then waited. I stumbled through the sounds of the words.

More Latin I didn't understand, then the smiling priest slammed his Bible shut, switching into Spanish. "Congratulations. You are now man and wife."

I stumbled on my cloak as Luis led me down the aisle. Neither of us spoke, but I raged against myself on the walk back, even as I wolfed down the cheese and dried meat Luis bought for me from a vendor, taking no comfort in the warm sun on my face, the lush flowers lining the street. I should have tried harder to escape. I should have stolen a sword and hacked my way from the palace. Oh, there's a great plan. One slash of the sword and I'd be minus a leg. No, I should have figured out earlier that 1085 ran by a set of rules that befuddled me. None of the skills or knowledge I'd acquired over thirty years of living meant anything.

At the palace gates, Fadri and Enzo left us. I tugged off my veil and licked my dry lips as Luis motioned toward a small bench in the shade of a massive yew tree. We sat quietly until I said, "You trembled."

Luis tried to smile. "I have never married before." He rubbed sweaty palms along his thighs.

I paused. "But you have been with women before."

Luis looked me in the eye. "I have never married before."

"Oh."

Several Moors trimmed the hedges near the palace walls, quietly crushing off the wayward branches. Neither of us mentioned Luis's offer of a marriage of convenience. Six weeks ago I would have insisted on it, but now I didn't know. Yesterday I'd bravely sworn to do things my way, but after reflecting on the whole Walladah mess, it seemed my way could get me killed. Marrying Luis was a short-term solution, but I still had a dangerous journey ahead of me, one I owed myself. But what would I find when I made it home? Anna might have given up and gone on with her life. She'd always had a major crush on that beautiful English professor at school, so perhaps I struggled to return to a life that no longer existed. I'd been gone nearly two months. How long would Anna wait? And did I even want her to? Damn. Today was not a day for thinking clearly about anything.

Luis and I sat in silence for an hour, watching horses come and go. A man ambled past on a dirty white horse, and I chuckled. "*You* don't have a white horse, do you?"

Luis leaned forward, hands on the edge of the bench. "No, just Matamoros. Why?"

"You always seem to show up just when I need help, my knight on a white horse."

Luis snorted, eyes twinkling in the shade of the heavy branches overhead. "I am no caballero. I am just a soldier."

I traced the embroidered leaves on my cape's edge. "Well, it's still true you tend to rescue me. You stopped Gudesto the day he nearly tricked me into leaving. You killed the man kidnapping me after the banquet—"

"For which you yelled at me, wounding me deeply."

I returned his smile. "And now, when Walladah was determined to kill me, you stepped in, my knight in shining...mail."

Luis threw up his hands. "I could not help myself."

I considered my words carefully. "Much as I appreciate these rescues, it's very different from what I'm used to in my..." The word "time" lay fully shaped in my mouth, waiting for release. No, he'd never believe me. "...in my country. I'm used to taking care of myself." My headache eased as I got this off my chest.

Luis gazed across the palace yards, nodding pensively. "You are a strong woman, that is true." We watched as a fabric merchant rattled by with his cart, loaded with gold, olive, and dusky orange bolts of linen and silk. "Are you asking me to stop rescuing you?"

I laughed, a little embarrassed at how that actually sounded. "Well, no, not exactly. I just feel strange that you always rescue me."

"Perhaps you could some day rescue me."

I laughed. "I'd be happy to."

"Until then, however, how will I know *when* to rescue you? When the moon is full? Only if you speak some mysterious incantation?"

I slapped his knee, ignoring his hearty laugh. "Don't be ridiculous."

He leaned closer, setting my heart pounding in my ears. "What will our secret incantation be?"

I growled a warning, but he wouldn't stop until I gave him one. "Okay. Lion King," I said, which in Spanish is 'King of the Lions.'

Luis raised his right hand, placing the other over mine. "I will only rescue my wife when she cries 'Lion King!' At all other times her bravery, strength, and sharpness of tongue will be all she needs to vanquish her foes."

We laughed, but being a lesbian feminist in 1085 wasn't easy, so every victory, no matter how small, made me feel less like a confused, helpless woman.

Two messengers arrived from a nearby castle, more carts passed, and veiled servants ran errands for palace dwellers. After so long within the harem walls, the view was too rich to keep to myself. The children had to see this. Liana had to see it. "Luis, could you escort me back to the harem?"

Luis stretched his back. "I am enjoying the warm day. I want to remain here."

I glared at him. "And I'm supposed to wait patiently like a good wife?"

"You know the way." I stared at him, feeling as stupid as I'm sure I looked. Luis's shy smile made me want to caress his smooth cheek. "You are now the wife of a Christian soldier. You are no longer in the harem. You may come and go as you please."

"I can come and go from the harem?"

"The harem, the palace. You are safe now that you are married. You may wander Zaragoza, but I would hope you would not do so without me."

I stood, brushing grass from my cape. "How odd. I win my freedom with marriage." I winked at him. "I guess there are a few benefits to marrying you after all."

Luis winked back, now the bold warrior I had first met. "Perhaps one day you will count more than a few." I swatted at his head as I walked by, but he ducked, chuckling.

❖

Once in the harem, I peeked into my room. A different divan rested near the wall, but otherwise nothing had changed. For a second I wondered if I'd imagined someone hacking up my bed, but the breeze rolled a few bits of stuffing along the floor, and my heart jumped. I whirled back into the courtyard to search for Liana.

Still in her blue cloak, Liana flung her arms around me just outside the kitchen. We squeezed each other tightly, and my heart expanded "Kate," Liana whispered, still clinging to me. "How do I thank you?"

I held her away from me, enjoying that her sallow cheeks glowed once again, her hazel eyes sparkled. "You owe me no thanks, my friend. Because you saved Babieca, Rodrigo didn't ship me off to Burgos like a package of Zaragozan linen. I just returned the favor."

Liana brought her fingers to her mouth, eyes wide. "My lord says I to be in shop near stables to help with horses and town animals. I can leave harem few hours every day."

Liana's excitement swept me along. "Bring the children and let's go there now. I'm sure it's the building where I paint. We can work together."

"I cannot take children with me when I leave harem. Mu'tamin knows I no leave palace grounds if my children here."

"But it's such a lovely day—"

Liana grabbed me. "And you married. I forget myself. My deepest congratulations." She kissed me loudly on the cheek. "Take the children with you for awhile. They would love it." She called Hazm and Tayani from the kitchen, where they'd been building a structure out of the cook's bowls, and we headed for the harem entrance.

Like magic, Suley and Abu stepped aside, tiny smiles flickering across stoic faces as my heart soared. I really was free. I breathed deeply as we stepped out into the arched walkway. Sticky hands clung to mine as we walked through the stables, petting as many horses as we could. First the children climbed a scrawny olive tree, then Hazm wanted to run all the way around the palace. I followed behind, holding up my skirts and robe so I could keep up.

Luis still sat in front, watching me as the children climbed another tree, hid behind the hedges, then chased me down the stone pathways. I pointed at everything, saying the words in Spanish, then they would tell me the Arabic. We found the livestock corrals behind the palace, where sheep and goats grazed. As I watched Hazm and Tayani chattering at the animals, I imagined Arturo showing Hazm how to play soccer, helping Tayani climb a tree. I let the fantasy run wild, and finally had to shake my head to clear the confusing vision.

The children taught me *zadwah*, a game of throwing nuts into a hole. I taught them hopscotch. By the time I returned the children to the harem, we'd worked out our own pidgin Spanish-Arabic code. Liana and I agreed to meet the next day at the new "Aljafería Vet Clinic and Art Studio."

"May you find love tonight," Liana said slyly as I left her room. My heart burned as I hurried down the hall. I didn't need love. I needed to find my way to Santillana, and while I had saved my life by marrying Luis, I was no closer to my goal. But at least I was no longer a prisoner. Many stones had piled up at that bottom of that well, so surely I had to be closer to the top.

Suley, Abu, and I exchanged salutes as I left the harem. "Free May Come Next" each said with a smile.

"You said it, men."

❖

Dinner was hell. We sat side-by-side on the floor with ten of Luis's men, and if not for a visiting Frenchman on a pilgrimage to Santiago de Compostela, things could have been worse. The men, led mostly by Fadri, whispered and stared at me all through dinner. At one point Fadri cupped his chin in his hand, giving me a silly, moony-look until Luis fired a tangerine at his head.

"Animal," Luis muttered.

The man next to Luis chuckled. "What is the matter, El Picador? Are you not up to the job ahead?" As snickers ran down the table, Luis cuffed the man and they ended up rolling on the floor. It was my seventh grade lunchroom all over again. The pilgrim, a tall, rangy Frenchman named Grimaldi, politely ignored the banter, telling me in simple, broken

Spanish of his travels through the Pyrenees. I only half-listened, for the other half of my body jumped whenever Luis accidentally bumped me and tingled when his arm rested near mine.

Jocular, downing glass after glass, Luis gave the appearance of a confident warrior about to conquer his maiden, but he kept his hands out of sight as much as possible. They trembled wildly in his lap. Was I so daunting a woman?

Mid-meal, Rodrigo entered, grunting as he dropped to a cushion and began stuffing himself, smacking loudly. Apparently table manners had not yet occurred to Christians, so I looked away as grease ran down the man's chin.

"Navarro," Rodrigo finally said between bites. "Mu'tamin needs more men, so he is *recruiting* more troops. You will train them."

Luis winced. "Training boys stolen from their villages is nearly impossible."

Rodrigo shrugged. "You and the lances at this table are my best men. Mu'tamin will increase our payment by one-third for our troubles. Marrying will not get you out of this."

"I never expected it—"

"When they arrive, train them twelve hours a day. We do not know how soon we go into battle." Rodrigo leaned forward, glaring down the table at me. "Navarro runs my army. You will not distract him with wifely complaints and female tantrums."

Good grief. "Only women married to you have complaints and tantrums," I snapped. That set the table laughing again, and even Rodrigo joined into the raucous discussion of women and marriage. Someone get me *out* of here.

Toward the end of the meal, Enzo grew serious. "Luis, what of the first rights?"

The table fell silent as I frowned in confusion. Luis scowled into his plate. "It is an old-fashioned custom and we are no longer in Castile."

Everyone looked at me, then back at Luis. "What are first rights?" I asked. In a world devoid of any discussion of civil rights or human rights, I was intrigued. Maybe there was hope for these people.

The men looked at each other, then down at their plates. Luis blushed furiously but said nothing. Rodrigo picked at a fingernail. Grimaldi finally coughed delicately, touching his prematurely silver hair, tied back with brown leather. "Perhaps they no do custom in your home, but is tradition here for the lord of lands under his control to spend first night of marriage with new bride."

My eyes narrowed. "What?"

Grimaldi waited for Luis or one of the others to explain, but suddenly eating required their total concentration. He sighed. "Long years ago many believed that...ahem...breaking virgin maidenhead too dangerous, so lord bravely step in, saving groom."

"Brave, my ass," I said loudly.

"Now tradition give noble first night with bride. First rights."

My face burned. "That is the most barbaric, medieval, stupid, inhuman thing I've ever heard," I nearly shouted. "Why do people put *up* with that?"

Luis finally found his voice. "For some, it is tradition. For others, it is power. The noble owns the land, has the power, so he gets first rights."

I snorted. "And who is your noble? Who is the great, powerful landlord who will not *ever* sleep with this bride?"

Luis gulped down the rest of his wine, then looked directly at me. "The land of my family in La Rioja falls under the protection of the eldest nephew of Count Ordóñez. Gudesto Gonzalez."

"Shit a brick," I sputtered in English. I raised up on my knees, pounding the table with my clenched fist so hard a few cups clattered against plates, and I switched back to Spanish. "The day Gudesto Gonzalez thinks he can collect his first rights with me is the day Father Manolo gives him his *last* rites."

My fury somehow broke the tension, which only enraged me more. Chuckles swept down the table, and Rodrigo shook his head. "Oh, Navarro, what have you done? May you survive to dine with us again tomorrow." Raucous laughter erupted, and even Luis shook as he turned away from me, probably to hide a stupid male smirk. I thumped him once on the back, drawing even more laughter.

Jesus. I sat back down, closing my eyes. I was truly in medieval Europe, smack in the middle of the Dark Ages. That society had survived at all to reach the twenty-first century was a damn miracle.

Dinner finally over, Luis helped me to my feet. We both ignored the last minute suggestions Fadri and the others contributed.

Heart pounding, I stepped inside our room. Luis bolted the door.

Silence.

"That first rights thing is disgusting," I said.

"I agree. The thought of Gudesto...well..."

"Well—" we both said.

"I suppose..." Luis trailed off, licking his lips nervously. He jumped to help me off with my cape, folding it carefully and stacking it in the corner next to his own things. "Kate, would...could we sit and talk for awhile?"

"Absolutely." Relieved, I sat cross-legged on the bed, which was jammed into one corner. We each leaned against the longer wall, sitting side by side. Why was I suddenly contemplating consummating the marriage? Would my need to keep Luis on my side take me that far?

"So."

"So."

I licked my lips. "I've had an amazing stay here at the Aljafería. Accused of being a spy, nearly kidnapped by a crazed Moor, nearly kidnapped by that slimy Gudesto, recited a poem, pretended to save a horse, stole a woman's soul and gave it back again, nearly got killed by Walladah's thugs, apparently escaped the totally forgettable tradition of first rights, and now, here I am married to El Cid's first lieutenant."

"Will your family be upset you are married?" Luis asked.

I contemplated my hennaed hands, then let my head drop back. "Dad died in an accident ten years ago. Mom got sick and died a year later."

"So you lose both parents too."

"Yeah." Long before they died.

"Any siblings?"

"No."

Luis sat forward, tugging his tunic off over his head, leaving only a white linen undergarment. Well-defined biceps pushed against the thin fabric. "Hot in here," he muttered, then exhaled slowly. "As the only child, you must have had to work very hard. Our mama had all three of us doing daily chores as soon as we could walk. My...sister started to feed chickens and gather eggs when she was three, to empty slop buckets when she was four. By five she was helping Mama bake bread."

"And you?"

"Ahh, chop wood, plow, slaughter meat, hunt."

"Oh." Modern children had no idea how easy life was. "I am so sorry your family is gone."

Luis reached under the bed and pulled out a tiny carved ivory box, reinforced at the corners by gilded copper braces. He handed it to me and I brought it close. Small carved figures adorned each side, with an arched courtyard on one end. I ran my fingers over the smooth bas relief carving, marveling at the craftsmanship in a box that fit entirely within my hand. "May I?" I asked softly.

Luis nodded, moving closer. "This is the ring of my sister, and a nail Father made for the house, and a piece of the shawl of my Tía Solana." The small broken knife handle he showed me was Tío Mingo's. Then he lifted a lock of dark brown hair. "My brother Miguel." My throat tightened. The lighter lock still in the box must be his sister's.

"Oh, Luis," I murmured. He smiled sadly as we put everything back in the box. My fanny pack lay hidden under my clothes in the far corner. Just three steps and I could unzip it, showing some of my mementoes—the purple flashlight, the postcard, the Lion King key chain, the photo of Arturo, a pack of Benadryl, Arturo's drawing, Paloma de Palma's note. Desperate to share my secret, I gathered my legs underneath me to stand, then stopped. He'd think he'd married a mad woman. Heavy with thoughts I could not share, I dropped back down onto the bed.

"And you?" Luis asked as he tucked the box away again. "Was your childhood hard?"

My childhood had been easy physically, but incredibly lonely. "Mostly I spent my childhood waiting for my parents to come home." I shifted a little, accidentally knocking Luis's foot with my own. I jerked back.

"Tell me about your parents' marriage." Luis pulled off his boots with a grunt; they thudded softly against the tile floor.

"Mom was the strong one, Dad was pretty calm." I shrugged. "They were happy. They laughed a lot. They weren't afraid to have fights."

"Fights are good?"

"They can be. If they don't get ugly, fights are a good way to stay honest."

Luis took my hand, tracing the outline of each finger. "Then, my pearl, we will fight many fights."

I chuckled. "I'm not sure *planning* to fight is necessary. How about your parents?" My entire hand tingled, a sensation that began working its way up my arm.

Luis shifted closer so he could trace my other hand. I closed my eyes. "My father was strict with all of us, even Mother. No one dared disobey him."

"I hope that's not how you will be," I said, breathing more slowly as Luis's fingers, still trembling, stroked the inside of my wrists, then my elbows. I opened my eyes and turned my head, falling into two brilliant pools, sliding across curved cheekbones, aching for his parted lips. I had to do this. Not sure why, but fate landed me right in this man's path. I would play it out.

The kiss was soft, gentle at first as Luis slid his hand around my waist. Mid-kiss a searing heat spread across my chest and down into my belly. He kissed my neck, my ears, my throat as I offered myself. My breath came in shallow pants as his tongue circled slowly at the base of my neck, then he pulled back my robe to kiss one shoulder, then the other. My body swelled and hardened.

Hands still trembling, he slipped my robe off, murmuring. His hands and tongue and breath seared my skin through the thin fabric of my chemise.

"Oh, god." I struggled to take off the chemise, but part was bunched under me, part under Luis. Finally he grabbed the neckline and ripped the thin fabric. Jesus, I'd married a bodice-ripper. He laid me back on the bed as he followed the henna maze with his rough tongue. The wet path he left cooled deliciously as he danced close then slid away.

"Stop teasing," I pleaded.

"Am I teasing?" He raised his head, eyes warm.

"No, you are torturing."

He chuckled and took me in his mouth and the ache so filled me I could not breathe. I clasped my arms around his back, feeling some sort of bandage wrapped around him. He gently removed my hands, tucking them under my hips as his mouth explored my ribcage.

"Why the bandage?" I managed to ask.

He ripped the chemise open the rest of the way. If he answered, I didn't hear it over the roaring heat as Luis moved lower and I groaned.

"My pearl," he murmured as he found what he'd been looking for.

Fire raced through every nerve and shot out my fingertips and out my mouth and out my toes and just before my bones all melted, he moved on so swiftly I gasped. "Jesus Christ." This man knew what he was doing.

"So sorry, I torture again." His voice was husky, deeper. As we kissed, something hard pressed against my belly, then Luis leaned over and blew out the oil lamp, throwing us in complete darkness except for the moon patch high on the opposite wall. Walladah had been right.

"It's so dark. I want to see you." Trembling now, I struggled with his tunic's laces.

"It is better this way." Luis lifted up on one elbow; I could feel him untying his waistband with his other hand, so I slid my hand down to help him.

"No," he commanded, moving my hand back to my chest.

Wait a minute. Making love meant touching each other, not laying back like some limp rag doll. Luis shifted over me again, kissing my ears and neck while I chewed the inside of my cheek. I might have married a man, but I was no rag doll.

When Luis took my head between both hands, giving me the opportunity I needed, I reached down and firmly grasped his penis.

"No!" Luis shouted. He leapt backward, something snapped, then he tumbled off the bed. But I still held his penis in my hand.

"Oh my god!" I cried, sitting up.

Luis scrambled on the floor, swearing angrily as he searched for something in the darkness. I reached for the oil lamp, my blood chilling at the whoosh of a sword being drawn from a scabbard, the scabbard clattering to the floor.

Hands trembling, I lit the lamp just as I was pinned against the bed by the ice-cold tip of Luis's broadsword pressed against my throat. Luis's steel eyes looked at me down the length of the sword. In my hand was a brown leather facsimile of a penis.

Neither of us moved. Luis held the sword with an ice-steady hand, more frightening than if it had trembled. Outside a late party broke up in front of the palace, the laughter drifting in through the window while I lay there with cold steel pressing against my jugular.

"I am not going to yell out," I whispered.

Luis said nothing, chest heaving, sword steady.

Struggling against panic, I hefted the leather, obviously filled with something granular.

"Sugar?" I managed to ask. Luis's fierce frown convinced me I could be run through with the sword any moment now. Moving very slowly, I lay the leather on the bed. "It's okay. I'm not going to tell anyone."

Lamplight illuminated the face before me. Jesus, how could I have missed so many clues—incredibly thick black lashes, full red mouth, the curve of the cheekbone, the graceful neck. I drew in a surprised, shuddering breath, then licked my lips. With two fingers, I slowly lifted the cold metal away from my chest.

Eyes never leaving my face, the woman let me rest the tip of the sword on the bed next to me. "Why did you *do* that?" she snapped.

"Because I don't like swords that near my neck." I slowly sat up.

"No." His—no, her—eyes darted to the leather beside me.

"Oh. Because I wanted to touch it."

"No one has ever wanted to touch it," she snapped, then swore in Arabic. "What am I going to do with you?"

"Nothing. I told you, I won't reveal your secret."

The woman who used to be Luis shook her head. "I vowed to kill every person who discovered it." No wonder Luis had known in such great detail the punishment meted out to women who lived as men.

I inhaled sharply. "How many have found out?"

"Including you?"

I nodded.

"One."

We stared at each other. Same low, melodic voice. Same eyes. Same lips. But the person before me was a stranger. She was not Luis, yet she was.

"I am glad you are not a man." My lower back burned, but I didn't dare shift my body, afraid of the eleventh century equivalent of an itchy trigger finger.

She frowned. "You are the first. All the others were glad...in the dark...that I could..." A ragged sigh escaped.

"I told you I loved women. I would rather lie with a woman than a man. I thought you understood that."

She licked her lips, then lowered the sword all the way. "Then why did you marry me? Why did you...respond when I first kissed you? You thought I was a man."

I wanted to pull something over my naked breasts, but could see nothing nearby. "I don't know. I found you...it felt..." I exhaled loudly, giving up. "I don't know." For a few seconds I was able to hold the image of Luis as a woman, but then like a computer-manipulated image, she shifted back into a man. My eyes crossed as I struggled to see her as a woman.

She sat back on her heels, rested the sword across her knees. "What am I going to do?"

"First, you're going to hand me my robe." I gratefully draped it over my body, suddenly feeling stronger, since being naked wasn't good for anyone's personal power. "Then you are going to relax. I am not going to tell anyone. I married you, remember. That must mean something."

"It means you needed a way out of Walladah's path."

"If Fadri had asked me to marry him, I would have taken your dagger and shaved him between the legs."

She didn't smile, but the frown lessened just a touch. "Your point?"

I shifted my body, tucking in my tailbone against the wall. "I wouldn't have married just anyone."

"Why *did* you marry me?"

She was right. The bald truth certainly wouldn't calm the swordswoman's fears. "Why did you marry me?" I countered.

Her eyes drilled into mine, but I couldn't read them. No answer.

"How long have you lived as a man?"

"No details."

"What is your real name?"

"No details. Be quiet. I must think." She leapt to her feet, dragging a blanket over to the door. "Enough talk," she said. "Sleep."

Yeah, right. I've learned the man I married was a woman. I've had a massive sword pointed at my throat. But I pulled the robe over me, sliding down onto my side, closing my eyes. Luis fighting by the river. Luis slashing that man's throat. Luis chasing me through the woods. She had been a woman even then.

CHAPTER TWELVE

Two crowing roosters woke me up. As I stretched, the blanket slid off my naked chest, and I suddenly remembered where I was. Luis was gone. I scrambled for my clothing but she'd ripped the chemise beyond repair, and the wedding robe and cape seemed inappropriate. After burrowing through his—her clothes, I found another shirt that covered my hips, but just barely.

The door latch lifted and I leapt back into bed, drawing the blanket over my bare legs. Luis entered with a tray of food and a small bundle, latching the door behind him...behind her. "I see you are still stealing my clothes."

I let myself smile. "Yours are so much more practical. And besides..." I nodded toward the ripped chemise.

"Oh, yes. Sorry." His-her eyes sparkled under her fierce black brows. "I guess I got carried away."

"I like that in a woman."

Shaking her head, she set the tray down, then settled cross-legged at the foot of the bed, long fingers deftly peeling the orange. I flushed to think the body of a woman moved beneath that leather tunic. Did a woman's heart beat there as well, or had it been too long buried? As she expertly removed the peel in one pungent spiral, I frowned, unable to think of Luis as a woman, then took a deep breath. "So what happens next?"

She tossed me half of the peeled orange. "All night I watched you sleep." She slid a plump, dripping orange slice into her mouth.

"And?" I focused on my orange sections so I wouldn't be so aware of his, of hers. Goddess, I suddenly hated pronouns. "She" didn't fit, but "he" wasn't right either. Did I follow the transgender conventions and call her "he"? Did she want to be a man, or was she just living as one?

"I decided I will not kill you."

I snorted. "I'm touched." I wiped juice from my chin and waited.

"I believe you will not tell. Your story about traveling through the Pyrenees to Santillana never made sense to me. I believe you, too, hide a secret."

I poured us each a glass of mango juice and sliced off two hunks of cheese. "So because I have a secret, I will respect yours."

The man who was now a woman nodded.

"And if I tell?"

The dagger flew from its scabbard, whizzed past my ear, and thudded into the wall behind me. "Jesus!" I yelped as I jumped to my knees. "What did you do that for?"

He-she shrugged, her mouth full of food.

I leaned forward on my hands and knees. "I am *not* Walladah, understand? No threats necessary. That is such a male thing to do." Her gaze dropped to the neck of my blouse, which in my position revealed everything. I scooted back. "And so is *that*."

"Sorry. I have lived as a man for so many years, I *am* one...except for the obvious."

I buttoned my blouse. "What am I supposed to call you?"

She grimaced and popped another slice into her mouth. "Luis. What else?"

"That's not your real name." How did he, no she, get those slender scars on her nose and cheek?

"It is now."

"How long?"

"How long what?" She was obviously enjoying herself now.

"How long have you been Luis?" I couldn't take my eyes off her, still stunned. How on earth had I not seen this earlier? Her voice lacked testosterone, but her expression was hard, almost as if she were challenging anyone to dare suspect her true gender.

She scratched her head, running her hands through the short black hair so vigorously it nearly stood on end. "Since I was seventeen... about ten years ago."

I stopped eating. "You were seventeen when your family was killed."

She nodded, but only looked at her hands.

"Look, I know your secret, so you might as well tell me everything."

She finished her orange, then wiped her hands on the saffron cloth. Her face revealed nothing as she stared at me. "I have never told another soul. Why should I tell you?"

"Why shouldn't you?" Was there a woman more exasperating in this entire century?

She stood, moved to the window, and concentrated on the action outside. I waited, and finally her tight posture relaxed, and with a heavy sigh, she turned and met my eyes. "This is not easy." I nodded sympathetically. She dropped down on the bed beside me. "If you tell another soul, I will have to kill you."

I flashed a wry smile. "We've been through that already."

After another measured glance, she rubbed her face. "I met Lucinda at the waterfall, just as I told you. I found the bodies of my family. I did bury them all."

I drew in a deep breath. "Your parents, your aunt and uncle, your brother Miguel, your sister."

A muscle twitched along her jaw as I waited. A story held in so long took time to tell. "*I* was the sister. I buried my little brother Miguel, and my older brother...Luis." The blond lock of hair in the ivory box. She leaned against the wall, hand shading her eyes. "As I dug, I planned my vengeance. But what could I do as a woman?" Her voice grew hard. "Nothing. I could not fight in a skirt. If I stayed on the farm, Ordoñez would marry me off to one of the men from Anguiano or take me as his mistress."

"So you became Luis." She wasn't transgender, but a woman who'd figured out what she needed to do to survive.

Eyes dry, jaw firm, she nodded. "Before I buried Luis, I stripped the bloody clothes from his body, put them on, hacked off my hair, and became my brother."

My skin crawled to think of putting on clothes soggy and cold with a dead brother's blood. Ten years living as a man. Hiding that she had to squat to pee. Menstruating in an army of men. It seemed a nearly impossible secret to keep, but since the Christians rarely bathed, I could believe she'd somehow managed all these years.

"So, what is your real name?"

A half-smile flickered across her features. "I told you already. Do not be so stubborn."

"I am not stubborn."

Her delighted laugh startled me. "You have been nothing *but* stubborn since the day I rescued you at Mirabueno."

"You *rescued* me?" I slammed the glass down onto the tray. "Excuse me, but that time you *kidnapped* me."

"But I thought I was your knight in shining mail?" I ignored her irritating grin, and in a flurry of bare legs I kicked at the covers, but before I could rise, Luis pinned me back down on the bed, her body heavy on mine. "During the night, I thought about your question, Why did I marry you." She settled her hips between mine, igniting a fire between my legs. "Seeing you in nothing but my shirt reminds me of a very good reason."

Her kiss sent shock waves careening through me. When I responded hungrily, our mouths fused, open, wet, smooth. I slid my arms around her and pulled her to me. She moaned as one of her hands found my breast. But as our bodies melted together, I felt Luis's leather, still tucked into her tights, against my thigh.

"Luis," I struggled for air, finally rolling her off me. I raised up on one elbow, heart racing at the raw desire in her eyes, tracing her cheek, running a trembling finger over those lips. "I know your secret. We are both women. We don't need..." I tapped her groin. "...this right now. Maybe later." I touched her chest. "Let's just get to know each other's bodies first. You can take off your bindings, take off your leather."

Did fear briefly flicker through her eyes, then disappear? "No, I will pleasure you."

"Why can't I touch you?" Okay, now I was getting pissed.

She raised up to face me, brow furrowed. "This is who I am, Kate. Judging by your response to my kisses, you *like* who I am."

"Yes, but now that I know you are a woman, I want Luis the woman, and all of her."

Her voice was thick. "I cannot do that."

"Why not?"

Her tan, burnished skin flushed, her deep Arctic pools suddenly clouded over, then she rolled to her feet, retrieving the dagger still stuck in the wall behind me, sliding it into its scabbard. "It is enough you know my secret. You cannot use my...my attraction to you to change me."

I threw up my hands. "I'm not trying to change you." I lowered my voice at her threatening glare. Luis's room was in a quieter section of the palace, but servants and slaves still passed outside. "You already *are* a woman," I whispered. "Why won't you let me touch you?"

Luis strapped on her sword. "It is who I am."

Without thinking, I rose to my feet and pulled a "Walladah," unbuttoning my shirt until it slipped off and pooled around my ankles. "And this is who *I* am."

Luis stepped back, eyes wide, a thin glow of perspiration on her forehead. She stared at my body, breathing heavily now. Then she shook her head, as if she'd drunk too much ale. "I cannot," she finally said.

"Yes, you can." This was ridiculous.

The woman before me became a soldier used to winning, back ramrod straight, eyes fierce. "Then it would seem, my pearl, that ours will be an unconsummated marriage after all." She whirled on one heel, flung open the door, and slammed it behind her.

❖

I barely spoke to Liana as we made room for her in the shed. She teased me once about my wedding night, but my glowering silenced her. She, on the other hand, floated as giddy as a kid on the first day of summer vacation as I moved my paints to a space by the window, then sat down to paint. I had to do something with the weird energy sparking through me, but I wouldn't use shading or perspective. Strictly two-dimensional from now on. My deal with Mu'tamin nagged at me, for I didn't know how he intended to use the portrait of his brother.

I sketched the scene outside the window, struggling to keep the yew tree in the distance the same size as the rose bushes lining the walk to the palace. It looked awful, but I'd learned my lesson. I spent the rest of the morning trying to focus on painting rather than wondering if all of Luis's hair was as black as the hair on her head.

Word spread fast, and soon Liana glowed with the deep joy of finally doing something useful, of placing her small, sure hands on animal after animal. People came with sick chickens, one sneezing donkey, and a man with a limping dog. As Liana probed the dog's hip, the man complained about the weather, Father Manolo, taxes levied on Christians and Jews. He finally stopped and stared at my paintings. "Did you train in a monastery?"

"I beg your pardon?"

"Your skills. I am amazed they taught such skills to a woman."

"It was a progressive monastery. The Most Holy Brothers of Sts. Peter, Paul, and Mary."

The man frowned. "Must be a new order." He pointed to one with sheep dotting the hills behind Zaragoza. "I would like to buy this painting. How much?"

As a Christian living under Moorish rule, he paid the annual tribute to al-Mu'tamin, yet still dressed in fine lightweight linens and new, kid leather boots. I blurted out "ten dinar," a ridiculous price, then watched, stunned, as he dropped ten gold coins into my palm. I was still staring at them when the man gathered up the dog and the painting, and left.

Money. I could buy a horse. I could hire a guide. My diaphanous skirts swirled as a warm breeze came through the open door. I could buy my own clothes. I could leave. My fist curled around the coins, warming them.

"Kate?" I jumped. Liana stood at my elbow. "You are suddenly pale. Are you ill?" I shook my head, squeezing the coins hard enough they pinched my palms. Money. Cash. Freedom. Hope. "Perhaps it is the heat," she said. "Sit outside for a bit."

Nodding, I wandered out of the shed and into the shade of the nearby yew tree. Money. I would find someone to make me a split skirt of linen or cotton. And a jacket made entirely of pockets.

Hamara found me daydreaming about steel-toed work boots and a Lands' End squall jacket.

"Babieca is doing very well," he said, dropping to the ground beside me.

"Thanks to you and Liana," I said, fanning myself.

"I still cannot believe Rodrigo did not have you killed for pretending to heal Babieca."

I sighed, watching the palace blacksmith stoking his fire. "I am very lucky." Horses snorted from a corral nearby, and the smell of fresh manure settled over us. For all my dislike of horses, the scent had become bearable, just part of my life.

Hamara nodded. "Yes, you are. You are now the happy wife of Luis, the brave El Picador." Brave, my ass. She might be fearless on the battlefield, but confront her with one naked woman and she froze solid with fear. Hamara picked self-consciously at the front of his robe. "Please tell me about love."

"Love?"

A furious blush reddened his ears. "I see how you look at Luis. How did you know it was love?"

My blush matched his. The poor boy confused lust with love. I thought about Anna, but came up just as blank. How long did love last? I let my head tip back, and caught sight of Luis conferring with Alvar and several other lance corporals at the far side of the yards. Her cropped black hair shone like ebony in the sun. "I'm no expert on relationships, I'm afraid."

"When you love someone, does it hurt to be separated?"

Actually, being separated from Anna didn't hurt that much anymore, a thought that made me sad. The thread connecting me to Anna hadn't broken because Luis had captured my attention, but because I could see now that my relationship with Anna was never meant to last in the first place. Guilt more than pain plagued me. "Yes, it can hurt, a great deal. But, Hamara, who have you been—" Suddenly, his wounded hazel eyes and thin face told me all I needed. "Aisha?"

He ducked his head, looking fearfully toward the palace, then nodded. "My chest hurts so badly I am afraid something is wrong inside."

Aisha had been gone less than twenty-four hours. I couldn't bear to tell him the pain would grow worse, then fade until it was as distant a memory as Aisha herself. "Aisha slipped from the harem to visit you." Briefly Luis and I locked eyes across the courtyard.

"Yes."

"But when we met by the river, you acted like you'd never seen a woman's knees before."

Hamara adjusted his turban so he wouldn't have to look at me directly. "I had not. All Aisha and I had done was hold hands and kiss. But then I realized her knees would be as...beautiful as yours."

I half-listened as I watched as Luis stood there, hands on her hips, nodding while Alvar waved his arms emphatically. She seemed terribly vulnerable.

Hamara touched my arm. "So when I returned from the raid on Ordóñez's...I...we..." He slumped forward, head in his hands. "We had not planned to be caught. I cannot believe she is gone. I should have stood before Mu'tamin and declared my guilt, and my love. I should not have let her go." Without a nod or wave to me, Luis disappeared into the camp at the far side of the palace grounds. "I cannot stand to think of her at Lerida." He choked off a sob. "She will be frightened. Other men will—"

I patted Hamara's hand. "Hamara, there was nothing you could have done. Besides, not all affection we feel is really love. Sometimes it is just physical. Sometimes it is just convenience." Luis had not reappeared.

The boy's bleary eyes met mine. "You are wrong."

"Usually." I sighed heavily.

"Perhaps I understand love better than you do." Mouth grim, he stood, brushed off his robe, and turned toward the stables.

Before I could respond, a dozen Moorish horsemen galloped into the yard, and Hamara leapt toward them, hollering to the stablehands. I drew the veil across my face against the dust as Hamara grabbed the beribboned halter of a massive white horse. The small, pinched man astride the stallion leapt off, barking commands at his guards, his jeweled rings flashing in the sunlight.

I felt Liana's gentle presence at my elbow. "Hayib," she whispered as the prince and his entourage swept into the palace, white, red, and yellow head scarves billowing behind them, curved swords at their sides. If I was to keep my promise to al-Mu'tamin, this was my best chance.

"I need to return to the palace," I said, unwilling to tell her why. I grabbed a few sheets of linen and my pencils, and followed the scent of rosewater and jasmine still marking Hayib's dramatic entrance.

Before I reached Mu'tamin's quarters, I attached my veil. No use pissing anyone off. The less conspicuous, the better. Chaos reigned in Mu'tamin's receiving courtyard as servants scurried around. Luis and five other soldiers stood protectively near Mu'tamin, every hand on every sword hilt. The room bristled with the tension of Moors who hated each other, Moors who hated Christians, and from the look on Alvar's face, Christians who hated Moors. Luis's solemn face betrayed nothing.

Hayib did not bow before Mu'tamin, which only deepened the scowls of Mu'tamin's men. I slipped into a back corner and settled myself on a cushion, well-concealed by nervous servants. Walladah and Musta'in sat behind their father, eyes glued to Hayib.

Hayib's angular face had enough planes that his three-dimensional countenance would practically jump off the page. Hayib spoke in rapid Arabic, but I did catch two words—Alfonso and Toledo. Judging by Mu'tamin's pale drawn face, and the grim, satisfied look in Alvar's eyes, the news was not good. When Rodrigo entered the conversation, all switched to Spanish. "Toledo fell hard under Alfonso's assault," Hayib said. "Thousands of Moors have fled."

Mu'tamin calmly listened to Hayib's descriptions, but terror had stiffened every servant in the room. Walladah's lovely jaw had set in a determined line, and Musta'in appeared short of breath. Even Rodrigo's flat face was grim. "Alfonso will not stop at Toledo," he remarked when Hayib took a breath. The muscle along Luis's jaw twitched, but she would not look at me. The only women in the room were Luis, Walladah, and myself. If any of the warriors knew a woman stood beside them in male dress, planning battle strategies with them, wearing a sword...I hunched over my drawing, terrified my eyes would give her away.

Somehow the ill emir found the strength to dominate the room. His voice rang out through the courtyard. "Alfonso has plucked the most precious of pearls from the greatness of al-Andaluz." He glanced at Rodrigo. "Which jewel shall be next? Valencia? Malaga? Granada?"

Even I knew enough geography by now to know Zaragoza was the next pearl strung on the necklace of Moorish cities snaking throughout the Moorish lands. And Zaragoza was defended by El Cid, the man King Alfonso loved to hate. I drew furiously as Hayib continued. "I propose an alliance between us to repel Alfonso's certain attack. Allah willing, we will send the infidel crawling back to Burgos." The turbaned men around him murmured approvingly. "When we reclaim Toledo it will be as it was in the time of Rahman," his voice rose. "Moors together expanding the glory of al-Andaluz."

I stopped sketching as Mu'tamin clearly measured his brother's offer. "You cannot have Zaragoza in the bargain."

The hated Hayib bowed slightly so I couldn't see his face. "Understood, my brother." Walladah scowled darkly behind her father. "Our alliance will be for the glory of al-Andaluz, for the glory of Allah."

I knew Mu'tamin would have stood, but risked revealing his illness.

Walladah leaned forward. "Father, we cannot—" She stopped

when Mu'tamin raised his hand.

"To you, my brother, I say this: our father gave Zaragoza to me, and Lerida to you. That will never change. But we will combine our forces to repel the barbarian, Alfonso of Castile."

As the leaders began discussing the details, I rolled up my sketches and slipped from the room, aware that only one pair of eyes, ice blue, watched me as I left.

❖

That evening Luis and I sat together at dinner for appearances' sake, Rodrigo and Grimaldi across from us. Fadri, mouth full of half-chewed meat, smiled at me. "So, Señora Navarro, are you pleased with your choice of husband?"

"Very," I replied curtly.

"If he fails to please in any way, let me know." Snickers ran up and down the table. Rodrigo smirked as Luis glared at Fadri.

"No need. Luis is very sweet. In fact, he's just full of sugar." Luis choked until I thwacked her none-too-gently on the back.

Grimaldi passed Luis the jug of water. "Drink, good man. And tell me news. The priest in town, he excited all day, but make no sense."

Rodrigo snatched at another hunk of meat. "Alfonso has taken Toledo, which means he will come for Zaragoza next. The only thing that might alter his plans is if the Almoravides return."

Grimaldi looked at me, thick brows pulled together, but I was equally confused.

Luis finally found her voice. "The Moorish emirs have sent word to Ben Yusef in northern Africa, leader of the Almoravides, that Alfonso threatens al-Andaluz. The Almoravides may come help defend Zaragoza and the other cities."

I scooped up the last of the rice on my plate. "So why is the priest upset? Aren't the Moors and Almoravides both Arabs?"

Rodrigo belched, which released a rash of belches from his men. I made no effort to hide my grimace. "Yes, Señora Navarro, but they are far from the same. The Moors are weak as women compared to the Almoravides."

"You know little of women, Rodrigo."

He dismissed my dig with an impatient wave. "The Almoravides are cold, fanatical killers. They could crush Alfonso as I crush this grape." Red juice dripped from his massive fist onto the white cloth.

"So that should make the Moors happy."

Enzo leaned forward. "Each time BenYusef crosses over from Morocco to bail out the Moorish kings, he may decide to stay."

"...crushing them as completely as he could Alfonso," Luis finished. As my gaze moved from face to face, watching for any sign the others might know Luis's secret, I suddenly realized how truly dangerous it was that I knew the truth. One slip of my tongue, and she would be yanked from the closet, so to speak, and likely be killed. I wiped my sweaty hands on my seat cushion.

Grimaldi poured me a glass of sparkling white wine. "So our friends the Moors are caught between the Christian King Alfonso and the Almoravide Ben Yusef."

Rodrigo nodded, then patted his full belly. "The Moors must choose their enemy and their ally. But since Mu'tamin told me this morning he'd rather be a goatherd in Morocco than a swineherd in Castile, he has chosen King Alfonso as the enemy."

Nervous laughter rippled down the table, but I thought Alvar's eyes would pop from his purple face. "I would rather be six feet under than fight against Alfonso, my sworn king."

Rodrigo waved him off impatiently, but the look Alvar and Luis exchanged made it clear Alvar was perfectly serious. I could feel the tension in Luis's body. Thanks to her devotion to Rodrigo, Luis would find herself fighting alongside the Almoravides, fighting against a Christian king. Would she be forced to fight Alvar as well?

"Are the Almoravides less tolerant than the Moors?" I asked.

Rodrigo glared at Luis. "You have forgotten my advice; wives are for the bed, not the table."

"Yes, well..." Luis did not look at me, but her back was ramrod straight. I bit off a retort; embarrassing Luis wouldn't change Rodrigo.

Grimaldi leaned forward. "Moors very tolerant, and let Christians and Jews worship because those religions have only one god too. Our only fault we no accept Muhammad as prophet." Grimaldi's smooth voice had taken on the same professorial tone Anna used when lecturing me, and soon Fadri's head rested in his hands, his eyes struggling to stay open. "Moor tolerance ends when prophet is badly spoken of. Do you know of Cordoban martyrs?"

My legs, folded under the table, began to cramp. I shifted and my knee bumped against Luis's, but I refused to move. Our bones pressed painfully against each other. "No," I replied.

"Over one hundred years after the Moors conquer this peninsula in 711, monk Isaac come down from mountain at Tabanos, and tell Moors in Cordoba Muhammad was fool."

Fadri's eyes were open now. "What did they do to him?"

"Cut off head. Next day, Sanctius do same thing. Cut off head." The room fell silent. "Six more men say Christ was one true god above Allah, and Muhammad was not prophet."

Rodrigo snorted. "Fools. I'll bet every one lost his head."

"By one week eight men lose heads." Murmurs ran through the men. "Then more martyrs—three men then two women."

"That's insane," I sputtered. "What does dying on purpose accomplish?"

"It shows the power of God in their lives," Alvar said quietly.

Grimaldi smiled ruefully. "A level of devotion I not yet reach. Over the next years, Moors in Cordoba chop heads off eighty-five men and women."

"Stupid," Rodrigo and I said at the same time.

"No," Luis said, her voice calm and so soft my jaw tightened at the fine-edged sword she walked every day. "It makes perfect sense. If you are not willing to die for your faith, there is little reason to live."

Rodrigo and Luis locked eyes; Enzo and Fadri shifted uncomfortably. "Money is the way to change things," Rodrigo said, "not praying or volunteering to have someone chop off your head. Money *is* god, Luis. Remember that." Tension as charged as a downed electrical wire ran up and down the table. Luis's mouth stretched into a thin, firm line, then a weathered soldier at the far end of the table farted.

Amid jeers and friendly insults, the diners dispersed. As we stood, Grimaldi bowed and kissed my hand. "Unlike Señor Rodrigo, I *do* like hear what women say. Perhaps we walk Zaragoza, with husband's permission."

"I would be delighted," I said, "but I do not need Luis's permission. I have a shop near the stables. Come visit anytime."

Luis grabbed my elbow and steered me toward our room. The setting sun shot through a huge keyhole window at the hall's end. At our door, Luis let go. "I will sleep in the stables. Goodnight."

"What about Walladah?" I twisted the end of my veil around my finger.

"You are safe. I spoke with her today and she accepts what happened." Luis breathed heavily, her chest rising and falling. "Goodnight."

I stopped her with a light touch on her arm, encouraged by her obvious struggle. "What will you do if the Almoravides come?"

She sighed impatiently, but stepped closer. "The Almoravides *are* coming. Hayib and Mu'tamin will join forces with them."

"Can you trust Hayib?" I leaned closer, concerned.

"No, of course not. But we have no choice. First I will train the recruits of Hayib, then we march south."

"And then?" My heart pounded in my ears.

"Then we take up arms against King Alfonso, Count Ordóñez, Gudesto Gonzalez, and any other Christian lords he has with him." Her gaze lowered, two melted pools resting on my lips.

"Why don't you stay here tonight?"

"Do you open your robe again to tempt me?" Her soft voice was edged with steel.

Shame burned hot across my face. "Don't throw that in my face," I snapped.

She moved closer, her warm, scented breath close enough to feel.

"Luis," I whispered just once, and with a strangled cry of frustration she pulled me to her, strong hands gripping my arms. Her kiss left me gasping as she pressed me close. My body tingled where she touched me, my lips swelled as she took them greedily between her teeth. "Come inside," I whispered.

She bit my neck, then grazed my neck and ear lobe. "If I can come as myself," she murmured, one hand slipping between my legs.

"Yes," I breathed. "That's what I want. Remove the leather. Let me touch you as you touch me. Come as yourself."

She stepped back with an exasperated growl. "No, I mean come as who I am now."

Stunned, I tried to gather up my wits. "We clearly want each other. Isn't that enough?"

Luis scowled, eyes burning. "I cannot be a woman."

I thumped her chest in frustration. "You stubborn jerk! You already are one. You don't have to give up who you are."

An angry mask slipped over her features. "Latch this door behind you." She thrust me into our room, closing the door between us. I dropped the latch, listening to her footsteps fade down the hall, willing them to return, but they did not.

Chapter Thirteen

Two hours later, I still couldn't sleep, so I swung open the round window grill, wincing at the squeaking hinges. The wind carried the thump-thump of the river's flour mill working even at night to feed the 15,000 souls packed into the city. I closed my eyes, visualizing the traffic on Chicago's turnpike, the snarl of honking cars near downtown, the steel skyscrapers towering over Lake Michigan, the slums, the racist graffiti, the brown smog.

I knew Luis had to be careful, but in this room with the door latched, why wouldn't she let down her guard with me? Perhaps I would never understand the pressure she'd been under for ten years, but wouldn't that make her all the more eager to stop pretending, if even for an hour or two?

At the single sound of hoofbeats on the veranda below, I opened my eyes. Hamara led a small black mare from the stables onto the grass, where her hooves became silent. Two swords and a bulging saddlebag made me gasp. The fool was going after Aisha. When Hamara sprang onto the horse and slipped through the palace gate, I flung on a robe and raced down the hall.

My footsteps echoed as I ran down the walkway and into the stables. I opened the first stall I reached, then led out the occupant, a medium-sized but gentle speckled mare. I tied her to a post while I ran for a saddle blanket. Then, grunting, I dragged a saddle over and by cursing and pushing, I settled the massive saddle over the horse's back. Oddly-shaped, the saddles had high ridges on both the front and back.

"Running off because I will not bed you?" Luis leaned against a stall door behind me, straw clinging to her muscular, tight-clad thighs.

"No, you jerk. Hamara just left for Lerida. He's gone to rescue Aisha."

"He will be killed," she said, yawning widely.

I struggled to tighten the saddle's cinch. "I *know* that. I've got to stop him."

Luis pulled me back from the horse. "This will never work," she said.

I yanked my arm free, planting tight fists on my hips. "And why *not*? Because I'm a *woman*?"

Luis gave me a dangerous look, brows pulled together, eyes smoky. "No, because you have the saddle on backwards."

"Oh."

With seemingly little effort, she reversed the saddle, tightened the leather cinch, then leapt into the saddle.

"Hey," I cried. "I'm coming too."

"I think not. A sack of oats can ride better than you." The horse pranced in place. "I will make better time without you." Before I could protest, the horse sprang forward and I was alone in the stables.

I paced for at least an hour. Luis should have caught up with him by now. Hamara might be riding at break-neck speed, suicidal at night. What if Luis's horse threw her down some ravine along the Ebro? A few horses whinnied, confused by my pacing. Not even the smell of warm horses and fresh hay calmed me. Finally, feet aching from walking the hard-packed earth, I found an open stall with a blanket draped across a pile of straw. I rested there, straining to hear hoofbeats, but must have fallen asleep.

When something landed with a thud on the floor next to me, I sat up, heart racing. "Luis?" An oil lamp flickered to life and Luis hung it on a nail. Hamara lay sprawled in the straw, face and robe caked with dried blood.

"Oh, my god! Who did this?" I dropped to the boy's side.

Luis sat down heavily on the straw. "I did."

"You were supposed to stop him, not beat him."

Luis let her head roll to one side, revealing a bruised cheek. "He started it," she said.

"Shit. I can't believe this." I ran for a clean rag and dipped a bucket of water from the well, then started cleaning Hamara's face and neck. "What happened?" I asked more quietly.

"Never come between a fool and the woman he loves."

"He is very brave."

"He is very stupid." Luis winced as she fingered her ribs, while I bent over the unconscious Hamara, cleaning the gash on the top of his head. "Sword hilt," Luis added helpfully. "Finally had to either run him through or knock him out cold."

"Can you see nothing but violent options?" I moved the bucket to Luis's side, dabbing roughly at a cut above her black eye.

"Ouch! You were gentler with an unconscious boy."

"Are your ribs broken?"

She shook her head wearily. "No, just bruised."

I cleaned the dried blood from her face, scrubbing none-too-gently across her cheeks and down her neck. "I want you to teach me to ride. I will not be left behind again."

She moaned, then stretched out over the straw, sword clanking against the wall. "Kate, one hundred recruits arrive in just a few hours, most of them so young they are barely off the teat." She rolled onto her back, sighing deeply. "I have to turn them into soldiers in just a few weeks. I have no time for riding lessons."

"Barely off the teat...lovely expression. I cannot believe how you denigrate women." I squeezed out the rag over the bucket. "This whole place is a nightmare for women. It's making me crazy." I stopped. Luis's chest rose and fell rhythmically. Hamara stirred, then rolled onto his side, eyes closed, mouth open. Slowly, lightly, I touched Luis's chest, the linen shirt rough to the touch, the bandages still binding her. Sighing, I stood, doused the oil lamp, then made my way back to the palace as crimson streaks shot into the early purple-dawn, a sight so moving I stood outside the entrance and watched the sun rise. Despite the violence, the ridiculous oppression of women, now and then the colors, tastes, and people of this time, of this divided country, pierced my heart.

❖

That morning the stables burst with horses and men; the palace grounds filled with tents. Enzo tried to commandeer our shed for sleeping quarters, but I literally chased him away with a broom, Liana watching wide-eyed from the shed's front door.

"You are not afraid of him?" she asked.

"Of course not. He's just trying to intimidate us." I raised my broom. "But I have vanquished him with my sword."

Liana giggled and slipped back inside. This art studio was my only way to earn money. I'd sold ten more paintings, none for as much as the first, but enough to weigh down my fanny pack, which I wore under my skirts now. The gentle pressure against my belly reassured me. As Suley and Abu liked to say, "Free May Come Next."

I stood outside and smiled as a young boy, his brown eyes reminding me of Arturo, dragged a reluctant, limping goat toward the shop. Funny how after five years of being together, my connection to Anna could be so easily severed; but the five minutes I'd spent with Arturo in the orphanage continued to haunt me.

Late that morning I wandered Zaragoza in search of a seamstress, thoroughly enjoying the sharp, spicy smells of the market, fresh pomegranates, piles of dark brown baskets, bolts of pure white linen, the sounds of the commerce down by the river, the feel of the cobblestoned streets beneath my feet. Oddly energized, I felt safer wandering these streets than I'd ever felt in my own neighborhood.

Finally, after asking at shop after shop, I found the small house a few blocks from the central market. The wooden door rattled alarmingly under my knock, and I braced myself to catch it, but it stayed hinged as it swung open, revealing a woman bent with age, skin weathered and brown. "Are you Señora Tolón?" I asked. At her cautious nod, I plunged ahead. "I live at the palace. I'm married to one of the Christian soldiers, and I would like some different clothes."

She touched my sleeve, fingering the silky fabric. "But these are such fine clothes. Why would you want any different?"

"May I show you?"

She escorted me into the simple apartment, one room with a small bed in one corner, a table with two chairs, and a fire pit in the corner. She pulled out a chair for me.

"I would like clothes that are made of stronger fabric." I unfolded the drawings I'd made earlier. "Maybe linen, or a heavy cotton. I need a skirt that I can wear when riding a horse." I pointed to my drawing of the mid-calf split skirt, biting off a smile as her eyes widened. It was pretty radical for 1085. "I need a few tunics, one long-sleeved, one short-sleeved, and finally, a coat." I was especially proud of the coat, almost a safari jacket with its two breast pockets, two patch pockets, loose fit, and belt.

Señora Tolón sat silently, pouring over the drawings. "I have never seen designs like these."

"I would really appreciate it if you would give this a try."

Caught up in the challenge, she asked a few questions about construction, then color. I shrugged. "I don't care. Just something bland. Nothing bright."

"A green linen would look lovely against your skin." She nodded. "Yes, I will take the job." I stood quietly while she measured me with a ragged brown string. We agreed on a price, and I counted out the dirhems so she could buy the cloth. I couldn't wear pants, even though I ached for a pair of comfortable jeans, but I had to get out of these blasted silks.

❖

Luis did not appear for the evening meal. "Where is Luis?" I asked Enzo as I stood by the table crowded with hungry lance corporals.

"He will be gone for a few days. Did he not tell you?"

My ears flamed at Alvar's concerned clucking. "Oh, dear, trouble between the lovers already?"

"Alvar, bite me," I muttered in English, then filled a plate and took it back to our room to eat in peace.

By late afternoon the next day, Luis still hadn't returned. Men roiled around the courtyard, but their numbers were fewer. I asked one soldier if he'd seen Luis, but he just blushed and shrugged. Finally I caught up with Fadri as he entered the stable, hot and sweaty.

"Fadri, I need a riding lesson."

He frowned, then shook his head. "No time." He swung a bag of oats over his shoulder, almost shy without an audience to entertain at my expense. I'd almost stopped thinking of him as the Blond Moron.

"Just the basics. How to saddle a horse, how to sit on it."

"Luis can teach you later." He ran a hand nervously through his rat-nest of hair.

I touched his fithly arm. "I'm sorry I punched you when we first met."

He rubbed his jaw, then smiled. "I might have deserved it."

"Put down the bag. You can take a short break. I just need the basics."

The large man pursed his lips, then shrugged off the bag. "If Luis finds out, you must tell him it was your idea, not mine."

"Absolutely." He reached for a woman's sidesaddle, but I stopped him. "No, a real saddle." Then he chose a deep chestnut mare with a black tail and mane, who stood calmly as I awkwardly flung the saddle over her broad back. I'd read *Don Quixote* in college, and had always been entranced with his quest. Once I learned to ride, I would set out on a quest of my own. I rubbed the mare's velvet nose. "Your name will be Rozinante, the same as Don Quixote's horse. The only difference is you are much more beautiful."

Fadri proved to be surprisingly patient, teaching me how to tell a saddle's front from its wider back, helping me mount, tapping my knees and back, guiding me so I sat on the horse properly. "Very good," he said.

"At least until the horse moves," I said. "Then Luis says I ride like a sack of oats."

Fadri laughed, walking my horse outside along the path. "Luis trained me by insulting me daily. And by pinning me to the wall a few times with his knife when I needed it."

"Do you fear Luis?"

Fadri looked up at me. "Luis is not the strongest of men, but he is the quickest, the bravest, the smartest, the fairest I know. But no, I do not fear him."

I shifted my hips, trying to find the horse's rhythm as we walked. "And what of Rodrigo? Why do you follow him?"

Fadri stopped, shading his gray eyes against the sun. "Rodrigo pays us, that is all. We *follow* Luis." He led me forward again, then stopped to adjust my foot in the stirrup, his hand lingering a touch too long on my calf.

"Fadri," a voice growled, "find your own woman."

The young man jumped and whirled toward the icy voice. "Luis! I came for the oats, and she..." He waved toward me.

"Fadri, I will finish this *lesson*." Luis's grim face was smudged from two days' travel.

With my thanks, Fadri shouldered the oats again and trotted away. Luis led my horse back to the stable. "What about the rest of my lesson?" I asked lightly.

"Lesson over," she said, grabbing my waist and pulling me roughly off the horse.

"You're pinching me." I jerked free and stepped back.

"How dare you flirt with one of my men?" Luis's voice was low and hard, her eyes narrowed and cold.

"Flirt?"

"I saw you with him. How can I maintain the respect of my men if my wife—"

"Look," I whispered. "I was just talking with him. I was just being myself, something *I'm* not afraid to be."

"Enough." Luis flung the reins to a waiting stable boy then grabbed my arm, hustling me back to the palace.

"Let go," I snapped as we fought our way up the stairs. "And where have you been?"

"None of your business." She shoved me into our room, then latched the door behind us. "You are my *wife*," Luis snarled. "Just because the relationship has not been consummated does not mean you can parade around—"

"Parade around? That's ridiculous. What are you so afraid of?"

"I am not afraid of anything," Luis said, face red. "But you tease, you taunt, you distract. Fadri cannot concentrate with you—"

"You mean *you* can't concentrate," I said. "Don't blame me just because you want—"

She grabbed me by the shoulders and shook me hard, her voice trembling. "I want to forget I ever found you." I struggled to push her away, but her scabbard tangled in my skirts and we both fell to the floor in a chaotic bundle of legs and arms. Hands out to break my fall, I landed on Luis's chest, my lips only inches from hers.

Time froze. Her eyes snapped as my heart thudded wildly in my ears. I hung, suspended, our breath mingling as we waited for time, or gravity, to decide our fate. My arms began to shake with the effort, so I slowly, deliciously, yielded to gravity, lowering myself to find her lips open, tender. A moan escaped me when Luis pulled me down, clutching me in her iron arms. As we wrapped ourselves around each other, our bodies thrust against each other and I forgot to breathe. Thigh against thigh, I gasped as the pressure between my legs threatened to explode. I rolled away, gulping for air. When my vision cleared, I took her warm face between my hands.

Luis squeezed her eyes shut, but not before I'd seen the fear. "No one has ever touched...me."

Sudden sympathy welled up in my chest. By taking off her leather, by letting someone touch her, Luis would feel more exposed and vulnerable than any woman, something a soldier could not bear. Bizarrely, now that she offered, I could not be the one to strip her so bare, to put fear into those blue eyes. Her very life depended upon being Luis *all* the time.

"I'm sorry, Luis. I keep forgetting how different things are for you. You don't feel safe, I—"

She silenced me with a finger to my lips, then smiled ruefully. "I have never lost a battle...until now..."

My heart raced. "You are willing to meet me half way?" She nodded, fingering my hair. "You won't regret it."

She kissed me long and slow. "Oh, I am very sure I will."

I carefully unlaced her tunic. When she didn't stop me, I slipped it off her broad shoulders. Wide-eyed, she watched, barely breathing, as I carefully removed the bandage wrapped around her chest. Two small perfect breasts glowed in the last of the daylight, two rosebuds closed tight against the world. I stripped off my own top, then slowly leaned into her until we touched. A small gasp escaped her. She didn't take her eyes from mine, but licked her lips. "Holy Santiago," she whispered.

I kissed her gently, tugging her lower lip into my mouth. "You ain't seen nothing yet, baby."

She reached into her tights, untied Mr. Sugar, and tossed it into the corner, then I helped her pull off the leggings, inhaling sharply at her thick black triangle. "I...ahh...have not bathed or changed since our wedding." Her voice shook slightly.

I lay her down on the bed, dipped a cloth into the corner basin, then drew the cloth across her belly and up the entire length of her arm. I washed under each arm, stopping only to tease the tight hair with my lips. Luis was silent until I washed between her legs, when she let out a brief gasp. "Now you wash me," I said. The air chilled my moist skin but I didn't care.

"I am starting to understand why the Moors bathe so often," she said, dribbling a few drops of water across my chest until I stretched in delight. Nothing in the last eight weeks had felt normal, but now, lying here with a naked woman in my arms, for the first time I felt whole, not ripped into pieces by the unthinkable divide between the eleventh and twenty-first centuries.

I lost track of time as we covered each other with kisses, wrapping ourselves around bodies soon slicked with sweat. I kissed the small tattoo on her right shoulder, a cross that ended in a sword point, topped with the letters "CV." "What does this tattoo mean?"

Luis grimaced gently, the corners of her eyes crinkling, her lashes so long Liana would have said she required combs for her eyes. She nibbled at my ear. "Why were you at Mirabueno?"

I snickered into her warm neck. "So many secrets." My hand brushed lightly across her belly, then lower.

"Kate," Luis gasped at being touched, and I flushed with the memory of my own first time, of electricity coursing through my legs, shooting out my fingertips. Even the ends of my eyelashes had felt on fire.

Once Luis got past the strangeness of someone actually making love to her, not just the other way around, she couldn't get enough, and we soon forgot about life, time, or the rest of the world.

Later, exhausted, we lay entwined like two kittens, our chests rising and falling together. Light as feathers, suspended in time, we lay there until I drifted toward a deep, luscious sleep, barely stirring as she kissed my eyes, my nose, the corners of my mouth. Her breath was warm on my forehead. "Goodnight, wife."

CHAPTER FOURTEEN

Consciousness came slowly as the pink sunrise filled the room. I didn't smell coffee, so Anna was probably still in the bathroom. That was okay; we had plenty of time before work. My limbs felt like sandbags—fluid, heavy, limp—as I snuggled deeper into my cocoon, gasping when a hand, rough-skinned and larger than Anna's, slid firmly *and* possessively up my naked hip and around my waist.

My eyes flew open as the warm hand cupped one of my breasts, sending a hot flush down my belly. Not Anna, but a black-haired woman who called herself Luis.

I lay perfectly still. I'd been so hell-bent on seducing Luis I hadn't stopped to consider the complications. But now guilt, remorse, and yes, embarrassment, rushed through me. I had *never* cheated on Anna, or any other lover, for that matter. Not one stolen kiss; not even one imagined affair, except for that great dream I had about Sophia Loren, and I told Anna about that to make sure we kept no secrets. I tried to picture Anna's face, but it flickered in and out of focus. What was she doing right now?

That safe, secure feeling I'd awoken with fled. I was in the wrong bed with the wrong woman in the wrong century. Luis nuzzled my neck as she stroked me. Damn. Why did the wrong *everything* have to feel so good?

With a pathetic "Oh," I rolled out of bed and reached for my clothes, feeling Luis's gaze as I tugged the flimsy gray skirt over my head, and then the embroidered tunic.

"You move faster than a startled rabbit," she said. "What is your hurry?"

I turned to face her, feeling ridiculous as I slipped on my sandals. "Liana probably has patients waiting, so I should help. You have soldiers to train."

Luis sat up, letting the blanket slide down into her naked lap. For a woman who hadn't revealed her body to anyone before, she was remarkably comfortable, unaware her pink, smooth skin glowed. "The sun is barely up." She patted the mattress. "Let us talk."

Now she wanted to talk. I shook my head. "No, I..." I snatched up my cloak and unlatched the door, which sent Luis grabbing for the covers. "I must go."

Feeling like a character in a campy, B-grade movie, I hurried down the hall, my cloak billowing dramatically behind me. Of course, no one waited in the shed; far too early for that. I shooed away a cluster of red hens pecking the ground in front of the door, then let myself in. At least in here, by myself, I could think.

But my thoughts were just as muddled as they had been while I was lying next to Luis, or whatever her name was. Why didn't she just tell me? I could be trusted not to blurt it out in front of anyone.

I stretched a few canvases over the wooden frames I'd made from scraps behind the stables, then began a new painting. A few days ago the light had shone through one of the higher keyhole windows, turning the main courtyard's arches and columns into a forest of glowing tile. Twice I had to start over because I'd let perspective slip in and give the painting depth, so I bent over the canvas, determined to think as flat and two-dimensional as I could.

Would I trust Luis if our roles were reversed? What if it'd been 1943 in Nazi Germany and I'd be sent to a concentration camp for being gay? Would I have dared trust anyone with the truth?

I stared at the canvas. What a mess. Nothing was working. I flung my brush down and begin pacing the shop. I was not really married. There was no reason to stay in Zaragoza. Santillana, Santillana, I chanted. I'd let myself get swept up into a passionate affair with Luis because I was lonely. Separated from my life by over nine hundred and twenty years, I needed someone. Until I figured out how to get out of this mess, I needed Luis. She was strong, fairly sensitive, kind. I flushed when I remembered her other qualities, loosening the top of my tunic to get some air.

"I am jealous." I jumped at Walladah's voice coming from the open door. "You have the flush of a woman well-bedded. I'd hoped to be the one to turn your white petals such a deep red."

"Walladah." Behind her the courtyard was empty.

"Don't worry, my Kate. I am not here to harm you." She pulled her cloak tighter against the morning chill.

I moistened dry lips. "Hard to believe you entirely."

She had the good grace to make a wry face. "I was very angry. I do not always think clearly when in this state. No one has ever refused me before." She stepped into the shed, then lightly touched objects as she strolled around the room. "My only regret is that I drove you right into Luis's arms."

"They are good arms."

She stroked a clay pot filled with dried dandelion leaves. "Yes, but always clothed and in the dark, no?"

I couldn't help it. "Lamp lit, clothes off." Who knew I was such a braggart?

Her eyes widened. "My, my, now truly I am jealous." She stopped directly in front of me, a wicked half-smile on her face.

"I am married to Luis," I reminded her.

"I know." She sighed, tossing back rippling auburn waves. Weariness replaced the teasing in her eyes. "I come to offer congratulations and to ask for Liana's help."

"She isn't here."

"Who isn't?" Liana chirped as she bounded into the room, yellow silken robe flowing, arms full of fresh herbs. She froze and stepped back when Walladah turned toward her.

"Please do not be afraid. I come..." Walladah's face contorted. Asking for help from a harem woman wasn't something a princess did. "My father grows weaker every day." She looked down at her hands. "You heal animals. Perhaps you can heal my father."

Liana bowed belatedly. "Most respected Walladah, I am not a—"

"Please." She touched Liana's arm gently. "Please just come see him. You will not be punished if you cannot help. But his doctors are useless." I caught Liana's look of panic, and wearily, I agreed to accompany them. I already knew what we would find.

We stopped outside Mu'tamin's quarters. "He has been smoking opium for the pain, but even that does not seem to help any more." She turned to me. "If my father dies, Zaragoza will fall. My brother is too weak to defend us. So it is not just the loss of my father that I fear."

Musta'in sat in the corner of his father's bedroom, reading, eyes flickering briefly over me and the mother of two of his children, then back to his book. Three men in white robes attended to the emir, who looked terribly small in his enormous bed.

Walladah commanded the men to leave, eyes glowing fiercely, but they only went as far as the door. As Liana stepped up to the bed, I entertained a tiny hope that she could help, but at the sight of Mu'tamin's sunken cheeks and yellow skin, his ragged breath barely lifting his thin chest, my heart sank. Uncle Kevin all over again.

Liana bowed slightly, then bent over Mu'tamin, talking quietly with him. When she backed away, and a withered hand beckoned me closer, I bowed, then knelt at Mu'tamin's side. "So, my lovely friend. We must play chess again soon."

I smiled bravely. "I would like that."

"Perhaps I will let you win this time," he said weakly. He clutched at my hand, pulling me closer. "I saw you in the meeting with Hayib." I waited for his coughing fit to pass. "Have you finished the painting?"

"Not quite yet, but soon."

Mu'tamin's eyes fluttered closed, his voice the barest echo of a whisper. "Yes, it will be soon."

Once outside the bedroom, Liana's grim face told me I'd been right, but terror gripped her as Walladah expected an answer. Liana tried to speak several times but nothing came out. She pleaded at me with her eyes, clutching her robe in tight fists.

"Walladah, I'm so sorry," I finally said.

"What? He is not dead yet. Can Liana not help him?"

The harem woman took a deep breath and faced her princess. "My lord Mu'tamin has been ill for a very long time. I have seen this in others. I do not know how to help him."

The taller woman's jaw was set, her back straight. "He has only been ill for two weeks. I do not believe you."

Musta'in appeared in the hallway. "My woman might be right. He came down with fever last year after the raid on Calahorra."

"But he got better." Walladah's voice rose to a high, thin wobble.

"Remember the last Ramadan, when he felt too poorly to attend the feast?"

"He had a bad stomach that day, that was all." She glared at her brother. "You snake, you castrated goat. You want him to die."

"I do not," he snarled back, spittle flecking his thin lips. "I pray to Allah that my father recovers. But if he dies, then I will rule Zaragoza."

Walladah's fierce frown was venomous. "And when that happens, Alfonso will take Zaragoza. He will turn the mosque into a cathedral. He will let that ridiculous priest run the city. He will force us to convert to their filthy religion or die. He will close down every public bath."

Musta'in clenched both fists and raised one. "No, our uncle Hayib will help us."

"Hah. Hayib will only help himself...to Zaragoza."

Musta'in shook his head. "You are wrong. Besides, I have been studying defensive techniques. I—"

"Bah. In your position the only thing you can study is your own anus."

With a quick look back at the dying man, I gently steered Liana down the hallway and away from the furious siblings. Mu'tamin's children would never get along.

❖

My stomach began to growl around noon, but I was afraid to eat the noon meal in the palace in case I ran into Luis. I needed a little time, a little distance. I wandered through the marketplace, buying a steaming bowl of spiced lamb, a thick wheat roll, and a skin of wine, then pushed my way through the crowds until I reached a side street that led to a grassy ridge overlooking the Ebro. I'd just gotten settled, far enough back from the steep bank to feel comfortable, when a friendly voice asked, "May I sit upon your grass?"

Grimaldi, arms full of a meal similar to mine, waited politely.

When I waved him over, he grinned, revealing a missing lower tooth. "Good. This is favorite spot."

"It is beautiful."

"Clear is water, charming is banks, serene is sound." His loose-limbed body folded itself next to mine. "I fish here."

"Catch anything?"

"Never, but I hope muchly to catch something one day. But today, a meal by the river with you is just what I need." He settled his brown robes around his knees.

"Bad day at the Parish?" A family of ducks floated in the river below us.

Grimaldi rolled his bleary, round eyes, and it felt good to laugh. "Father Manolo is making me want to be crazy. I copy for him every record. I clean for him every window. It still not enough."

I chewed my lamb thoughtfully, savoring the garlic and rosemary. "Not enough for what?"

"He thinks pilgrims must do penance along the way. Helping him is penance. But I think I am slave instead." Grimaldi guzzled his wine. "I cannot stay Zaragoza for never-ending. Must keep going. Finish pilgrimage and return to France."

"And then?"

Grimaldi's eyes sparkled, erasing years from his weathered face. "Pigeons."

I bit into a slab of cheese, hiding my smile.

"I'm liking the pigeons. Send messages everywhere. Is good."

"How long will you stay in Zaragoza?"

"Three weeks more."

"Then where will you go?" I asked, offering the poor pilgrim half of my bread.

"Hah! You be sorry you ask. I have map. I love map." From inside the folds of his robe, Grimaldi pulled a roll of leather, then gently spread it on the grass before me. "Long ago I take boat from France to Gerona. Go to Ripoli, then bishopric at Urgel, then Vick, San Cugat, Barcelona." He jabbed at Zaragoza. "Am here now." His eyes twinkled. "Feel like here forever."

I smiled back. "You poor thing. Where do you go from here?"

He traced a path north, then west to Pamplona, Burgos, Sagrajras, Leon, then finally Santiago de Compostela near the west coast. As Grimaldi began to tell the story of St. James and Santiago, I stared at the map. Finally I interrupted the gruesome tale. "Grimaldi, do you know Santillana del Mar?"

He threw me a hard, appraising look, then his eyes warmed again and he tapped the northern coast an inch above Burgos. "Lovely coast. I like see, but no time." He sighed. "I see so much. I miss even more."

My heart beat faster as I stared so hard at the map the Burgos and Santillana points nearly merged into one. I was learning to ride a horse. I had ordered real clothes. And now, here, was my guide for a huge part of the journey. "Will it be dangerous?"

The pilgrim raised one gaunt shoulder, then pointed to a string of ducklings floating by in the fast current. "Every journey is risk. This one have no more or no less. But I not worry about future. I want to live *now*."

Grimaldi was a visionary. One thousand years from now he could make millions teaching people to live in the present, including myself. "Yesterday is history, tomorrow is a mystery, but the present is a gift," I quoted some card I'd read long ago.

He snapped his fingers. "Yes...a gift. What will you do with today's gift?"

I pondered my options while I finished my meal, then gathered up my leftovers and tossed them to the ducks. "I think I'll go look for my... husband." I'd made my bed, so had better lie in it. Until I found my future again, I had nothing but the present.

"Excellent." Grimaldi helped me to my feet. "And I will spend my gift studying. Only I will study in the mosque today. The good father will not think to look for his slave there." With a wink and a kind pat of my hand, Grimaldi strode away.

❖

As Rozinante and I walked up the hill, Luis stood alone, hands on her hips, watching her troops in mock battle below, dull sticks thumping awkwardly against leather shields, hoarse cries exploding when the sticks found their mark.

She threw up her hands. "Enzo," she shouted down the hill. "Tell them they fight like women!"

"That's pretty funny coming from you," I said softly behind her.

Luis jumped, then smiled in spite of herself. "You know what I mean."

"I'll forgive the insult, but only if you take a break and come riding with me. I need the practice." Luis's cheeks were ruddy from the sun, and had lost their pale glow from this morning.

She held my gaze for a moment, then looked back toward the mock battle. At her shrill whistle, Enzo looked up and nodded at her hand signals. "Effective communication," I said. We headed toward our horses, happily grazing in the shade.

"Shouting during a battle gets us nowhere." She helped me mount, then swung herself easily into her own saddle.

I tried to hold the posture Fadri had taught me as I followed Matamoros. "I take it your army needs more work."

"Relax your spine. Move with the horse. Yes, they do. Some days my task seems impossible."

"Today is one of those days."

She nodded. We rode along the Ebro, then turned north across a lush green meadow sprinkled with white clover and a plant with slender cornflower blossoms. It struck me again how clear and pure the light was in this country. Perfect for painting. "Any word on Alfonso?"

"No, but our messengers from Cordoba say the Almoravide Ben Yusef will cross into the peninsula any day."

"And then?" My lower back muscles began to burn and my knees ached. Why did Rozinante have to be so wide?

"Like water flowing downhill, soldiers on both sides will flow toward each other." For nearly half an hour, we rode while Luis explained the complicated politics of the emirs, the Christian kings, and the Almoravides. It made my head spin, but it was a conveniently impersonal topic. Besides, I'd simplified everything in my head, making whatever side Luis fought for the good side. But since Luis and El Cid were mercenaries, that side could change at any time.

Finally I shifted in my saddle, raising up to rub my backside. "I don't think I'll ever get comfortable."

Luis stopped. "When you left so quickly this morning, I..." She stroked Matamoro's thick black neck. "I thought you regretted last night." Her voice was low and serious.

"Last night was incredible."

Luis's intense gaze and lips parted in surprise made me smile. "Then why did you leave?" With her eyebrows knit so tightly together, her scowl could intimidate. Our horses started walking again up a slight incline, where a grove of trees rose up from the meadow like a layered wedding cake. I had no answer to give. "It's Anna, isn't it?" A muscle twitched along her jaw.

"How did you—"

"Soon after we met you mentioned Anna. I had thought you were friends only, but now wonder if you were...more."

"Yes, we were...are...were." Past tense. Yes, that felt right.

Luis dismounted at the edge of the trees and tied her horse. I did the same, groaning as my wobbly legs threatened to collapse. "Why did you marry me if you have Anna?"

My hand fit well in Luis's as we walked up a narrow rocky path weaving through the dark, cool thicket of trees. Rabbits fled before us, and the white tail of an alarmed deer disappeared among the trees.

"We each know each other's reasons for marrying," I said. "Anna and I grew apart." There was no denying to myself any longer. More than just time separated me from Anna.

"But you still care for her?"

"Yes, I will always care for her." I couldn't see Luis's expression as she looked straight ahead. We walked in silence until the path leveled out into a small clearing, a grassy patch of land surrounding a kidney-shaped pond, its edges lined with granite boulders. Flakes of mica and quartz flashed in the sun. Deep yellow movement caught my eye as finches flittered among the trees. A tiny spring gurgled as it fed the pond. We'd stepped into a magical grove, the kind you read about but never expect to see.

I dropped Luis's hand and ran forward. Sun sparkled across the surface of the clear, deep water. Tiny minnows darted away as I leaned across a warm rock to dip my hand into the ice-cold water. "This is delightful," I cried, gasping as I splashed water onto my face.

Luis leaned against a nearby tree. "It is where I come when I get tired of...of Moors and politics and Alfonso and battles, and..."

"And men?"

She returned my smug smile. "Perhaps." Totally secluded, the pond was hidden high above the meadow we'd crossed. Luis made no moves toward me, gave no hand signals as she'd given Enzo, yet I stood, dried my hands and face on my cloak, and moved toward her.

Luis's nostrils flared slightly as I stopped inches from her. "So you've brought me to your secret place." She nodded. We touched only on the mouth, but that was enough to set off a mad throbbing between my legs. Her tongue traced the edges of mine as her arms slid around my back. Breaking off the kiss, I lifted her tunic and unfastened the drawstring of her leggings. "I don't supposed you'd undress."

She chuckled, looking around the grove. "Do I look like a woman gone mad?"

"No, I guess not. This will have to do." I kissed her again, still startled at my own hunger. Our kiss deepened. My feet melted into the sandy ground, anchoring me as we wrapped ourselves around each other. How could she fit so perfectly within my arms? Finally pulling back for air, I smiled at Luis's naked desire. "My cloak will hide us," I said as I tugged Luis's leggings down her hips, "just in case we have visitors."

When Luis eventually found her voice some time later, she whispered, "Kate, I can no longer stand."

Giggling, I helped her slide to the ground, where she stretched out on her side, one hand pressed between her legs. "Warriors should *never* do this," she said.

"Why not?"

"If my life depended on it, if *your* life depended on it this very minute, I doubt I could lift my dagger, let alone a sword." She sighed happily.

"No matter," I said, resting on my side. "I would defend us."

Luis snorted, her face soft and blissful. "Your tongue would stop the first advance of any man, but he would soon return, sword drawn."

I sat up. "Then maybe you should show me how to use a sword, to throw a dagger."

"Swords are not for women." I raised one eyebrow and waited. "Perhaps not all women, but you, my pearl, are not strong enough"

I leaned forward, my blouse falling open slightly. "I'm stronger than you think." Before she could react, I pinned her to the ground with my hands and knees. Luis's eyes widened when she couldn't free herself. "Not strong enough, huh?" I said smugly. "What would people say if they saw the magnificent El Picador pinned to the ground by a mere woman?"

She stopped struggling, a chagrined smile revealing those pearly white teeth, the tip of her tongue. "They'd say the poor man has been bewitched." She licked her lips slowly, turning them ruby red and plump and wet. "Care to bewitch me again?"

Mesmerized, I lowered my mouth toward hers. Big mistake. My weight shifted, Luis rolled free, then grabbed for me. I slid away, squealing when she caught my ankle. Laughing and kicking, I only tangled myself in cloak and skirt. Luis flipped me onto my back, pulled up my blouse, pinned my flailing arms beneath me, and lowered her mouth. Another victory for El Picador.

Later, as I nestled against Luis, the world seemed far away, as if the grove had been carved from the earth and lifted into the heavens. "Tell me about Marisella," I suddenly asked, needing something to stay awake.

She refused, but I persisted until she sighed. "Not much to tell. A ward of Count Ordóñez, she was engaged to Gudesto. Before our exile, I spent a great deal of time at Gudesto's castle trying to raise money for Rodrigo's army. I was not having much luck, given Count Ordóñez's feelings about Rodrigo. I was bored, Marisella was afraid of Gudesto, and we started spending a few afternoons together walking around the castle." Luis sighed. "I had no intentions of seducing her, but one night, she came to me. I was lonely. She floated into my room, pale and beautiful, and I...Did I mention I was lonely?"

"You poor thing," I chuckled sympathetically.

"We spent the night together, but judging from her behavior and the lack of blood on my sheets the next morning, I had not been the first she had visited at night."

"Gudesto found out about you."

"Marisella told him. She thought I would marry her myself."

"You beast. Bed the wench then run away."

Luis lifted her head. "I was poor. I had nothing to offer her. And I was not really a man."

I bit her finger. "You married me."

"I was desperate." She laughed as I growled menacingly.

"So then what?"

"Gudesto tried to kill me, giving me these scars," she pointed to one on her arm, the slender one alongside her nose.

"And what damage did you do to him?"

Luis sighed heavily. "It was an accident, of course. I sliced toward his belly, but I slipped and well, I fear I might have cut off his penis."

I laughed so hard tears formed. "The whole thing?"

Her chuckling bounced my head up and down. "I haven't really asked him. I just know I connected with that part of his body, he screamed, and passed out."

"How did he survive?"

"He should have died, but he pulled through."

"No wonder Gudesto hates you." I dried my eyes, snuggling back against Luis's warm body.

"I left for exile with Rodrigo soon after, and Gudesto has been trying to stick me with his sword ever since. The closest he came was a few months ago. We had finished our raid on La Rioja when Gudesto and his men found us. That's why we took the southern route past Mirabueno, where we found you. The rest of my encounters with Gudesto you know about."

"What a nightmare," I said, rolling lazily on top of Luis.

"But from that nightmare, one glittering star emerged." She stroked my cheek, tracing my jaw, my neck, coming to rest in its hollow.

"That is so poetic," I said.

Her eyes narrowed playfully. "You wound me, woman."

I kissed her again to take the pain away, then reluctantly, we put ourselves back together, retrieved our horses, and rode slowly back to Zaragoza.

That night I awoke suddenly, freezing at the haunting sound. Had I dreamt it? I moved closer to Luis, then stopped. The half whimper, half moan that had dragged me from my dreams came from her side of the bed. I sat up in the waning moonlight. Luis's strong hands, curled under her chin, twitched rapidly; her eyebrows bunched together over closed eyes. I reached to wake her.

"*Laa*," she muttered, Arabic for "no." "*Laa*," she continued, mumbling something more I couldn't catch. I pulled my hand back. "*Laa, laa*," she repeated, then spoke words that raised goose bumps along my arms. A violent spasm rippled through her, then she fell silent, her face once again smooth and untroubled.

I rolled onto my back, pulling the covers up under my chin, feet and hands now icy cold in the moist summer air. I would have to check with Liana, but with my basic Arabic, it seemed Luis had said, "No, no, let me live, let me live."

CHAPTER FIFTEEN

Liana gave me an odd look but confirmed my first translation, "Let me live." As the days passed, I couldn't banish Luis's nightmare from my mind. She woke me twice more with loud moaning. I considered broaching the subject with her, but couldn't. Did I really need to know everything about her life?

A week later, after the third nightmare, Luis took me behind the stables, set up a row of small, round, pebbly-skinned melons on a few stumps and handed me a dagger. "This is yours," she said simply. I hefted the new dagger, disturbed by how well it fit my hand. "Consider it a wedding present."

I grimaced but nodded. Learning to defend myself made sense, but I doubted I would ever have what it took to stab a six-inch blade into another human's body. The ridges of thin, overlapping leather wound around the hilt were strangely comforting. As I tightened my grip, I expected the ridges to rub and grate, but the soft leather melted into my warm hand, reshaping itself to fit my crooked pinkie, my long thumb. "A Moorish dagger?"

"My design, but Moorish-made. Mu'tamin's sword-maker owed me a favor."

I ran a fingertip over the scrollwork etched down the blade's center, sliding lightly over pearls spilling from an open oyster shell. The edges of the blade gleamed from contact with a grinding stone. The dagger's scabbard, a small brown leather sheath, belonged around my calf, so I hoisted my skirt and tied the slender laces. "I feel like Indiana Jones," I muttered.

Luis showed me how to stab upwards under the ribcage. I imagined my sixth-grade Visible Woman model with the organs tucked neatly inside the clear plastic body, and I decided the liver/spleen wouldn't appreciate such a jab. Approaching my victim from the back, I was to stab downward between the ribs, near the backbone to avoid the collarbone, which would only deflect my stab and totally piss off my victim. "How's Mu'tamin?" I asked as I pretended to destroy my lover's kidneys, unsettled by the growing realization that every time Luis looked at me, my vibrating skin sent out wonderful tingles that started at my wrists and ended up caressing my neck.

"He weakens every day. Rodrigo curses him hourly." She turned my wrist, insisting I twist once I'd sunk the dagger in to the hilt. Her touch now had the same effect as her gaze, and my body buzzed pleasantly.

"Odd thing to do as a friend dies."

"Here, practice overhand on my back. Mu'tamin's son does not like Rodrigo, so if Mu'tamin dies, so dies our connection to this city, and we must look elsewhere for our living." Luis sighed. "Much as I hate to admit it, I shall miss Zaragoza."

I practiced my downward jab, stopping just before Luis's leather tunic. "Where are you going?"

"If Rodrigo leaves, we will follow."

"We?" I squeaked.

She showed me how to deflect a knife attack using one hand gripping the other wrist. "Of course," she said with a wink. "I have always wanted a camp woman to keep me warm at night. My bedroll is big enough for two."

"Animal." Rodrigo's moving campground, if it happened, certainly wouldn't head west and north to Santillana. As Luis showed me a few more stabbing movements, I searched for an opening. "Why are you so accomplished with the dagger?" I asked quietly.

Luis stopped to clean my blade, which I'd dropped in the dewy sand. "Had to be." She smiled ruefully, handing me back the dagger. "I am not strong enough to win a long sword fight, so I learned to shift my body to absorb a blow's impact with my hips and legs. But when swords become locked overhead—" she stopped, smiling. "Nuño nearly killed me the first time we trained together." She held both our hands overhead. "My power rests in my hips, but they are of no use to me in this situation." She dropped one hand to her side, retrieved her dagger, and touched the cold tip against my vulnerable belly. "But this is."

El Picador. In the future, that nickname would also apply to the person who pricked or stung the bull in a bullfight with long, colorful sticks. "Very effective," I said as we dropped our arms and I shook the blood back into my fingers.

By now we'd attracted every young boy running around the stables and a few from outside the palace walls. They dashed in front of me, I'm sure daring me in rapid Arabic to try to stab them. In just a few years, Arturo would reach this reckless age. Good lord, what was I in for? Would I be able to manage a teenaged boy? Would he even still be in my life at that age? Since I might move, or Anna might move, I had no guarantee my relationship with Arturo would even last.

I shook off my thoughts and focused on a more immediate worry. "So have you ever...let someone live?" Luis's face paled, then she bent her head to study her dagger.

"Come. Now we practice throwing." Luis shooed the boys off to one side and stood back, the tip of her dagger poised in the air. Frustrated, I said nothing as the knife flew from her hand and sunk hilt-deep into the melon with a satisfying "slush." An appreciative murmur rose from the boys, who slapped and punched each other.

"Now you try," she said. "Never take your eyes from it. Stare at it until your eyes burn."

I held the dagger gingerly by the tip. Luis had more secrets than her sex. As I raised the knife, the boys scattered with alarmed shouts, disappearing around the stable and over the walls.

"Thanks for the confidence, boys."

Luis stepped back off to one side. "Keep your eye on the melon."

I stared at the tan melon, sitting just below eye level, visualizing my lovely new dagger sliding into the firm flesh. I had learned to swing a golf club for Anna's sake; I should be able to toss a dagger thirty feet for Luis's.

Too early, the slippery dagger flew from my fingers, but I stared at the melon anyway, determined the knife would be where I'd aimed it. "Damn, where'd it go?"

"Into my arm."

"Shit!" The blade pierced Luis's left bicep. She looked down, amused, and pulled it out. Blood blackened her sleeve as I ran to her side. "Oh my god! What have I done?" I ripped off my cap and veil and wrapped it around her arm.

"Nuño warned me marriage could be dangerous," Luis said as I tried to stop the bleeding.

"Sit down. Hold this against your arm. Liana has salve and bandages in the shed." I helped her settle back against the white-washed courtyard wall. "I'm so sorry."

She pulled me to her with her good arm, kissing me roughly. "Sorry enough to give me whatever I ask?"

"I already *do* that," I responded with a light shove. "Wait here."

What a dolt. A golf club can't slice through human tissue. I jogged down the lawn and around the corner. My heart still raced as I bounded into the shed, stopping to let my eyes adjust to the dim light. On Liana's well-organized shelves I found the smelly salve and roll of rags almost immediately. As I reached for an herb Liana had said was good for pain, the door squeaked shut behind me. "I told you to stay sitting down," I scolded.

But when I turned, the shape of a large man was barely visible in the dim light. He stepped forward, leather creaking, mail and scabbard clanking, into the patch of light from the window, revealing sun-bleached hair, the long, Roman nose.

"Gudesto Gonzalez." My blood froze. My palms began to sweat. Calm down. He wouldn't harm me right under Luis's nose. My pulse pounded like a piston in my head.

"Ah, you remember me. I am deeply honored." His bow was shallow and insolent. He reached for my hand but I jerked back.

"How did you get in here?" I asked, thighs pressed against the table edge behind me. My nose wrinkled at the man's smell.

"As a messenger for Alfonso, I have a certain flexibility. But before I officially announce my presence, I wanted to first congratulate you on your marriage to Navarro."

"I'm deeply touched, but I'm busy, so why don't you go about your business." My hands felt clammy.

"Oh, I am, Señora Navarro, I am." As he stepped closer, his eyes narrowed so dangerously my heart skipped a beat. "You see, I am here to collect something."

His lurid smile told me exactly what he had in mind. He stepped in too close, violating my personal space. "In your dreams, prick," I sputtered in English. Grinning now, Gudesto reached for me, slammed one filthy hand over my mouth and grabbed my arm with the other, twisting it back cruelly. White pain shot up my arm, sucking all the air from my lungs. My knees buckled but he held me tight, roughly caressed my breast, flicking the nipple painfully, then probed my crotch through the flimsy skirt with his rock-hard fingers. Black dots clouded my vision as I gasped from the pain. Gudesto could dislocate my shoulder with little effort.

"I think, however," his voice barely penetrated my fog of pain, "that I will take you elsewhere to collect first rights. You will not cry out with pleasure," he chuckled lewdly, "but I certainly will. Let us find a more private place, where Luis will not interrupt our fun. I will certainly tell him later this is how he must pay for breaking his vows. Come, and watch your mouth. I would hate to harm such a lovely bride."

Luis! my mind cried out as Gudesto hustled me from the shed, down the path and out the palace gates. My shoulder, arm, and back burned, but as I stumbled along next to Gudesto, he tightened his grip even more, sending lightning-sharp stabs through my back. I moaned as he half-dragged, half-carried me across the main road toward the river. No one tried to stop us—a Christian soldier with a palace harem woman under his arm sent people scurrying away. He dragged me to a block of abandoned shops at the edge of town, then through tall grass that slapped my arms and face. When Gudesto finally flung me down, I curled up in the grass, clutching my throbbing shoulder, frantically searching for options. The low roar of water and the mill's loud "thump-thump-thump" told me we were right on the bank of the river. Luis— damn it! How long would she wait for me to retrieve a simple rag?

Gudesto flipped me over onto my back as easily as if I were a paper doll. "No one can hear our joyful cries," he said, eyes bright, breath ragged with excitement. I kicked and clawed and slapped, but when he slammed a fist against my face, the world exploded into yellow and black stars. Stunned, I shook my head. No one had ever hit me before.

Seconds later, the world came into focus again and I instantly regretted it. Gudesto knelt over me, his swollen penis released from his leggings. A thick white scar ran from the purple tip all the way to the base, but the penis was all there and clearly functioning. Unfamiliar panic rushed through me as Gudesto flung himself on me, pinning my arms beneath me with his weight. I growled in frustration as he whispered terrifying suggestions in my ear. "This is Luis's fault, you know," he murmured.

"Fuck you, you filthy bastard. Now get off me." I struggled to kick, but he'd pinned my legs.

"You tell Luis an oath is an oath." I could feel him hard against my thigh, and I suddenly realized there was nothing I could do. Not one damn thing. I had no sword, no dagger, no knight in shining mail, only, as Luis loved to point out, my sharp tongue.

A hand snaked up my thigh, raising my skirt with it. Focus! screamed my brain. Chuckling, Gudesto grabbed himself, lifted his hips, and thrust forward. At the pressure between my legs, I twisted and lifted my hips, sending his disgusting penis between my buttocks. He reared up with a roar and slapped me hard.

Blind with instant tears, I steeled my voice. All I had was my sharp tongue. "Your penis is ugly," I managed to gulp.

"You can also thank Luis for that," Gudesto grunted as he grasped my hip with one hand, the other wrapped around my wrists.

"Marisella wasn't a virgin," I said. He froze, lifting himself off me with his free arm. "Luis told me. Marisella had been with lots of men before him."

"You lie," he growled, but his distraction gave me the second I needed to twist underneath him and free my hand long enough to grab a testicle and torque it as hard as I could. How many more times would I be forced to harass this man's genitals? Gudesto doubled up and rolled off me with a strangled cry. I scrambled on my hands and knees through the tangled grass, then seconds later the earth turned to air beneath me.

I yelled as the river rushed at me, then I took a breath, splashed into the Ebro, and went under. Cold water and darkness and sudden quiet. Tumbling in the current, skirts swirling around my face and neck, lungs bursting, I saw light above me and kicked to the surface. Gasping and coughing, hair plastered across my face, I fought the current but could not reach the bank. One roar of frustration came from back where I'd fallen, but nothing more.

I tried the crawl stroke, but my clothes tangled in my arms and I gagged as water filled my mouth. I tried to dog paddle, but the swift current held me in its grip. After just a few seconds, my arms grew heavy, my legs refused to move as I bobbed up and down. Cool water washed over my head and I kicked wearily back to the surface. I went under again and again, each time my wooden limbs responding more slowly.

Then, somehow, I saw it, right in my path. Grunting with the effort, I lunged for the slender rope rising straight up from the water. Got it!

"Mon dieu!" The voice sounded far above me. I twisted the taut rope around my wrist before my strength gave out. The current pulled at me but the rope held. "I caught big one. Mon dieu! Help! Help!" I held my face out of the water. I was nearly drowned and he was crying for help. "Dear God, it is woman!"

Warm air hit my chilled skin as the jerking rope yanked me from the water up onto a muddy bar. I crawled from the water, my sodden clothes dragging through the mud. "Kate! Oh Kate!" Grimaldi's welcome hands reached for me, pulling me farther up the bank and out of the water. "Mother of God, I catch you like fish."

I sank to the ground, cold water dripping from my hair, running off my nose, then I lay back in the warm sun, eyes closed, as I struggled to breathe normally. The tall, lanky man sat patiently by my side until I finally stopped coughing, but I began to shiver violently. "Gudesto," I croaked, my throat raw from swallowing all that water. "Gudesto tried to collect his first rights."

Grimaldi grunted with anger. "I hate that custom. You choose river over soldier pig?"

"More or less." When Grimaldi helped me to my feet, we both noticed my soaking harem clothes clung to my body like a flimsy wet handkerchief.

"Ahh, here, you take cloak...Oh dear, yes, you cover." He lay the light cloak across my trembling shoulders. "You go back to palace," he said. "Dry off. Sleep."

I pulled the cloak tighter, clenching my teeth to stop the chattering. "Yes, but first I have one stop to make." Grimaldi escorted me back, steadying my elbow. But the nearer to the palace, the stronger my legs felt. Fury replaced fear and trembling. I waved Grimaldi off at the gate and stomped toward the stables, my sandals squishing, my damp skirts slapping against my legs.

Luis sat right where I'd left her, head back, snoring softly. "Hey!" I shouted.

Luis's eyes flew open and she leapt to her feet. "Holy Santiago!" she cried, looking me up and down. Mud-streaked hair, stinging welt across one cheek, soggy, muddy clothes, arm cut from rolling off the bank.

"Don't 'Holy Santiago' me! Where the hell were you?" I balled up my fists, and Luis's forehead wrinkled in alarm as she looked from me toward the shed and back again. "I fell in the river, Luis," I growled, my voice hard. "Which was damned lucky for me because Gudesto was about to rape me."

"Gudesto?" Suddenly alert, her eyes darted across the courtyard.

"Yes! Gudesto! With a penis!" I stomped my foot, too angry to care how petulant I looked. "Why didn't you come looking for me?"

Luis spread her hands innocently. "I'm sorry. I thought you were still in the shed, maybe talking with Liana. I did not hear anything."

"I *couldn't* scream. Gudesto was breaking my arm and ranting about you breaking an oath. What the hell is that all about? And why didn't you come?" I ignored the pain flashing through her eyes. "Were you waiting for me to call 'Lion King' before you got off your ass to check on me?" I was sputtering now, pounding my fists against her chest.

She pulled me to her, disregarding my soaking clothes and hair, and held me until I stopped ranting. We stood, quietly, while I took deep, shuddering breaths to slow my pulse finally to normal. Drained of adrenaline, my body slumped against Luis, and I began shivering again.

"Where is Gudesto now?"

I didn't know. But at a clattering of hooves and shouts outside the palace, we turned. Gudesto and four other soldiers entered the palace, flags flying, shields and armor glittering in the sun. Stable boys ran for the horses and three of Mu'tamin's soldiers approached. Gudesto's entrance was public enough that he could deny it was his second entrance into the palace yards. He dismounted, handed off the reins, then scanned the courtyard. He could not miss Luis and me clinging to each other at the far end. The asshole actually smiled at us, nodded politely, then headed inside.

Luis reached for her sword with a growl, but I restrained her. "No, not now."

She stopped, turning to face me and take my hands. "I will kill him some day," she said, voice colder than her sword, "for touching you." I shrugged wearily, so exhausted my body felt like lead. It was over. Luis's face was serious. "I have learned one thing from this terrible event, however." I waited, recognizing that twinkle. "I have learned you *can* save yourself."

I snorted, but returned her kiss anyway. All I wanted now was a good scrubbing by Ali, a soak in the warm tub, and a deep, long sleep in the steam room to cleanse my skin of mud, river water and Gudesto's touch.

❖

That night, as I nestled in Luis's arms, the warm evening breeze gently banging the unlatched window grill, Luis recounted that Gudesto's visit to the Aljafería was short but explosive. While I had rested, safe and secure in the harem bath, Luis refereed a shouting match in Rodrigo's quarters, where Gudesto had come with a directive from King Alfonso. Even though he was exiled, Rodrigo and his men were still sworn subjects of Alfonso, and Gudesto announced that whoever took up arms to fight Alfonso would be permanently exiled from Castile. A price would be set on all their heads. Their families would be thrown out of their homes, forced to beg for food. Rodrigo called Gudesto a lying, whoring pig, and Gudesto called Rodrigo a devil infidel dog. "Very creative," I murmured. "Then what?"

Luis sighed as she stroked my hair. "Then Alvar started yelling at Rodrigo, I yelled at Alvar, and Enzo and Fadri started in on Gudesto. Quite an ugly scene, actually. Alvar nearly drew his sword on Rodrigo."

Anna had called Alvar Fáñez "Rodrigo Díaz's most trusted first lieutenant." I closed my eyes, uneasy to know a tiny sliver of Luis's future without understanding what really happened or why.

"Finally, Gudesto drew his sword, his men drew, we drew, and the room held more bare steel than good sense." Another poetic thought, but this time I bit my tongue. "No one moved. Ten drawn swords in Rodrigo's office leaves no room for mistakes. Finally, slowly, I sheathed my sword." She stopped. "I just knew if I did not, we would soon slash each other to shreds."

Woman as peacemaker. I considered pointing out women's skill in resolving conflict without violence but held my tongue once again. "Gudesto wanted to run me through, but he, too, sheathed his sword.

Rodrigo and the others followed, then we returned to fighting with words. Gudesto tried to convince Rodrigo that Alfonso has raised an army of twenty thousand to fight the Moors and the Almoravides and that we will be slaughtered."

"You don't believe him?"

"Not entirely, no."

My eyes wouldn't stay open. "Then what?"

Luis had never talked so much. Her voice, usually low and calm, sparked with nervous excitement as she continued the story. I'd thought it was just the day's events, but then I realized it was more. The approaching battle could kill or maim her, and yet she trembled with anticipation. "Gudesto and his men left, Rodrigo punched Alvar in the face, and then we sat down to dinner."

I sighed. "You like to fight, don't you?"

Luis rolled on her side, throwing one leg over my hip. "Not really. Battles are bloody, noisy, confusing, and terrifying. But I love winning."

"What about when you lose?"

Luis kissed my nose. "Has never happened."

My mouth dried out to hear the quiet confidence of a soldier who had never known defeat. A perfect record was difficult to keep, and in the long run, the odds were against her. A night owl hooted from somewhere above us on the palace's roof. Luis finally talked herself out and fell asleep, but I lay awake, afraid for her, and afraid of how I felt whenever I was with her—so damned happy I thought I'd burst. Yet soon I would, of my own accord, walk away and leave her behind.

❖

We developed an easy pattern over the next week. In the morning I painted while Liana worked, then she returned to the harem, sent the children out, and Hazm and Tayani played ball and chased butterflies. Luis was gone all day, returning late at night, face and arms caked with dried sweat and dirt. We'd eat a light supper, walk briefly through the palace yards or by the river, then retire to our room, where Luis would collapse, too exhausted to undress. I would fall asleep quickly, but then wake up in the middle of the night thinking about Arturo, about Laura, about Anna. This relationship with Luis had changed nothing. I still needed to escape. I still needed to find my way to the Altamira cave. I still needed to get home.

One afternoon when the children and I re-entered the palace, Tayani skipped toward Mu'tamin's quarters. She didn't stop at my call, so Hazm and I hustled after the little imp, following her into the deserted throne room. Sun poured into the courtyard, converting the reflecting pool into a lake of diamonds. Tayani stopped, cooing in delight.

"May we play here for awhile?" Hazm begged.

Other than a few servants passing through, we wouldn't disturb anyone, so I nodded, dropping down onto a velvet cushion. Tayani and Hzam knelt at the pool's edge, pointing to the fist-sized goldfish flashing by.

I leaned back against the pillar, letting the sun warm my eyelids. Something unfamiliar washed over me; I tasted it, sniffed it, poked at it, and finally named it. Contentment. I was living over nine hundred years in the past in a Moorish palace with a female mercenary soldier and I felt content? I hadn't had a can of Diet Coke in weeks and could barely remember its taste. No Melissa Etheridge or Frou Frou or She Pirate CDs. No M&M's. I'd missed so many episodes of my favorite TV shows I'd never catch up, but I didn't seem to care.

I opened my eyes, smiling. The children had stripped leaves from a nearby palm tree and floated them in the pool, jabbering in Arabic. Anna had lectured me about being more attentive when we had children, and she'd lectured me about swearing less and kissing her in front of Arturo. I lay back on the cushion, trying to forget the damn lectures.

"Aiyee!" I jumped up at Tayani's cry and wet splash, covering the distance in seconds. Tayani's thin, dark arms flailed as she struggled to keep her head above water at the pool's edge. I grabbed both wrists and yanked her out, then dropped to my knees. Tayani pushed wet hair from her eyes, coughing and sputtering with laughter. "I fell in," she giggled.

Hazm hooted along with her. "Mama will be angry with you for getting wet," and this made him laugh even harder.

My heart still in overdrive, pistons crashing in my ears, I wrung out as much of her sodden skirt as I could, my hands trembling. "You sure you not hurt?" I finally said in halting Arabic.

Tayani rubbed her eyes, then tried to pull away, reaching toward the pool. "I lost my branch. It floated too far."

"Enough pool," I said, grasping each child's hand and leading them back to the harem. Liana only laughed at the sight. "You look like a monkey," she teased Tayani.

"I am so sorry," I whispered.

Liana patted my arm before stripping off Tayani's wet clothes. "This is how children learn, Kate. And what did you learn, my wet monkey?"

Tayani jumped up and down, spraying us with her dripping hair. "I can swim, I can swim."

"Tayani," Liana warned.

Tayani's dark eyes sparkled as she tried to look serious. "I learned not to lean out so far over the pool."

That night when Luis returned, I made her peel off her filthy clothes, which I gingerly moved into a far corner. "They will not bite," she said wearily.

"You don't know that." Then just as on our first real night together, I washed the grime from her face, dipping the rag in cool water, then stroking down her arms and legs. "Tayani nearly drowned in Mu'tamin's pool today. I wasn't watching and she fell in." God, I was *so* not parent material.

Luis stretched, unconcerned, as I scrubbed her back. "Children must learn."

I stopped. "You don't understand. It was my fault."

She arched forward so I'd start rubbing again. "Kate, you are marvelous with Hazm and Tayani. Life is dangerous, and we cannot protect a child from every danger. That is why they must learn."

No lecture? I stared into Luis's clear eyes, ran my hand through her cropped hair. Why had I ever expected Luis to be like Anna? I wet down her hair, brushing it briskly with another cloth, then I slid into bed beside her. But instead of slipping into my usual position nestled under her arm, I opened my own arms, patting my shoulder. "Come here."

Her eyebrows shot up, so I pulled her down close, wrapping my arms protectively around her. Stiff and tense, she didn't move. "Wait a minute. Don't tell me no one has ever held you."

A brief pause. "No one has ever held me."

"That's terrible." I stroked her damp hair, my heart aching for her ten years of secret life.

"I was the man to most women, so I held them."

I ran my hands over her back until she finally melted into me, settling her hips next to mine. We just lay there, breathing quietly. Then Luis drew in a long, shuddering breath. "What?" I finally said when she didn't speak.

She nuzzled even closer as my arm tightened around her. "Nothing," she murmured. I gave her a squeeze, waited until the brave, fearsome El Picador slept, then joined her.

❖

The Almoravides entered the Iberian peninsula two days later. As I headed for the harem to pick up Hazm and Tayani, two voices from around the corner ahead, low and tense with controlled fury, caught my attention. I tiptoed closer, hugging the wall so my shadow wouldn't give me away.

"The Almoravides are coming, Alvar. This is it. You swore an oath when you joined this army. I will not let you break that oath." I could imagine Luis's face, as stone cold as her voice, mouth grim. "We fight with Rodrigo, alongside the Moors, alongside the Almoravides."

Alvar's voice was more agitated. "What about the *first* oath you took? Have you forgotten?"

"Silence!" Luis snapped.

"Luis, I swore an oath to help you and Rodrigo fight *against* the Moors, not *with* them. This is not what you said would happen."

A pause. "I know, but we must stick with Rodrigo. He always wins. One day he will return to Castile, and we will fight for Alfonso again."

The young man snorted. "Your faith in Rodrigo runs deeper than mine, but stop and think. What are we doing here? You are the best tactical knight I know. You can devise sneak attacks that work. You can inspire untrained troops to throw themselves into battle. I follow you, not Rodrigo."

"This is just one battle. As Mu'tamin weakens, so do our ties to Zaragoza. Alfonso needs more men, despite what Gudesto claims. He must lift the exile soon."

Alvar dropped his voice even lower, enough so that I was forced to creep forward, feeling a touch guilty for eavesdropping. "Look at what we have *become*, Luis. We were the Four Caballeros de Valvanera, who swore to vanquish the Moors, one infidel at a time if we had to. But now look at us. Nuño was in Santiago when we were exiled, then became swept up in Alfonso's recruitment net. You and I live in a damned Moorish palace, eating their food, working *with* them. Gudesto is Alfonso's puppet, and hates your guts."

I stifled my gasp with a hand over my mouth. Four Caballeros de Valvanera. Luis, Nuño, Alvar, and Gudesto. Jesus. Luis and Gudesto had deeper ties than just Marisella. I held my breath as a scabbard knocked gently against the tile.

"Luis, this is wrong. Before we took Rodrigo's oath, we swore an oath to each other."

CV. Caballeros de Valvanera. Nuño, Alvar, and Gudesto—I shuddered—all likely had the same tattoo Luis did, a cross that ended in a deadly point as sharp as a sword.

"Mu'tamin pays us well. The chances we face Nuño and Gudesto in battle are slim, but frankly, I welcome the opportunity to fight Gudesto openly. I am weary of his games."

"Is it true he threw your wife into the river?"

"No, she jumped in to escape his...attentions."

The tone of Alvar's voice softened, and I grimaced in frustration not to see Luis's face. "She is just a woman, Luis. She cannot lay the claim to you that Valvanera can."

"You have never been married to her." Luis's voice was barely above a whisper, so I pressed closer, even though I knew I shouldn't be there. I didn't want to know any of this.

"You care for her that much?" Before she could answer, I whirled, appreciating my quiet slippers, and scurried back down the hall. I flew down the stairs and out the back entrance toward the pastures. Two shepherds and a dozen sheep looked up in surprise as I paced back and forth in front of the little-used exit. It was not my concern that Luis might feel anything more than healthy lust for me. We married to save our skins, that was all. And what I was feeling certainly couldn't be love—it didn't hurt, didn't make me crazy, didn't make me want to tear my hair out. Muttering, I resolved to pull back. It wasn't fair to Luis. Long distance relationships just did not work, especially one that stretched across nine centuries. Besides, my path led to the cave at Santillana del Mar, where I would leave this new life behind.

❖

To avoid Luis that afternoon, I played with the children in the palace yards, but out of sight of the stables. Hazm gripped the stick, facing my pitch with grim determination on his six-year-old face as I tossed the wadded ball of rags. Hazm connected with a thump, sending the ball bouncing, but his triumphant cry died as the ball rolled to Tayani's feet and she picked it up, giggling wildly as she ran into the orchard. The chase was on, and I rested in the shade while their laughter rang through the trees.

I took advantage of the peaceful moment to consider why I'd wanted to adopt Arturo. Part of it was pressure from Anna. I could see that now. But perhaps another part was because my own childhood had been so lonely that I ached to set it right by raising Arturo, giving him the attention a child needed. My heart had never burned to be a parent, which was why Laura had tried to tell me adopting a child with Anna would be like trying to put out a fire by throwing gasoline on it. "A person doesn't dabble in parenthood," she'd said. "Is having a child what you want, or just a way to keep Anna with you?"

"Kate! There you sit. I hear children and look for you." Grimaldi loped around the corner, reminding me of a Great Dane puppy I'd seen once, all legs and no coordination. He bowed politely then sat on the bench next to me. "You have been restored from swim?"

I nodded, smiling.

"I am to be sorry I think you big fish." He spread his massive hands. "I wait so long for fish." I offered him grapes from my bowl and asked about his work. "Father Manolo is so afraid of Almoravides it make me afraid. They kill Christians in towns they control. I go soon, before big war happens."

Damn! He couldn't leave yet. "How soon?"

"A week, perhaps. I must start gather supplies."

I wondered why my pulse beat so fast. "Grimaldi, could I come with you?"

Delight, shock, then embarrassment flashed across his long face. "Kate," he stopped, licking his lips nervously. "I flattered, deeply honored, but I steal wife of El Picador, my life be snuffed out like candle."

I laughed, patting his arm. "No, no. I just want to be your *traveling* companion. I must get to Santillana, but Luis cannot take me because of the exile."

Grimaldi leaned back, considering me through narrowed gray eyes, revealing a spark of something I'd never seen before. "What in Santillana?" I had the odd feeling he expected a particular answer.

I took a deep breath. "A boy."

The pilgrim's mouth formed a surprised "oh." "You have child?" he asked after recovering.

"No...maybe. It is complicated. I want to bring him from Santillana to live with us." I hated lying to such a decent soul.

"But I no go to Santillana."

I nodded, then swung my veil from my back to reveal my fanny pack. I hefted it so he could hear the coins. "I know, but I have money from selling my paintings. I can hire a guide in Burgos to take me."

Grimaldi stared at the fanny pack, face white as the palace walls. Then he met my eyes with such intensity I shivered. "I will take you to Santillana."

My heart leapt at my luck. "But it is out of your way."

"I want see cave paintings near Santillana. I go with you." When I slumped with relief, he patted my hand kindly. "This our secret, no?"

I nodded. "If we could leave after Luis and the army has left for battle, then he will not worry about me." Or be able to stop me.

"Does Luis know you have son?" I shook my head. "Why you marry Luis?"

With my admission of Arturo, this man already knew more about me than most. "To save my neck and his."

"You no care him?" Grimaldi watched the laughing children run toward us.

I couldn't answer, so I opened my arms to receive Tayani's hug. I didn't know the answer.

"There you are." Grimaldi and I both jumped with guilt as Luis appeared, straight and strong astride Matamoros. She nodded to Grimaldi, a relaxed satisfied smile on her face. "Grimaldi, may I borrow my wife for an hour?"

The poor man leapt to his feet, as guilty as if Luis had caught us naked in bed, and bowed. "Señor Navarro, I never keep man from such a lovely wife."

"I must stay with the children," I said lamely. Distance, Kate, keep your distance.

Luis leaned forward, saddle creaking. "Take them back to the harem. I want to show you the men. They actually look like soldiers today." Her eyes gleamed with pride.

I adjusted Tayani's tunic, then kissed her flushed cheek. "I do not have the energy to battle a horse today. I—"

"No problem." Luis slid back, patting the saddle in front of her. "All you need do is sit."

"I play children, take back to harem," Grimaldi offered. "Make great horse." He dropped to his knees and both children squealed with delight as they climbed on. It would seem I had no choice.

Luis dismounted, helped me into the saddle, waited while I arranged the stupid skirt around my legs, then mounted behind me. A tight fit, but not uncomfortable. I snickered to feel Mr. Sugar pressed against my buttocks as Luis headed us for the palace gates.

"You are impressed with my sweetness, eh?"

My snicker turned into helpless laughter as we rode through the gates, Luis's arms lightly around me holding the reins. Eventually I relaxed, letting my body move with the horse's gait. Luis took us up a few small hills, deeper into a small forest, along a path worn bare by hooves. Finally we reached the top of the hill and stopped. With the trees at our back, a deep valley stretched out below us, and sun sparkled on the narrow river that must feed the Ebro. On the far side, I could barely see women tending a vibrant vineyard clinging to the steep valley. Well below us in a huge clearing, looking like toy soldiers, Luis's new recruits marched, shields straight, heads high, as a drum beat a cadence. With a command from Enzo, the men broke formation, drew swords, and began sparring in earnest. Steel rang against steel.

"Impressive," I said, wondering why Luis was removing my cap and veil, draping it across her saddlebag. Then she swept all my hair back, baring my neck. "You've really shaped them up," I said. Warm lips pressed against my shoulder, then parted as she bit gently. "Ummm, Luis, your men—"

Her arms tightened around me, then my name, spoken huskily in my ear, shot shivers to the tip of every limb. Distance, Kate, keep your distance. "Here? I don't think—"

Her hands slid up and boldly loosened my chemise, baring my breasts to the sun and anyone in the valley who cared to look this far up.

"On a horse?" I croaked, cursing the weakness sweeping over me as she cupped my breasts.

"Why not?" she replied. Her fingers roamed and I responded. Damn. One touch from this woman and I wanted to rip off all my clothes.

"Luis, someone will see." I struggled to breathe normally.

"So? We are married." One hand reached down for the hem of my skirt, then slid up along my thigh.

"But what if..." Gasping now, I couldn't seem to form a complete sentence.

"First, no one will look up this far. But if they do, they will think me highly creative and innovative to pleasure my woman while on horseback." Her chuckle tickled my neck. When she gently took my earlobe into her mouth, then slid her hand even higher, all pretense of distance fled as I planted my feet on Matamoros's broad back and I no longer cared if all of Spain watched.

CHAPTER SIXTEEN

The days flew by as Luis prepared her men for battle, and I prepared for my journey. During a quiet moment I tried to sketch Arturo's face but couldn't remember what he'd looked like. Our time together had been so short, and even that sometimes now played in my head as a dream, not as something that had really happened.

I sold fifteen more paintings, a few in the shed, but most to Señora Tolón's customers after I brought some to her shop during one of my fittings. My clothes were almost done, and I nearly wept with relief when Señora Tolón draped the half-finished jacket over me for a fitting. As I wove my way home through the crowded, dusty street, I couldn't stop thinking of Luis's nightmares. She'd had another last night; the same plea again—"Let me live, let me live." Was it her own cry, or someone else's?

Liana and I suddenly had more business. When Grimaldi came in one morning with the priest's dog, I smiled at Liana's shy flush. They must have met when Grimaldi returned the children to the harem for me. Grimaldi's gray hair, freshly brushed, shone, and his cape was free of burrs and mud. The next morning he returned with a neighbor's goat, bloated from too much grain, then a shopkeeper's prized hen. Between his weak Spanish and Arabic, they could barely communicate, but the shop pulsed with electric energy whenever Grimaldi appeared.

"He is very nice," Liana said casually, cheeks even redder than usual.

"Very nice," I replied, hiding my sad smile. A harem woman had little choice in love. To pursue it meant slipping out secret passageways, risking sure death. I shuddered at the image of Liana's lovely head adorning a spike on the palace wall.

I finished the portrait of Hayib, working in the shed when Liana wasn't there. The painting wouldn't win any juried shows, but Hayib virtually leapt off a three-dimensional background so real even I wanted to reach my hand into it. Defeated, Hayib held a sword broken off at the hilt, blood dripping from the jagged cut as if the sword were bleeding. A bit dramatic, but I think I knew what Mu'tamin wanted. When the painting had dried, I rolled it up and tried to deliver it to al-Mu'tamin, but when I arrived, he lay unconscious, and Walladah and Musta'in argued in the corner. My first commission and Mu'tamin may never see it.

Painting had become a glorious escape as I slipped out of my skin, seeing through an artist's eye. I continued to experiment with colors, mixing soil for a yellow ochre, crushed aquamarine for a manganese blue. I began noticing the differences in whites. The whitewashed palace walls contained a hint of yellow, the white Zaragozan linen sold in the market held a whisper of rose petals.

One day I paced inside the shed, unusually agitated. In a few days Luis and her men would ride for Albarracín, then Grimaldi and I would flee Zaragoza. I began having frightful visions of Luis impaled on Gudesto's sword in the middle of a battlefield. Once Luis took her army to the southwest, Grimaldi and I would head northwest, so I would never know if she lived or died.

Finally I forced myself to sit down and attack the arch study I'd struggled with for days. Frustrated, I gave in and let perspective rule my brush. No one would see this painting anyway. The grove of graceful arches and columns from the palace's central courtyard came to life, and the sun cast a similar forest onto the tiled floor. I tried to capture the softness of a low afternoon sun filtering through a half-opened window screen.

Concentration is a marvelous thing. I forgot time until a few hours later. After washing out my brushes, standing, arching my back, then stretching my legs in a few side lunges, I turned back to the painting.

I gasped and took a step back. I'd been too focused on the individual details to notice what I'd done. This was the painting Carlos had shown Anna and me on our tour of the Aljafería, the one found so well-preserved. I sank to my chair, knees trembling. Which had come first—the chicken or the egg? Did I only paint what I remembered seeing, however unconsciously? Or was this painting the very one that had survived through the ages to end up in a museum?

I pressed my icy hands against my face, closing my eyes to imagine

Carlos's painting. Faint, but legible, the initials KV marked one corner. Me. And the painting had been inscribed "To E—," most of the letters worn off. At some point in the future, did I learn Luis's real name and inscribe this painting? That meant with each day she didn't tell me her name, she would live to tell me another day. But after I learned her name and inscribed it in paint, then what?

❖

That afternoon as I hurried to Señora Tolón's after siesta, the streets were clogged with people as the day's commerce began again. When I slipped into the soft cotton blouse, forest green skirt, and matching jacket, I felt like Katharine Hepburn, Joan of Arc, Amelia Earhart, Sally Ride, Ann Bancroft. My reflection in Señora Tolón's cloudy mirror blurred at the edges, but I could see enough to know I would conquer whatever lay between here and Santillana del Mar. I would find the ledge in the cave, survive that sickening dizziness, and walk from the cave into the twenty-first century. To do all this, however, I must leave Luis behind.

New clothes safely tucked inside my bag, I stepped from the side street, and was immediately swept up in a crush of people flowing nearly as fast as the Ebro toward the palace. A sudden cry came from up the street near the palace and was repeated by those around me. "*Sallimna!* Mu'tamin has died!" shouted hoarse voices. "Alfonso comes! *Sallimna!*" screamed a woman. Others took up the "Save us!" cry, and panic erupted as behind me people pushed forward, screaming and yelling, clawing their way toward the palace gates. Someone stepped on my skirts, knocking me off balance, and with a yelp, I went down as the crowd swarmed over me. Dust choked me as I struggled to my feet, only to be knocked down again when someone tripped over me. Defensively I curled up into a ball around my bag, crying out as feet tripped over my back, kicked my head.

I finally felt two strong arms grab my own and drag me off the street into a narrow doorway. I slumped to the ground, coughing, as a prematurely gray head bent over me, his ponytail falling into my face. I clutched at Grimaldi's hand, struggling to slow my breath.

"Kate, are you okay? I saw you go down, but couldn't reach you right away." He wiped dirt from my face with a trembling hand. "I thought you were done for. This crowd is wild with fear." I fingered my torn blouse, panting as heavily as Grimaldi. He was right. I could almost smell the fear. "We must leave soon, Kate. I've planned our route so we will go north a bit to clear Zaragoza, then head west. We'll have hard days of riding, but the more distance between us and Zaragoza, the better."

"Thank you for saving me once again, Grimaldi." I stared hard at the man.

"It is my honor. I am so relieved you weren't harmed."

I wiped the dust from my eyes. "Grimaldi?"

"Yes?" His breathing had returned to normal.

"You are speaking perfect Spanish. No accent. No grammar errors. Every definite and indefinite article is in place, every verb conjugated correctly."

The tall man flushed. "Oh. Must be excitement. I no speak goodly before." He tried to smile but I wasn't buying it. "Perhaps I can be rescuing beautiful women more times to be speaking more better."

I glared at him through narrowed eyes, but he only pulled me to my feet, towering above me. "Grimaldi, who are you?"

"I take you back palace." I waited, but he said nothing more, instead gazing out onto the street, now empty as the noisy throng must have filled the palace yards.

"I can get back just fine on my own. We leave in two days. What about Liana?"

"Two days," Grimaldi confirmed. "We go Santillana." Then he winked. "Then I return Zaragoza and Liana."

❖

Early evening, after I'd changed into clean clothes, Luis found me in the shed. I smiled at the sight of her tanned face peering in through my open window. "Did you hear about Mu'tamin?" she asked.

I nodded, surprised at my sadness, then lightly touched Luis's hair as she slumped against the windowsill. Finally she looked up, eyes weary. "The Moors do not have funerals, but there will be forty days of mourning." She rubbed her face. "I would like to take a ride with my wife. Would she come with me?"

"No," I winked, "but *I* will. If we slip out now, she'll never know."

Chuckling, Luis grabbed my hand and kissed it. "Oh, what a difficult choice—you or my wife. I cannot say who is the more lovely."

"Better be me," I growled happily, grabbing my veil and shutting the door behind me.

"Luis!" Alvar Fáñez thundered up in a cloud of dust and flung himself off his sturdy roan horse, nearly bouncing when he landed. "Mu'tamin is dead. There is nothing to keep us here."

Luis straightened, but weariness etched around her eyes and forehead. "You and I will not cover this territory again."

"Rumors are flying that the Almoravides have already retreated. That Alfonso has one hundred thousand men. That Moorish mercenaries join Alfonso to fight against us."

"All rumors. We stick with Rodrigo."

Alvar's face was dark with fury. "My lance and some of the others will *not* fight with you and Rodrigo."

Luis's sword appeared before Alvar could blink and pressed against the base of the man's neck. Still furious, but now white-faced, Alvar froze. Luis's voice was iron-hard. "As commanders of this army, we must show absolute faith in our leader. If we show doubt, the men fight poorly. If they fight poorly, they die." She lowered the sword slowly. "I want my men to live." Tension crackled between them. Finally Alvar blinked once, then stepped back. Without another word, he mounted and charged back the way he'd come.

Luis said nothing as I saddled my horse, but when we cleared Zaragoza, I broke the silence. "What will Alvar do?"

Luis sighed heavily, eyes focused on the far horizon. "He is too honorable to just take his men and desert, so he will likely challenge me either on the journey down or on the battlefield."

"So you will have to watch your back. Hard spot to be in with a friend." I wanted to ask about the Caballeros Valvanera, but found myself unable to form the question. I didn't want to know any more about Luis's connection with Gudesto than I already did. Besides, if I asked, he'd know I'd been eavesdropping. "Is your army ready to leave?" She shook her head. "Then why take time for a pleasure ride with me?" The path we took led, I knew, to the grove of trees with the pond.

Luis looked down at her hands, lightly gripping the reins, then into my eyes. "I leave in two days. While not probable, it is possible I will not return to you. If my time is to be short, I want to spend it with you, not with a bunch of sweaty, terrified soldiers." She smiled. "Besides, the image of you in this light will warm me even if I lay stone cold on the plain of Albarracín." She held up her hand to cut me off. "I know, I know. But if I am poetic, it is your fault."

We argued good-naturedly as we approached the trail at the base of the hill, then dismounted and walked up the path through the trees, but sadness nagged at me. What did Luis feel for me? Or me for her? We laughed a lot, we shared her secret, we kept each other company at meals, and found immense pleasure in exploring each other's bodies.

In the hidden meadow we lay in the cool grass beside the largest rock, sun heating the water, frogs croaking. Something passed between us as we gazed into each other's eyes, something I did not want to admit. No, no, no. Falling in love was not in my plan. It would ruin everything and make it all the harder to leave. I would ignore the intense tug deep in my gut whenever I saw Luis. I would banish from my mind the image of two pieces of a jigsaw puzzle happily clicking together with relief that they'd found each other.

Luis kissed me slowly, deeply, both of us in control. But when her hands fumbled at my strings, I tried pulling her tunic off over her head.

"No," Luis said, tugging it back down.

Fire swept through me, and I forgot all the good reasons to be cautious. "You leave for battle," I moaned, slipping my hands under her tunic and stroking with my thumbs. "Who knows what will happen." She struggled weakly, but I persisted until, urged on by each other's frantic breathing, we both lay naked in the grove.

❖

Later, curled up in her arms, I drifted toward sleep, relaxed, unbothered by the days to come. If I could bottle that feeling, it'd sell better than alcohol to any crowd. Part of me knew we should get dressed and return to the Palacio, but I didn't want this to end.

I woke up completely when Luis stiffened. "Wha—?" She cut me off with her hand. Voices. Male voices. Coming up behind us on what must be another path to the meadow. In a matter of steps they would arrive to discover two naked women.

"Stay here," Luis hissed as she scrambled toward the pond and slid into the water with barely a splash. I pulled my chemise over my head just as two men appeared at the trail head.

"We can get fresh water in the pool. Hey—Bareja! Look what else we can get at the pool."

I tugged the chemise down over my hips and reached for my skirts. The men, dressed in filthy leggings and tunics, whooped and covered the thirty yards between us in no time, so focused on me they ran right past Luis's clothes and sword resting on a rock by the pond. The shorter man, beard grayish and straggly, grabbed my skirts and flung them aside. "You won't need these for awhile."

I fought down a familiar panic, knowing I couldn't outrun both of them. This rape scenario got old quickly. My dagger was under my cloak, which we'd been using as a blanket. The taller man, face scarred and gnarly, knelt before me. "We're in a hurry, but we can always take time to court such a pretty lady." He stroked my calf and I slapped his hand away.

"In your dreams, prick," I snapped in English, my standard line in 1085.

His eyes widened as he circled my ankle with his hand. I tried scooting back, but now he held both ankles. I kicked and he flipped me backwards, leering up my chemise. At least that distracted him from looking toward the pond. My mind raced as I felt for the dagger beneath me. I had to get us out of this.

The shorter man began unbuckling his scabbard. "Me first, Dariz. You went first last time."

Dariz smiled, nodded, but didn't take his eyes from me. "It is a puzzle, a nearly naked woman, here, alone. Who will protect such a lovely flower?"

"I can protect myself. I—"

"Take your slimy hands off her."

The men whirled at Luis's voice, confused, until they saw her in the pond, only her head above water, her eyes fierce. "Holy Saints! El Picador!" Both men stepped back and I scrambled for my skirts. "We are sorry, Navarro. We did not know," Dariz sputtered.

"Bareja, Armendariz, you are a long way from Alfonso's army. What brings you here?"

"Business, Luis, nothing more."

"Leave now and I will let you live despite the insult to my wife."

Bareja moaned, slapping his forehead. "Your wife. Bullocks, we didn't know. We will go."

"Wait," Armendariz said, squinting at Luis, then back at me. "Why do you stay in the water? Why did you not come out and strike us dead?" I gathered up my cloak, finding my dagger and hiding it in the folds of fabric. Jesus, could I use it?

Luis laughed, sending shivers down even my spine. "Because you pigs are not worth interrupting my swim. I could come up there and carve out your eyes, slice your cocks in two, cut you each a new asshole with my dagger, but I am busy. Go now, before I lose my temper and do all that and more."

Bareja, sweating heavily, tugged at the other man's sleeve, but Armendariz, wary, shrugged him off. "Could it be the great El Picador has grown soft in his time with the infidels? Is he afraid to fight Alfonso's men? We are but lowly captains, but surely we are at least worthy of a small skirmish." My heart pounded in my ears, and I bit my lip when Armendariz grabbed me by the hair and yanked me to my feet. "Would you not even interrupt your swim to save your precious wife?"

"No, Luis, don't!" I shouted, struggling. I thrust the dagger at the man, but he slapped it aside with a laugh. He pinned my arms behind me. "Stay where you are," I yelled.

But she didn't. She swam forward with strong, even strokes, then stopped in the shallow end of the pond. "No, don't." I held my breath as she slowly stood, revealing broad white shoulders, firm upper arms, then two round perfect breasts.

"What?" Bareja cried.

She stepped up onto the grassy bank, water running down her small but female hips, dripping from her dark hair. Both men stood, transfixed, unable to understand why the head of El Picador topped a woman's body. Luis calmly picked up her scabbard, unsheathed her sword and raised it, totally naked, yet so glorious and beautiful in her anger and courage my throat tightened.

Armendariz recovered first, chuckling roughly. "So that is how things are. Well, the man who tells Rodrigo Díaz that his trusted El Picador is a mere woman will be highly rewarded." He drew his sword casually. "Bareja, you go first with this whore of a 'wife.' I'll slice up this black-haired cunt then take my turn."

He sauntered toward Luis, but then I had my own troubles as the fat man grabbed my hair and flung me back. "Let me go, you asshole." He grabbed at my breast and I kneed him, shouting a curse Luis had taught me, the one about the penis and a meat grinder. But the man was so fat he barely felt my knee. Onions and rotting food blasted me as I struggled. While steel rang near the pond, I searched the grass for my dagger, now beneath me.

As Bareja fumbled at his crotch, laughing and cursing, I slid the dagger from the scabbard. He flopped down on me and I wrapped my arms around him, dagger in hand. "That's more like it, cunt."

I groped for his backbone, but when I felt a confusing patchwork of metal, I realized he wore mail under his tunic. I couldn't stab him in the back. Suddenly, pressure and sharp pain between my legs.

"No!" I cried. Just as quickly as it began, however, the pressure disappeared as Luis kicked the man and shoved him off of me. She took my dagger and sliced the man's throat from ear to ear while I screamed as blood splattered over me.

Luis yanked me to my feet. "Quickly." She ran for her clothes, but I could only stare at the white, exposed windpipe, watch the twitching legs as a pool of blood soaked the grass. I picked up my cloak, sheathed the dagger, but couldn't move.

"Kate." Dressed, she grabbed my wrist. "There might be more of them." We ran for the path, stopping at the edge of the pond where Luis pulled her sword from Armendariz's dead chest. We flew down the path, leapt onto our horses, and thundered toward the river, my heart beating triple-time to the horses' hooves. A half mile from the pond, Luis suddenly reined in her horse and slipped to the ground, trembling violently.

"What's wrong?" I cried, dismounting awkwardly. Eyes massive in her white face, she touched my eyes, my face, my lips, my arms, with shaking hands. "I'm okay," I said. "I'm fine." I threw my arms around her to still the trembling. She held me so tightly my ribs ached, but I said nothing, squeezing her as tightly. She buried her face in my neck as I stroked her back, whispering soothing sounds, then I lifted her face, kissing her roughly. "I'm fine."

CHAPTER SEVENTEEN

By the time we'd returned to Zaragoza, Luis still shook, but from the fire in her eye, it wasn't from fear. We unsaddled the horses, then she stormed toward the palace. I ran to catch up with her. "Luis, what is the matter?"

She flung off my hand, giving me a look so cold I shivered. Now furious myself, I struggled to keep my voice down. "If you're angry with me, tell me why." But she kept walking, and I had no choice but to follow her to our room. She locked the door behind us.

Luis's glare unsettled me. "I was stupid to let you undress me." She slapped an open palm against the door, setting off a terrible rattling of the weak hinges, then leaned her forehead against the door. I leaned in closer, not sure what to say, since she was right, of course. Two men were dead because passion had carried us beyond reason. I reached for her, but she backed away, eyes black, mouth grim.

"Luis, what happened wasn't your fault."

"I know," she said coldly.

She might as well have slapped me. Heat rose up my neck and face. "You think it's mine."

She leaned forward, eyes snapping. "You led me to the grove. You seduced me again. You took off my clothes."

"That's unfair," I said, hands on my hips. "We did that together."

"I teased you once about bewitching me. I do not believe in witches, but I do believe I lose my head when you are near." She glared at me, her lean face grim. "A soldier cannot afford to lose her head, especially when her woman already has."

"Well," was all that could escape my tight lips. Luis swung the door open.

"I must go tell Rodrigo we saw Alfonso's men in the forest. Then I will sleep elsewhere tonight."

"Fine," I snapped. "Just fine." But when I lay down on the bed, alone, I started to shake with the memory of Bareja's heavy body pressing down on mine. My body ached, and the fact that I'd nearly been raped bothered me less than my inability to even wound the bastard who'd tried it. Why hadn't I sunk the dagger into his throat, his arms, his ass even?

Because I was pathetic, that was why. Because I didn't belong in this century. I curled up into a ball, trying to ignore the empty place on the bed next to me. But it mirrored the hollow burn in my chest.

The next afternoon the entire palace gathered in the massive courtyard while I hung back in one of the side chambers, still numb. Al-Musta'in stood on the raised tiled platform, his narrow face as pale as his white robe and turban, a man clearly determined to fill his father's slippers. Walladah stood next to the city officials, her jaw tight, her deep magenta tunic and skirt screaming in anger as al-Musta'in was officially named their father's successor in a brief ceremony. I missed al-Mu'tamin's calm, wise presence.

Other than a haunting song sung by a small group of musicians, few spoke as Musta'in walked among city and palace officials, acknowledging their bows and good wishes. Exhausted, I slipped down the hallway toward my room, but stopped at loud voices near the main entrance, arguing about Musta'in's right to lead.

I felt Luis beside me, but I did not turn. "It is getting more dangerous in the city," Luis said softly. "Stay in the palace from now on. People are on edge since Mu'tamin's death."

I did turn at this. "Don't order me around. Besides, I am not afraid."

"*Please* stay in the palace. You will be safer here, especially after I leave for Albarracín."

"And you will be safer once you leave." The words slipped out too quickly to take back or disguise as something else. "I won't be able to put you in any danger."

Luis's strong hand gripped me like a talon. "No more talk of yesterday, woman."

The "woman" set me off instantly. I flung her arm away, aware the fringes of the crowd had begun to stare. I stormed to the deserted end of the hall, Luis right behind me, so I whirled on her.

"So what if those two men died? You like killing. You do it all the time. It's your job, for Christ's sake. You kill Christians, and you probably kill Moors, too. You named your horse the Moor Slayer, after all." I leaned closer, poking her chest with my finger. "There's a lot I don't know about you." She raised one eyebrow, waiting. "For instance, you have a CV tattoo. I've seen it. Why this tattoo? And Luis, you talk in your sleep and have nightmares. Why is that?"

Inhaling, Luis stepped back as if I'd slapped her. The blood drained from her tan face. I'd never meant to bring this up in anger, but I couldn't stop now. "You say 'Let me live, let me live.' What does *that* mean?"

Luis bent over in pain, eyes wide, then almost immediately straightened, growling as she did. She grabbed the back of my head and pulled me close. "Do not ever say those words to me again."

"Who said those words, Luis? You? A Moor? A Christian?" My voice rose as the events of the last few days piled too high for me to handle.

She gripped my wrists and locked me in a furious gaze. "I may have once shared my bed with you, but the rest of my life is none of your business." With that she let go, stepped back, and strode away.

❖

The next day might have gone easier if Luis and I had woken up in each other arms, but instead, I slept alone, my body tired as I replayed our argument in my head. Why hadn't I been more sensitive? When a bulldozer drives through a greenhouse, not many tender plants survive. She'd been totally right. Hidden in that grove with Luis, I'd traded caution for passion and nearly gotten us killed. Yeah, I *so* belonged in this century.

Early morning sounds in the courtyard below finally cut through my fog—men shouting, oxen lowing, women yelling. I opened the wooden grille over the window and looked down at the courtyard filled with people loading wagons, saddling horses, shouting orders.

Our door banged open to reveal a wide-eyed Luis, face tight and focused, as if holding back a hidden pain. "Scouts report that Alfonso is advancing faster than expected. We leave today." She grabbed a cloth bag and began stuffing in a change of clothes.

"Today?" I squeaked, all oxygen suddenly squeezed from my lungs.

"Now." Done, she tied the bag shut and tossed it aside. She stood, a small, heavy sack in her palm.

"Now?" What about time to make up? To apologize for fighting? To talk long enough to work out the heavy knot in my stomach?

"Kate, listen to me. If I die in battle, I asked Rodrigo to cremate me immediately. I told him it was for religious reasons, but really, I could not bear to have my men find out my sex. So if I die, you will not have the burden of my body to bury."

"Luis, I—"

Coins clinked together as she put the heavy sack in my hands. "This is some of the money I have earned as Rodrigo's lieutenant. You will find he has been generous in sharing his spoils."

"No, I can't—"

"If I do not return, you must have this money. I also ask a favor of you. Should I die, send a message to Nuño Súarez, either at Burgos or Calahorra. Tell him the lands of my family are his, and that…" She swallowed suddenly. "…and that his friendship has given my life its only light." She touched my cheek. "Until you, that is."

My brain spun. How could she be poetic at a time like this? "This is too sudden." Just one more walk, one more teasing about poetry, the chance to fall asleep in her arms one more time. Outside the shouts grew louder and more strident. I flung my arms around her. "I'm sorry," I murmured.

"Me, too," she whispered, then she drew me into a long, deep kiss that warmed my core. Finally she pulled away, smoothing the hair back from my face. "Sparks fly between us, my pearl, but the fire will never go out." She kissed me again. "I must go. Come see us off."

Terrified, I practically ran to keep up with her as chaos reigned in the yards. Oxen bellowed and swung their heads as a Moor tried to harness them. Shields and helmets shone despite the gray day. Most of the horses were adorned with long drapes to make them harder targets. Some had dull gray mail hung across their broad necks and over their faces, two round holes revealing massive black eyes.

Hamara appeared with Matamoros, already saddled. At the far end of the yard, Rodrigo pranced on Babieca, Alvar mounted at his side motioning to the men, seemingly quite anxious to be going for a man so set against fighting Alfonso. The Zaragozan soldiers wore striped or solid robes with white, brown, or blue turbans, the white turbans a sharp contrast to burnished skin. The Christian garb was muted, but practical—chain mail hoods under their helmets protecting neck and throat. Shoulder and elbow plates, tied on with leather, flashed in the emerging sun. I clutched at Luis's hand. "What is the plan? Where will you go?"

With a terse roar, Rodrigo stood in the saddle, thrust his arm forward and somehow, about two-thirds of the horses, men, and wagons sorted themselves out and followed, raising such a cloud of dust they disappeared from view even before they left the grounds.

Luis held my hand. "Calm down, Kate. I have explained this before. Rodrigo and Alvar ride southeast to meet with Hayib, then on south to Albarracín. I take my men west to the border, just in case Alfonso tries to sneak in an attack of Zaragoza, then head south to join Rodrigo and the others. Hamara, have you decided?"

"I ride with you, not with Musta'in." The young man handed Luis the reins, then returned to the stable for his horse. A group of roughly-clad women gathered around another wagon loaded with fruit, sacks of flour, and cloth-wrapped meat.

"Why are these women by the wagons?"

"We may be gone a week or more, so they are along to cook, do laundry, bandage wounds, and..oh...generally meet the men's needs."

"You're kidding me." ·

Luis leaned closer, brushing my cheek. "No, but do not worry. After being with you, I could never return to...what I did before." Enzo and Fadri sat on their horses, waiting.

How could I slow this moment down? It would be my last, *our* last. "Luis, this is too sudden." She crushed me against her chest, mouth against my ear, while I held my breath, terrified at what she might say, heartsick at what she might not.

"I will return to you, my pearl. Alfonso shall lose this battle, lift the exile, then we will build a life together."

"Oh, Luis, I—" She cut me off with another kiss, ignoring the catcalls of her men, then let me go, gathered her reins and swung easily into the saddle. Unlike Rodrigo's dramatic exit, all Luis did was nod once and the entire group, with shouts and chickens scattering out of their way, flowed through the gate.

After the dust cleared, I ran to the gate, leaning weakly against the wall, aware that the rough stone grated against my skin but unable to move. The army disappeared down a small valley, then reappeared as they ascended the next hill. Red and gold mingled with the dull chain mail and Christian capes. At the top of that hill, a lone rider held up a hand, then broke away, galloping back toward the palace. As the rider neared, I recognized the flowing purple drapes on Matamoros.

Luis galloped up, reining in sharply, then slid nimbly off the saddle and pulled me into another kiss that left me breathless yet bursting with something I could not name.

"Kate." She brushed my hair back, then leaned forward, mouth brushing my ear. "My name is Elena." Then she was gone, flying back down the hill toward her men. My vision blurred and I struggled to breathe. She must live. She must live. I was not in love with her. I was not in love with her. I would never see her again. Ever.

Elena. Elena. I don't know how long I sat there, skin burning in the bright sun as I leaned against the wall, until Liana found me, helped me back to my room, gave me a glass of juice with a white powder mixed in, and I fell immediately into a dark, dreamless sleep, where I remained for hours.

❖

The palace and yards were oddly silent when I awoke on our bed, wishing a breeze would swoop down through the open window and cool me. Maybe then this horrible cold twist in my muscles would abate.

I slowly sat up. It must be the middle of siesta, which meant I'd slept for hours. With a heavy sigh, I rolled to my feet, knowing what needed to happen next. The future demanded it, and I would obey. I uncovered the three-dimensional painting of the arches, mixed a bit of black powder with water, and dipped my brush. "To Elena," I wrote, bold and heavy so it would cling to the canvas for ages. I signed it "KV."

Elena. I waited while the paint dried. A name as beautiful as she was. And I would never whisper that name in her ear while we made love. She'd finally told someone her name, but she would never hear me speak it. By the time she returned from Albarracín, if she did, I would be in Santillana, or Chicago.

After the paint dried, I took the canvas off the frame, rolled it up in a linen cloth, then sat back on my heels. Now what? The answer came almost immediately. I grabbed the edge of the secret door leading upstairs to the harem, and grunting softly, swung it open. With my purple flashlight I searched the walls of the dark passageway until I found a loose brick. I pulled it out, wincing as the rough stone grated against my flesh, then dropped the painting down behind the wall. It might have been fun to drop the flashlight down there as well to really mess up future archeologists and historians, but I decided I might need it, so I shoved the brick back into place.

I sat on the floor of our room, contemplating the incredible beauty of the carved window screen. Just last week it had split a shaft of sunlight into diamonds, ovals, and arcs of light that had danced across Luis's naked body. No. Across Elena's body.

She was really gone. I drew my knees to my chest, squeezing as hard as I could, but the tears still threatened. How could I leave the woman who'd captured my heart more quickly, and more completely, than anyone else? If Laura could have asked me to explain how I felt about Luis, I wouldn't have found the words, but would have just held both hands over my heart and rocked.

That was how Liana found me when she knocked sharply and pushed her way into the room bearing a tray of food. "You should eat." I sat up and wiped my eyes, ignoring Liana's concerned gaze. Nearly everyone had left to fight the upcoming battle, but the delicious food never ceased. The goat stew tasted surprisingly good and I emptied the entire bowl.

"Thank you," I said, "for everything."

Liana nodded. "I knew sleep be good for you."

I reached for her hand. I'd already lived through the hardest good-bye, so I might as well get all of them over. "Liana, I leave tomorrow with Grimaldi. He is taking me to Santillana del Mar."

Her black eyes widened, then narrowed into a deep frown. "I do not understand."

"I must go to Santillana. My son is there."

"Your son!"

I repeated the same lie I'd given Grimaldi. "My only hope of reaching Santillana is Grimaldi, for Luis is in exile and would be killed as soon as he appeared in Castile."

"Will you return to Zaragoza?" Her voice dropped to a whisper.

I sighed. "No." She glared at me harshly enough that I looked away.

"Does Luis know?"

"No." I lifted her delicate chin, now forcing her to look me in the eye. "And he must not. If he returns, tell him I left with Grimaldi, but please do not tell him where we go."

She sucked in her cheeks, biting them gently. "He will be angry. He will be hurt."

I swallowed. "I know, but you must promise." I waited for her nod. "Luis will understand, Liana. We married each other to save our skins, not for deeper reasons. He knew it was never meant to be a real marriage." Then what the hell was this deep ache in my bones?

Her eyes glowed as she considered me. "I do not believe you."

"To what lengths would you go to find Hazm or Tayani?"

"Until I breathed my last breath."

"Then you should understand. I don't know if I will find Arturo, but I must try." She nodded. By shifting the discussion to Arturo, I stood on firmer ground, both in Liana's mind and mine. "Liana, while I will not return, Grimaldi has said he will."

She nodded, eyes watery. "Will you say good-bye to the children?" A dose of children was exactly what I needed, so I left the dismal gray room and followed Liana to the harem.

❖

Slowly I packed up my bag with a few small paintings, two-dimensional to be on the safe side, a blanket, and my new clothes. Only when I finished did I recognize my nervous excitement. Life at the Aljafería had held its terrifying moments, for sure, but overall it hadn't been too bad. The palace was beautiful, the food incredible, the peace heavenly. Laughing with Luis, no, with Elena, every day had lightened my heart, something I realized only after she left. Life with Anna had not been nearly as joyful, but blind determination continued to push me down the path I'd chosen.

I dug out the painting of Hayib and rolled it up, sticking it into the waist of my skirt. One more duty, then I could leave.

Walladah stood in the middle of a crowd of servants, snapping out commands. Her quarters had become a hive of activity, quite a contrast to the courtyard outside, so I waited until she saw me. She waved away the servants and stood by the window waiting for me as I approached.

"You are busy," I said. Her brother had left the city in her charge while he was away fighting with Luis and the others.

"I am going to make the most of my brief time without His Weakness running things." She smiled, making it hard to remember that only weeks ago she'd wanted me dead.

"Are you afraid, with everyone gone?"

Her lifted chin and sparkling eyes answered before she did. "It is a relief to be in charge, if only of a skeleton army and a city emptied of all men of fighting age. I am taking steps to ensure Zaragoza will not fall while I rule in Musta'in's absence."

I ran my tongue across my lips. "I have a gift...from your father." She turned, delicate eyebrows raised. "I don't know if you will need it, or if it will even help, but..." I pulled the canvas from my skirt and handed it to her.

A strangled cry escaped when she unrolled the painting of al-Hayib. "My uncle, that bastard." She looked behind the painting, then at me. "You have captured Hayib's soul as you did Shajar's." Her eyes shone with awe at the terrible power she thought I possessed.

"No, at your father's request I just painted him. But if he or others believe that soul business, perhaps you can use that."

"You are right. This will help." She smiled sweetly. "I am so glad I did not kill you."

I snorted. "Me, too."

I returned to our room, and waited, too keyed up to do more than doze. Even the night owls and chattering monkeys fell silent in the late night, yet I could not sleep. My pulse seemed irregular, off, so I could not relax. But after a few weeks of hard travel, I would be home again. "There's no place like home," I muttered, finally drifting into an uneasy sleep where I wandered through my dreams, terribly excited and terribly sad.

CHAPTER EIGHTEEN

When the dark, swaying masses in the courtyard became almond trees, it was light enough to leave, so I looked once around the room to make sure I left nothing of the future, then closed the door behind me. My fanny pack rested under my skirt against my belly; my shorts and Doc Martens were packed in my saddle bags for my return to the future.

The stables were nearly empty except for a handful of Mu'tamin's horses and Rozinante, who nickered as I approached. Fingers trembling from the cold or fear, who knew? I slipped on her bridle, saddled her, strapped on my bags, and led her from the stable.

The few merchants up and about this early nodded politely, eyed me curiously, but said nothing as Rozinante and I wove through a labyrinth of side streets, blue and cool in the early dawn, until we reached the north gate.

Grimaldi, already mounted on a roan mare, waved from outside the gate. He'd abandoned his pilgrim gear for travel clothes—loose brown pants, brown leather tunic, brown cloak. "Good you come now. We leave before Zaragoza awake."

I swung my leg over the saddle, delighted with my split skirt. The pilgrim raised one eyebrow at my outfit, but said nothing. We crossed the stone bridge spanning the Ebro, the horses' hooves clomping softly. I turned to see if anyone would stop us, but as the city began to wake, no one gave us a second glance. I'd never imagined leaving Zaragoza would be so easy, and at the same time, so hard.

The narrow road ran alongside a stream that fed the Ebro. "We go straight north," Grimaldi said, "because Alfonso is west, Hayib is east, Almoravides south."

The mountains jutted toward the clouds, a soft mauve in this light. At the base of those mountains we would turn left, toward Calahorra, and eventually join the trail of pilgrims to Santiago. Before Burgos we would encounter the Ebro again and would turn north with it, toward Santillana.

In my brief time in the city, I'd forgotten how wild it felt out here—few roads, massive trees, danger possibly waiting at every corner. I must have gone temporarily insane to think I could have made this journey on my own.

We rode at what must have been a leisurely pace for Grimaldi, but my backside and knees had gone numb hours ago, and if I didn't stop soon, my bladder would burst. Grimaldi found a small clearing in the woods just a short distance from the trail. "It is cool here, a good place to rest in the heat of the day."

After squatting behind a bush, I felt better. Sitting cross-legged on the ground, Grimaldi shared slices of sausage, and I cut up the cheese I'd brought. After our stomachs were full, and we'd washed everything down with wine from Grimaldi's leather pouch, I lay back. The sparse grass tickled my neck as light flickered through the dancing green-yellow leaves above me. Birds chattered overhead, and some sort of jay scolded us from a low branch.

"So, Kate, what's in your fanny pack?"

I shot bolt upright. He'd asked the question in English, perfect English. And used the word "fanny pack." "What?"

"You guard that fanny pack like it's packed with gold from Fort Knox. Or maybe stock in Microsoft." He stopped, smiling at my confusion. "Or maybe Microsoft is no longer the investment it used to be. It's been awhile since I've read a *Wall Street Journal*."

"What?" I stared so hard my eyes watered. "You...you know?"

He stuck out his hand. "Walter Williams, Flagstaff, Arizona, but please, continue to call me Grimaldi."

My pulse roared through my head as we shook hands. "Oh my god, I'm not the only one."

"No, you're not. I came back in 1997."

"Nineteen ninety-seven," I repeated stupidly. It had never occurred to me there might be others trapped here as well. "How did it happen?"

My fellow time traveler stretched his legs, leaning back on his elbows. "Accident, of course, much the same as I'm sure yours was, in Mirabueno. But when I'd recovered from the shock, I saw what a great opportunity this was. My only family was a brother who never called, an ex-wife, and a girlfriend who I'd just discovered had been cheating on me with the UPS delivery guy. So I decided to stay awhile." He smiled crookedly. "I've always been a history buff, and what better way to study history than to live it?"

I rubbed my eyes. "You came back at Mirabueno but have never tried to return through Altamira?"

He shook his head, long, gray locks brushing his shoulders. "Not until now. Early in my stay, I tried to return via Mirabueno, just in case, but it seems to be a one-way portal. When I saw your fanny pack and realized how desperate you were to reach Santillana and the Altamira cave, I decided to take you there myself."

I chuckled softly, shaking my head. "Just like the Wizard."

"Beg your pardon?"

"The Wizard of Oz. Dorothy needed to get back home to Kansas, so the Wizard decides to take her there himself in his hot air balloon."

Grimaldi's guffaw echoed through the woods. "Exactly. Yet I have no hot air balloon, and no ruby slippers, I'm afraid."

I felt strange, almost light enough to float. "That's okay. I can't tell you how wonderful it feels to know I'm not alone."

"You don't have to. I already know that feeling." He pulled a few blades of grass and began braiding them. "When you asked so intently about Santillana, I realized you were from my time. I nearly burst with questions, but thought I should wait until we'd left Zaragoza."

"My butt still hurts too much to get back on a horse, so ask away."

The sun passed overhead and slipped toward the west before we'd exhausted nearly every topic possible. Sports, politics, world affairs, September 11, Iraq, medicine, new books and movies, hot stocks, and the latest food craze, which in Chicago had been breaded green peppers dipped in raw garlic juice. He explained how he'd wandered for a few months, trying on different personas until he found one that worked. He decided he was less threatening with a halting, foreign accent than if he spoke perfect Spanish, which he did thanks to his college major and an Hispanic aunt.

"Don't you miss anything from the future?" I asked. Movies, French silk pie, and books popped into my mind. Latin, Hebrew, and Arabic were the only written languages here, and I didn't read any of them.

Grimaldi sighed, cracking his massive knuckles. "*The New York Times* and peanut M&M's." Laughing and comparing junk food favorites, we ate another meal, then Grimaldi considered the sun. "We are hours from Zaragoza, so why not camp here?"

I agreed, grateful, yet embarrassed my tender behind was slowing us down. "I will toughen up as we ride more, right?"

After Grimaldi assured me I would, I gathered twigs for a fire, and we spent the rest of the evening reliving the future, or rather, our pasts. I told him about Roberto and his strange warning. We both agreed Roberto must have fallen back through Mirabueno. That he'd returned to the future must mean the passage at Altamira worked. I told him about Anna and Arturo, and explained the events leading to my marriage with Luis.

"That must have been hard for you, as a lesbian, to marry a man."

I chewed on the inside of my cheek. "Yes, it was."

"Yet you care for him." I nodded, terrified the cold cramp in my chest had not lessened since Elena had whispered her name. Damn it. I more than cared for her. I'd found that elusive other half of myself, and I'd left her behind. If returning to the future meant this ache would never leave, I wasn't sure I was strong enough to bear it.

We laid our blankets across from each other near the fire. "Grimaldi, what do you know of the Knights of Valvanera?"

Grimaldi rested his head on his hands. "Not much, other than their reputation for violence. They are before their time, actually, because the orders of knights don't really start forming for another century. The groups were formed to promote Christianity, but if I remember my history correctly, they also help pull all these kingdoms into a real country some day. Valvanera is a bishopric southeast of Burgos, in La Rioja region. Apparently Father Ruiz used to be good with a sword, so he attracted many young men with strong arms and a fierce motivation to fight." We talked until my bleary eyes could no longer focus on the slender thread of smoke curling up into the black sky.

❖

The next morning, suddenly impatient, I resolved to ride hard all day, no matter how my butt felt. "To Oz?" Grimaldi cried with a wink.

"To Oz," I replied, and we set off.

We'd only ridden a few miles, however, when Grimaldi reined in his horse and pointed to the east. "Ten bucks says that's no Boy Scout camp." A mile away in a kidney-shaped hollow in the woods, Christian soldiers moved about camp, taking down a small blue and white tent.

I stood in the saddle to see better. "What are Alfonso's soldiers doing way up here?" Dozens of Moorish soldiers mingled at the edges of camp. "With Moors."

"Zaragoza." Grimaldi swore softly. "They've come to take the city from al-Musta'in."

I dropped back into the saddle with a painful thump. "Oh no. Walladah. Alfonso and Hayib must be working together."

Grimaldi grimaced. "It makes perfect sense. Alfonso sent most of his troops to fight the big battle, knowing that Musta'in and Rodrigo will do the same. Then he sends a few select troops off to Zaragoza to catch her at her weakest."

Liana, Hazm, Tayani. "Is it too late to warn them?" I asked.

"I'm afraid so." Grimaldi nodded over my shoulder. "Especially since we now have trouble of our own." I whirled to see four horsemen galloping up the trail toward us.

With a grunt I dug my heels into Rozinante's side and hung on for dear life as she followed Grimaldi's mare. I leaned forward over her neck, grateful for the sturdy boots holding me in the stirrups. My eyes watered as my hair whipped across my face and the angry shouts behind us grew closer. Rozinante's pounding vibrated up my arms and legs as she ran neck and neck with the roan.

"Can we outrun them?" I shouted. Grimaldi's only reply was a grim shake of his head. A quick glance told us both we were losing ground. Then, without warning, something black and round slammed against the back of Grimaldi's head, and with a strangled cry he fell off his horse, rolling and tumbling like a body without bones.

"Grimaldi!" I struggled to rein in Rozinante and turn her around. Grimaldi lay twisted and quiet in the middle of the path, a pool of bright red blood spreading beneath his head.

"No! Get up!" I flung myself off Rozinante, grabbed a veil from my bag and ran toward him, passing an iron ball covered with spikes. Before I could reach Grimaldi, a soldier arrived, barely reined in, then grabbed my arm. I kicked as he pulled me onto his horse, dropping my veil as the man nearly ripped my arms from their sockets. "Let me go. He may still be alive."

The soldier crushed me to his chest. "You think so, m'lady? Hey, Aldonzo, the man wearing brown might still be alive."

Aldonzo slid from his horse, drawing a wicked dagger from beneath his mail. He casually knelt, smiled up at me, then before I could scream or plead or even breathe, he buried the dagger in Grimaldi's side. "Not any more, he is not." The man stood, then went for Rozinante's reins.

I gasped for air, but could not get enough. "No," I moaned. The man holding me whirled and galloped past Grimaldi's body, where a black wetness stained the front of his tunic.

"He is a Christian!" I struggled for air. "Does that mean nothing to you?"

"Not today," the man growled.

The ride to the soldiers' camp was brief but battering. I barely noticed when the horse stopped and I somehow ended up on the ground, my face pressed into the cool, loose dirt.

"Don Gonzalez, I bring you a whore to keep you warm tonight."

Someone pulled me to my feet and I found myself looking into the cold steel green eyes of Gudesto Gonzalez. Jesus Christ. Not again.

"Now, now, Martin, is that any way to talk about my future wife? And look, you beast, you have made her cry."

I slapped the hand that tried to wipe those tears away. "Bastard. I am already married. And I cry because your stupid Aldonzo killed a man for no good reason."

"Aldonzo, did you kill this fair woman's friend for no good reason?" His gallantry made me want to vomit.

"No, m'lord. He wore brown," came the amused reply.

"Tsk, tsk." Gudesto turned back to me. "One should never wear brown on Thursdays. Aldonzo always kills brown on Thursdays." He leaned closer, not a trace of amusement in his narrowed eyes. Gold stubble did nothing to hide the triumphant set of his jaw. "And since Luis will die at Albarracín by Alvar's hand, you will be a widow and free to marry me. Or maybe I will just make my own harem, starting with you."

"You are a sick bastard." I slapped his face as hard as I could, refusing to listen to his lies. Gudesto smirked and I threw my best punch, which only grazed his chin.

"Good. I like a woman with fire in her belly." He blocked my arm as I raised it again. "Martin, I have a special job for you. Take m'lady back to Hayib's. Keep her in the harem until I return and have time to deal with her. No one is to touch her. Is that clear?"

I pulled free and crossed my arms. Running would do me no good now.

"But m'lord, you chose me for Zaragoza. If I take this woman all the way back to Lerida, I will miss the battle."

Gudesto smacked the man's back. "You shall share in the spoils, my good man. Perhaps a bag of Moorish gold, or a harem woman?" The man grinned and agreed to Gudesto's request. Someone brought Rozinante, her sides still heaving from our flight, and I practically spit in Gudesto's face. "I am not going to Lerida. Take me back to Zaragoza with you."

Gudesto threw back his head, laughing heartily. "My dear, you delude yourself if you think you have any control over your fate from this point forward."

"And why is that, you prick?" I itched for Luis's sword. I could run him through. I would do it.

"Because," he shrugged, "you are a woman."

Anger surged through me as he tied my hands to the saddle. "You do not fear me because I am a woman." I leaned forward until I was right in his face. "That is exactly why you should fear me, asshole." He smirked and I vowed I would some day beat this man. Then he tied my ankles to the stirrups. "I cannot dismount."

"We can only hope, my lovely Kate, that you drank little this morning. Speaking of water, Martin, keep her away from rivers." He patted my knee and I squirmed away as best I could. "My lady swims like a fish." He seemed to notice for the first time my split skirt, which drew attention to my crotch as I sat on Rozinante. He smiled, winked at me, then slapped Rozinante's rump.

Still stunned over Grimaldi, I found myself led at a fast trot by a man disappointed he couldn't cut off a few Moorish heads. We headed east. Away from the caves. Away from my Wizard of Oz, who lay dead or dying in the middle of the road. Away from Luis/Elena, El Cid's most trusted First Lieutenant. Fear shuddered through me. Luis might suffer the same fate as Grimaldi at the hands of Alvar Fáñez, the man history recorded as El Cid's most trusted First Lieutenant.

❖

After two hours of picking our way southeast on a twisting, narrow trail, we reached the road that ran alongside the Ebro, and the horses began to gallop. At first I used my legs and knees to hold myself correctly on the slapping saddle, but soon my strength gave out and I bounced like a floppy, old teddy bear. After an hour I pleaded for a break, which he consented to only for the horses's sake. "I need to relieve myself," I said.

"We are not stopping. I might make it back to Zaragoza in time for the victory party."

Two hours later I had no choice. Urine warmed my thighs, soaked my skirt, and trickled down the back of my calf. Exhausted, sick, I slumped forward in the saddle, glad I was tied on because otherwise I would have fallen under Rozinante's pounding hooves. The man rode us hard, only slowing to a walk now and then to rest the horses. Once he must have led the horses to the river to drink, for Rozinante's neck stretched out low, but I wasn't able to lift my head or open my eyes. I willed myself to lose consciousness, but could not. I felt every jolt, every bump, as I struggled to keep Luis from my thoughts, but soon I could not hold back the flood of images, both real and imagined. Every time my traitorous mind showed Luis dead on the battlefield, I forced that image aside, replacing it with her astride Matamoros, leaning on her saddle, eyes twinkling at something I'd just said. She would not let Alvar kill her. She couldn't. El Picador would keep her guard up during the battle. But what about afterwards?

The sun sank behind us, yet we rode. The man stopped once to dribble water into my parched mouth, then we rode. Alternatively chilled then drenched with sweat, I gave up all hope of ever getting off Rozinante.

Not until the road ahead blazed with the gold of the rising sun did we near Lerida. An ugly gray castle, solid and foreboding, rose from the hilltop. Brown and red homes, looking meaner, rougher, without the whitewash applied throughout Zaragoza, circled the base of the hill. "Why a castle?" I finally croaked out through dry lips.

The man jumped, surprised I had a voice. "Lerida was Christian before the Moors ran it over." He grimaced. "It will be Christian again."

I coughed, wiggling fingers numb from gripping the saddle. "You resent the Moorish presence here, yet you plot with them to take over Zaragoza."

The man led Rozinante up a wide path leading to the castle. "Hayib is a useful ally, for now." Two soldiers greeted us at the gate, one on crutches, the other with a patch over his eye. My captor tossed the second man my reins. "This is Gudesto's woman. She is not to be touched or Don Gudesto will slice you open like a pig. Keep her in the harem until he returns. I'm going back to Zaragoza." Without a backward glance, the man took one of the guard's horses and headed back down the path to the main road. I pitied such bloodthirsty devotion to battle.

When untied from my horse, I collapsed on the ground, unable to walk. The men dragged me a few feet, threatening me, then finally, out of fear of Gudesto, the one-eyed man carried me to the harem and dropped me into a corner. I slid to the icy marble floor, ignored the grit and stench, and blissfully slid into an unconscious stupor.

CHAPTER NINETEEN

When I awoke, a young blond woman with dimples wiped my brow with a cool cloth. The face was thinner, sadder, but Hamara's beloved still lived. "Aisha," I whispered, clutching her hand. She nodded, smiling slightly, then looking to make sure no one had seen her do so. Her Spanish was bad, my Arabic was worse, but we struggled until we could make ourselves understood. "You are Kate, the foreigner from the Aljafería. Why you here?"

We were in an alcove of a larger room. Cold and gray, the walls repelled sound so the voices of thirty women echoed forty feet above us against the ceiling. I tried to explain how I'd ended up there, but gave up. "After you left, Hamara tried to rescue you."

Her hazel eyes flew open. "He would be killed."

"Yes, that's why Luis stopped him. Hamara misses you. He loves you."

Aisha bent her head, eyes brimming. "Life here is bad, but only because I cannot see Hamara every day, feel his touch..." She swallowed hard, raising her chin. "We will be together. Our love too strong, not be stopped." I didn't know whether to smile at her innocence or envy her strength. I closed my eyes, wearily welcoming the darkness, then opened them again when Aisha fingered the ring on my left hand. "Luis?"

Good guess. "How did you know?"

She shrugged. "When I use secret passage to Luis's room—you know about passageway?" I nodded. "He always ask how you are, what you doing. I see in his eyes he feel much for you." I said nothing, but gratefully drained the soup she offered me, even though it tasted of soap and rotting vegetables.

Stuck in a stupid harem again. Since I had gotten myself no closer to the cave at Santillana, only farther away, my despair cozied up to my anxiety and had such a party I began to think that I might really die, here, in the past.

Three days passed. I ate little, and not because it was the worst food I'd ever tasted. The two goons who guarded the door glared at me fiercely whenever I approached, making Abu and Suley seem like cuddly teddy bears. The large open windows revealed the bleak, barren horizon, which sent my spirits tumbling even lower, if that were possible.

Three stories down jagged rocks waited for anyone foolish enough to jump, so that exit route was out. If I ever got out of here, I could give up on Santillana. I could live in this time with Luis, if she survived Albarracín. What kept me flailing toward Santillana? Arturo, or sheer stubbornness? I did notice that Anna rarely entered my thoughts these days, which on some level horrified me, but also brought some relief. Although my commitment to Arturo was a slender rope pulling me back to the future, sheer stubborness drove me as well.

Finally one morning the two goons barked an order and all the women scrambled to their feet, adjusting robes and fastening veils. When one of the men tried to put a cap and veil on my head, I snapped it off, stomped on the cap, and ripped the veil in half. His eyes opened in alarm, but he left me alone after that.

When they marched us from the harem down a wide, echoing hallway, it became clear the castle was nearly empty, with ragged moth-eaten tapestries hanging on the walls, corners filled with piles of rotting wooden furniture. The cold and lifeless castle filled me with dread. Hayib didn't live here; he merely squatted in the castle until he could claim Zaragoza's Aljafería, a sparkling diamond compared to this lump of coal.

We entered a throne room which Hayib had transformed into a Moorish courtyard, where a large reflecting pool ran down the center of the room, and the columns had been topped with Arabic carvings. Hayib sat at one end of the pool, surrounded on the cushions by a handful of Moorish officials. In front of Hayib were the contents of my saddle bags. Thank goddess the fanny pack was still around my waist, since no one thought to search a woman for weapons. I was escorted to him while the other women flocked behind me.

Hayib held up a two-dimensional painting of Rozinante. "You paint this?"

"Yes. Why are you not fighting with your men at Albarracín?"

"Silence. It is not a woman's place to question what I do. Besides, I am in mourning for my brother al-Mu'tamin. I like painting." He motioned to the endless bare walls. "I may have you paint for your food."

"No."

Hayib's cruel mouth twisted. "You think you are under Don Gudesto's protection. You are not. Speak to me again like that, I will abuse you, slit your throat, and toss you from this cursed castle." The men laughed, and he waved me off, so I stepped back, jaw tight with rage. My mouth would likely get me killed, but it was getting harder to bite my tongue.

Hayib had kept his fat ass right here, waiting, while Rodrigo and Luis and Musta'in did his fighting. Even Gudesto fought while Hayib played. "You four," Hayib snapped. The young women selected stepped forward, and the rest of us were herded to large cushions in a far corner. The four girls removed their clothes, letting the silk fall around slender ankles. One girl was so young her breasts had barely begun to fill out. They lowered themselves into the waist-deep pool and began swimming, their forced laughter thin threads of sound curling above the pool as they "played" for the guests.

"I think I am going to be sick," I said.

"Gets worse," Aisha replied.

Hayib reached into a small, blue velvet sack and threw a handful of sparkling bits of color into the pool. With real shrieks of delight, the girls began diving for the pool's bottom, revealing everything of *their* bottoms. "Jewels," Aisha whispered. "Emerald, rubies, and garnets, easier to see in the water than diamonds."

Now I really was going to be sick. The men laughed and leered, discussing each round bottom, each "dusky rose flower."

"At least we get to keep the jewels." Aisha took off her slipper to show me hers. "Hamara and I will use these to start a new life together." I lay back on the cushion, hand on my forehead, stomach churning. Would Hayib kill me if I threw up?

Shouts down the hallway distracted Hayib from his sport, and forty Moorish soldiers, filthy from the road and battle, rushed into the throne room, followed by a small group of Christians led by Gudesto. My heart sank. I'd hoped he'd been killed.

"My lord!" A tall Moorish soldier dropped to his knee, dipping his head respectfully. "Zaragoza still stands."

Aisha and I squeezed each other's hands. Somehow, Walladah had held them off.

"Impossible," Hayib roared and the soldier winced, probably because Hayib was just the kind of man to kill the messenger.

"My lord, the townspeople fought back. They'd all taken refuge behind palace walls and repelled our every advance."

"Shopkeepers and wives? You were defeated by weaklings." Hayib spat at the man. "My niece was in charge. You were defeated by a woman."

The men bowed their heads to this most painful of insults. Gudesto stepped forward, his cloak heavy with dried mud. "Al-Hayib, bombs of burning fire rained on us. Arrows flew. They would not break."

Hayib stamped his wide foot. "Then you should have stayed. Worn them down. Are Alfonso's men as weak as my own?"

The Moorish soldier stood. "Also, Musta'in and his men had begun to return." I sat up straighter. Was the battle of Albarracín over? "And, m'lord, our men saw a terrible thing and lost all heart. I scaled the wall and ripped it down." Hands shaking, the man removed a canvas from his robes and began unrolling it. Shit. This would not be good.

I couldn't see Hayib's face, but when his own image confronted him, he staggered backward. The officials with him cried out, and a number of the harem women screamed. Not exactly the reaction to her work an artist likes to see. I held my face in my hands.

"When we saw Walladah had captured your soul, we thought you dead," the soldier pleaded, on one knee again. "The men ran, terrified. I could not stop them."

"You imbeciles!" screamed the raging man. He drew his heavily-jeweled sword and began slashing the painting. When he'd shredded it completely, he raised the sword high above the poor soldier's head, who closed his eyes in resignation. Aisha buried her face in my shoulder, and at a terrible thud, the women around me moaned softly.

Aisha whispered in my ear. "When Hayib starts killing, he does not stop."

"This deed was done by someone with a knowledge of the arts, by a spy, a sorceress," Hayib shouted, now speaking in Spanish. A chill ran down my arms. "Someone from the Zaragoza palace." He turned to face me, setting off more terrified moaning from the women. All but Aisha slithered away from me. "Bring her to me!" he bellowed, spittle flying from his mouth.

Gudesto reached me before Hayib's goon, yanked me to my feet and flung me over his shoulder, knocking the wind out of me. "My lord, this evil witch was to be my wife, so I feel responsible." He headed for a side exit. "I will deal with her."

"Peel the skin from her flesh."

"Yes, m'lord." He gripped my kicking legs. "Stay still," he hissed at me.

"Pulverize every bone in her body."

"Of course, my lord." He dropped his voice. "I'm trying to save you. Stop fighting me." As far as I could tell, upside down and struggling in the folds of Gudesto's cape, we left the throne room.

"Put me down," I snapped. Gudesto said nothing but quickened his pace. I lifted my head a few times, but recognized nothing, just more dreary hallways. We entered a more remote part of the castle with even fewer signs of life. He stopped before a massive wooden door, pulled a key from a hole in the wall, and unlocked the door. Inside, he dumped me on the floor.

I cussed as I landed on my hip. Gudesto's chest heaved. "I will do my best to keep Hayib from you until he calms down."

I stood, brushing the grit from my legs and hands. "What, you aren't going to peel the skin from my flesh?"

"Stay here," he barked, locking the door behind him. The only window in the narrow, rectangular room was ten feet up the wall, so darkness pressed around me. I felt along the damp wall until I found a stone bench, where I gratefully sank down.

Before I had too much time to feel sorry for myself, Gudesto returned with a rope and a lantern. I stood. "Excellent idea. Lower me out that window."

Gudesto put down the lantern and pulled me to him. "You are in a big hurry to leave. Why not spend more time with me?" He forced a kiss, hard and dry, which I paid back by jamming my knee toward his groin. He twisted to avoid me, then, with a disgusted snort, he let me go, sighing heavily. "Take off your clothes."

"Kiss my ass," I said in English.

He drew his dagger and pressed it against my throat. The cold metal stung as I held my breath. "Take off your clothes."

Slowly, carefully, I did, keeping the fanny pack hidden in the skirt as I slipped it down my hips. I tossed the pack and clothes onto the bench, then turned to glare at him, daring him to comment on my naked body. But instead, he grabbed my wrists, tied them together.

"Let me go," I pulled away but he held me fast. He stepped back, tossing the end of the rope over a massive oak beam overhead. "What the—" My arms flew up as he grabbed the end and yanked. My shoulders pinched as he tugged hard enough that my feet left the floor. "Put me down," I gasped. He lowered me a few inches, just enough for my toes to touch, then tied the rope off on a wall cleat. "Damn it, this *hurts*."

"Yes, I imagine it does." Gudesto stepped back, watching as I twisted slowly, unable to get much purchase with my toes.

"Let me *down*." What might have passed for sympathy crossed his face, then without touching me further, he left, locking the door behind him.

"Hey! Come back here!" I reached my toe for the bench but it was beyond my reach; the walls were even farther away. I yelled and cursed Gudesto until I was hoarse, then I added Hayib and screamed every Spanish curse I knew, every Arab curse I'd learned. No one came. My arms throbbed. I dangled there, hands and arms now totally numb, toes cramped from supporting part of my weight. How long could I hang like this?

Hours must have passed. I yelled and screamed but still no one came. I sang "The Star-Spangled Banner." I sang "Heard it Through the Grapevine" and "It's My Party." I dragged myself through the entire "One Hundred Bottles of Beer on the Wall." I recited "Jabberwocky" over and over, even trying it backwards.

My ankles swelled as the blood drained from the upper half of my body. My bowels cramped. Jesus, what had happened at Albarracín? Did Luis live? Had she returned to Zaragoza to find me gone? I squeezed my eyes shut. She was tough. She would be angry, and yes, hurt, but she would get over it. She had her career with Rodrigo, and her feud with Gudesto. Even if she didn't hate me for leaving, she couldn't help me. I'd told Liana we were heading west, so Luis would never come east to search for me. Or was it Elena that would never search for me?

Where the hell was Gudesto? With a sob of frustration, I finally released my bladder, grateful for the warmth on my legs. But the urine soon cooled and I trembled violently, damned tired of pissing on myself, then I translated *Green Eggs and Ham* into Spanish for Arturo. "And Arturo, this is your room," I babbled. "Max can sleep in here with you, but not on the bed. No dogs on the bed. And this is your closet. I don't go in closets anymore, but you can have one."

The light from the window above faded, and still I hung. My bowels cramped again and I grit my teeth. When I got my hands on Gudesto, I would squeeze his neck until his face turned blue. I would run him through with his own sword. I would kick his balls until he could no longer breathe. Would Arturo like baseball? Could I learn to play soccer with him? "My, you are a beautiful woman. May I call you Elena?" A horrible buzzing started in my head and persisted no matter whether I let it drop back or forward.

Finally, sometime in that endless night, Gudesto returned, his flickering candle pulling me out of my fog of pain. "Oh dear," he said with a delicate sniff.

My bowels had exploded earlier; there'd been nothing I could do about it. I raised my heavy head, snarling. "What did you expect? You left me here hours ago." The effort to form those words robbed my mouth of its last moisture. My lips felt fat, my eyes bleary.

"Here, let me lower you a bit."

I groaned with relief as my feet touched the cold floor, not caring what I stepped in. I lowered my hands to my chest, sending shoots of pain into my hands, a welcome change from numb. I gasped as Gudesto doused my lower body with water, cleaning the floor beneath me as well. He approached with a warm rag and began to clean me. "No," I sobbed with shame, but his touch was gentle and it did feel good not to be soiled. I swayed dizzily as he held a bowl of soup to my lips. I guzzled half the bowl, ignoring the liquid spilling down my chin and chest. "This is terrible," I choked.

Gudesto nodded. "Hayib's cook should be run through for what he does to food." I finished the soup, then drank the entire mug of brackish water he gave me. Enough feeling had returned to my hands that I could hold the mug myself.

Gudesto sat on the bench as I drank. I had to get out of here. "You know, Luis is not the person he seems," Gudesto said mildly. I choked on the last swallow of water. "You see him as this valiant knight, this great leader, but he has a dark side, a black murderous side." His mouth twisted unpleasantly as he chuckled. "That's the part I'll miss the most."

At least Gudesto didn't know Luis's true sex, but he used the past tense when he spoke of Luis. He couldn't know if she were dead, so he had to be bluffing. I struggled to focus. "I know about the Caballeros de Valvanera," I said. "I know you bear the same mark as Luis."

"You know nothing," Gudesto snarled, springing to his feet and ripping open his tunic. Where the tattoo should have been, a chaos of jagged white scars nearly obscured the small black cross. He closed the tunic, flexing his chest muscles as he did. "Since Navarro's cowardice ruined everything, I am no longer a Caballero."

Heavy exhaustion rolled over me in waves and white dots blurred my vision. "Please let me down," I breathed.

"I am doing my best to keep Hayib away," Gudesto said. "He is still furious and rants about you hourly."

"I'd rather face him than hang here," I said weakly.

"I am so sorry you had to wait so long for food. Hayib insisted we describe the failed siege in great detail. It will not be so long next time." He began gathering up the bowl and empty bucket.

"No, Gudesto, don't do this again."

"I must, dear Kate, but I will be back." He stroked my cheek briefly, tightened the rope again, then left.

I tried to shout, but had little voice for it. My back screamed. Snatches of memory tormented me. My mother's face. My father's voice. Their funerals. The silky touch of Luis's lips on my skin, or was it Elena's lips? Were they the same thing? Arturo's face, fuzzy and vague, a stranger's face, then I felt Max's wet tongue licking my ears. Hours later my body trembled and shook, hot one moment, then shivering the next, then just as quickly sweat would run down my back. The buzzing was so loud I could barely hear the rope creaking over the beam or my own feeble whispers…"Luis, Luis." Once, between sobs, I even whispered our coded plea for help, "Lion King, Lion King."

❖

Delirium. Nothing but pain. Images of the oak tree protecting my parents' backyard. Trees. Trunk. Strength. Laura's words that day we walked Lake Michigan's shore, "You're a strong tree, Kate, but every day Anna saws away at your trunk, little by little." Ridiculous, I had muttered. "Ridiculous," I muttered in my dank prison. "Not with a chain saw," Laura had said. "You'd hear that. But with a nail file, so you won't notice." Anna with a nail file smiling. Didn't care. Couldn't care. Nothing mattered but those pain-free moments when Gudesto lowered my arms. I lost count of how many times he came. At each visit he gently cleaned and fed me. After the longest interval ever, when he walked in I nearly sobbed with relief. "Gudesto, thank God." When he lowered my arms, I fell against his welcome warmth and he held me up, lifting me off my swollen feet. I lay my head on his broad chest, the leather cool against my feverish cheek.

"Hayib asks to see your severed head, but I put him off," he said, lightly stroking my back.

"How long have I...?" Buzzing filled my head.

"Four days," Gudesto said, his deep voice almost gentle. "But you have not always been conscious." Too fuzzy-headed to think, too exhausted to answer, I sighed once, then fell asleep in his arms.

When I awoke, Gudesto had gone, but had barely tightened the rope, so he could lay me on the bench, which he'd dragged under the rope. When I stood, I could lower my hands nearly to my waist and could stand. Filled with gratitude, I clung to the rope and slept in fits and starts, dreaming of nothing, thinking of nothing but Gudesto's next visit.

Hot flashes and chills continued to plague me. Exhaustion fed the buzzing in my head. My tongue swelled up. "Bwead!" I cried when Gudesto returned, what seemed to be the next morning, judging by the dust motes floating above me when I let my head drop back; or maybe it was the morning after. He broke off a small piece of the dry, brown bread, but my mouth was so dry the bread stuck to the roof of my mouth and I could not swallow. The next piece Gudesto put in his own mouth, moistening it, and I greedily took it when offered. I leaned against him as he fed me, murmuring appreciatively, weak with pain.

Then he untied one of my hands, letting it drop completely while the other remained raised above my head. I whimpered into his chest as he gently massaged my hand, arm and shoulder. Needles shot through every nerve, but in a short while I could wriggle my fingers.

"How much longer?" I asked, leaning into his strength.

"Soon, my love, soon," he said, stroking my hair, my naked back. He kissed me gently on the lips, and I responded, a surprising tingling running between my legs. I snuggled closer, desperate for his warmth.

"You are almost ready, my lovely Kate," he murmured into my hair. "Soon you shall be my jewel." He kissed the top of my head, sending delicious shivers down my spine. I sighed, resting my free hand on his chest, relieved the buzz in my head had receded a bit. His jewel. Diamonds. Emeralds. Pearls.

Pearls. Wait. I opened my eyes. Almost ready? My eyesight was as cloudy as my mind. He was protecting me from Hayib. Ready for what? Kate, my pearl. Then, like flood waters rushing over the top of a dam, reason returned in a blinding, tumbling rush. Jesus Christ, what was I doing? I stayed perfectly still, but my heart pounded so loudly I feared Gudesto would hear. My torture had nothing to do with Hayib. He'd just used the moment to confuse me. I was here because of Gudesto and no one else. I gasped as everything became painfully clear, but Gudesto, unaware, stroked me gently.

Christ. He didn't rape me when he could have. Instead, he set up this sick torture scene so I'd soften toward him. I moaned. Until this moment, his plan had worked. Today I was in Gudesto's arms, but tomorrow it could easily have been his bed. What better way to hurt Luis Navarro than to bed his willing wife?

Gudesto would not go through this elaborate scheme unless he knew Luis was alive. Adrenaline raced through me. Luis was alive. And since I was sure I'd hurt her enough by leaving, I would not multiply that pain by succumbing to Gudesto's plan. My breathing became ragged as I flexed my right hand while Gudesto's thick, grimy fingers played with my hair.

"Soon, my love, you will be safe and I'll have both your sweet arms around me."

I slipped my hand to his waist, as if to pull him to me. With a silent prayer and a deep breath, I grabbed the hilt of his sword. With a furious roar I drew the sword, stepped back, and swung wildly, one arm still tied above my head. Anger provided me with strength I should not have had.

Shouting, Gudesto stumbled back out of my reach as I cursed and swung the massive sword hard enough it whistled through the still air. "Come here, you filthy bastard. I'm going to kill you." My swings were wild and weak, but deadly enough to keep Gudesto back. He frowned, totally puzzled. He'd begun to believe his little charade as much as I had. "It's not going to work," I said, my voice as cold as the solid floor under my feet. "I am not going to sleep with you. You cannot hurt Luis that way."

Realization flashed through his eyes, followed by regret. He had felt for me what one would for a vulnerable, dependent puppy. But then his face set into firm grimness. "You will regret this," he said softly.

"Never," I snarled.

He paused, not entirely sure of me, then reached for the door with a sigh. "So be it. I shall bring things to a rapid close then."

"How?"

He stopped. "By telling Hayib where you are." The door closed and locked.

I swung the sword over my head but could not keep it there long enough to saw through the rope. I slashed toward the rope above the cleat on the wall with no more success. Finally, patiently, I used the tip of the sword, fully extended, to begin unwrapping the rope from the cleat attaching the rope to the wall. Every few seconds I lowered the sword, resting it on the floor until my arm stopped trembling, then I would lift it again.

Finally the last loop snaked free and I collapsed. Gasping in pain, nearly crazy with relief, I willed myself to stand, to move my legs, but I could not. I rolled onto my back and the world dissolved in a rush of white dots.

❖

"Señora Kate, wake up."

When a hand rocked my arm, I came to, confused at the cape thrown over my body. "Señora Kate, you must get up. We have little time."

I opened my eyes. Hamara's flushed face hovered above mine. "Hamara," I mumbled.

"Come, you must dress." He rose, bringing me my clothes from the bench. The fanny pack fell out, but he said nothing. I sat up, staring dumbly at the boy, sure I hallucinated. "Gudesto will return soon. You must dress."

My hands fumbled for my blouse as Hamara rose and turned his back. Every muscle in my body screamed as I slowly, painfully, dressed. "Hamara, I don't understand."

"I came to rescue Aisha, but when I found her, she would not come with me until I found you as well. It has taken me two days of avoiding Hayib's men to search all the rooms in this horrid place."

I could not manage the movements necessary to slip the jacket on, so Hamara helped me. "What of Luis? Are you back from Albarracín?" My voice was weak and thin.

"I am sorry. I do not know Señor Navarro's fate. I left him soon after we departed Zaragoza and rode for Lerida because I knew it would be my best chance to rescue Aisha. It took me longer than I thought because I had to avoid Alfonso's men." He helped me to my feet, but my legs, swollen as tree trunks, barely responded to my brain's commands. "Quickly, I hear them coming." Leaning on the boy's thin shoulders, I struggled to stay upright. He opened the door and a rush of fresh air filled my lungs. "Hurry, Señora Kate, we must hurry." Boots clomped in a nearby hallway.

I clutched at Hamara's arm as I half-walked, half-fell, down the stairs to the landing, turned to continue down the stairs, then stopped. Two Moorish soldiers, curved swords drawn, stood at the bottom of the stairs. Behind us, in a swirl of royal robe and Christian cape, Hayib and Gudesto appeared at the top of the stairs. Hamara slowly lowered me to the ground, drawing his sword.

Hayib guffawed. "This is beautiful. A Christian woman and a Moorish boy. Perfect."

Gudesto and I locked eyes, something passing between us that sent a flush up my neck. I'd almost fallen into his trap, and almost was as bad as doing so completely. We'd been intimate in a way I would never be with anyone again, and I hated him for it. Hayib was speaking, but I heard nothing as our stare continued. I hated myself for letting myself feel what I had, even though I knew what happened had nothing to do with sexuality and everything to do with power. Jesus, I even kissed him. Gudesto's bland, self-satisfied smile set my teeth on edge.

"—so they will make a fine example," Hayib continued. "It has been too long since our last beheading. Ibn, take them to the dungeon of this pig of a castle. Let them rot there for a few days until I can make the arrangements." He rubbed his hands together. "We can use this to weaken Zaragoza. Things may work out as I'd planned after all."

CHAPTER TWENTY

I gagged as the guards dragged us deeper into the bowels of the dungeon. The acrid urine, feces, vomit, and mold burned my nostrils as Hamara and I were flung into a dark cell. Something under the straw squealed and ran into the corner as I thudded heavily onto the floor. The cell's rusty iron bars swung shut with a harsh clank.

I struggled to sit up, but it was slow work; my body had forgotten how to move. Finally I was able to join Hamara at the iron bars, wincing at the damp cold as I grabbed one for support.

In the weak torchlight the nearby cells were clearly empty. "Halo? Anyone else here?" Hamara's voice echoed alarmingly against the dank, crude rock walls.

I sank back to my knees. My eyes stung to feel so weak—I'd always been proud of my strength and stamina, but Gudesto Gonzalez had stolen it all. "You should have fled with Aisha when you had the chance."

Hamara crouched beside me, warming my frigid hands in his. "And leave you behind? Never. You have done me far too many kindnesses for that."

I laughed softly. "Like sending Luis after you to bash you over the head."

The young man blew on my hands as I sank deeper into my body, shivering. "I would rather die by Hayib's blade than look El Picador in the eye and tell him I'd abandoned his wife."

I leaned back, coughing. "I think Elen—El Picador survived Albarracín."

"I am sure he did," Hamara said soothingly as he crawled away, scooping up great armfuls of filthy straw. "We must not give up hope." He began piling the disagreeable mass over my feet and legs, gently restraining my feeble attempts to stop him. "The straw will keep you warm. You must stay warm." I gave in when a vague warmth spread up my legs, so I snugged down deeper into my nest of matted, urine-soaked straw, and mercifully, slept.

❖

When I awoke, my nostrils were so plugged from the ammonia released by decomposing straw and manure, I could barely breathe. My eyes watered, my body ached as if I'd been run over by a herd of stampeding horses, but I was alive. Hamara slept fitfully, curled up in a tight, shivering ball beside me. Slowly, each muscle in my body protesting, I shifted my nest until I spooned behind Hamara's back, smiling as the lithe body unconsciously relaxed against my warmth. I pillowed straw under my head, prickly stalks jabbing my skull. Other than rats scrabbling over straw in the nearby cells, and a dull thumping above us, the dungeon was silent.

I closed my eyes and tried to sleep. What a mucked up mess I'd made of things. In 1085 people traveled all across Europe, Africa, Asia, yet I was too incompetent to get myself a few hundred miles to Santillana without pissing off some Moors, getting married, being attacked, kidnapped, and tortured, and now thrown into a filthy dungeon straight out of some swashbuckler movie. I railed at my lack of useful skills. I couldn't hunt. I couldn't kill anything, man or beast. I could barely ride. I could not seem to master the task of staying out of trouble in 1085.

We both drifted in and out of sleep since there was nothing else to do. I lost all sense of time, missing desperately the tiny shred of light filtering above me in Gudesto's cozy room. I was only vaguely aware that sometimes Hamara would leave our nest to relieve himself in the corner and pace the cell, then curl up beside me again, any horror at being so familiar with El Picador's wife long since abandoned in the bone-chilling air.

Luis. God, I missed her. Was she relieved she no longer had such an incompetent nincompoop for a wife? She was now free to search for someone who wasn't so stubborn, so reckless, and the thought sent jealous goosebumps down my arms What if I died in this dungeon and never made it back? Anna would care for Arturo. While she may not have been the best partner for me, she adored kids. She'd make an excellent parent. I was sure she'd already adopted Arturo, and they were both happy and safe in Chicago. How was I going to fit into that picture? Maybe I needed to let go.

Hamara mumbled in his sleep, and I shifted on the hard ground, grateful I could only breathe through my mouth, since I was sure Hamara and I smelled as bad as the straw. I tried to sleep, but could not. God, I had taken so much in my life for granted—no *everything* in my life for granted. I had often stressed over a few extra pounds, a boring assignment at an old job, a disappointing painting, a slight from Anna, without ever giving a single thought to how hard it might actually be to stay alive.

Later, the creaking hinges on the dungeon door woke Hamara up, and we both struggled to our feet, stiff with cold. Would this be more bread and water, or would it be an escort to the executioner's block? Part of me trembled in fear as the footsteps approached, another part no longer cared.

This time it was our food, which we snatched from the guard's hands, then settled onto the floor to eat slowly, savoring each bit of moldy bread, every sip of fetid water. I lowered my mouth into the cup, and let my parched, pursed lips rest in the cool water. Neither of us spoke as we finished, then we crawled back to our nest. Each meal might be our last.

❖

"Kate!"

I awoke in a daze, confused by the frantic whispers filling the cell. Strong arms swept me to my feet, and I stared into the most beautiful blue eyes I'd ever seen. Luis. Elena.

"Oh my god," I managed before she clasped me to her, breath hot and ragged as she pressed her face against my neck.

"Saint's Blood, I despaired of ever finding you." One of us sobbed, but my mind so reeled I couldn't sort out who. Our tears mingled as she kissed my ear, my cheeks, until I turned aside.

"Please, I'm filthy."

"You are alive," Luis/Elena said softly. "Do I have your permission to rescue you?"

I actually chuckled, which turned into a deep, rasping cough.

"Permission granted." That's when I noticed Hamara in a tight embrace with Aisha. "How?"

"Later. First we get out." She tapped Hamara and the two lovers separated. I squeezed Aisha's hand gratefully, and she tore her gaze from Hamara long enough to smile at me.

There was nothing like a rescue to pump up a person's courage and resolve, so I followed Luis from the cell and down the corridor of flickering orange torches. A Moor lay on his back by the door, throat slit. We stepped over him, then climbed the narrow stone steps, passing three more Moors with vacant eyes and bloody pools beneath them. I must have clucked or something at the third body, because Luis stopped. "Are you going to chastise me again for killing Moors to save you?" Even in this dim stairwell, lit only by the torch in Luis's hand, I could see the glint in her eyes.

"No." Fresh cool air brushing my face told me we'd left the dungeon, but no light save Luis's shone in the massive hallway. A night rescue. Feet tingling, I struggled to keep up with the others as we passed another half dozen bodies. Dazed, heart pounding, I half-expected Gudesto to loom up before us.

Since Luis had chosen her path well, no one appeared as we fled out a back entrance, mounted the four waiting horses, and slowly picked our way around the guard station, which was eerily quiet because, of course, that would have been Luis's first stop.

I somehow stayed in the saddle, and we rode in the moonlight for hours until we reached a small, protected grove. "We will be safe here tonight," Luis said. Hamara and Aisha dismounted, grabbed their bedrolls, and scampered off into the trees.

Luis caught me neatly as I fell off my horse. But when I leaned gratefully toward her, she held me off, her eyes cold as dungeon iron in the moonlight, her relief replaced by something sharp-edged and raw. Tension and pain wedged itself between us. My breath caught in my throat when I realized how desperately I missed our easy banter, our private warmth.

"I have dried meat if you are hungry," she said, releasing me when I found my balance. "There is a spring about fifty feet that way, where you can wash if you want. We cannot risk a fire, but I will give you an extra blanket."

I watched, stunned, yet on some level not surprised, as she set out both bedrolls a good ten feet apart. I found a rag and clean clothes in my saddlebag and stumbled toward the spring. I deserved this treatment, but it still stung.

The spring formed not much more than a puddle, but I stripped and plopped right down in the middle, nearly laughing in hysteria at the feel of water on my body. I scrubbed every inch of skin and hair, washing away grime and stink and urine. The only thing I couldn't remove was the sick feeling left by Gudesto. I dried my hair as best I could using leaves, then I dressed in the harem clothes, sighing at their silky thinness, but grateful they were clean.

Noises in the brush off to my left told me Hamara and Aisha were wasting no time getting reacquainted. I returned to Luis, awkwardly accepting a piece of dried meat. "Eat slowly," she advised. "I imagine your stomach is empty."

"You got that right," I muttered. Salt and garlic filled my mouth as I chewed, sure that I was devouring a slice of heaven. The noises in the bush now reached an embarrassing level, and Luis refused to meet my eyes.

Despite my ordeal in the dungeon, I practically hummed with happiness now that I was clean, full, and Luis sat here with me, alive and in one piece. Not even her dark scowl could dishearten me, since the Universe was gifting me a little more time with her.

"Elena, I—"

"Never use that name. My name is Luis." She stomped over to her blanket, rolled herself up with her rigid back to me, and said no more.

Groaning, I crawled to my own bedroll, curled up under the wool blanket which almost immediately warmed me to my core. I slept deeply, safe again.

❖

The sky had just begun to lighten, a pale blue free of clouds, when I woke up, inhaling wet grass, warm horses, and a sweet-blooming tree off to my left. My mind spun with thoughts of Elena, of Luis. How was I supposed to think of her? As Elena? As Luis? Luis felt more normal, but she'd told me her name and I wanted to use it. I sat up, stretched my arms to soak in the freedom. I started, however, at the sight of Elena sitting in the dawn's shadow below a cork tree, watching me. Her drawn face was blank and cold, sending shivers down my arms.

"Good morning," I said. She nodded, eyes hooded. "Hamara and Aisha still asleep?"

Elena stretched out her long legs. "No, they have left."

"What?" I scrambled to my feet, relieved I could stand. Only Matamoros and Rozinante grazed the moist grass in the clearing.

"If they return to Zaragoza, Musta'in will send Aisha back to Hayib."

I brushed dirt and grass from my skirts. "Where have they gone?"

Elena clenched her jaw. "South, to Cordoba. But why do you ask? So you can follow them and leave me again?"

I ignored the dig and shook out my blankets, concentrating on rolling them tightly so I wouldn't have to meet Elena's steady gaze. "Because I care about them, that's why."

Her guffaw was raw and cruel. "Oh, so you do care about *some* people."

My pulse raced as I turned to face her. "Elen—Luis. Of course I care. I care very deeply. But sometimes circumstances lead...people have to...I *had* to. Just *accept* that."

Elena leapt to her feet, face incredulous. "Accept that? Do you have any idea what I have been through?"

"You!" Blood boiling now, I flung down the bedroll hard enough it unfurled, then I jammed my fists onto my hips and squared off with my furious lover. "How about what *I've* been through? I saw Grimaldi murdered. I've spent days starving in a dungeon."

Elena waved her hand contemptuously. "Nothing compared to—"

"Nothing!" My voice rose to a shriek. I had hurt her terribly, but she had no right to do this. She closed the distance between us in two strides and grabbed my arms in her vise-like grip.

"You *left* me, Kate. I survived Albarracín, yet I came back and you were *gone*."

"Look, I'm sorry I hurt you."

"Hurt me? Why would it hurt me to have the woman I marry leave without saying a word? The woman I exchanged vows with, promised to honor and protect my entire life?"

I struggled but her fingers only gripped me tighter. "I can't tell you my reasons, but I had to go. I—"

"We are *married*. You can tell me anything."

"Elena, we are both women—"

"Call me that again and I will cut off your tongue. You endanger my life with your carelessness, as usual."

I was almost too angry to admit she was right, but she was, so I forced myself to see her just as Luis. "Look, *Luis*, we can't be married. We went through that ceremony to save our necks. That—"

Luis jerked me close, eyes blazing, and even through my fury I registered how beautiful and terrifying she was, her face only inches from mine. "That is not why *I* married *you*."

I tried pulling back. "No, Luis, don't."

Her icy eyes bore into me. "I married you because, from the moment I saw you at Mirabueno, half-dressed, spitting nails, bringing my best soldier to his knees, my heart was no longer my own."

I tried to cover my ears. "Luis, we can't—"

"God ripped my heart from my chest and put it in your pocket." She shook me again, lips thin with anger, but her eyes suddenly lost their chill. "I *love* you, Kate. That is why I married you."

I struggled to breathe. We couldn't be saying these things. They could not be taken back. Tears blurred my vision and I stomped my feet, breaking free. "Just because we love each other doesn't mean we get what we want. There is more at stake here. I—"

She clutched my hand, eyes wide. "You love me too?"

I whipped my arm free, my voice frantic. "Of course I love you! I can't stand to be apart from you. I hate it when I make you angry, which seems to happens a lot. You make me feel—" my voice cracked and I stopped. "But none of that matters because I can't stay."

This time she grabbed me by the shoulders and pinned me against the massive tree trunk, shaking me so hard my brain rattled. "You rip me wide open, showing me what it means to be loved *by* a woman, what it means to love *as* a woman, and you cannot stay?" The raw pain on her face shot through me, and I suddenly saw, with blinding-white clarity, what it had cost *Luis* to let down her guard and become Elena in my arms.

"No, I can't stay. *We* can't be."

With a deep growl of pain, Luis pulled me to her, our hearts hammering against one another. "We belong together, you and I. We are like two trees, entwined. We show our strengths to the world, our weaknesses to each other." My knees gave way at her words, and I sank against her chest. "I am strong and can fight and hunt. You cannot even catch a rabbit." She held my trembling body close, murmuring next to my ear. "Yet you have strengths I could never hope to possess."

I felt my resolve melting as she stroked my back, nuzzling my neck with her now soft mouth. Give in, my body breathed. Stay here forever, the trees whispered. You love her. You love this country. The air, the trees, the light, the color, the people. Stay, stay.

"No!" I shoved myself back. "I must go."

Luis reached for me, but I twisted away so fast all she caught was the hem of my skirt, enough to bring me down with her on top of me. The cold dew soaked through my clothes as I kicked myself free and leapt to my feet. It wasn't fair. I hadn't wanted to fall in love. I hadn't looked for any of this. I couldn't stay. I couldn't leave. She shouldn't make me feel this way. I don't know what to do, my mind screamed. I couldn't *take* this!

"Kate." Luis reached for my tear-streaked face, and I flung off her hands.

"I can't stay here. Don't you see? I don't belong here." I pounded my head so hard with my balled up fists that pain shot behind my eyes and a violent rage spread through my body. "I'm from the future. I have to go back."

Luis frowned.

Fury at myself, at Luis, at Anna, at Gudesto drove me on. "Yes, the future." I nearly screamed. "Guess when I was born. 1972." My laugh sounded near hysteria. "I won't be born for another eight centuries. *Centuries*, Luis, not years. By then you'll be dust. What kind of a future does that relationship have?" Through my ravings, I registered Luis's wide eyes and nostrils flaring in stark terror. She thought I'd gone mad. "I sat on a ledge in Mirabueno in 2006, and found myself back here. Insane but true! But my son—" I choked back a sob, "—or someone who could be my son, is back in the future, not here. Do you understand?"

Whatever she thought, Luis recognized hysteria and reached for me, arms open wide.

I jerked back. "You must listen. That is why I left you. My way back to the future is at Santillana. Grimaldi was taking me there when we were attacked." I began pacing the clearing, frightening both the horses and Luis. "I have to make you see. You must believe me."

Luis stood, watching me. "It is all right, Kate. We will go home. You need rest."

"No, wait!" I lifted my bodice, fumbling with the clasp of my fanny pack. "Come here." I dropped to the ground, pulling Luis with me. "Have you ever seen one of these?" Her eyes widened as I tugged the zipper pull back and forth, the black plastic teeth miraculously clicking into place. God, what a marvelous invention. "I'd wanted to show you this on our wedding night, but I was afraid." I opened it and drew out the postcard of the Aljafería. "Do you recognize this?"

Luis's breath drew in sharply. "Mother of God, did you *paint* this?"

"No, it's a photograph, an exact image of the palace using light and a camera and chemicals." My knowledge of photography stopped there. "Look." I turned it over. "Look what it says. 'Newly restored, the Aljafería is one of the few remaining examples of the Moorish palaces of the eleventh and twelfth centuries. And what's this date?"

Her eyebrows forming a fierce line across her forehead. "2005." She rubbed her eyes.

"And this." I pulled out the Lion King key chain. "This is the Lion King. He is a character in a...story from my time. He's made of rubber." Her mouth formed a perfect "o" at the tiny, bendable lion.

"And this," I said breathlessly, "is a flashlight. It is a type of... torch." Luis jumped back when I projected the small, narrow beam onto her chest. She ran her fingers over the smooth purple plastic.

"Is this carved of some gemstone?"

I laughed weakly. "No, it's called plastic, and in the twenty-first century, everything is made of plastic, even cars."

"Cars?"

"Never mind." I left the note from Paloma de Palma but pulled out the photo of Arturo and his drawing. Luis held my hand as I poured out the whole story about Anna and me, the orphanage, the cave, my childhood, Arturo. As I finished, a deep weariness settled in my bones. I could barely keep my eyes open.

"So Anna is waiting for you to return."

I sighed. "I doubt she's waiting, not after this long. And besides," I met Luis's clear gaze and held it. "Even if I do get back, I cannot...be with her any more. Not after...us." I cleared my throat. "But Arturo, my friends, my life, my dog, my future, my paints…"

By now the sun had lifted high enough so that our clearing had dried of dew and was beginning to heat up. I could barely lift my head. "We should go," I mumbled. But Luis drew me into her strong arms and held me until we were both soaked with my tears. Exhausted, I finally stopped, breathed slowly through my mouth, willing time to stop, to keep me suspended forever in this blessed relief, incredible release, and absolute safety.

❖

I must have slept for hours but finally awoke, wrapped in my blanket. Birds chattered happily in the grove around us. Luis sat beside me, the flashlight disassembled in her lap. When she saw me stir, she held up the battery. "Does this light up the plastic torch?"

"Yes," I said, grinning sleepily at the intense wonder on her face. "It's called a battery." She put the flashlight back together, but it no longer worked.

She gasped. "Holy Saints, I have broken it."

I showed her the positive end of the battery needed to connect to the copper disk inside the flashlight. She sighed with relief when it lit up at her touch. Then she returned it to my fanny pack, opening and closing the zipper several times. Finally she took my hands in hers and I gasped at the power of her simple touch. Now that the word love had actually been spoken, it was as if every pore in my body had swelled, plump and satisfied.

"You really are from the future," she said.

"Yes."

She nodded pensively, then brushed my cheek lightly. "If people knew the future held such beauty, they would try to live forever."

My blush started, but I held her gaze. "You must recite something at the next banquet."

She snorted, then smiled. "El Picador has a reputation to uphold, but that does not include poetry." She pursed her lips. "I have been thinking while you slept. The night Nuño and I caught you trying to escape—"

"I was trying to get to Santillana."

"And when you got most intimate with Walladah even after I warned you?"

"I was trying to get to Santillana."

"And when you left with Grimaldi?"

"I was trying to get to Santillana."

She wore a pained expression. "Not having much luck, are you?" I shook my head. She stretched out her legs, then flashed me a wicked grin. "Your luck is about to change."

"Says who?" I replied, suddenly grumpy. "Are you my fortune teller?"

She jumped up and pulled me to my feet. "No, I am your guide." She held my hands to her chest, eyes serious again. "The only way to ease your pain, my pearl, is to take you to Santillana del Mar myself."

"But—" She silenced my protest with a kiss so fierce it left us both breathless. When I pulled away, there was no mistaking the determination on Luis's face. She was totally serious.

If Luis set out to get me to Santillana, I would reach the Altamira cave. I would find a ledge, sit down on it, pass out with dizziness and end up back in the twenty-first century. Instead of jubilation, however, deep sadness filled the marrow of my bones. I was going home.

CHAPTER TWENTY-ONE

An hour later, as Rozinante slowly followed the narrow path winding through the forest, I tried to talk Luis out of it. "We'd have to go right through La Rioja, where Gudesto hates your guts. Then we'd have to go through part of Castile and León, where Alfonso hates your guts. It's too dangerous." She shrugged off my concern, and pointed to a herd of tiny deer moving parallel to us, barely visible through the underbrush.

Despite her stubbornness, I was almost giddy with relief Luis knew my secret. But now that my return to my own time was practically assured, I didn't know what I wanted anymore. I didn't belong in this century. I couldn't feed myself. I couldn't defend myself. I couldn't travel. I was pathetic. I couldn't do anything without help. As a woman I had no real rights. Chocolate didn't exist, at least not on this continent. Luis lived a beyond-dangerous life and could be killed at any moment. Only a fool would choose to stay.

But to leave this century was to leave Luis.

"What makes you think we can reach Santillana?" I lifted my face toward the sun as the elm trees fell away into a meadow of switchgrass. "Grimaldi and I could not."

"I am not Grimaldi," Luis said, and my heart fluttered at the look she gave me. I'd never known a heart could do that. I'd thought it was just a cliché romance writers used. But when she looked at me with such strength and desire and need, my heart's rhythm faltered until I pressed a hand against my chest, reminding my ticker to keep ticking.

Luis squinted in a patch of sunlight. "Kate, I need to ask. You spent days in that dungeon. Did Hayib or Gudesto harm you?"

I pressed my lips together. I had expected this. Yes, Luis, he did, but not in the way you imagined. I hesitated, unwilling to reveal my near capitulation. "No." Her body relaxed. "Both were cruel and obnoxious, but Gudesto did not collect his first rights." My heart ached to think how weak and malleable I'd been. Torture aside, I should have seen his game sooner than I did.

I watched the muscle jump in her smooth cheek, then took pity. "So, how did you find me?"

The breeze ruffled the full sleeves of Luis's red shirt. "Liana told me."

"She promised not to tell," I cried.

"Some promises are best not kept. When I heard you had headed north the day before Hayib attacked Zaragoza from that direction, I—" She stopped, swallowing hard as she gazed at me. "I feared the worst. Then I found your veil in a clearing, and a large pool of blood."

I straightened. "You did not find Grimaldi's body near the blood?"

Luis shook her head. "I searched an ever-widening circle, thinking you were injured in the brush. I found no one, but Grimaldi could have crawled into a thicket and been invisible." An odd mix of hope and despair zapped through me as she continued. "I decided Hayib's men must have taken you to Lerida, so I rode hard."

We reached the edge of the Ebro, which we would cross then follow west to Zaragoza. Luis found a shallow spot and we urged the horses across. My skirts swirled as the cold water reached my knees. "And then?" Goose bumps snaked up my cold flesh as the sun warmed my arms as I emerged from the river. Once back on the trail, I found Rozinante's easy gait had become almost as relaxing as sitting on a porch swing.

Luis continued her story. "I found Aisha in the harem, she told me Hamara had not returned from his search for you, and you know the rest." She smiled cheerfully. "You are looking much more comfortable on a horse these days. We might make a horsewoman of you yet."

I chuckled. "Let's not change the subject quite so fast, El Picador. Back up. How did you get into the harem to talk with Aisha? It was guarded by two very nasty men."

Luis flushed as red as her shirt, then took a deep breath. Finally she met my eyes and laughed weakly. "I still cannot believe I did this. I stole the clothes of a servant woman off the line and put them on over my own." She shuddered. "It was horrid."

I threw back my head, laughing with a deep joy I hadn't felt in years. Luis's answering grin was half-embarrassed at the image, half-delighted she'd made me laugh. I wiped tears from my eyes as Luis described awkwardly trying to conceal her sword under the thin skirts, avoid the amorous attention of one of Gudesto's men, and keep Aisha quiet, for the poor girl had started to laugh uncontrollably when she realized it was truly Luis under all those veils.

The sun set below the hills ahead, so we stopped for the night, choosing a quiet clearing a good distance from the Ebro and the road. We sat in companionable silence while Luis gutted and skinned the two rabbits she'd killed with a slingshot and two rocks. I wanted to look away, but decided it was time this modern woman faced her meat directly. Soon two rabbits roasted over a small fire, and Luis slipped away to dispose of the fur, skin, and internal organs.

I didn't think I'd be able to eat something I had seen alive an hour earlier, but by the time the rabbit was done, hunger ruled me, and I bit into the crispy, fire-darkened meat with relish. Until that night, I had never truly appreciated the sacrifices nature made to keep me alive.

Over this humble meal came the question I'd been expecting since my confession. Done eating, Luis wiped a sleeve across her face. "Kate, I..." Her measured gaze told all, but I said nothing. "Kate, could you tell me about the future?"

I chewed thoughtfully then swallowed. "What part? Nine hundred years covers a lot of history."

She looked down at her boots, digging one heel into the soft soil. "The part about this peninsula, and the Christians and the Moors. Does Rodrigo..." Her eyes burned with hope, but her tense tone revealed doubt. "Do the Moors ever leave us and return to Africa?"

I wanted to leap to my feet and pull her into a victory dance, shouting "Yes, yes, it takes nearly four hundred more years, but it will happen. Your Rodrigo is a hero at Valencia, then Ferdinand and Isabel drive the last Moors from Granada in 1492." But I'd watched enough shows on the Sci-Fi channel to worry about that whole space-time continuum. What if giving Luis knowledge of her future changed that future? What if something she knew or did interfered with Rodrigo's capturing the crown of Valencia in 1094? Much of history really stunk, but it wasn't up to me to change it.

I shifted my foot until my dusty boot touched hers. "I'm so sorry, Luis, but I cannot say."

She sighed, nodding. "I suppose too much knowledge can be a dangerous thing."

"If you alter your life based on anything I tell you, it may alter the path of history."

She held up one hand, smiling. "No, I am not that important in the scheme of the world."

"Probably true," I said, "but everything could change and if my parents do not marry in that new future, I won't be born, so I could disappear from your arms in a blink."

"Erased from history?" At my nod, El Picador shuddered. "You are right. It is best I know nothing. I am sorry for asking." Ahh, another way in which Luis differed from Anna. I remembered Anna that day in Zaragoza wishing she could change history. No one deserved to wield that kind of power, and Luis was wise enough to recognize that.

I nodded, picking meat from my teeth. "I would have been disappointed if you hadn't. It's natural to want to know." I guzzled water from Luis's leather pouch, then lay back by the fire. "Speaking of wanting to know, what happened at Albarracín?"

Luis snorted loudly. "Not one cursed thing." She wiped her greasy hands on her leggings. "All that drilling, all that practice, and we missed the whole battle." She shook her head, brows fierce in frustration. "We met Rodrigo and the others, but before we even reached Albarracín, scouts reported Alfonso had been routed, that he had tucked his cowardly prick between his legs and fled back to Toledo. Ben Yusef and the Almoravides had begun the journey back to Africa."

"Yusef didn't pursue Alfonso? He could have taken control of so much."

"His cousin was dying, so Yusef needed to return. Besides, Yusef has not grown impatient enough with the infighting between the Moors. Some day he will conquer all the emirs and consolidate al-Andaluz again. When that happens, God help us all."

"So none of your men even drew a sword."

A deep pain settled around her eyes. "One did."

"Alvar." At her startled look, I explained Gudesto's prediction I'd be a widow soon.

"The second night on the journey back, I awoke to find Alvar's steel pressed against my neck. Saint's blood, that sword was cold." She sat forward, stirring the dying coals with a stick. "I told Alvar to kill

me, that I would rather be dead than never be able to trust him again."
A deep sigh seemed to drain her, but I waited patiently. "His sword
started to shake so violently I feared he would slice me open by fear
alone. Finally, he stepped back, stuck his sword into the ground beside
me, fell to his knees, and begged my forgiveness."

"...and?"

"I rolled away from him. I could not. I cannot."

I stared into the coals. It had to come out eventually. "You two have
been friends for many years." She nodded sadly, her lids heavy. I took
a deep breath. "You have shared much...including, I suspect, the same
mark on your back." Her head shot up, body tense as a startled deer.
"The same mark you also share with Gudesto. The Four Caballeros de
Valvanera." Luis paled a ghostly white. "I suspect the fourth Caballero
is Nuño." Her jaw worked, but she said nothing, so I plunged ahead.

"You and Alvar are both Caballeros." She set her lips and turned
back to the fire. "That's why Alvar couldn't kill you."

Stony silence, then a look so piercing I nearly jumped. "I will not
talk about this. I cannot. Leave it rest."

"Yet Gudesto has tried to kill you, repeatedly, all because you
seduced his fiancée? It doesn't make sense. It must have something to
do with being a Caballero."

Luis shot to her feet, face now red. "I said I will not talk about this.
Do not push me. This is none of your concern."

I scrambled to my feet as well, pulse racing. "None of my
concern?" My voice started that dangerous slide upward. "I love you. I
need to know what's going on."

Luis grabbed my hands and pulled them tight against her chest.
Her heart beat like thunder under my palms as she struggled for control.
"Within days, you will enter a cave at Santillana, and..." She swallowed
hard, then pressed her lips against my knuckles. "I cannot bear to have
the truth follow you into the future."

I opened my mouth, then stopped. Silently, I nodded and took her
into my arms. Nearly frantic with relief, Luis began kissing my face, my
neck, my lips. I responded, forcing the Caballeros de Valvanera deep
into the musty recesses of my mind, where I also stored the knowledge
that my time with Luis was nearly over. Grimaldi and I had talked about
whether someone born in this time could travel to the future, and he
thought it doubtful. I did too.

Later, as Luis slept, I listened to the frogs singing along the river. The grass whooshed softly in the breeze. Without a moon to dull them, the stars filled the sky, and my throat tightened when I recognized the Big Dipper. Luis mumbled as her arms and legs twitched slightly. "Let me live, let me live."

❖

I almost regretted it when the shiny white towers of the Aljafería came into view the next day, because now that this journey had ended, another would soon begin. When we arrived at the palace and Luis left me in search of Rodrigo, I hurried straight to Liana's shop, just in case she was working through siesta.

"Kate!" She threw her arms around my neck, and I squeezed her tightly, loving her roundness, her spicy scent. "What happened? Did Luis catch you and Grimaldi?" She noticed I was alone. "Did Luis harm him? Where—"

I touched my fingers lightly to her lips. "Grimaldi and I were attacked by Gudesto's men north of Zaragoza."

Her full lips began to tremble. "Attacked?" she managed to whisper, but just barely.

"They knocked Grimaldi out, then—" I knew no other way to say this. "Then stabbed him. I was dragged off to Lerida and was there until Luis rescued me."

Her eyes glistened as her gaze wandered from me to the table to the window to her hands, yet I doubt she saw any of it. She began winding her veil around a finger.

"Luis found where...it happened, but did not find Grimaldi's body. The forest is so thick Luis thinks Grimaldi might have crawled into a thicket before he..." My heart ached as I pulled the silent woman into my arms. "Liana, I am so sorry." Her tears dampened my sleeve as I choked back my own. I held her for a long time, rocking gently from side to side. Then she pulled back, wiping her eyes. "Allah did not intend for Grimaldi and me to be together." She drew in a shuddering breath. "What is, is." She reattached her veil, and turned toward the palace.

Happy endings were a crock of shit. Hamara and Aisha were the only ones who would end up together, yet even they faced a mountain of obstacles. And as for Liana, Luis, myself, what would prevent us from growing old and bitter because we were denied love, either by death, or by nine hundred years?

I did nothing for a few days but sleep, eat embarrassingly large amounts of sinfully rich food, and soak in the hot baths for hours. A woman could really get used to this sort of treatment. Luis started calling me her "wrinkled pearl," and Ali even clucked impatiently when I showed up for my fifth bath in two days. Gudesto's touch had gone deep.

The soaking and steaming cleansed me enough, however, that Luis said I looked like myself again. Only then would she agree to Walladah's daily demand that I appear before her.

Walladah greeted me warmly as her servant escorted me into Mu'tamin's throne room. She clasped my hands with a strong grip. Her dress was tailored, more practical. Here was a woman too busy to fuss with silks and sashes. "Your painting worked beautifully."

"So I heard." I nodded toward the raised platform. "So what happens now?"

Walladah's fine features hardened, and my heart filled with hope for Zaragoza. If this woman grew up and stopped bedding anyone with a pulse, she could be a great leader. "Musta'in and I are...negotiating. If the last week has taught us anything, it is that I was born to rule, not he." No trace of false pride marred her smile. Her back was straight; her eyes lacked their usual bored insolence. "My brother has not fully accepted it yet, but we will rule Zaragoza together. Over half my father's court prefers me, but I do not need to be proclaimed my father's successor as long as I have real power."

"And what will you do with that power?"

"Keep Zaragoza independent. I will keep the army strong so no one—not Alfonso, not my uncle, not that goat Count Ordóñez—will ever lay claim to my city."

I smiled. "Your father would be proud."

Startled, Walladah bowed her head. "*Shukran*, Kate." A servant interrupted us, speaking rapidly to Walladah. She threw up her hands. "An Aragonese ambassador? Here?" She glared at me. "My stupid brother. We will *not* pay protection money to Aragon. If Sancho Ramírez thinks we are as weak and as stupid as my uncle, he....he..." She stopped, then laughed at me. "He can sit on his sword and spin."

She strode from the room, flashing me a quick, joyful smile as she passed. Yes, ma'am, Zaragoza would be just fine.

CHAPTER TWENTY-TWO

A week flew by as we made our preparations, and I entertained myself with thoughts of Arturo. It felt good to think about Anna taking care of him back in the twenty-first century. This probably didn't make sense, but it comforted me to imagine the eleventh and the twenty-first centuries happening simultaneously. As I breakfasted on fruit and dried goat meat, I imagined Anna scrambling eggs for Arturo or toasting him a bagel. As I fell asleep every night, I knew that at the same time, only nine hundred and some odd years away, Anna was reading Arturo a bedtime story. She was becoming his mother, and that was good.

Luis disappeared again for a few days, shrugging slyly when she returned, but refusing to explain. Fall had brought a sharpness to the air, stirring my need for change, for starting something new as I soaked up the crisp sunny days. Arturo would be in school now. When we visited schools last spring, Anna had been great, grilling the teachers on their philosophies, how they felt about Arturo having two mothers, whether they were open to her volunteering in their classrooms. I had little patience for those details, but Anna knew just what kind of school she wanted for Arturo.

What would Laura and Deb be up to? Would they think I'd died? I tried to imagine their faces when I showed up on their doorstep. "Hey, guys, guess where I've been?" Book group would still be meeting the first Wednesday of the month—I'd have a lot of catching up to do. How bizarre it would be to read a book about this time period and know what people looked like, how they smelled, what this world sounded like.

Each night in our room, Luis and I held each other, wordlessly making love with an intensity that frightened me. Each morning she rolled over, brushed the hair from my eyes, and seemed to drink me in as she gazed at my face, lightly touching my eyebrows, the bump in the bridge of my nose, my jawline. Only when I started trying to memorize her features did I realize she'd already been doing the same. Each day was one long catch in the throat, a slowly-releasing sigh, a deep, shuddering breath. We spoke with our eyes, our hands, our bodies.

Then one morning at the end of the week, the spell broke. Luis rolled over and kissed me brusquely on the nose. "You have recovered your strength," she said.

I shook my head. "No, I'm still weak."

She laughed for the first time in days, her eyes sparkling. "A weak woman could not have pinned me as you did last night."

I blushed. "I'm still weak."

"A weak woman could not have made love for all those hours."

"It's a sporadic weakness," I said. "It comes and goes. I expect it's coming back soon."

She snickered softly, nibbling my ear. "I am glad we had last night then." She kissed me, eyes serious again. "Because we leave tomorrow."

I bit my cheek, saying nothing as she rose and dressed. Strong thighs disappeared beneath gray-green leggings; high round breasts became wrapped in cotton strips; muscular broad shoulders slid under a green blouse and rusty brown leather tunic. "We leave at dawn."

I crawled out of bed after she left, irritated my compliant lover could so swiftly morph into an efficient soldier in charge of a mission, especially one that would separate us forever.

Too edgy to paint, I flitted between helping Liana treat a colicky horse, to playing ball with Hazm, to taking a steam bath, to just sitting in the main palace courtyard by the fountain, letting the gentle mist tickle my palms.

As I listened to the falling water, trying to capture every sensory detail of this palace, Moors and Christians passed through the courtyard, slippers scuffing on the tile, voices bouncing off the slender columns. None paid me any attention, except Rodrigo. Twice he passed me, glowering deeply both times. Finally, the third time he approached, lowering himself onto the marble bench next to me with a soft grunt.

I waited, meeting his fierce scowl.

"I do not like that Luis returns to Castile," he said, shifting his gaze to the courtyard arches. "It is too dangerous."

"I know."

"I need him here with me."

"I know, but he insists."

Rodrigo rubbed his salt and pepper beard. "No man is as stubborn as he, not even me." He paused, looking at me from under his bushy eyebrows. "And why it is so important to get to Santillana is beyond me." He frowned when I didn't explain.

Why was Rodrigo suddenly so chummy? Other than our few meals together, he'd done his best to ignore me since Luis and I had married. He cleared his throat several times, then finally drew a small pouch from under his belt. "Luis is my best soldier, my first lieutenant, but he has a blind spot where money is concerned. He thinks his faith and his sword will be enough, but you..." his gaze was direct. "You are a practical woman." When he tossed the pouch into my lap, heavy coins clinked together. "Events may go as Luis has planned, but should they not, you will need money."

I nodded, unsure what to do or say, but was I overcome with gratitude that Rodrigo cared so much for Luis. Would the same be true if he ever learned her true sex? "Thank you."

He huffed a few times, nodded, then abruptly rose and lumbered down the hallway. That afternoon I put the pouch of coins in my fanny pack, then walked the roof, taking in the incredible view of the city for one last time, trying to memorize the raw sienna thatched roofs on the huts, the phthalo blue tile roofs of the wealthier homes, the hills rising beyond, the delicate archway leading to the stables. I froze, however, at the sight of two familiar figures facing each other in the open courtyard below, Luis's back to me, Alvar facing me. I could not see Luis's face, but could tell she was speaking.

The gestures of both grew more exaggerated and twice Luis stepped threateningly toward Alvar. The third time Alvar's smooth face crumbled, and he dropped to his knees, nodding, burying his face in his hands. I raced closer, bending low behind the parapet.

"How *could* you?" Luis growled. "You were a soldier, and now you are nothing more than Gudesto's puppet."

"I know, I know," moaned Alvar, tears streaming down his dusty face. He lifted his head, then staggered to his feet, wiping his face.

"What am I going to do with you?"

Alvar drew his sword, then flipped it over, handing it hilt first to Luis. She took it. "See that justice is done. I have drawn my sword at Albarracín against the man I admire more than King Alfonso himself. I am too weak a man to live."

A breeze ruffled Luis's tunic, Alvar's long locks. I held my breath, still peering over the parapet's edge. If either turned slightly, they'd see me.

Finally Luis flung the sword off to the side, then grabbed Alvar and drew him close, now speaking so softly I heard nothing. Alvar's good eye widened, and a look of fear, then awe crossed his dark features. He shook his head, but Luis nodded vigorously. Finally Alvar pointed to himself. "Me?" he clearly asked.

Luis nodded, and Alvar dropped his head, made the sign of the cross, then knelt before Luis, whispering a reply. She pulled him to his feet, then they threw their arms around each other and headed out of sight under the canopy below. A sick coldness settled in my chest.

Luis's words that night didn't chase that coldness away. "I have asked Alvar to serve in my place while I'm gone."

"But he attacked you."

"He is a good man at heart. He lost his way, but has returned. He will do a fine job."

"So Alvar Fáñez will be El Cid's First Lieutenant."

She chuckled, blue eyes warm. "Only for a few weeks. That is not a position I intend to give up. Alvar will serve Rodrigo well, but it is *my* job."

So this was how Alvar would become a permanent entry in the history books, and Luis Navarro would disappear. I rode a supersonic fate train, swept along on a ride I was powerless to stop.

❖

The day before we were to leave, I sat in our room and slowly, meticulously, folded the few clothes Luis and I had, always the first step before packing for a journey. I decided I needed to wash my split skirt, which I was wearing, so I had pretty much undressed myself when Luis burst into the room.

"What?" I said.

"Nothing. I just wanted to see you. Holy Santiago, but you are a beautiful woman." She dropped the latch, crossed the floor in three strides, and flung us both back onto the bed, directly onto the folded laundry.

"Your clothes are beneath us," I said.

"I know," she murmured, then we proceeded to perform various acts not normally conducted on piles of neatly folded laundry.

❖

Luis shook me awake at dawn. "Time to go," she said gruffly.

I pulled the blanket over my head. "How about next year?" I mumbled, eyes stuck shut.

Cold air prickled my skin as the blanket was suddenly gone. "No, now. How long will it be before you leave me again, desperate to get to Santillana?" Roughly, she pulled me to my feet and thrust my traveling clothes in my arms. "We leave now."

I slipped my skirt on, shivering and muttering. "You can hardly wait to be rid of me, can you?" Now where had *that* come from? I winced at the stunned look on her face. We finished dressing in silence.

Liana was the only one up early enough to see us off. As she and I hugged, I stroked her curly hair. "Are you going to be all right?" I whispered.

She leaned back, looking up at me. "Love is more durable than we think." She tapped her chest. "Grimaldi will always be with me." I didn't want to let my friend go, the woman who'd helped me survive as long as I had, but when Luis said it was time, Liana stepped back, eyes shining. My own vision was so blurred I could barely mount Rozinante.

"Allah be with you," Liana said softly.

"And with you," Luis replied. We left Zaragoza through the west gate, and half an hour later I looked back, gasping softly as the rising sun blanketed the white palace in a wash of warm pink. This stunning work of architecture, the only home I'd know in the eleventh century, would survive, in some form, into the twenty-first century.

Soon the sun warmed our backs as we alternately walked then trotted the horses, and smells of fish mingled with that of wet leaves along the Ebro road. Fall's chill was taking longer and longer to fade every morning. We stopped several times to relieve ourselves, water the horses, and chew on dried meat. Finally, I could take the silence no longer. "I love you."

Her eyebrows raised. "You have a strange way of showing it."

"I know. I'm just tense. I'm sorry."

She nodded, then remounted. "What is, is. I have accepted that. You need to return to your own time."

❖

On the second day we moved off the main road, instead following a narrow path that paralleled the Ebro, but we were high above it on the opposite shore. The days blended together as we moved past stunning vistas, and across slender streams so clear and blue I actually teared up once. We ate dried meat, fruit, nut balls, and cold rice because Luis didn't want to start any fires, but it all tasted so good. The closer we got to Castile, the busier the Ebro became. Small rafts and barges floated by, the rafters shouting to one another, or singing raucous songs about Maria or Jimena. Rickety wooden carts pulled by rusty brown donkeys traveled the road, transporting wheat, fruit, and other produce to Burgos. The farther from Zaragoza, the cruder the farmhouses, the more primitive the farming methods, the less creative the use of water for irrigation. We were leaving behind the land of the Moors and entering Christian territory.

The third evening, as dusk settled around us, we sat against a tree sharing an orange. The ground was hard, but at least it wasn't a horse. Luis tossed the perfect, one-piece spiral aside, then looked around us for like the tenth time. "Nervous?" I asked.

"No," she smiled, popping a juicy section into my mouth. But an hour later, when a twig snapped in the forest behind us and I jumped, Luis snickered and raised her voice. "A cow could move with more stealth than you."

The answer was a muttered curse, then a man appeared in our clearing, leading his horse. "A cow could not climb the hill I just scaled. Why in blazes did you pick such a stupid rendezvous?"

Nuño Súarez glared at Luis, then unsaddled his horse.

I looked from Nuño to a grinning Luis. "I don't understand. Why are you here?"

The man's long strides brought him to my side, his riding cape billowing dramatically. He clasped me around the waist, his face serious. "Luis requested that I come. Apparently you are more woman than one man can satisfy, so I am here to help." I neatly sidestepped his attempted kiss and smacked his arm.

"Back off, big guy," I snapped, but couldn't help smiling. "I didn't know you were such a flirt."

"Only with my best friend's wife," he replied, winking. He greeted Luis with a bear hug that nearly lifted her off her feet. "Welcome back to Castile, my friend."

We talked late into the night. Luis had disappeared that week and the one after our marriage because she'd snuck off to the frontier to meet Nuño to keep each other posted. This last meeting they'd decided Nuño should come with us. Only when Luis and Nuño began discussing in detail our complicated route did I understand why Nuño had joined us. Now that we'd crossed some invisible barrier into Christian Spain, it would take the skill of both natives to get me to Santillana, and Luis back to Zaragoza.

❖

Luis seemed to glow when Nuño was around. The only time I'd seen them together was the night I'd tried to steal a horse and escape from Zaragoza, so I was surprised when their easy banter, their ability to pick up a conversation started months ago, sent a tinge of green running through me. But their friendship was oddly comforting, since it meant Luis would not be totally alone after I left. Just like Arturo would not be totally alone if you stayed here, my mind screamed. Shut up, I screamed back.

That morning the trail hugged the top of a narrow ridge above the Ebro. Now and then the road below appeared through a break in the thick underbrush, but not often enough for me, since I hungered for some sign of civilization, even if it was a dusty donkey cart. So during a break, I wandered to the edge of the ridge, staying hidden behind a broad maple already ablaze in its fall yellows. The traffic on the road was moderate.

One man rode alone, a wide-brimmed brown hat pulled over silver hair. I gasped. Was the man's hair pulled back in a ponytail? His face was shadowed by the hat, but the lanky build was the same. It had to be.

I ran for Luis. "Come quickly." We peered around the tree.

"It could be Grimaldi," Luis said. "I am not sure from here."

"I must know."

Nuño grabbed my arm as I ran toward Rozinante. "No, I will go," he said. "You should not be seen."

"Hurry. Bring him back here."

"No," Luis said. "We don't have time for reunions."

By the time Nuño and his horse had scooted off the ridge and swum the river, the man had nearly reached the curve in the road taking him out of sight. Legs and boots dripping wet, Nuño approached him. After a brief discussion, the man scanned the ridge. He flung off his hat and his ponytail fell into view. It *was* him. Thrilled, I stepped out from the tree's shadow, and Grimaldi, hundreds of yards away, threw his arms in the air, then clasped them together as if in grateful prayer.

I wiped my eyes, smiling and laughing as we stared at each other, too far away to yell, and yet it was too dangerous to get closer. Grimaldi placed both hands on his heart, then his lips, then reached toward me. "Oh, Grimaldi...Liana," I whispered, then repeated his motions. A team of oxen rumbled into view, and Luis gently drew me back into the shadows.

I paced until Nuño returned and slid from the saddle. "That is the last time I am scaling this ridiculous hill," he snapped.

"Your horse did all the work, you lazy sot," Luis teased.

I raced to Nuño, words tumbling from my mouth. He held up his hand. "Let me catch my breath...Well, your friend is a lucky man, apparently. After Gudesto's men stabbed him and spirited you away, he crawled back down to the Ebro road, collapsed, and was found by a passing Christian merchant, who put him into his wagon and took him home to Calahorra. He drifted in and out of consciousness, but recovered quickly, thanks to the merchant's wife. The dagger missed all his organs. As thanks, he helped the man transport his wares to Burgos. He is still weak, but has no 'fection,' whatever that is."

"Infection," I crowed. My heart swelled. "And now he goes...?"

"He now returns to Zaragoza. Apparently a woman and something about pigeons?" I threw my arms around Nuño in a bear hug, and he held me tight, chuckling. "Oh, Luis is a lucky, lucky man."

"Back off, big guy," Luis growled, pulling me away as we all laughed.

That night, curled up in my bedroll next to Luis, I dreamt I struggled through a long, dark tunnel. When I finally emerged, dressed in a suit of mail with a sword heavy against my right hip, I rang the doorbell of our Chicago home and walked inside, scabbard thudding against the doorframe. Arturo played with Max in the living room, Anna and the English professor sat on the sofa holding hands, looking like a happily married couple. All three looked up when I entered.

"Who are you?" Arturo asked as the English professor looked down her nose at me, not threatened in any way by my arrival.

"Why are you here?" Anna said. "I don't understand."

"C'mon, Max, let's go play outside," Arturo said in perfect English. He slid open the glass door to the deck, then turned toward me. "Cool sword, but I don't need you here. I already have a family, so why are you here?"

"I'm not sure," I said, and I woke up.

CHAPTER TWENTY-THREE

We passed Calahorra, a dark blot on the far plateau. North of Burgos, at Ona, we would turn right and head north for Santillana, a two-day ride from there. The closer to that turning point, the quieter Luis and I became. Nuño, bless his heart, did his best, weaving stories and riddles throughout the long days, but eventually he gave up and we rode in silence. My thoughts turned to Anna, her patience playing with the neighborhood kids, her skill at whipping leftovers into incredible meals, her passion for history, her desire to raise a child. I returned to the future as Arturo's parent, but not as Anna's partner. My time with Luis had stripped the truth clean down to the bone: Anna and I would be friends, but nothing more.

But how would I parent Arturo? He'd live with Anna, of course, so I'd be the every-other-weekend mom, the one a kid merely tolerated, or used to punish the primary parent. What was I thinking? How could any of this be good for Arturo? I was fighting to get back to my own time in order to what—give Arturo a broken home? My doubt wore at me like a persistent mosquito buzzing my face.

One week after Nuño joined us, we reached Ona, a quiet spot of buff-brown bluffs that grew into mountains to the north. We skirted the town and made camp in a small clearing not far from the Ebro. Even before nightfall a heavy fog settled over the area, dampening my hair and my clothes, and Luis finally agreed to a fire, for the fog would hide the smoke.

Thanks to Nuño and Luis's hunting skills, we ate a warm meal of fresh rabbit and finished off Nuño's wine pouch. A number of times Luis caught my eye, her smoldering gaze weakening me more than the wine. I hugged my knees to my chest, grateful for the fire's drying warmth, wondering how to be intimate with Luis in our cozy threesome.

She'd tried a few nights earlier, but with Nuño only ten feet away, I just couldn't.

When dinner was over, however, Nuño stood, stretched, then tossed his bedroll over his shoulder. "You both are fine company, but I need more privacy," he said, winking so lewdly both Luis and I blushed. "See you in the morning." He walked north on the narrow trail we would take tomorrow, then judging by the rustling, he must have left the trail a hundred yards up and tamped down a place to sleep.

With the darkness and the fog, it was as if we were in a quiet room. "How considerate of Nuño," I said evenly, my eyes on the fire.

"I told the big lout I'd run him through with my dagger if he did not give us tonight." And then I was on my back, Luis's shaking hands fumbling with my blouse, my own hands busy as well. She bit my neck, my shoulders, frantically kissing me and touching me everywhere, moaning softly.

For the next hour, every caress, every whisper, every sigh, every deep gaze, created a layer of sadness over my passion. How many nights did we have left? Two, by Nuño's estimate. Jesus, how could I walk away from this woman?

The stars pulsed above us as Luis finally regained her breath, then settled down into my arms, turning toward the glowing embers. "Thank you," she said softly.

"You're welcome," I replied, voice husky.

She snickered, lifting up on one elbow. "I do not mean for tonight. I mean...for everything."

"Oh." I sighed, trembling slightly, but not from cold.

"Do you like oysters?" she asked suddenly.

I nodded. "They're okay."

"Have you ever gone pearl diving?"

I nibbled on her ear. "I just did."

She snorted and took my hand, eyes serious in the firelight. "Oyster divers harvest oysters, but they also seek their entire lives for that one huge, luminous, unforgettable pearl. Most never find it; some go crazy, some grow bitter." She kissed my fingers. "I gave up on happiness long ago. But then I found *my* unforgettable pearl. No matter what happens, I will be happy the rest of my life."

I couldn't push any words past the lump in my throat, so I swallowed hard. "Luis, how can I—"

She stopped me, her lips barely brushing mine. "Because I live a violent life, it is not likely to be a long one. But I will always carry you with me, even while you live so far into the future." I opened my mouth, but my heart was too full to speak. We clung together, our faces buried in each other's neck. Exhausted, we finally lay down, and sleep came.

❖

I awoke to the same thick, moist blanket of fog, and cold feet. When I rolled over, tucking my legs up under the blanket and rubbing them together briskly, I smelled of campfire and wet hair and woman. I snuggled deeper into my cocoon, but at a gentle, polite cough, I opened my eyes.

Nuño sat on the ground across the firepit from me, rough-cut bangs falling into his eyes. "Sleep well?"

"All night," I said, not quite awake.

"Not from what I heard."

He yelped as I sat up and flung a charred hunk of log at him. Luis's bedroll was no longer beside me. "Has Luis gone off to catch us breakfast?" I rubbed my face, inhaling her scent. Nuño didn't answer, but looked down at his massive hands. "Where's Luis?" I asked.

My heart lurched when Nuño's soft brown eyes filled with sympathy. "He left in the night."

"What do you mean, 'left?'" My brain felt fuzzy.

"He left. I am to take you the rest of the way myself."

Reality punched me in the stomach and I gasped. "Luis left? Just like that?" I struggled to my feet, kicking off the blanket.

Nuño rose as well. "He thought it best for both of you."

"Best?" I looked wildly around. Only two horses grazed in the clearing. Suddenly fury pulsed through me. "We have two more days. I didn't tell her everything I needed to. How could she *do* this to me?" I clenched my fists. "How could she *do* this?"

Nuño grabbed my arm. "She?"

Shit! Oh, God, no. I clutched my head. What had I done? One stupid slip.

"How do you know Luis is a woman?" he barked.

"Because I *married* her," I shouted, now waving my arms.

"I assumed she would keep that from you."

"She?" Panic nearly set it. "Did *you* know she's a woman?"

Nuño grabbed my flailing fists. "I have always known."

"What?"

"If you'll calm down, I will tell you." Nuño offered me a tin cup of water, which I guzzled without a word, not caring when it dripped down my chin.

I began to pace, pulsing with a weird energy, "So, I don't have to kill you?"

Nuño's guffaw faded quickly in the heavy air. "No. I have kept the secret for ten years. I think I can be trusted."

I grabbed my blanket and wrapped it around me. "Does she know?"

Nuño shook his head and began stacking moist twigs for another fire. "He has no idea I know." While Nuño coaxed the spark into a tiny fire, I sat down across from him.

"I have never told anyone this story." When he scratched his beard thoughtfully, I nodded, heart thudding, then leaned toward the column of heat. My heart hurt. Luis had left without saying good-bye. "When I was fifteen, I ran away to study with the greatest swordsman of the day, Father Manolo Ruiz, at the monastery at Valvanera. I was still young, and because I was not as good as the other students, they often tormented me. So one fall afternoon, to prove myself, I decided I would stay out in the forest until I shot a deer."

Nuño pulled dry bark off the stump behind him and fed the fire. Where was Luis now? I closed my eyes for a second, rocked by a thought: Arturo could be fine without me. Anna could be a wonderful parent. I struggled to focus on Nuño's story.

"I sat up in the crook of that damned tree, bow and arrow ready, until my legs fell asleep. Then a horse and rider appeared on the path below me. The boy was about my age, but his clothes were darkened with dried blood. He dismounted, falling off more than anything, then pulled down his leggings as he squatted. I considered making a rude noise to embarrass him, but when I heard urine hitting the ground, I held my tongue. I'd never known a man to squat and pee. He stood, but before he pulled up his pants, I got a good look at why he peed differently than I did."

"She didn't hear you?"

He shook his head. "I held my breath. I was so excited I knew something the other boys didn't. I also had never...seen a woman before." His smile was wry.

I could picture an exhausted young woman squatting in the quiet forest, hungry, unused to her new identity as Luis, full of despair at having lost her family and being forced to flee her home.

"Why do you use 'he' when you know she's a she?"

Nuño tugged his thick beard. "To avoid revealing his secret by accident. I have always thought of Luis as a he. I do not trust myself." He smiled. "Especially after a few mugs of ale."

I had already figured out I faced the same problem, but for obvious reasons just couldn't think of Luis as a "he." It was a good thing I was leaving, or I could easily mess up in front of the wrong person and get Luis killed.

"Luis left, and showed up at Valvanera later that night, passing himself off as a boy who wanted to learn to fight with the rest of us. I kept my mouth shut thinking I could use what I knew to blackmail him."

"Let's see. 'Have sex with me or I'll tell everyone you're a girl?'"

Nuño flushed. "Something like that."

"But you didn't do that."

He studied his hands. "More passion for killing ran through Luis than through any of us combined. He threw himself into every drill, every sport. He taught me to shoot my arrows straighter. He was smaller than the rest of us, so learned to be quicker. He saw the other boys picked on me, so he made me his special friend. We became the team to beat. Everyone respected Luis. He was fair, honest, and devoted to killing Moors."

"So you waited longer to expose her."

Nuño scratched his beard. "The longer I waited, the harder it became. One word from me and he would lose everything. But I found I could not do it. I respected him too much to destroy all he'd built. He was...and is..." He looked me in the eye, dropping for an instant the veil hiding his own pain. "...very special to me."

Breathless, I could not speak. For ten years this man had pushed aside his deep feelings for Luis's sake. Exposing her would have destroyed her; yet maintaining the illusion she was a man meant he could never act on his own feelings. I held his gaze, touched by the depth of his compassion. "Luis could have no better friend than you."

"I know," he said simply. "And he could have no better wife than you." I looked at my hands as Nuño stirred the fire. "Kate, this may be too private, but I am very curious how you discovered Luis's true sex."

"On our wedding night, by accident." I smiled, remembering the scene that seemed so ridiculous now.

"Most women would have exposed Luis if they'd been in your situation."

"I was relieved, actually."

Nuño's brows knit together. "So you are one of those women who—"

"Yes, I am...and so is...Luis."

The big man nodded quietly. "I thought as much." He smiled ruefully. "That explains why he had many more conquests than necessary to establish his reputation as a ladies' man. Oh, sorry."

I nodded, then stood, my limbs strangely heavy with my thoughts. I retrieved meat from my saddlebag and we built up the fire. "You, Luis, Gudesto, and Alvar met at Valvanera."

"Yes," came his cautious reply.

I took a deep breath. "So whose idea was it to form the Caballeros?" Nuño started as if I'd slapped him. "I know about the tattoo on your back. I know you took vows to conquer the Moors." I hesitated, then took a shot in the dark. "I know everything."

Nuño's eyes widened as he struggled to swallow his mouthful of dried goat. Then he shook his head, clearly amazed. "Luis must really trust you."

I kept my voice light. "What's done, is done."

Luis's best friend scowled into the fire. "Yes, that's true, but the killings never should have happened."

"Sometimes we start things that go wrong." Jesus, what killings?

Nuño stood and began pacing. "No, we intended to kill from the start. That's why Luis formed the Caballeros in the first place."

"How many of you were there?" Nuño seemed not to notice, or at least not to care, that I did not, in fact, know everything.

"We were ten at first. Ramón and Panchi died at Tudela, Marcos died of a wound received at Calatayud. Raul was killed over a woman.

Miguelito and Oso died in the last skirmish near Osma." He sighed. "But we killed at least three score of Moors."

I did the math. "Oh, my god. That's sixty people." My hands turned moist.

"A conservative estimate," Nuño said. "When we'd learned all we could from Father Ruíz, we were twenty years old, and ready. Luis was hungry to lead, and we were hungry to follow. He led us on raid after raid into the frontier."

"Killing any Moorish soldier you met?"

Nuño suddenly sat back down and pressed his forehead against his knees. "Killing any Moor we met."

Silence hung between us. "How long did this go on?" I finally asked.

"Two, three years, I guess. Neither King Alfonso nor his brother Sancho before him interfered. More and more often, our paths crossed Rodrigo's. We heard he was a great warrior who could beat any foe. We only stopped killing...after the family."

I froze, my heart a slow, loud thump in my ears. "The family?"

Nuño raised his head. "Luis did not tell you of them?" He snorted at my silence. "Luis told you nothing, did he?"

I leaned forward. "I figured most of it out myself, but you might as well tell me the rest, or I'll pester Luis until she tells me herself."

Nuño exhaled in frustration, contemplating the smoke curling up between us. "This knowledge remains between us." I nodded. "You will not bother Luis about it." I nodded again. "Good, because it gives him great pain." He gripped a stick in his massive fist, stirring the coals into a red-hot pile. "We still mourned Miguelito and Oso, so roamed a short section of the frontier near Tudela, looking for a fight. Rain plagued us, soaking cloaks, bedrolls, everything. We went nearly mad fighting the mud for two weeks, and still no Moorish soldiers wandered into our net. But then..." The silence was stifling in the heavy fog.

I bit my lip.

"...then a Moorish family came up the Ebro just as we'd left Tudela, where we'd purchased more supplies. We saw them, hunched over on their horses, as wet and as miserable as we were, and we..." He stopped, Adam's apple rippling frantically. "You must understand, Kate, we were young. We thought of the Moors as animals, beasts outside the Christian faith, not as people." He sighed wearily. "We slaughtered them. It was over in seconds. All I remember through our blood lust were the shouts of the Caballeros, and the quiet whimpering of the woman. How I heard that in all the noise, I will never understand, but her words continue to haunt me."

I whispered, "Let me live, let me live," and Nuño's mouth dropped open. "Luis has nightmares," I said. "She repeats those words over and over."

Nuño closed his eyes briefly. "Gudesto had yanked the woman off the wagon seat and stood over her, sword drawn. Luis rode up on his horse and for a second I thought he was going to stop Gudesto, but it was too late. Gudesto slashed the woman open." Nuño's pain filled the small clearing, but I could do nothing to eliminate the horrible story now hanging in the air like a heavy fog. "That night I heard Luis vomiting in the woods. His lust for blood died with that family."

"Too much revenge."

"Kate, I am not proud of what we did. Killing that family was cowardly. We drifted for awhile, still hating the Moors, but having no more stomach for outright killing. Luis grew pale and nearly stopped eating. I was terrified he would die, so I kept suggesting we join Rodrigo, for he had an army. He had power we Caballeros would never have."

"Did all four of you join up with Rodrigo?"

"At first, but then things began to fall apart. Gudesto inherited land so he returned to La Rioja. Rodrigo sent me on a journey with some of Alfonso's men, and by the time I returned, he had been exiled, and Luis and Alvar had followed him."

"Where Luis had to work and live with Moors."

Nuño leaned against the gnarled tree. "His penance for his sins. He cannot see a living Moor without remembering the Moors we killed."

"And the others?"

"Gudesto paid by losing his faith, and perhaps his mind. Alvar lost an eye. And me?" He gave me a sad smile. "My great punishment, and my great joy, is to see Luis madly in love...with you." There seemed to be no good reply to that, so we both looked toward the horses and the blue sky which had begun to appear through the dissipating fog.

As we sat there in silence, deep within me I felt the future's hold on me snap like a rubber band stretched beyond its limits. I flushed hot with the truth I had known for weeks but could not let myself acknowledge. Everything I thought I needed back in the future fell away like dried paint flaking off a canvas. Anna could care for Arturo without me. In fact, I would just get in the way. We'd fight over every detail in the poor kid's life, like we had seemed to fight over everything else, and we might even turn into those horrible ex-spouses who used their children to wound each other. No, Arturo's future looked rosier and less complicated if I remained as I was in his drawing—not really there.

Besides, Anna's gritty determination, her unshakable self-confidence, and her intense love of children could serve her well. Luis, on the other hand, was a woman who had no idea how to be one. She was alone. She needed me. Goddess, I needed her. I could not, I would not, leave her.

My hands trembled with excitement and I knew, deep in my soul, this was the right choice. I had never really been parental material, even though I'd been willing to give it a try. Anna and I should have ended it months ago, maybe even years ago. I could live without flush toilets and Cheetos and airplane rides, but I couldn't live without Luis. "Nuño, I have changed my mind. Forget Santillana."

He stared at me, eyes wide. I repeated my words, and Nuño groaned, dropping his face into his hands. Not even his exasperated look deterred me. "After all this? Why can I understand Luis, but every other woman baffles me? I do not even know why we travel to Santillana in the first place." I said nothing, so Nuño sighed. "He will be waiting for me back at Miranda. We are to meet in five days." He shook his head but grinned widely, seeing now his new role. "The greatest gift I can give Luis is to deliver you to him, not to Santillana."

I held my hand over my racing heart, marveling at how light I felt. I had to let go of Arturo. He had Anna. Luis had friends, but as Elena... Elena had no one but me.

Nuño began putting out the fire. "You want Luis even though you now know the truth about the Caballeros?"

I stood up straight, hands on my hips, mind clear, heart full. "I will not be the cause of another deep wound in her life. Please take me home—to Luis."

CHAPTER TWENTY-FOUR

We rode as swiftly as the trail allowed. "He has about twelve hours' lead," Nuño warned, "so do not expect to overtake him."

I shifted in my saddle, then ducked under a low branch. "Maybe she will go slowly. She has five days."

"Not Luis. He will push himself to Miranda, then wait for me."

My heart ached at the intense loneliness likely gripping Luis right now. I experienced it the moment I realized she'd left, and the bottom had dropped out of my world. But now I urged Roz faster, anxious to ease Luis's pain, to hold her, to be together for the rest of our lives. As we rode, I soaked up the smells and sounds of my new home. God, this was a gorgeous country. I could be happy here, as long as I didn't have to catch, kill, and cut up my own food.

The next day we approached Miranda, where a cacophony of sounds drifted up from the Ebro, then we headed north to the rendezvous point. As we rode closer, even Nuño was excited. "I cannot *wait* to see Luis's face when you ride up behind me." At the base of the hill we were to climb, Nuño stopped me. "One thing, Kate. I do not want Luis to know that I know the truth."

I had already been puzzling how to handle this. "It might be easier for her if she did."

Nuño wagged his shaggy head. "No. He must keep his guard up at all times. He cannot let it down, not even for me."

"That's why you haven't asked her real name."

"Our relationship is simple—we are brothers. In battle, at a tavern, in council with Rodrigo, I cannot stop to think which name to use. One day I may use the wrong name. I do not want that fear to come between me and Luis."

I nodded, the same fear plaguing me since I'd decided to remain with Luis, and I urged my horse forward. I protected Luis's secret; I would protect Nuño's as well. As Rozinante lurched up the hillside, I gripped her sides with my knees, then followed Nuño into a small clearing. A hawk squawked above us, and two deer fled the far edge, but that was it. Nuño scowled as we dismounted and walked farther into the clearing. He bent over, peering at the ground. "Look. Hooves have broken off the grass here, and here, and here."

Once I knew what to look for, a quick survey revealed hundreds of hoof prints. A dull throb of fear began pulsing at the base of my skull. "Luis?" I called. Nuño cussed violently as he spun in a circle, searching for Luis. I licked my dry lips. "Maybe other travelers use this spot."

He stopped his wild tirade. "Not all at the same time. And not all in the last few hours."

We searched the entire clearing. Perhaps Luis had not even arrived yet. She took a long detour. She changed her mind and was on the trail to Altamira. Then, near a small charred fire ring, I found an orange peel, all in one piece, still coiled in a spiral.

"Luis," Nuño said, voice tight.

Damn. My heart pounded as Nuño and I stared helplessly at each other. "Miranda," I finally said. "Maybe someone knows what happened here."

"Yes." Nuño swung into his saddle. "Stay here. I will be back."

"Like hell I will," I snarled as I threw my leg over Rozinante. "We both go. Luis may be down there."

He started to protest, but I kicked Roz into a gallop and he had no choice but to follow.

Miranda was a mean little town on the Ebro with huge corrals of sheep, crude wood and stone buildings, and noise, lots of it. Men shouted by the river and squealing children dodged between rumbling carts.

We passed a few homes, then Nuño pointed to a small tavern, a crude *vino* sign over its open doorway. My pulse raced as we dismounted. This was Christian Spain, to me a foreign country. Inside, three windows and the open door provided the only light, huge yellow rectangles that revealed two men passed out over a table, and a short, plump woman, her hair in a greasy bun, clearing off tables. The air burned my nostrils, as it was heavy with wine, sweat, and judging by the yellow piles on the floor, vomit.

"We're closed," the woman snapped.

"We seek only information," Nuño replied.

"We're out of ale. That Pedro, my bastard of a husband, is too *busy* to get more." She slammed another tankard onto her tray. "Son of a bitch leaves on a lark. How am I supposed to sell ale when we ain't got any?"

"Señora." Nuño began stacking bowls beside her. "We seek a man with very short, black hair, very blue eyes, and a scar along his nose. He wears a green shirt and brown tunic. He—"

The woman laughed bitterly. "Well, get in line, mister, because there's lots more ahead of you that wants a piece of him."

I stepped forward. "You've seen him?"

"Seen him? He's the reason I've got such a damned mess here. Bunch of the King's men rode in this morning and wanted to celebrate. 'Your best wine!' they cried. 'More ale!' they whined." She thrust a finger at me. "Rudest bunch of assholes I've ever served. 'El Picador falls,' they toasted over and over again. Kept the poor bastard, a damned handsome fellow at that, tied up in the corner. Didn't give him a drop to drink."

Nuño's anger matched my own. "Was he wounded?" he asked.

"A bit beat-up around the head, cut lip, but seemed in one piece otherwise. But then talk started up about taking him to Burgos to be drawn and quartered, and Pedro, the bastard, decides he wants to go along to watch." She lifted the tray to her shoulder, glaring at us. "Stupid asshole." She stomped into the kitchen, still swearing.

Nuño and I spoke as one. "Burgos." He followed the woman into the kitchen and managed to buy a long sausage and a hunk of cheese, then we mounted and headed for the main road. Caution be damned now. Speed was everything.

❖

Whoever held Luis must have gotten their celebrating out of the way at Miranda, for they really moved after that. We rode hard all day but never caught up with them. Nuño finally made me stop for a few hours to rest the horses, but I couldn't sleep. *I* had brought Luis into Castile, and for nothing. If I'd had the courage to make the right choice earlier, we never would have left Zaragoza.

It rained the next day, and by afternoon I no longer even cared that I was soaked and muddy and cold. My teeth hurt from the pounding hooves, my skin hurt from the driving needles of rain, yet we pushed on.

When we stopped that afternoon under a tree to eat a few slices of sausage and cheese, the rain slowed to a drizzle, then stopped. I successfully relieved myself behind a bush, but when it was time to mount my clothes were so wet and heavy, and my limbs so tired, that Nuño had to push and shove me up into my saddle. Luis would have gotten a good laugh over that.

Located on a plateau, Burgos had overflowed its city walls with dozens of crude shacks spilling out the major gates and onto the surrounding pasture. No one took notice of us as we rode through the main gate. The smell of rot hit me first, then manure. Two and three story gray buildings lined the muddy streets, pressing in so closely they almost appeared to touch overhead. An open sewer ran alongside the street, women casually stepping over it, skirts dragging; barefoot children ran through it as they chased one another. Two men fought in a narrow alley, their faces bright with blood. A wide wagon piled with hay nearly forced us and our horses into an open doorway. A young boy defecated next to a building.

"Welcome to Burgos," Nuño said, a touch of pride in his voice.

"Not exactly Zaragoza, is it?"

"No, but these are good people. You'll see. Come." Nuño led me past a crowded market, then up a narrow street. "I have a room in Señora Lazcano's home."

"*Agua va!*" a woman called from above. Nuño neatly moved his horse between me and the building, where a woman leaned out the second story window and dumped her chamber pot. It splashed against the building wall and Nuño's leg.

Nuño's room was small, simple, but fairly clean. "Señora Lazcano cleans as part of my living fee," he said with a weak smile. "I am quite a slob otherwise." The bed was a straw mattress on the wood floor. Next to it was a table and two chairs, a bowl as a sink, and a chamber pot in the corner. "I hope you will be comfortable here. I know it's not the

Aljafería, but it's dry and out of the mud."

"We'll do just fine," I said bravely.

Nuño's eyes widened. "No, I cannot stay here with you. Luis—"

"Oh, for Christ's sake. Forget my reputation. If we are going to find Luis and help her, we need to be together."

He gave in but did insist on hanging a sheet across the chamber pot corner for my privacy. Then he sternly took me by the shoulders. "I must insist you stay here. That divided skirt draws attention. Gudesto may be here. He may have given Alfonso's men a description of you. You cannot help Luis if you are captured, and you could provide Alfonso with a way to hurt or torture Luis even more."

"He hates Luis that much?"

"Alfonso's anger is for Rodrigo, and while he does not dare harm Rodrigo's wife and children, he can build enough false charges against Luis that not even Rodrigo could sway the court's opinion."

"Will you get me some other clothes? I need to help."

"First I go to the castle and find where they're holding Luis. Perhaps I can even see him. When I return, Señora Lazcano can help us with your clothes."

With a grim nod, he closed the heavy door behind him. I ran to the window and watched as he entered the crowded street then turned left up the hill toward the stark, imposing castle. I shivered. We had to get Luis *out* of there.

❖

I very nearly wore through the floor pacing until the sun set, turning the room into an icebox. I wrapped a musty blanket around myself and kept pacing. Nuño finally returned hours later, and collapsed at the table, head in his hands.

"Did they let you see her?" I perched nervously on the chair next to him.

He looked up and I gasped at the total despair in his eyes. "I couldn't *find* him," he whispered hoarsely.

"What?"

"I looked *everywhere*. Alfonso wouldn't see me, of course. I'm no one to him. But I have friends among the castle guards, and they insist no one has even *seen* Luis." He rattled the table with a pound of his meaty fist. "I got down into the dungeon. The keeper said he'd never seen him, but I accused him of lying and threatened to remove his face, so he let me look into every cell. No Luis."

"Maybe Alfonso has hidden her in another dungeon, or another castle."

"No, they brought him to Burgos." He sighed. "I talked with the guards at every city gate, and all said they'd never seen him. I finally bought the truth from one guard, who admitted seeing something. Luis was brought in last night through the same gate we used. The guard saw them head for the castle, but now no one in the castle will admit to ever seeing him." He shook his head wearily. "I have tried to see prisoners before and been turned away, but no one has ever claimed the person wasn't there."

My mind flailed for ideas, but none came. "Why would Alfonso want to keep this a secret? He can't use Luis to hurt Rodrigo if no one *knows* about it."

Nuño pulled at his hair. "Something is very wrong."

I pushed down my rising panic. Think. Think. What came next? "Nuño, we need clothes for me. And perhaps Señora Lazcano has something we could eat."

With great effort, Nuño pushed himself to his feet, and took me downstairs. "Señora Lazcano, this is Señora Navarro." He explained my husband was missing, and that I needed extra clothes for my search.

The old woman peered at me doubtfully with bleary gray eyes. "Señora? Bah. Don Súarez, you know I am not running that kind of house here. You can just take this young—"

Nuño touched her arm. "Señora, remember my friend Luis? Luis Navarro?"

A wistful smile flickered briefly. "Luis—that nice young man with the blue eyes."

"This is his wife. It is Luis who is missing."

"Oh!" I was rewarded for my good choice in husbands with a wet kiss on each cheek, a bowl of warm stew, and a heavy black skirt, brown blouse, and black shawl.

Stomachs full but hearts aching, we returned to Nuño's room. He insisted I take the bed, and lay down by the door before I could disagree. Despite the constant city noises that had continued after sundown, I fell asleep.

When I woke up in the middle of the night, I thought at first it was because of a barking dog, or a woman's drunken song up the street, but it was the dry, frantic gasps coming from Nuño. I knelt by his side on the hard, gritty floor. "Nuño?"

"Cannot...breathe...no...air."

I held his hand. "Nuño, you are hyperventilating. You must calm down. Breathe more slowly. Breathe with me. Breathe in...breathe out...breathe in...breathe out." Gradually his breathing slowed to match mine.

Finally he squeezed my hand. "Kate, I fear they have already killed him."

I refused to believe it. "No, Nuño. She is here, somewhere. We will find her. I have a plan."

He sighed deeply, closing his eyes. "You have a plan."

"Yes."

His breath slowed more. "Good," he mumbled. I sat with him until his breathing evened out completely and he began to snore softly.

I felt my way back to the lumpy mattress and collapsed. Eyes wide open, I lay awake the rest of the night, trying to think of a plan.

CHAPTER TWENTY-FIVE

My creativity failed me. By morning all I could think of was a direct approach—convince Alfonso to reveal what he knew about Luis Navarro. He surely knew something; his men had captured her.

Nuño and I did not speak of his brief bout of panic. After we both wolfed down Señora Lazcano's thick, warm porridge, I gave him my hard-earned painting dinars and dirhems, and he left to find a money-changer. The market for Moorish cash flourished but stayed underground to avoid attention from Alfonso and his men. I kept the large gold coins Rodrigo had given me. They were too impressive to give up just yet.

After Nuño left, I changed into Señora Lazcano's dowdy clothes, draping the shawl over my head and around my neck, relieved it hid my filthy hair. I'd given up on being clean, but I was not alone; all of Burgos smelled of sweat and body oil. I ran my hands over the skirt. Despite its coarse scratchiness and heavy smell of someone else's body, at least it was practical.

The streets were already teeming with people, horses, and carts. After two nasty surprise splashes, I learned to run to the center of the street at the cry "*Agua va!*" from above. An occasional bright pot of begonias hung from balconies, and I passed ornately carved wooden doors that led to inner courtyards. The smell of garlic and rosemary emanated from one, and a small group of women chatted in a doorway, their deep laughter lightening my mood.

The crowd thickened near the castle. One man tried to sell me a smelly fish, and I elbowed my way through the carts and stalls. Another held out a gnarled hand for money, but I kept my head down and joined the people flowing into the castle.

Once inside, everyone strode purposefully in different directions to work or conduct business. I tried not to stare at the massive vaulted ceilings, the vibrant tapestries hanging on the wall, and walked until I found the circular staircase Nuño had described. I trudged up the wide, stone steps, slowing when I realized two bored guards stood at the top of the stairs, stopping people to ask their business. I pretended to drop something and bent over, heart racing, until both men argued with and then subdued a wild-haired woman who insisted she tell Alfonso the world would end in eleven days. I slipped past.

The guards had stopped most people, so I was nearly alone as I shuffled along the corridor, trying to blend in with the gray stone. The white and black marble floor, though grimy, stunned me with its strong geometric design.

The main corridor, also lined with tapestries, led to a wide open door, lined with columns and two more guards. Behind them stretched a massive vaulted room, voices bouncing off the high arches as small groups of men and women lounged, chatted, laughed, and generally looked gorgeous in gold-embroidered dresses, fur-lined cloaks, and perky headpieces with long veils. The yellows, greens, and blues were welcome relief from the earthy tones of Burgos commoners. I sighed. No one in the room was dressed like me.

"I would like to see the king," I said.

"Old woman," the taller man said wearily, "the King only sees his subjects on the first Tuesday of the month. Marcos, is this the first Tuesday of the month?"

"Hell, it ain't even Tuesday." Both men smirked, pleased with their supposed wit.

I dropped the old woman pose, standing straight, pulling the shawl off my head. "I need to see the King. It is very important."

The man called Marcos rolled his eyes. "Everyone thinks their business is important. Hell, I gotta crap and I have two hours left on duty. I think *that's* pretty important." The assholes chuckled.

One of the groups at the far end of the room shifted, revealing a slight man wearing a dull gold crown, a red and white tunic and a cape. Alfonso. Shit, he was less that one hundred feet away. Some in the nearest group watched me with amusement, others barely glanced at me. One woman sitting near the king, probably offended by my appearance, looked away quickly, her long blond hair becoming a curtain shielding her face.

As I glared at the guards, I realized I was willing to do almost anything to get through the door, but I didn't even get the chance to offer.

"Be gone, woman. Alfonso can only stomach you pathetic folk one day a month." He grabbed my arm and as he hustled me back to the top of the stairs, I struggled but he just gripped tighter.

"Let go, you pig," I snarled.

"Julio, stop sleeping at your post," the man snapped to one of the stair guards. "Do not let her up here again." He shoved me toward the stairs and I grabbed the cold wall for support. "Unless, of course, it is..."

"The first Tuesday of the month," all three morons chortled.

I hurried down the stairs. There had to be another way in. But after three hours, all I'd done was run into more guards, a cranky housekeeper, and four nasty Doberman type dogs. I'd gotten hopelessly lost twice and had even startled a servant straining over his chamber pot. "Try prunes," I muttered before slamming that door shut and trying another. The guards were wary even during siesta, so, exhausted and discouraged, I dragged myself back to Nuño, who paced in the street near Señora Lazcano's. He read my face and didn't need to ask. Once in the room, he handed me a pile of Castilian coins, explaining the value of each.

"We will need more money, so I am going to start calling in some favors," Nuño said. I nodded, then collapsed on the bed.

For three more days I tried getting into the castle, stomping around the room in frustration every night. Then for the three days King Alfonso left the city to hunt boar, Nuño scoured the city and even began visiting castles and monasteries nearby, talking with friends, pleading for information. I got into the castle kitchen one day, posing as a cook, but had to flee when the cranky housekeeper recognized me and screamed I was trying to poison the king. The castle depressed me with its walls covered with religious paintings—sorrowful virgins and martyred saints.

"Why is this asshole so well-guarded?" I had cried one afternoon.

Nuño had shrugged. "If you'd been able to kill your brother, King of Castile, because he was poorly guarded, you would make damned sure the same didn't happen to you. Alfonso does not trust anyone."

As our despair grew, it was oddly comforting to talk about Luis. I told Nuño about the day by the pond when we'd been discovered. One evening after too much wine, I described our wedding night, and Nuño had sputtered and coughed up his ale, stunned Luis hadn't killed me on the spot.

He shared stories of long, hard journeys together, of nights when they'd drunk jug after jug and had sang themselves silly.

On our seventh day in Burgos, we knew no more than the day we'd arrived, and I could barely eat with worry. But Nuño had me almost laughing with stories of Luis's near catastrophes.

"A few months after Luis arrived in Valvanera, Alvar and I walked the woods near the abbey and saw a small pile of rags browned with dried blood." Nuño blushed. "I have sisters, so I knew immediately whose and what it was." He smiled. "I told Alvar they were my rags, that Luis had bloodied my nose in a fight."

"Fast thinking."

"I had to do a lot of that. No one ever noticed that Luis supposedly punched me bloody about once a month. And of course no one ever said a word to Luis—they didn't want him to start punching them instead."

What a life Elena, as Luis, had led. She had gone through so much. If still alive, could she get through whatever she was facing now?

A polite knock on the door interrupted our stories. Señora Lazcano, a small basket in her arms, asked Nuño if he'd deliver this food to her friend Maria, whose husband was very ill.

We found Maria's house without difficulty. In her cozy front room, lit by two small lanterns, her two teenaged daughters bent toward the feeble light, stitching. Maria accepted the food gratefully, and inquired of Señora Lazcano's health. As she and Nuño talked, I approached a lovely green dress and cape hanging on the wall. Gold and silver stitching ran up the front, and down the sleeves. Intrigued, I stroked the smooth, shiny fabric. Now this dress could get attention.

I gasped. Of course! John Malloy's *Dress for Success*, the businesswomen's mantra. Tailored suits, sleek shoes—clothes that exuded confidence, competence. Clothes that murmured, "Ignore me at your peril, you pathetic little man." An idea thrilled through me.

I whirled to face Maria. "I would like to buy this dress."

"I'm sorry, but Señora Menendez—"

"I will pay you twice what she has offered." Nuño's eyebrows raised slightly. I turned toward the woman's daughters. "And I need two ladies-in-waiting, who need to be as well-dressed as I."

"My daughters? But—"

"I will pay you and them well. Do they have appropriate dresses?"

The girls giggled and looked at each other's drab brown muslin dresses. "No," the younger one said, "but we know where we could... borrow two."

"Claudia!"

"Mama, that spoiled brat will never know she's missing two dresses. You know she has dozens. We've sewn them all."

"I don't—"

"Maria, the girls will be perfectly safe. I just need a few hours of their time in the morning. Tomorrow, you see, I go to see the King."

❖

The next morning I breathed a sigh of relief when Maria and her daughters arrived and both girls' faces, necks, and hands were scrubbed pink, their hair clean and pulled back in demure buns. They'd *borrowed* two lovely dresses from the spoiled client who lived several blocks away—the soft greens complemented my own dress. I had scrubbed myself as well.

"Impressive," Nuño said, and as we set out, I struggled to hold my stiff skirt above the mud.

At the castle entrance I asked Nuño to drop back. "If you are along, the guards will pay no attention to me." Scowling, Nuño did as I asked, then the girls and I, after discussing their behavior—eyes down, hands clasped, no giggling, no speaking—swept into the castle.

Two different guards stood at the top of the staircase. With my nose in the air and two maids following respectfully off to my sides, I didn't even look at the men, but marched right past. God damn. Dress for success. Why hadn't I thought of this sooner?

Marcos and his asshole friend again guarded the throne room, but they did not recognize me.

"Señora Sophia Loren of Valvanera to see the King. He expects me."

The men looked at each other, then nodded politely. "I'm sorry, señora," Marcos stammered, "but he said nothing to us."

"I bring news from his exiled knight, Rodrigo Díaz of Vivar."

Beads of perspiration sprung to each forehead. "I do not know if we should—" I moved next to Marcos, slid my dagger out of my cloak sleeve and pressed it between his legs. "Jesus!" the guard jumped then froze. The girls gasped behind me.

"Do you like your penis?"

The white-faced man nodded, then licked his lips. "Very much," he finally whispered.

"Then waste no more of my time. Announce me to Alfonso." Marcos nodded, turned on his heel, and strode down the black-marbled center of the hall. I replaced the dagger, then followed, dignified and serene.

Marcos bowed as he reached the group gathered around Alfonso. Ten curious faces turned toward us. "Señora Sophia Loren of Valvanera, who brings news from Rodrigo Díaz of Vivar." I moved forward, then curtsied, not too shallow to be rude, not too deep to be fawning. I forgot to ask Nuño if royalty expected to speak first, so I waited.

"So, news from the great Rodrigo. What could it be?" Alfonso grinned at his audience. "Has he fathered a Moorish bastard?" As his courtiers laughed and clapped, Alfonso leaned back in his massive gold chair, its red velvet worn bare along the edges. "Paloma de Palma predicted he'd come crawling back on his knees. She's never been wrong yet," he crowed.

For a split second I thought of Anna and her beloved pen name— Paloma de Palma. A spasm ran down my back. No, Anna was back in the twenty-first century caring for Arturo. Terror for Luis pushed everything else aside.

"Your highness, I have come to discuss—"

"Paloma, my new *advisor*—" No one attempted to hide their lewd chuckles. "—says that I will outlive Rodrigo Díaz by years. I think you should return to my dear friend Rodrigo and tell him that." His audience laughed again, and I realized I'd never get anywhere this way.

"Your majesty, if you take the security of your realm that lightly, then clearly I waste my time and yours. I will go elsewhere with my information." I curtsied, then began to turn away.

"Just a moment, hasty woman." More chuckles from the peanut gallery. "Come, sit with us. Your beauty graces this court."

Rigid with anger and frustration that this joker was my only link to Luis, I stood before him. "What I have to say is for your ears only."

The others continued to laugh, but I finally had Alfonso's attention. With a jerk of his head, he dismissed the courtiers, who left, muttering loudly about my manners and I dismissed the girls. Heart pounding, I turned to face Alfonso. Adolescent acne scarred both cheeks, and his chin was sharp as a dagger, but otherwise he was an ordinary man. Perhaps I'd expected him to be bigger-than-life, instead of average. I would not be afraid. He lifted his palms, impatient.

I took a deep breath. "You were lucky at Albarracín."

His eyes narrowed as he considered me. "We lost."

"You could have lost much more. If Ben Yusef had not returned to Africa, he would have retaken Toledo."

The king shook his head. "No, that—"

"He will return. He will fortify Zaragoza, Valencia, and Cordoba. He and his hordes will sweep into Christian lands—Barcelona, Aragon, Castile, León, Asturias. He will drive you like rats to the north until you fall into the sea."

Alfonso's cheeks reddened. "No one dares speak to me in this—"

"Musta'in, Hayib, and the others have built a massive army, larger than any reported to you. Zaragoza is a rich city and has spared no expense. I have seen it. I have seen their new weapons, more lethal than anything ever devised."

"Why are you here?" Alfonso's eyes flew around the empty room, perhaps regretting we were alone.

"You need Rodrigo Díaz on your side. He has never lost a battle." I paused. "Ever. When Ben Yusef returns, when the Moorish emirs band together, you need Díaz to fight with you, not against you."

The king licked his lips, shifting nervously. "I have a strong and powerful army."

"Children with sticks compared to the Moors." I sweetened the pot, removing the pouch and spilling the brilliant coins into my hand. "Rodrigo Díaz is a very wealthy man now, as are all his men. Mu'tamin rewarded them generously for their efforts. This great wealth could return to Castile and León if you lift the exile." I handed one of the coins to the eager king, but put the rest back in the pouch and returned it to my belt.

Alfonso leaned back in his throne, turning the coin over and over. "And what does Rodrigo Díaz of Vivar expect in exchange for his renewed allegiance to me?"

I paused, waiting for his full attention. "He expects the safe return of his first lieutenant, Luis Navarro."

The man nodded. "Yes, I expected as much." My heart raced so fast my hands and head tingled. I struggled to hide my anguish but failed as Alfonso studied me, holding me with his steady gaze. "I wonder, however, why Rodrigo would send a woman with this message. So unlike him." The man shifted on his throne. "I suspect you came of your own accord...but why?"

The only way through this seemed to be the truth. "I am not really Señora Sophia Loren of Valvanera."

His eyes widened, then relaxed. "Of course not. I heard rumors Navarro had taken a lovely but overly spirited wife. You are Señora Navarro, yes?"

My nostrils flared as I sought more oxygen. "Yes."

Alfonso rubbed his chin thoughtfully. "Paloma has warned me not to lift the exile. She predicts Díaz will bring trouble if I allow him to return."

"You have no choice if you are to save Castile, León, and Asturias. You have no choice if you ever hope to expel the Moors from this peninsula." Our eyes locked and I held his gaze, willing him to see that lifting the exile and releasing Luis were his best options. I barely breathed.

"Your highness," a timid servant called from the side door. "Señora Paloma de Palma has returned from her morning ride."

Alfonso raised his hand for silence as we stared at each other, measuring, plotting, hoping. "I will see her shortly. Leave us." My heart pounded so loudly that surely Alfonso would hear and somehow use my fear to his advantage. But his gaze dropped to the coin in his hand. He stood, stretched, then walked to a blank spot on his wall, hands behind his back. "I hear you are a painter."

From whom? "Yes."

"If I tell you where your husband is and lift the exile, Rodrigo and his wealth will return. He will agree to be my loyal subject and fight where and when I demand he fight." I nodded, fairly certain, but at this point not caring what El Cid did. Alfonso pointed to the wall. "A painting showing King Alfonso victorious over the Moors would look very nice here, don't you think?"

"Done," I said, mouth dry.

Alfonso returned to his throne, oozing confidence now that the tables had turned. He controlled our meeting now and he knew it. He took his time setting back into the chair, folding his cape carefully around his knees. "My fair-haired Paloma is a beauty, but she worries too much, so I will lift the exile. I suspect you are right in this matter, and I will not gamble my realm's future."

I did not move, terrified any small movement or change in my expression might interfere with what had to come next. Luis's life depended on it.

"Your husband is in a castle just to the west of Burgos, on the hill between Burgos and Tardajoz. Gonzalez assured me he would come to no harm."

"Gudesto Gonzalez?" I gasped, staggering forward.

"Just as my men brought in Navarro, Gudesto appeared and suggested he take him to Tardajoz in case someone, such as yourself, attempted to free Navarro." I could not breathe as fear gripped my lungs, squeezing, pumping. "Calm yourself, Señora Navarro. I know your husband is Rodrigo's favorite. He lives. Gudesto would not disobey me."

I clenched my fists. No, Gudesto would not kill Luis. But if he discovered her sex, he could do much worse.

CHAPTER TWENTY-SIX

Memories of those endless, dark hours hanging from a rope by my wrists flooded back. Pain shooting up my arms, heavy head, sheer exhaustion. What if Luis had suffered the same fate? Why hadn't I told her that Gudesto was capable of torture? I could barely focus as the girls helped me down the castle stairs and to the waiting Nuño, who paid the girls and dismissed them. I leaned against Nuño as the girls scampered away. Oh, Luis.

"Gudesto has Luis," I whispered. "He took her the day they arrived in Burgos."

"No, God, no." He took my arm as I stumbled toward a puddle. "Where?"

"The castle at Tardajoz."

Nuño cursed. "That was one of the first places I checked. My cousin serves the owner." Anger boiled to the surface. "But my cousin is like a brother to me. How could he lie?"

"Nuño," I restrained his gesticulating arm. "Gudesto would not keep her with other prisoners."

"I don't understand."

"I'll explain later." I changed out of my "rich woman" dress and back into my peasant clothes then we hurried straight to the stables, paid the keeper, and rode out the west gate of Burgos. Less than a hour's hard ride brought us to a small castle ringed by two dozen cottages and huge flocks of sheep. We left the road and approached through a stand of oaks, hanging back in the shadows. Ten soldiers guarded the front gate and dozens more walked the ramparts above.

"There were no soldiers when I came four days ago."

"Gudesto heard you sought Luis."

Nuño, eyes narrowed, watched the men patrolling the castle. "I can raise fifty men in Burgos who hate Gudesto and support Luis. We will storm the castle."

As I squinted against the sunlight flashing on the distant helmets, I could only see one way to do this. When Gudesto heard the exile had been lifted, he would kill or expose Luis, so I had to get to her first, and by myself. "I have a better idea. You raise ten men, storm the castle, and then surrender."

Nuño's eyes widened, but the determined set to his jaw did not change. "Luis said you had some odd ideas, but that is ridiculous."

I explained my torture at Gudesto's hands, leaving out the more painful details. "Luis will be held in a remote area of the castle. Her rescue must be quiet. I must be the only one to find her, or her secret will be revealed."

Nuño caught on. "So when we pretend to be overwhelmed by Gudesto's men and surrender, he relaxes. He thinks the only threat has been eliminated."

"You might even tell him I died or fell ill. Then I sneak in and bring her out." Easy as pie for someone from the twenty-first century who continually screwed things up in the eleventh. "But you will be left as Gudesto's prisoners."

Nuño shook his head. "No problem. My cousin will help us escape. He hates Gudesto."

I racked my brain as we stood, horses snorting softly, but no other option was swift enough, or private enough. We discussed the details, then Nuño slipped back through the trees and galloped toward Burgos. I would watch and wait.

❖

By mid-afternoon I'd worried my nails nearly down to the quick, and I had stared at the castle until my eyes burned, searching the windows for a sign. Late afternoon a firewood cart rattled past me on the road to Burgos, pulled by a tired donkey. Leading the animal was a woman bent with fatigue, a basket full of twigs bouncing on her back. Perfect.

I patted Rozinante's rump. "I'll be back, girl." I dashed through the woods until I came out on the road ahead of the woman. "Excuse me, Señora, could I help you?"

The woman's head shot up in alarm. "What?"

"Here, let me take that." I tugged the worn leather straps off her back and shrugged the pack onto my own back. "You look tired. I will carry this for you."

Eyes narrowed, she finally spoke. "I ain't sharing what I make wit you."

I nodded, shifting the awkward pack so it wouldn't poke me. "I want no money. But I've been walking alone for hours and would like some company." She merely grunted, then tugged on the donkey's lead. The massive pile of sticks shuddered but did not fall off the wagon.

We did not speak as I accompanied the woman to a number of cottages near the castle. I shivered when we passed into the shadow of the heavy stone. The woman haggled with each customer and complained bitterly about the prices, but I unloaded armful after armful, wincing as the sharp twigs pierced my clothes.

The guards at the castle gates glared as the old woman passed through the gate, but apparently, found her harmless. Heart pounding, I followed the cart. I was in.

The woman stopped at the stables, selling more wood, then headed for the back of the castle. As I walked next to a wobbly wheel, shouts rang out from the ramparts. "We are under attack!" Soldiers hustled to their posts, one nearly knocking me over. My pulse raced as I followed the now hurrying woman. A servant in a thin linen skirt emerged from the kitchens and began inspecting the wood. More shouts pierced the air, then the ground shook with thundering hooves. We were behind the castle; all the action was around in front.

"Release Luis Navarro!" came Nuño's furious cry. Swords began clanging together. More shouts and mysterious thuds and clankings drew me back to the castle's corner, but the fighting was over by the time I peered around the rough stone.

"Surrender, Súarez. You are surrounded."

Nuño's fury, his frantic whirling of his horse to seek a way out, his tense but proud bearing, the resigned drop of his head, convinced even me.

"Nuño, my old friend, I have been expecting you." Gudesto stood at a second story window so I drew back into the shadows.

"I have come for Luis. Release him."

Gudesto's laugh raised the hair on my neck. "You are in no position to make demands, old friend. Besides, I hold Luis for his crimes against Castile, his crimes against his sacred vows." His voice grew angrier. "But most importantly, I hold Luis for his crimes against God and against the natural order of our world."

I pressed my forehead against the wall, pushing into the sharp roughness. He knew. The bastard knew.

While Nuño and Gudesto exchanged insults, the painful kind only two people who knew each other well can wield, I raced back to the kitchen and slipped inside. Moist heat surrounded me as young boys stoked three massive ovens. I entered the main castle, found the corner staircase and headed for the third floor.

Thinking I was delivering firewood, no one stopped me, The pack dug into my back, but I didn't dare remove it as I flew along the corridor, checking doors, apologizing sullenly to a few surprised shouts. Nothing. This castle was smaller than Hayib's, and every room seemed to be used. Then I found a narrow stairway leading to the castle tower. I scrambled up into the tower, finding nothing but a chair, piles of pigeon droppings, and an incredible view.

But as I returned to the third floor, I stopped at a small stone door, identical to the walls, just beside the staircase. I rattled the doorknob, but it was locked so I pressed my ear against the cool, damp stone. Something rustled inside. "Luis?" I whispered, peering under the door to see a woman's bare feet, and what might have been men's boots off to one side

Luis! I pulled with all my strength, but the door and latch held. "Luis! Say something!" Nothing. Why wouldn't she respond? Shit. I slumped against the door. Only Gudesto would have the key.

I returned to the second floor, slowing to an old woman shuffle, offering wood to anyone I passed. When a woman servant said "yes," and I lowered my pack, Gudesto and two men walked by. My pulse pounded in my ears as I held my slumped posture, face averted, afraid to breathe.

"Good job, Julio. We'll let them think about their foolish rescue attempt in the dungeon for awhile." My hands perspired as I handed over the wood, for while I could handle downtown Chicago traffic cool as you please, this life and death stuff terrified me. As Gudesto passed, I noticed a brass ring of keys dangled from his left hip. "I feel like celebrating...for many reasons," Gudesto said as he disappeared into a nearby room. I accepted the woman's coins, then thought fast.

I could only get the key if Gudesto were dead, or asleep. How could I make him fall asleep in the middle of the afternoon? I needed to drug him. But how? I shifted my weight and my fanny pack pressed against my belly. The antihistamines in my fanny pack.

A servant emerged from Gudesto's quarters, and I followed him to the bustling kitchen, where he poured three large mugs of ale. "Hey," I croaked, "Cook wants you out back."

"Me? Why?"

I kept my gaze on the ground, subservient to the servant. "Don't know. Want to buy some wood?" With a snort, he left me alone with the mugs, and I emptied all twelve capsules, four in each mug, then hid behind a cabinet. The servant returned, shaking his head angrily, then took the tray upstairs, with me a slinking shadow behind him.

The hard part was waiting without loitering, risking expulsion by a conscientious servant. An hour passed as I hovered in a doorway several rooms down from Gudesto's, waiting until the laughter and talk died down.

Finally silence. I counted to one hundred, and still no sound, so I peeked in. Gudesto and his companions were each sprawled out in a chair, eyes closed, mouths open in raspy snores. Good. Eleventh century people were highly susceptible to twenty-first century drugs.

I was so damned scared I was sure Gudesto would wake at the sound of my chattering teeth. Indiana Jones I was not. I slipped off my boots, wincing at the icy stone floor, and set them on a small rug. One step. Two steps. Six steps and I stood at Gudesto's side, panting silently through my mouth. His shirt was wet with ale, and he smelled of sweat and leather.

Trying to suppress my tremors, I lifted the loop and slid off the ring, clutching the keys so they wouldn't rattle. I backed up. One step. Two steps. I picked up my boots and tiptoed from the room.

Excitement gripped me as I flew down the hall. I *did* it. I raced up the stairs, stopping only to shrug off the basket and tug on my boots. At the stone door I fumbled with the keys until one turned the lock with a dull click. Panting, I swung the door open and stepped inside.

A narrow bed ran along one wall, and a rope hung from the center of the medium-sized room. A woman, face in the shadows, sat on a bench, bare feet and ankles exposed under a heavy green skirt. Her chest rose slightly with each breath.

"Luis?" Mouth dry, I stepped forward, feeling in my fanny pack for my flashlight. The narrow beam revealed my fear—the woman seated in the corner was Luis. But it wasn't. I flew to her, hugged her to my chest, then touched her face, her arms, her hands. Everything intact. Except Luis. Her blank eyes sent chills down my arms as she looked through me. I shook her by the shoulder.

"Damn it, Luis, it's *me*." No response. I shook her again, then frantic, I half-slapped her cheek. Still nothing. "Luis, we have to leave *now*." I pulled her to her feet, and she stood, but her arms hung limply at her sides.

"What did he do to you?" I whirled on my heel, desperate for a clue. Her tunic hung on one wall, leggings on another, red blouse on a third, sword on the fourth. Elena's only defenses were her identity as Luis, and her sword. Gudesto's cruelty went deep, for he knew what to do. Strip her of all that, then display it just out of reach. Without her clothes, without her sword, Luis was Elena, alone, exposed, and vulnerable.

Furious, I yanked the clothes down and tied them into a bundle. "Honey, we need to leave." I stuck her dagger in my pocket, fastened the sword belt around my waist, jammed her clothes and boots under one arm, then half-supporting her, got her moving toward the door.

"Good day, my lovely Kate."

I froze, every nerve quivering as I raised my head.

Gudesto, groggy, stood in the doorway. "I dreamt a beautiful woman stole my keys."

I stepped back against the nearest wall, hugging Luis to me. Gudesto yawned, then stepped inside, casually closing the door behind him. Luis's muscles tensed against me, but otherwise she remained catatonic.

"You bastard," I spat out, struggling for breath. "What the hell did you *do* to her?"

He shrugged. "Same thing you and I did." I shivered. He made torture sound so intimate. "She was stubborn, but not as a strong as you. Even then it took me five days."

If I hadn't been supporting much of Luis's weight, I would have squeezed his throat until his eyes popped. "Five days for what?" But I knew.

Gudesto yawned again, then sauntered over, leaning beside me, eyes half-lidded. "There is nothing," he whispered softly, "*nothing* like spilling your seed in the womb of your enemy." His velvet tone barely hid the raw malice.

"Bastard." Fury pulsed through me. I growled. "You raped her."

"No, no. I am not a brute. Luis, or whatever her real name is, came to that bed over there willingly." He sighed. "It was incredible."

"How did she end up like this?" I had to keep him talking. How could I get us both out?

"God is punishing her for dressing as a man," Gudesto snapped, his face dark and blotchy. "I took her body, but God took her mind."

"When?"

A brief look of confusion flickered across his face. "I do not know. When I returned for our second encounter, I found her like this, insane. She was much less responsive that time, but I managed just the same, as I have several times since."

"You son of a bitch." Now my entire body trembled. My fists itched to smash his face, but the man was armed.

Gudesto moved closer to my right, and Luis slumped against my left. His voice hardened. "She deserves this. She fooled us all, living as a man. When I think of all the years I have known him...*her*. My god, how unnatural. It's a sin against God." He slapped the wall over my head. "I discovered his sex when I made him remove his clothing for a little friendly torture." His red face leaned in closer, suffocatingly close. "You are both disgusting, and you will pay for your sins."

"All because of Marisella." My left arm went numb with Luis's weight, the right not doing much better. Gudesto was too close for me to draw Luis's sword, but I could do nothing with it anyway.

Gudesto's staccato laugh hurt my ears. "No, you stupid woman. Luis broke his sacred vows to the Caballeros. He could have led us to glory, but he was weak. He lost his stomach for what needed to be done. He primed us, he honed us, then he abandoned us. *My* hate for the Moors will *never* die."

I could feel the weight of Luis's dagger in my pocket. "Luis didn't abandon you. The Caballeros disbanded. They—"

"Disbanded? Christ, woman, you do not break a vow sealed with blood." Gudesto's voice vibrated. "Luis *made* us. He gave us strength, purpose. When I rode as a Caballero de Valvanera, I did God's work, wreaking vengeance on his enemies. Luis ruined everything when he lost his nerve. Without the Caballeros…" His fist clenched as tightly as his voice, and he stopped.

Light broke through my fear. "Without the Caballeros, you are nothing." His narrowed, cold eyes told me I'd hit the bull's-eye. "Following Luis, murdering Moors. That's who you were."

"I devoted my life to Luis and his cause. We were the *Great* Caballeros. The entire frontier feared us. Then Luis decides that Moors are good, that Moors should live?" He pounded the wall above my head. "I do not think so. I will not stop until the infidels have been slaughtered or driven from this land."

Religious wars didn't make sense to me in the twenty-first century, and they didn't make any more sense in the eleventh. "What are you going to do with us?" I asked as I finally gave up and lowered Luis to the chilly floor. As I bent over, I slipped the dagger from my pocket and hid it in the folds of my skirt.

Gudesto straightened, shook off his twisted memories, then smiled. "I intend to marry, but Marisella is a whore, so I will not have her. Perhaps Don Pablo's daughter, as she is very wealthy. First, however, I will take your whore *husband* to Alfonso and reveal her sex. I'll make sure Rodrigo is there to witness it. He will likely want to strike the first blow. After the pretender has been vilified and humiliated, she will be executed for the crime of living as a man. God will punish Luis for abandoning me."

Sweat slicked my palms and forehead. The dagger handle warmed as I clutched it. My brain thudded painfully against my skull as cold sweat trickled down my back.

Gudesto moved even closer, arm against the wall by my head, leering down at me. "So you see, you'll be much better off with me. Besides, I require more than one woman." When he grabbed my breast and teased my nipple, I gasped. Given my earlier weakness in Lerida, he must have taken that as a sound of pleasure, for he smiled and leaned down to kiss me.

The dagger slid in more easily than I expected.

"Oh," Gudesto breathed softly. We both stared stupidly at my hand around the narrow hilt. Then I twisted the dagger sharply, drawing it out. Before the stunned man could respond, I flipped into an overhead grip and slammed it into the left side of his chest.

"Jesus," he cried as blood began spurting over both of us. "Not you." He staggered back and hope and fury and fear gripped me in such a spasm I stabbed again and again. He threw up his arms but nothing stopped my rage.

He finally fell back against the far wall, sliding to the floor. Blood stained his tunic, spurting from a slash over his heart. I collapsed across from him, nauseous from the smell of blood, my arms still tingling from the shock of the blows. I lay my head in Luis's motionless lap and waited, eyes locked with Gudesto's.

He struggled to speak, wincing with effort. "Someone else will... discover Luis's secret. He...she will never...survive." Blood ran from his nose and ears. "And when she is...killed, my spirit...will rejoice." He sank deeper into himself. We remained that way until, slowly, his gaze grew even more blank and empty than Luis's. I had killed a man.

My ragged sob echoed in the room as I wiped the sticky blood off on my skirt. I pulled Luis to her feet, wrapped my shawl around her head, grabbed her clothes, and half-led, half-dragged my lover from the castle. Nuño waited at the agreed spot behind the stables with two horses, freed by his cousin as planned. "Help me," I pleaded as we rounded the corner.

"Where is Luis? Why do we rescue this woman?" I pulled the shawl back to reveal Luis's face and blank eyes. "Mother of God. What—"

"Gudesto did this. Help me get—"

"I will kill him!" Nuño thundered, but I grabbed his arm.

"I already have. Help me get her into the saddle."

With a low cry of anguish, Nuño lifted Luis into the saddle and I mounted behind her. Together we galloped out the east gate and down the dusty road. No one tried to stop Nuño and two peasant women. We stopped long enough for Nuño to retrieve Rozinante, then we rode hard toward Burgos. Tears stung my eyes as I held my reins with one hand and gripped Luis around the waist with my other arm. It had been my turn to save her, to be *her* knight in shining mail, and I had arrived too late.

CHAPTER TWENTY-SEVEN

I pulled up short as Burgos appeared on the horizon. "We can't take her into Burgos in this condition."

Nuño looked at Luis, his Adam's apple working furiously. "No, we can't," he said hoarsely.

"I need a place where she and I can be alone for awhile. Maybe I can bring her out of this."

Nuño's gaze snapped to me. "He is not permanently insane?"

"She isn't insane at all. It's a type of shock. She could not accept what happened to her, so she shut a door in her mind, closing everything and everyone out." I struggled for an eleventh century metaphor. "What happens to a river mill when logs from up river jam it?"

"Shuts down."

"Exactly."

Nuño wiped an eye. "You can help him?"

"I must try."

A heavy sigh escaped his broad chest. "I know of a cottage near here. My mother's cousins lived there but abandoned it last year to move in with their children in Burgos."

We left the road and headed north around the city. The sun dipped low in the sky, stretching our shadows out like those in a fun house mirror. Burgos shone like gold in the last of the sunlight, and cool dusk had settled upon us by the time we reached the cottage. Nuño lifted Luis off the horse, then stood there, awkward, until I took Luis by the elbow and led her inside.

A fine layer of red dust coated the rough oak table and two chairs, the narrow bed, the single cupboard. "I will sleep outside," Nuño offered.

I sat Luis down on a chair, then motioned for Nuño to follow me outside. I dug my toe into the soft soil. "Nuño, I need to do this alone.

If you are here, she may not snap out of it."

He worried the inside of a cheek. "If he does recover, will he remember I saw him as a woman?"

"I don't know."

"You are not safe here. Luis cannot defend you." He stopped, one eyebrow raised thoughtfully. "Although you did kill Gudesto, didn't you?"

My fingernails were still brown with blood. "With a dagger. But I am useless with a sword."

"Few women can handle a sword," he said softly with a quick glance back at the thatched-roof cottage. "You need food. You need protection. You need privacy. I will provide all three." He scanned the horizon. "See that hill over there, the one that looks like a camel's hump?" I nodded. "I will camp there. I will bring supplies from Burgos. I will hunt for you."

"—and skin and gut the animal?"

He smiled. "Yes. I will be close enough to hear you shout, but far enough away Luis will not know I'm nearby."

I hugged Nuño, who flushed bright red in the near darkness. "Thank you, Nuño. Be patient. This may take some time."

"I would wait long after this beard grows gray, if there was any hope of restoring Luis." With a curt nod, he mounted and rode into the woods. I unsaddled both the horses, pulled up a bucket of water from the well for them, then returned to Luis.

❖

For two days I cleaned, cooked, and gathered firewood. I scrubbed the blood off my hands, arms, and clothes. I fed Luis, then led her outside into the woods where she would squat, relieve herself, and then I'd sit her in a chair in the sun. I talked to her constantly.

"Honey, Gudesto did the same to me. Torture can make you do things you wouldn't ordinarily do." I told her the details of my time with Gudesto and wished I'd had the courage to share this with her sooner. I told her fairy tales with strong women. At first, when her facial expression didn't change and her hands never moved from her lap, I lost heart so quickly I ran out of words. But after a short recharge, I started again. I just kept talking.

After I'd cut and fed her the cooked rabbit Nuño had left on the rock by the cottage door, I held her hand. "Luis, I am not returning to my time. You will not be alone. We will be together. We can make plans, build a life. It will be great." A huge weight pressed against my chest when I realized how alone Luis must have felt. She didn't know I'd changed my mind. When Alfonso's men captured her, when Gudesto discovered her, she was certain I had entered the cave at Santillana and been whisked from her life forever.

At night she lay on the bed beside me, flat on her back, her eyes fixed on the rough board ceiling until sleep finally closed them.

The third day her stare was as blank as the moment I'd found her. I had tried calling her Elena, but that hadn't worked, and I was running out of ideas. Then I found her bundle of clothes. Of course. I led her to the bed, and gently removed her filthy skirt and blouse. She went rigid at my touch but made no move to stop me. I tugged on her leggings, pulling them up over her waist, laced the boots, fastened the tunic, and even strapped on her sword. *Now* she looked like my Luis.

I took her for a walk, pointing out the wildflowers, chattering the entire time about the house we would have, the animals we would raise for food, the needy children we might help. Since Anna had sole responsibility for Arturo, it was the least I could do.

Later, I sat her on the bed while I gathered firewood. When I returned, she had not moved from that spot, but wore her green skirt and blouse again. "Hmmph," I said.

The next morning I dressed her in the leggings and tunic; by noon she had changed back. A sliver of hope shone through the dark tunnel ahead. Some part of her either didn't like the clothes, or didn't think she deserved to wear them. The third time it happened, I changed her again, then led her outside to my campfire.

"Luis, sit on this log. Good, now let's watch the fire for awhile. Oops! Look there. That ugly green skirt has fallen into the fire." The heavy fabric smoked, first white, then black, and I wrinkled my nose. "Oh dear, and look at that. I dropped the blouse as well. How clumsy of me." Luis stared straight ahead, but she left her own clothes on after that.

I made no more progress for days. Now and then a thin feather of smoke floated above Nuño's hill, but I never saw him, not even when he brought meat, fruit from Burgos, milk, and other staples.

At least once a day I talked about shame, and that it wasn't good to let it eat you up, that people could live through shame, that a person could grow *stronger* from difficult times.

Nothing. One morning, desperate, I stripped off my clothes and bustled around the cottage totally naked, covered only with goose bumps. Shameless, I leaned over her when cutting up her food. I pressed against her when I helped her stand. I moved the table to one side and sat across from her, legs splayed wide open while I gnawed on brown rye bread. I figured I'd get pneumonia, but the chilly day was worth it when, that evening, as I passed her in the lamplight, her eyes followed my body for a split second, then returned to their fixed stare.

I told her about my meeting with Alfonso, and that he'd lifted the exile. I told her I'd killed Gudesto and that her secret was safe. I told her Nuño was safe. I told her about strong women, and how they'd had to face adversity and move on. I told her strength comes from *not* winning every battle.

But Luis's resolve to remain shut down was strong. On the seventh night I curled around her in bed, exhausted, out of ideas. I'd talked and cajoled all week.

"Luis, you must come back to me," I murmured. "I need you." An owl hooted outside. I remember Luis's words in the forest after she'd rescued me from Lerida: We are like two trees, entwined. I pushed past the lump in my throat. Two pine trees entwined as one, their vulnerable centers turned inward, hidden from view except to each other, their strengths turned outward, stretching out to the world. Me and Luis.

Soon Luis's regular breathing told me she slept, but I lay awake listening to the wind whispering through the pines around us, thinking about her strengths, about mine, about how two people could share those strengths, and both be stronger for it.

Luis mumbled something so I rolled toward her. Was she back? "Let me live," she whispered, then fell back into a troubled sleep. I sat straight up in bed. Suddenly I knew what to do. Luis's log jam included much more than Gudesto; I had to free her from all her memories to bring her back.

❖

When Nuño arrived just before dawn with bread, cheese, and a baked chicken from Señora Lazcano, I was outside waiting for him.

"No change," he said as I accepted the food, a statement, not a question.

"It's time for drastic measures," I said. "Nuño, I need some of your clothes—leggings, blouse, and tunic. I need a sword, shield, and mail."

He frowned. "Now what?"

"When can you get these to me?"

"This afternoon. But—"

"Luis and I will nap during siesta. Leave them behind that tree. And Nuño—" I touched his arm to get his full attention. "No matter what you hear tonight, you must *not* come."

He rubbed his week's-growth of stubble, eyes weary. "You are the puzzle Luis said you were."

"No matter *what* you hear, no matter *what* you see. Will you promise?"

He squinted as if in pain. "I do not like it."

"My plan may not work. If it doesn't, it makes no difference what happens to me. But it will not work if you appear."

He blew out both cheeks, then glared at me. "I promise."

❖

The moon rose almost full, a luminous disk lighting the night and the cottage in soft shades of blue. I didn't know if the bright light would work to my advantage, or against it. I left a small candle burning on the table, then I lay Luis down on the bed, resting beside her for at least an hour until I was certain she slept.

Then I rose as quietly as possible, slipped outside, and changed into Nuño's clothes, shivering despite the unseasonably warm night. My body nearly floated to be free of my long skirt, but it came back to earth when I buckled on the heavy coat of mail. The weight would slow me down, but I dared not go without.

I strapped on the sword Nuño had left, pulling it from its scabbard with a groan. Damn, it was heavy. If I survived this little stunt, it would be one hundred percent luck and zero percent skill. Then I hid both our daggers behind the woodpile. El Picador was a dangerous enough foe without a dagger to use in a close kill.

I hefted the diamond-shaped shield, made of rock-hard cowskin stretched across a wooden frame. Damn, I should have asked for a helmet as well. I stood outside the cottage door, sword resting on the ground, heart pounding, adrenaline racing. Only the need to have Luis *look* at me again, not just through me, gave me the courage to open the door and step inside, closing it softly behind me. I blew out the candle, then tiptoeing, I lay Luis's sword on the floor next to the bed. Show time.

Earlier I had moved the table and chairs to one wall so there was nothing for me to fall over. That also meant Luis had a clear shot at me. I retreated to the window, but back in the shadows, took a deep breath, let it out in a ragged shudder, then began.

"Luis Navarro!" I shouted in as deep a voice as I could. "You coward! You bastard! I have your wife." The bedclothes rustled. "You cannot save her." A scrambling from the bed, then two boots hit the floor.

I screamed in my own voice—"Luis! Luis! Help!" My blood froze at the thin sharp sound of a sword sliding from a scabbard. I raised my shield. "He's taking me away. Help! I—"

A massive sword flashed across the moonlit room, wielded by a woman black with fury. The first blow across my shield nearly dislocated my shoulder. I swung the sword in my right hand. "I've got your wife," I said with a grunt as Luis blocked my sword with her own, ringing steel piercing the night. Somehow I deflected the next blow to the shield, but my arm was already so numb I could barely control it. I swung wildly, hitting only the wall, then ducked when steel whistled past my head. I dodged around her and dove under the table. With a roar of rage, she overturned it, forcing me to scramble to my feet.

I fended off blow after blow. Once I leapt back just as the tip of Luis's sword sliced across but not through my mail. If I couldn't fight back, I would die. With an exhausted grunt I swung the sword and cried out as it connected with Luis's, the shock of it rattling my teeth.

At one point our swords locked over our heads by the door, and I was close enough to feel her tremendous heat, smell her anger. Then the door fell open and we spilled out into the moonlight.

My legs nearly gave out as I struggled to avoid the slashing steel.

Our swords clashed again, but she flipped her tip around so quickly my sword flew from my nearly-paralyzed hand and clattered off into the bushes.

My shield began disintegrating under her furious sword. I fell to my knees, yelling as my shield finally snapped in two and her sword grazed my hip. I rolled to avoid the next blow, then scrambled to my feet. I had only one weapon left, and if didn't work, I was dead. I braced my back against the rough wall as a furious Luis raised her sword. "Let me live," I cried out in Arabic. "Let me live. Please, Luis, let me live."

I couldn't see her face but I heard the quick intake of breath, the small sound of surprise. My life hung suspended in the sharp sword above Luis's head. I raised my face to hers, suddenly unafraid. "Let me live," I whispered.

Silence rang in my ears. My breathing slowed. There was nothing more I could do. If Fate had brought me nine hundred years into the past only to be killed by the woman I loved, so be it. I was done in, defenseless, and out of options. I prayed she'd hit my jugular so I'd bleed out and avoid a slow, painful death.

Then, with a wrenching sob, Luis dropped to her knees, the sword thudding softly onto the ground beside me. Delicious joy rushed through me, but I reached for my head, just to make sure. Holy shit, I was still alive.

Luis touched my hands, my feet, babbling nearly incoherently in Spanish and Arabic. Weak with relief, I pulled my delirious lover close to my chest. "You have suffered enough. You are forgiven." She moaned weakly, then lost consciousness, dead weight in my arms. From my position, I couldn't see the camel mountain, but I knew Nuño was there. With Luis half across my lap, pinning down my legs, the rough stucco gouging into my back, I relaxed exhausted, tense muscles, closed my eyes, and slept.

❖

Morning came and went as Luis slept on the ground beside me. I relieved myself, ate a bit, but otherwise never left her side. I held her hand, stroked her pale cheeks, but not until siesta did she stir. She sat up, rubbing her temples, muttering to herself as if trying to shake off a nightmare. She turned toward me and with clear blue eyes, she looked *at* me, not through me. Disoriented, she scooted back on her haunches.

"Who are you?" she rasped. "You cannot be who I think."

"Luis, it is me."

"Kate," she gasped. "But you returned—"

"No, I want to stay here with you." My heart soared to say those words.

After a long pause, she drew in a deep breath. "It must be you," she finally said, voice raw with disuse. I held my breath, palms pressed against my stomach. "Because that was the worst swordplay I have ever seen."

I grinned. "Is that so?" I pulled her to her feet and we embraced in the blue light, now both holding on so tightly we couldn't speak. Luis pressed her face into my neck, her entire body shuddering.

Finally she raised her lips to my ear. "I nearly killed you," she whispered.

"I nearly *lost* you," I responded.

Luis touched my cheek. "I feel strangely light, as if three coats of mail have been lifted from me." She looked around. "Where are we? How did I come to this place?"

I kissed her lightly. "No details right now."

She rubbed her forehead, struggling to focus. "I feel new, like I have been touched by God's hand and cleansed."

"That's good," I said, lacing my fingers through hers.

"Somehow I have a new heart." I leaned against her, letting her peace melt into me. Even in the bluish half-moonlight, she looked calmer than I'd ever seen her. "I remember nothing after...Gudesto," she said softly. "Kate, he knows...of my sex."

"He will never tell," I murmured, horrified at the sickly thrill the memory brought. In 1085 survival was earned, not assumed.

"How can you be so sure?"

"I'll explain later. But he will never, ever touch you again."

Luis shuddered and pulled me close, our hearts pounding fiercely, separated only by the thin bark of skin and fabric, protected by our trunks entwined together. "Kate," she said gruffly, "I do not want to stop living as a man. It is the only way I can remain a soldier." She rubbed her cheek against mine.

"I know," I said softly into her ear.

"But I...I do not know how...to be strong...as a woman, and I want that as well."

I pulled back, meeting her troubled but clear gaze. "We will learn together," I said, then kissed her gently. "And as you can tell from my swordplay, I don't know how to protect myself."

Her answering kiss was so light tingles shot through my arms. "We will learn together," she said. We held each other for a long time, my chest expanding to fill every inch of me. Behind Luis, movement on the camel hump hill caught my eye. A lone rider and horse stood silhouetted against the white-blue sky. The rider raised his arms in triumphant joy, then melted into the darkness.

❖

It took a few more days before Luis felt ready to leave the cottage. She remained physically shy, jumping whenever I touched her. She did allow me to hold her both nights that she tried telling me what happened, but could not. "There is plenty of time," I murmured into her hair, stroking her back until she slept.

During the day I caught her staring at me constantly. "I am sorry," she said. "I just cannot believe you are still here."

"You are stuck with me," I said, kissing her gently enough she wouldn't pull back. "Forever."

Then she actually winked. "Poor me."

She never mentioned Nuño or asked how I'd found her. I had no idea how much of her time in shock she remembered, but there was plenty of time for that. Her face looked tired, worn, her eyes those of a woman who had, much to her surprise, lost her first battle, but would recover and go on, a woman free of ghosts.

We discussed the future. "I want to take you to La Rioja, where I grew up. And to Valvanera to meet Father Ruíz."

I nodded. "I want to learn to ride a horse better. I want to live in a castle. I want to learn to defend myself with a knife. I want to learn Latin. And Arabic."

"I can help with the knife and the riding. But the languages?"

"Everything here is written in Latin or Hebrew or Arabic. Maybe I'll learn all three. I want to be able to read."

"But why?"

I chuckled, thrilled at all we had to teach each other.

We finally mounted our horses one cloudy morning, but nothing could dampen our spirits as we rode. "I want to show you something," she said, which explained why we weren't headed for Burgos. As we rode in happy silence, grinning foolishly every time our eyes met, I considered my life. Both Arturo and Anna would be better off without me, free to bond without an *ex* complicating the picture. As for me, I could leave modern life behind. In fact, the longer I spent in 1085, the less sense the twenty-first century made. Those last crazy days with Anna—packing for the trip, meeting with Señora Cavelos—all faded into my distant past. I'd made my choice and knew, without a doubt, it was the right one.

Several hours later we left the road, crossing a wide pasture filled with sheep, then took a smaller trail to the Ebro, which we forded, then joined a small path. Déjà vu hit. "This is the path to Miranda," I said. Luis nodded, but refused to explain. That afternoon we finally entered the clearing where Nuño and I had searched for her so frantically. I shivered. "This is where Alfonso's men captured you. Why would you want to return?"

She shifted in her saddle, grinning. "When I decided to return you to Santillana, knowing I'd never see you again, I vowed to settle here, never far from this clearing."

I looked around. "But why?" Towering white spruce ringed the oval clearing. Sparrows scolded over our heads. Nothing seemed out of the ordinary, but I was drawn to the tallest, most majestic spruce at the clearing's edge. She smiled, nodding encouragingly, so I rode closer, then gasped. What had appeared to be one trunk was really two. I slid off Rozinante's back and ran under the tree, its lowest branches long since fallen. A bed of soft, sharply-scented needles crackled under my boots. I touched the cool, rough bark, then looked up. Light filtered through the branches, revealing two trunks, entwined sensuously, reaching up toward the sky together.

Luis reached my side, sliding her arm around my waist, shyness falling away in her excitement. "When I realized in Zaragoza how I felt about you, I remembered this tree." She pressed me gently against the tree, then kissed me so deeply my knees weakened.

Finally she pulled back for air, lifting my hair back off my neck.

"You and I are this tree." A sly smile slowly spread across her face. "Perhaps I will write poems about you and this tree."

"Welcome back," I murmured.

She only chuckled softly, then we kissed for a very long time.

Time. It had been my enemy for all these weeks, but now it would be my friend. I was an artist. An adventurer. A woman who could now ride a horse without requiring hip replacement surgery. A woman with a sharp dagger and an even sharper tongue. A woman who could admire Luis's strength during the day, and keep Elena's heart safe at night. Time stretched before me like a blank canvas, one Luis and I would paint together.

EXCERPT FROM *THE CROWN OF VALENCIA*

SEQUEL TO *THE SPANISH PEARL*

Ex-girlfriends. You can't live with them, and you can't get away from them, not even if you travel back in time over nine hundred years. Somehow, some way, they find you and wreck your new relationship and totally screw with your head...

Heart pounding, gasping to relieve my aching lungs, I marched up to the closed door and rapped my knuckles against the smooth wood. No answer, so I inhaled once for courage, then pushed down the heavy iron latch and flung open the door.

The small room held three benches, two tables, and one woman. She stood against the far wall, back to me, looking out the window as her fluttering fingers pinned up her fallen hair.

"Anna?" I asked. My blood bashed against my ear drums as I waited, praying when the woman turned around I'd see close-set eyes or the wrong-shaped face or a flat nose or a moustache...anything to show me I'd been wrong, mistaken, paranoid even. I wiped my mouth. False alarm. Please.

The woman's head dropped, then, gown rustling on the grimy floor, she turned.

"Oh, my god," I breathed. Same green eyes. Same little bump on the nose. Same firm chin. I stared stupidly at her, too numb to think. My jaw dropped as if broken.

"Kate." My former lover held out her hands as a confusion of emotions raced across her face. "I ran because I did not know it was you." She crossed the room, expensive gown and cape flowing behind her, then before I could stop her she flung her arms around my neck. "Oh, Kate, I finally found you. Now we can be together again."

Shit.

Instinctively my arms went around her, probably because I couldn't think of anything else to do with them, and because my brain flailed around like a caged animal. Holding her had once been the most natural thing in the world, but now I could scarcely breathe. She smelled of fish and a sickly sweet rose perfume. Slowly, gently, I unlatched her arms, stepping back to stare into the face I thought I'd never see again. Although it had been only nine months, it felt more like nine hundred years.

"Anna," I finally croaked. "Why are you here?"

"To look for you...and to just *be* here." A tentative smile flickered across her flushed face, then faded. "Kate, I was sick with worry. Can you imagine how I felt? You left for the cave, then never came back. You were *gone*, you'd vanished."

"It was an accident." I dug my nails into my palms.

"I asked Carlos for help. We tracked down Roberto at the orphanage, and that horrid little man finally confessed what he knew about the ledge in the cave."

I nodded, feeling as if I were stuck in one of those horrible nightmares you *know* is a dream, but you're powerless to escape, for you cannot force your mouth to open and wake yourself.

"Anna, where is Arturo?"

"God, I missed you so much." She leaned forward and kissed me, her lips warm and soft.

Slowly, as politely as I could, I drew back. She studied me with cool eyes, then made a small noise of disgust. "So that's why you didn't return to the future." Her jaw tightened and guilt about my choice to remain in the past flared like a torch. "You've found someone else."

"I tried to get back, Anna. God, I tried. But something always went wrong. And then, later, I knew Arturo would be fine with you. But where is he? Please tell me you didn't bring him back with you."

Anna calmly shook out her gown, then cleared her throat. "Kate, I don't know where Arturo is, and I really don't care."

The words hung in the air as I shut my eyes, unwilling to hear them. Oh, my god. I'd been wrong about everything. She hadn't taken him home to Chicago and put him in school and read him books every night and given him a wonderful life.

Arturo was probably still at the orphanage, and there was only one thing I could do to help him.

About the Author

Catherine Friend – After her careers as an economist and technical writer, Friend finally found her way to creative writing, and intends to stick around. The author of six children's books and one memoir, *Hit By a Farm: How I Learned to Stop Worrying and Love the Barn*, Friend also raises sheep in southeastern Minnesota with her partner.

The Crown of Valencia, her sequel to *The Spanish Pearl*, is due for release in November 2007. She is hard at work on her next novel for Bold Strokes Books, *A Pirate's Heart*.

Learn more about Friend's children's books and other books for adults at: www.catherinefriend.com

Books Available From Bold Strokes Books

Sequestered Hearts by Erin Dutton. A popular artist suddenly goes into seclusion; a reluctant reporter wants to know why; and a heart locked away yearns to be set free. (978-1-933110-78-3)

Erotic Interlude 5: Road Games eds. Radclyffe and Stacia Seaman. Adventure, "sport," and sex on the road—hot stories of travel adventures and games of seduction. (978-1-933110-77-6)

The Spanish Pearl by Catherine Friend. On a trip to Spain, Kate Vincent is accidentally transported back in time...an epic saga spiced with humor, lust, and danger. (978-1-933110-76-9)

Lady Knight by L-J Baker. Loyalty and honour clash with love and ambition in a medieval world of magic when female knight Riannon meets Lady Eleanor. (978-1-933110-75-2)

Dark Dreamer by Jennifer Fulton. Best-selling horror author, Rowe Devlin falls under the spell of psychic Phoebe Temple. A Dark Vista romance. (978-1-933110-74-5)

Come and Get Me by Julie Cannon. Elliott Foster isn't used to pursuing women, but alluring attorney Lauren Collier makes her change her mind. (978-1-933110-73-8)

Blind Curves by Diane and Jacob Anderson-Minshall. Private eye Yoshi Yakamota comes to the aid of her ex-lover Velvet Erickson in the first Blind Eye mystery. (978-1-933110-72-1)

Dynasty of Rogues by Jane Fletcher. It's hate at first sight for Ranger Riki Sadiq and her new patrol corporal, Tanya Coppelli—except for their undeniable attraction. (978-1-933110-71-4)

Running With the Wind by Nell Stark. Sailing instructor Corrie Marsten has signed off on love until she meets Quinn Davies—one woman she can't ignore. (978-1-933110-70-7)

More than Paradise by Jennifer Fulton. Two women battle danger, risk all, and find in one another an unexpected ally and an unforgettable love. (978-1-933110-69-1)

Flight Risk by Kim Baldwin. For Blayne Keller, being in the wrong place at the wrong time just might turn out to be the best thing that ever happened to her. (978-1-933110-68-4)

Rebel's Quest, Supreme Constellations Book Two by Gun Brooke. On a world torn by war, two women discover a love that defies all boundaries. (978-1-933110-67-7)

Punk and Zen by JD Glass. Angst, sex, love, rock. Trace, Candace, Francesca...Samantha. Losing control—and finding the truth within. BSB Victory Editions. (1-933110-66-X)

Stellium in Scorpio by Andrews & Austin. The passionate reuniting of two powerful women on the glitzy Las Vegas Strip where everything is an illusion and love is a gamble. (1-933110-65-1)

When Dreams Tremble by Radclyffe. Two women whose lives turned out far differently than they'd once imagined discover that sometimes the shape of the future can only be found in the past. (1-933110-64-3)

The Devil Unleashed by Ali Vali. As the heat of violence rises, so does the passion. A Casey Family crime saga. (1-933110-61-9)

Burning Dreams by Susan Smith. The chronicle of the challenges faced by a young drag king and an older woman who share a love "outside the bounds." (1-933110-62-7)

Fresh Tracks by Georgia Beers. Seven women, seven days. A lot can happen when old friends, lovers, and a new girl in town get together in the mountains. (1-933110-63-5)

The Empress and the Acolyte by Jane Fletcher. Jemeryl and Tevi fight to protect the very fabric of their world: time. Lyremouth Chronicles Book Three. (1-933110-60-0)

First Instinct by JLee Meyer. When high-stakes security fraud leads to murder, one woman flees for her life while another risks her heart to protect her. (1-933110-59-7)

Erotic Interludes 4: Extreme Passions ed. by Radclyffe and Stacia Seaman. Thirty of today's hottest erotica writers set the pages aflame with love, lust, and steamy liaisons. (1-933110-58-9)

Storms of Change by Radclyffe. In the continuing saga of the Provincetown Tales, duty and love are at odds as Reese and Tory face their greatest challenge. (1-933110-57-0)

Unexpected Ties by Gina L. Dartt. With death before dessert, Kate Shannon and Nikki Harris are swept up in another tale of danger and romance. (1-933110-56-2)

Sleep of Reason by Rose Beecham. While Detective Jude Devine searches for a lost boy, her rocky relationship with Dr. Mercy Westmoreland gets a lot harder. (1-933110-53-8)

Passion's Bright Fury by Radclyffe. Passion strikes without warning when a trauma surgeon and a filmmaker become reluctant allies. (1-933110-54-6)

Broken Wings by L-J Baker. When Rye Woods meets beautiful dryad Flora Withe, her libido, as hidden as her wings, reawakens along with her heart. (1-933110-55-4)

Combust the Sun by Andrews & Austin. A Richfield and Rivers mystery set in L.A. Murder among the stars. (1-933110-52-X)

Of Drag Kings and the Wheel of Fate by Susan Smith. A blind date in a drag club leads to an unlikely romance. (1-933110-51-1)

Tristaine Rises by Cate Culpepper. Brenna, Jesstin, and the Amazons of Tristaine face their greatest challenge for survival. (1-933110-50-3)

Too Close to Touch by Georgia Beers. Kylie O'Brien believes in true love and is willing to wait for it, even though Gretchen, her new boss, is off-limits. (1-933110-47-3)

100ᵗʰ Generation by Justine Saracen. Ancient curses, modern-day villains, and an intriguing woman lead archeologist Valerie Foret on the adventure of her life. (1-933110-48-1)

Battle for Tristaine by Cate Culpepper. While Brenna struggles to find her place in the clan, Tristaine is threatened with destruction. Second in the Tristaine series. (1-933110-49-X)

The Traitor and the Chalice by Jane Fletcher. Tevi and Jemeryl risk all in the race to uncover a traitor. The Lyremouth Chronicles Book Two. (1-933110-43-0)

Promising Hearts by Radclyffe. Dr. Vance Phelps arrives in New Hope, Montana, with no hope of happiness—until she meets Mae. (1-933110-44-9)

Carly's Sound by Ali Vali. Poppy Valente and Julia Johnson form a bond of friendship that becomes something far more. A poignant romance about love and renewal. (1-933110-45-7)

Unexpected Sparks by Gina L. Dartt. Kate Shannon's attraction to much younger Nikki Harris is complication enough without a fatal fire that Kate can't ignore. (1-933110-46-5)

Whitewater Rendezvous by Kim Baldwin. Two women on a wilderness kayak adventure discover that true love may be nothing at all like they imagined. (1-933110-38-4)

Erotic Interludes 3: Lessons in Love ed. by Radclyffe and Stacia Seaman. Sign on for a class in love…the best lesbian erotica writers take us to "school." (1-9331100-39-2)

Punk Like Me by JD Glass. Twenty-one-year-old Nina has a way with the girls, and she doesn't always play by the rules. (1-933110-40-6)

Coffee Sonata by Gun Brooke. Four women whose lives unexpectedly intersect in a small town by the sea share one thing in common—they all have secrets. (1-933110-41-4)

The Clinic: Tristaine Book One by Cate Culpepper. Brenna, a prison medic, finds herself drawn to Jesstin, a warrior reputed to be descended from ancient Amazons. (1-933110-42-2)

Forever Found by JLee Meyer. Can time, tragedy, and shattered trust destroy a love that seemed destined? Chance reunites childhood friends separated by tragedy. (1-933110-37-6)

Sword of the Guardian by Merry Shannon. Princess Shasta's bold new bodyguard has a secret that could change both of their lives. *He* is actually a *she*. (1-933110-36-8)

Wild Abandon by Ronica Black. Dr. Chandler Brogan and Officer Sarah Monroe are drawn together by their common obsessions—sex, speed, and danger. (1-933110-35-X)

Turn Back Time by Radclyffe. Pearce Rifkin and Wynter Thompson have nothing in common but a shared passion for surgery—and unexpected attraction. (1-933110-34-1)

Chance by Grace Lennox. A sexy, funny, touching story of two women who, in finding themselves, also find one another. (1-933110-31-7)

The Exile and the Sorcerer by Jane Fletcher. First in the Lyremouth Chronicles. Tevi and a shy young sorcerer face monsters, magic, and the challenge of loving. (1-933110-32-5)

A Matter of Trust by Radclyffe. When what should be just business turns into much more, two women struggle to trust the unexpected. (1-933110-33-3)

Sweet Creek by Lee Lynch. A celebration of the enduring nature of love, friendship, and community in the heart-warming lesbian community of Waterfall Falls. (1-933110-29-5)

The Devil Inside by Ali Vali. The head of a New Orleans crime organization falls for a woman who turns her world upside down. (1-933110-30-9)

Grave Silence by Rose Beecham. Detective Jude Devine's investigation of ritual murders is complicated by her torrid affair with pathologist Dr. Mercy Westmoreland. (1-933110-25-2)

Honor Reclaimed by Radclyffe. Secret Service Agent Cameron Roberts and Blair Powell close ranks to find the would-be assassins who nearly claimed Blair's life. (1-933110-18-X)

Honor Bound by Radclyffe. Secret Service Agent Cameron Roberts and Blair Powell face political intrigue, a clandestine threat to Blair's safety, and the seemingly irreconcilable differences that force them ever farther apart. (1-933110-20-1)

Innocent Hearts by Radclyffe. In a wild and unforgiving land, two women learn about love, passion, and the wonders of the heart. (1-933110-21-X)

The Temple at Landfall by Jane Fletcher. An imprinter, one of Celaeno's most revered servants of the Goddess, is also a prisoner to the faith—until a Ranger frees her by claiming her heart. The Celaeno series. (1-933110-27-9)

Protector of the Realm, Supreme Constellations Book One by Gun Brooke. A space adventure filled with suspense and a daring intergalactic romance. (1-933110-26-0)

Force of Nature by Kim Baldwin. From tornados to forest fires, the forces of nature conspire to bring Gable McCoy and Erin Richards close to danger, and closer to each other. (1-933110-23-6)

In Too Deep by Ronica Black. Undercover homicide cop Erin McKenzie tracks a femme fatale who just might be a real killer…with love and danger hot on her heels. (1-933110-17-1)

Stolen Moments: Erotic Interludes 2 ed. by Radclyffe and Stacia Seaman. Love on the run, in the office, in the shadows...Fast, furious, and almost too hot to handle. (1-933110-16-3)

Course of Action by Gun Brooke. Actress Carolyn Black desperately wants the starring role in an upcoming film produced by Annelie Peterson. Just how far will she go for the dream part of a lifetime? (1-933110-22-8)

Rangers at Roadsend by Jane Fletcher. Sergeant Chip Coppelli has learned to spot trouble coming, and that is exactly what she sees in her new recruit, Katryn Nagata. The Celaeno series. (1-933110-28-7)

Justice Served by Radclyffe. Lieutenant Rebecca Frye and her lover, Dr. Catherine Rawlings, embark on a deadly game of hide-and-seek with an underworld kingpin who traffics in human souls. (1-933110-15-5)

Distant Shores, Silent Thunder by Radclyffe. Dr. Tory King—along with the women who love her—is forced to examine the boundaries of love, friendship, and the ties that transcend time. (1-933110-08-2)

Hunter's Pursuit by Kim Baldwin. A raging blizzard, a mountain hideaway, and a killer-for-hire set a scene for disaster—or desire—when Katarzyna Demetrious rescues a beautiful stranger. (1-933110-09-0)

The Walls of Westernfort by Jane Fletcher. All Temple Guard Natasha Ionadis wants is to serve the Goddess—until she falls in love with one of the rebels she is sworn to destroy. The Celaeno series. (1-933110-24-4)

Change Of Pace: *Erotic Interludes* by Radclyffe. Twenty-five hot-wired encounters guaranteed to spark more than just your imagination. Erotica as you've always dreamed of it. (1-933110-07-4)

Honor Guards by Radclyffe. In a wild flight for their lives, the president's daughter and those who are sworn to protect her wage a desperate struggle for survival. (1-933110-01-5)